SWEETNESS

IN THE

SKIN

SWEETNESS
IN THE
SKIN

A NOVEL

ISHI
ROBINSON

HARPER

An Imprint of HarperCollinsPublishers

SWEETNESS IN THE SKIN. Copyright © 2024 by Tonisha Akua Robinson. All rights reserved. Printed in the United States of America. No part of this book may be used or reproduced in any manner whatsoever without written permission except in the case of brief quotations embodied in critical articles and reviews. For information in the U.S., address HarperCollins Publishers, 195 Broadway, New York, NY 10007, U.S.A. In Canada, address HarperCollins Publishers Ltd, Bay Adelaide Centre, East Tower, 22 Adelaide Street West, 41st Floor, Toronto, Ontario, M5H 4E3, Canada.

HarperCollins books may be purchased for educational, business, or sales promotional use. For information, please email the Special Markets Department in the U.S. at SPsales@harpercollins.com or in Canada at HCOrder@harpercollins.com.

Originally published in Great Britain in 2024 by Penguin Michael Joseph.

FIRST U.S. AND CANADIAN EDITIONS

Library of Congress Cataloging-in-Publication Data has been applied for.

Library and Archives Canada Cataloguing in Publication information is available upon request.

ISBN 978-0-06-333487-8
ISBN 978-1-4434-7110-7 (Canada pbk)

24 25 26 27 28 LBC 5 4 3 2 1

Hi, Mum! This is for you.

'Bad fambly betta dan empty pig sty'

'Better to put up with a bad family than be alone in the world'

Pumkin

My name is Pumkin Patterson.

Well, my name is Akisha Agnes Edna Patterson, but when my auntie Sophie first saw my yellow, jaundiced body she said I looked 'just like a little underripe pumpkin' so that's what she called me and it stuck with everyone else, except my mother, who never really called me anything at all.

If Auntie Sophie'd had her way, I would be a Renée or a Simone, an Amélie or maybe a Gabrielle. Names like those are feminine and gentle, she says. Names like those go to good schools, become lawyers and doctors, marry names like Sean and Damian and Craig and Edward, and give birth to names like Asha and Abigail and Jonathan and Michael. Names like those have lives filled with opportunities. But Akisha is harsh in your ear. A verbal attack, a karate chop, with its tough-as-nails *k* and that explosion of *sha*. You might have a picture in your head when you hear the name Akisha, and it's most likely not of a Supreme Court judge or a brain surgeon. When you're an Akisha, you have to unbuild the picture of you that someone's created in their head.

But if Auntie Sophie wants a thing you can be certain that my mother will do everything in her power not to let her have it. So Akisha it is, a nod to my father, Akil, who is the very definition of an absentee father so, sure, by all means, let us honour him through my name.

★

It's not unusual in certain parts of Kingston to have a name like Pumkin. We've got Cherrys, Peaches and Pudd'ns galore. There's Jim Livingstone up the road, who we all call One-y, ever since he lost his leg in unknown circumstances. There's Bigga, who is as thin as a steak knife turned sideways and runs a construction site for a big-name family, and Scallion, who is tremendously fat and drives a taxi, weighing it down so heavily that the tyre on his side is almost flat. Bubbles is the hairdresser two roads over, where my mother gets her weaves and extensions and gossip, and there's Stamma, who hangs around Bubbles's salon always hoping she'll take notice of him, but whose stutter holds him back from telling her how he feels. Nutty the peanut vendor, Broomie the broom vendor, Punceys and Biggas and Tall Mans and naturally, if you have buff teeth, Teetus. Not to mention all the people named, for example, Everton Ellis Brown but who are called, inexplicably, 'Robert'. 'Because him look like a "Robert",' his mother might say, if pressed. So no one blinked an eye at 'Pumkin'.

I am eleven years old and I live with my mother, my grandmother and my auntie Sophie almost downtown on Potter's Lane, an area that is not good but is not quite as bad as it could be. We are squished together in a tiny two-bedroom house made of concrete instead of clapboard, with a proper roof instead of a flat piece of corrugated iron that would save itself at the first sign of hurricane.

The houses on our street have a look about them, as if they're turning their backs on each other, each ashamed of itself. Some are propped up on piles of concrete blocks, 'Like dem wearing flood pants,' my grandmother, Cecille, likes to say. Some are painted in the brightest colours of the rainbow – pink and blue

4

and yellow. I like the bright colours but Auntie Sophie says they're the cheapest ones. A few, like the one my best friend Tamara lives in, are white and crisp, with flat solid roofs and deep brown lattice windows. 'Stoosh people house,' Gramma Cecille would sniff sometimes when we walked past. Gramma would prefer to live in one of those. Auntie Sophie wants to live as far as possible above the Half Way Tree clock.

Our house is somewhere in the middle, the top half painted sea-foam green, the bottom half rust-stained, exposed concrete, like the paint just gave up halfway. We have a bathroom so small you have to cotch on the sink to close the door but at least it's inside, with running water, although that's always cold. There are hollow concrete blocks that serve as steps to the front door and a warped, rusty gate that leads into a small front yard covered with gravel and a small back yard covered with crab grass, with a huge plum tree I used to climb.

Tamara's father is a successful mechanic and her mother's a dressmaker, like Gramma Cecille, except she has so much work she has three girls sewing for her. That's why Tamara lives in one of the better houses on our road, big and wide with a decent patch of grass in the front and her own room, even though she has a little brother. My mother had to share a room with my grandmother because Auntie Sophie needed her space to study and my mother was contributing nothing of value to the household, but once I came along Auntie Sophie was adamant that I share her room so I could also study and learn and be creative, so she could mould me into the person she wanted me to be.

Everything around me is noise: my grandmother's radio talk shows, in which she is an active participant, arguing aggressively with the hosts and the guests and the people who call in; the yells and shouts from our neighbours; the dance halls blaring music, the deep growls from the DJs hyping up the crowd almost every night of the week. My mother is rarely at home but, should she grace us with her presence, she plays the TV at top volume as she sits zoned out in front of it. If she's home at night, drunk and vicious after doing God-knows-what God-knows-where, the tension is so loud it presses against my ears. Although it's the sound of her fists against my skin that is the loudest.

The Young and the Restless

'Dat ooman too connunjin.'

I look up from my seat at the dining table, where my head is bent over a schoolbook. I'm in my first year at St Agatha's and conjugating French verbs under the watchful eye of Auntie Sophie, who is at the other side of the table reading a magazine. Sophie works at the French Embassy and she brings home magazines and comics and lots of cookbooks, which are my favourite because I love to bake, even though our gas stove is so old and weary it slumps to one side in a perpetual state of exhaustion. Sophie is adamant that I learn French because it is our dream, both of us, to go and live in France.

'One day, Pumkin,' she'd say, 'I'll be riding through the streets of Paris in a black and white striped shirt with a baguette sticking out of my bicycle basket, and you'll be perched on the back with your legs sticking out, waving your beret in the wind.'

And we would descend into a fit of giggles at the idea of it, because who ever heard of a girl from Potter's Lane making it to Paris, no matter how light the brownness of her skin?

'She, da gyal deh,' my mother continues, jutting her chin at the TV. 'Connunjin!'

She's standing in front of the screen, one eye on her soaps, the other on the iron as it glides over a tattered green skirt. It's her one good skirt, the one my grandmother forces her to wear to church. Her muscled arm flexes as she shoves the

7

point of the iron between the pleats. There are heaps of clothes piled behind her on the sofa, a deep burgundy monstrosity of a thing that dominates our tiny living room, wedged up against our low mahogany coffee-table and between a seemingly endless array of cabinets filled with knick-knacks. Having my mother home at this time of evening – doing something as domestic as ironing, no less – is a rare sight. But my grandmother caught her before she could leave the house again and there was an almighty row.

'Is weh yuh goin *again*, Paulette? Why yuh don tan a yuh yaad, eeh?' my grandmother yelled. My mother had muttered that the house was too small for all of us to cotch up in, my grandmother shouted that she should be grateful she had a roof over her head, my mother kissed her teeth, my grandmother smacked her on the side of her head, flung a pile of laundry on the couch and told her to iron every last one of them before she call down the hand of Jesus to 'smite her ungrateful dawta right cross side a di face' and my mother did not have the nerve to disobey. I snort a laugh at the thought of my skinny grandmother as the lion, and my mother, broad-shouldered, veins running like rope down her thick arms, as the wildebeest.

'Yuh fine summ'n funny?'

I'm startled to find her eyes on me and I crawl into myself, bending my head back over my book.

'What you mean by *connunjin*?' Sophie asks my mother, in her poshest voice. Her accent gets more stoosh when my mother has mispronounced something, which is almost all the time.

'Den yuh nuh know what *connunjin* mean, Your Eye-Niss? She a ginnal!'

Auntie Sophie and I glance at each other and giggle.

'I think you mean *conniving*, Paulette,' Sophie says, with a sound in her voice that I know drives my mother insane.

'Den ah nuh dat mi seh?' my mother shouts. 'Connunjin!'

'That's not even remotely what you said, Paulette,' my aunt says, turning back to her magazine, as if to say, I'm done with this foolish argument that you have lost. I can almost see the steam rising from my mother's dark skin and I think of her as a wildebeest again, and my aunt as a gazelle, and I laugh under my breath at the idea of it all, which, as you can well imagine, was not the right thing to do. Because the hunter will always choose the weakest prey.

'Di prablem wid you, yu see, likkle girl,' she says, pointing at me with the iron, 'is yu get likkle heducation and all of a sutten yu don't ave no respeck fi yu elders. Head eva eena one book, before yuh help me ayan de clothes dem, or sweep di house, or –'

'But you don't even do those things!' I say, startling my mother, my aunt and myself. 'Not unless Gramma makes you do it.'

I don't know why I did that. I don't know why I didn't follow the usual rules: make myself small, keep myself quiet, knowing as I did that it took only one innocent statement, a perceived slight, to pierce my mother's skin, burrow its way underneath, worm its way into her heart and cause her to explode. Maybe it was because my aunt was right beside me and my grandmother in the next room that I thought the herd would close around me, keep me safe. My mother stares at me for a moment, her eyes wide, the whites slightly yellow as if they smoked tobacco, and then she yanks the steaming hot iron away from the wall and throws it straight at my face.

I remember . . .

. . . *I am sitting on the carpet in front of the couch, on which my mother is sat. The TV is loud and blaring. I am making clothes for my doll, like Auntie Sophie makes for herself. Auntie Sophie is beautiful and fashionable and always makes new clothes. I don't have scissors to cut the scraps of fabric, so I am using a knife. I am cutting and cutting through the fabric, cutting and cutting, and then I feel a sharp, sudden bite on my thumb. The knife has bitten me. I don't feel anything, at first, and I look at my thumb, which now has a thin white line across it. As I watch, a bubble of deep, dark blood pushes through the line and it starts to burn and burn and burn. I feel it in my entire hand, all the way up my arm. I start to scream, holding my thumb out to my mother as the blood washes over it, spilling onto the carpet. It is burning and biting at the same time. I think my whole thumb will fall off. The figure of my mother is blurred through my tears but I can see she is looking at me.*

Her face is blank as she watches me, the blood running from my still outstretched hands, my wailing so loud in my own head. She is watching me and she does not move, does not change her expression, does not leap forward to hold my hand and stop the bleeding and hush my cries. She is just watching me and her eyes are like glass, like the eyes of my doll.

I feel arms swoop me up and my head is pressed into a soft chest. It is my aunt. 'It's all right, Pumkin, it's all right, my darling,' she coos, racing with me into the kitchen, my hand still outstretched. But I am looking over her shoulder and I can see my mother staring at me blankly before she turns those glass eyes back to the TV, and I know that it is not all right. It is not all right at all.

Is ghetto we come from

'Pumkin! Pumkin! Are you all right?'

I can still see the blurred figure in front of my face. I look down at my thumb but there's no blood, just a deep scar running down the side. I blink a few times and the figure sharpens. It's Auntie Sophie, her face a mask of worry, her hand pressed against the side of my head, which is wet and sticky. I smell something like barbecue.

'Oh, Jesus,' she says, exhaling. 'Are you okay?'

I try to nod but my head hurts, like someone threw a boulder at it, and then I remember the iron, which I can now see is lying on its side, like a wounded animal, over by the wall. There is something brown and crusty along the side of the hot part and I look away before I can think too hard about what that is. I turn away and throw up on the carpet and look at it and think that the vomit is actually an improvement, the carpet is so old and ratty.

'I think it fell on hard times,' I mutter.

'What?' says Sophie.

'The carpet. I think it started out fancy, but it fell on hard times.' I laugh, which makes Sophie's forehead crinkle. She must really be concerned, I think, to make her forehead crinkle like that because she spends a lot of time making sure there are no crinkles anywhere on her face. I hear a lot of shouting. My mother and grandmother are fighting. My grandmother has a rolled-up magazine, I think it's the same one Sophie was reading, and she's hitting my mother with it, her shouts synced with each meaty slap.

'*HOW! YUH MUSS! BUN! DIE CHILE! LIKE DAT?*'

Wap! Wap! Wap! Wap! Wap!

'*WHY! YU MUSS GWAAN! LIKE SEH! YUH A VIRAGO?*'

Wap! Wap! Wap! Wap! Wap!

There is something strange about seeing my grandmother beating my mother for beating me. My aunt mutters about scars and takes me to our bedroom, where she wipes the blood from my face, dresses my wounds and puts an ice-filled washcloth against my eye and tells me to hold it there before she heads back to the living room to join the war. Our walls are so paper thin that I might as well be standing in the centre of the storm. I think, again, that Sophie must be really mad because she's normally so worried about what the neighbours will think, although she claims, in the same breath, that she doesn't care what *these* neighbours think. The left side of my head is throbbing and burning and my eye won't open. I wonder if I will really have a big scar.

I feel restless just lying here holding this limp washcloth to my face, now that the ice has melted, so I get up and walk quietly to what passes for a corridor in our house to peer around the corner and watch the fight. There used to be a string of beads hanging here, like a curtain, but I played with them so much that most of them broke off, leaving random pieces of string hanging from the ceiling. I used to pretend they were pearls, draping them around my neck, acting like I was a princess in a fairy-tale castle.

'She ah nuh fi yuh pickney!' I hear my mother scream.

'Oh, that's *rich*, Paulette! She might not be my *child*, but

I'm the one paying for her school fees and for her books and her uniforms. *I*'m the one who buys her clothes and takes her out. *I* help her with her homework, help her improve herself – she's more mine than yours!'

'Im*prove* harself? Like seh, if she talk pretty like yuh, she gwen do what, Miss Sophie? Yuh tink cause yu brown and have puss eye and yuh talk like yuh come from farrin yuh betta than me?'

'Jeesas Christ,' my grandmother says conversationally, from the corner of the room where she is on her knees, praying. She is rubbing the left side of her chest, vigorously, her face in a grimace. She always says we give her heartache.

'I don't think I'm better than you, Paulette. I just want to give your daughter an opportunity to –'

'Happartunity! Eh eh! Is ghetto we come from, yuh nuh! Don't yuh still here? Yuh go university and have uptown fren and yuh skin cool like honey and yuh hair tall tall, but yuh still down 'ere, right 'ere in die ghetto. Don't it? Where yuh tink yuh going? When yuh fren dem haxe yuh where yu come from, is wah yuh tell dem? Yuh nuh betta than me!'

Sophie hesitates, a patch of red blooming from the base of her neck and crawling up to her cheeks. I strain my head forward, holding one of the last remaining strings of beads so it doesn't make a sound. I've met some of Sophie's friends and I've wondered that myself. Where do they think she lives? But instead her voice lowers and softens, like she's trying to calm a wild dog.

'Listen, Paulette. You know that I'm only here because of Pumkin. I've been working for a while now. I can afford to move out, get a small apartment for me and her, and you can have your own room here. You won't have to share with Mama any more. Wouldn't that be better for you?'

'She not going nowhere!'

'Why *not*, Paulette?' Sophie says, dropping her voice so low I can barely hear it. 'You don't even want her!'

'Dat don't mean dat you can have her.'

My mother turns and pushes her way out of the house, slamming the already weakened door behind her. A silence falls over the room that feels like pressure in my ears, my grandmother's praying sounding like white noise. I decide to make bread pudding.

I sneak into the kitchen and gather up the bags of slightly stale bread stuffed into our battered bread box. Sophie always buys too much bread so that some will go stale because she loves my bread pudding so much. She also loves my potato pudding, my coconut cake, my grater cake. But the bread pudding is her favourite, so I think now is a good time to make bread pudding so she will remember how much she loves it, and she will think about the fact that she won't be able to eat it if she leaves me here to live by herself.

I take out our misshapen baking dish and coax the oven up to 190 degrees. I butter each side of the bread with lots and lots of margarine – which I heard Sophie once say is so unhealthy that not even ants will eat it, but my grandmother thinks butter is too much of a luxury – then rip up the bread, spread it across the pan, sprinkle some raisins sparingly on top and repeat the process two more times. The tearing and spreading and layering and sprinkling makes me almost forget how bad my head hurts, and that my eye is so swollen that everything has a wavy double outline. When I lift the baking pan, my hands are shaking so much that it looks like it's dancing the strangest shoulder shimmy. Sophie comes in just as I start mixing the wet ingredients in a bowl. She leans against our ancient fridge as I fold the eggs and milk and all-spice and cinnamon and sugar and salt into a batter. It's when she holds up the pan for me to pour the wet ingredients over the dry that I see she is shaking too.

At least, a Chiney man

The way my grandmother tells it, before I came along, she lived with her daughters Paulette and Sophie in the same little house where we all live now. Cecille came to Kingston in 1966 from May Pen, a small city an hour or so outside the capital, to look for work, which she found as a housekeeper – or what we call a helper in Jamaica – for the Joneses, a high-class uptown family. They lived in Norbrook, a rich-people area in Kingston, where the houses sprawl over acres of grass so green and even it looks fake, and the roads are wide and sloping. My grandmother was a live-in, her tiny room and bathroom at the back of the house behind the garage, and the Joneses paid well, although they were somewhat standoffish and didn't mix much with the help.

'Dem did stoosh yuh see,' my grandmother used to tell me, as I sat between her legs, her rough hands pulling a brush through my hair. 'Nose right up in di air til yu cudda almos' see she brain, die missus.'

Mr Jones, who was so very light-skinned that he could almost pass for white, was a lawyer from a family of well-known and wealthy lawyers; his wife, who didn't have to pass for anything because she was, in fact, white, was an accountant for her family business, a chain of fancy hotels along the north coast. They had three boys, aged twelve, fifteen and seventeen, each one fairer than the last and all with green eyes. Gramma said Mr Jones was always on the radio shouting his defence of this or that uptown businessman who had been wrongfully accused of some bandooloo business. Mrs Jones was always in the *Gleaner* in a fancy dress, raising money for poor people. 'But axe har if she ever set one foot in a poor man house!' Gramma snorted. 'Dat ooman neva pass Half Way Tree yet, except fi go buy fabric at Miguel Fabric – an' is caws har rich fren own it!'

The sons all went to St John's College, one of the best all-boys' schools on the island, where most of the population were white, Chinese or brown, with just a sprinkling of black for a little flavour. The Jones boys had their futures planned: they would go to university in the States or Canada, earn a law degree, then come back and work at one or the other of the family businesses.

When my grandmother joined their household, she was twenty years old, unattached, unfettered, and a beauty. She was of medium skin tone with a button nose, big black eyes and a pronounced Cupid's bow, and was quick to tell people that her father had a touch of coolie in him. This little bit of Indian, she said, explained the wave in the shiny black hair she kept in one long braid down her back and the fact that she was – 'Tenk yu, Jesus!' – not too dark.

Gramma said that lots of uptown boys helped themselves to their helpers, if the latter were young and pretty enough. She had no shame in telling me that her beauty was 'hirri-sis-tible' to not one, but two of the Jones boys, whom she was more than willing to entertain.

'Den dem nuh was two big horse-steering man?' she said, when I raised my eyebrows at this part of the story. And since teenagers really *did* seem like big men to me, I just shrugged and asked her to carry on.

When her belly started to show she went to Mr and Mrs Jones and asked what was to be done. What sort of arrangement, she wondered, could they come to? Mrs Jones slapped her across the face, accused her of lying and fainted dead away, while Mr Jones ordered her to pack her bags and get out 'herewith and with haste!'

My grandmother, ever the pragmatist, calmly explained that she had nowhere to go and, in her delicate state, would not be leaving to roam the street like any and any ol' vagrant. She went to her room to watch *The Young and the Restless*, turning up the volume to drown out the noise of the shouting and crying that took place deep into the night. Plates were smashed and glasses were broken, 'and den is who yuh tink did haffi clean alla dat up di nex day?' she said, kissing her teeth. Mr Jones, his face 'grey like one rat', came to my grandmother with their decision: they would give her a lump sum of two years' wages to go away and never return. 'And wa' bout di baby, Missa Jones?' my grandmother wanted to know, only for Mr Jones to have 'the nerve fi come tell me seh, mi cudden *prove* dat is one of fi him son dem is di fadda. After is what him tek mi for, skettel?' and she kissed her teeth again. I never liked this part of the story, because she would comb my hair so roughly my head would hurt and she could complain I was too tender-headed.

In the end, Gramma said, she ended up with just enough money to buy the little house we all live in together now. But once she settled in with a few pieces of furniture she bought on layaway, she realized she'd got a raw deal. She would have to go back to work with no references and nowhere to leave her child.

When Sophie arrived in the world, pink as a newborn mouse

with soft, curly blonde hair and sea-blue eyes, my grandmother took one look at her and saw, quite clearly, that she was undoubtedly, most definitely a Jones. She marched herself right back to the family, baby in one hand, to change the terms of the agreement. In the other hand she held a birth certificate on which she had written Craig Jones, the oldest of the three boys, although she could not be certain if it was him or his brother, Adam, who had gifted her this cash cow. And she'd defiantly written 'Sophie Jones' on it too, because 'Jones she is an' Jones she name'.

It was plain to the pragmatic Joneses that (1) this child was quite clearly their granddaughter and (2) this woman was not going to go away. 'Me did know dem wudda radda pay me off than have a scandal,' Gramma said, nodding decisively. 'Nutten worse to uptown people dan scandal.'

By the time Sophie turned two, her skin had deepened to golden honey and her eyes settled on hazel green, which, according to my grandmother, was ideal. You don't want a too-white daughter 'hinvitin all kinda 'ooligan *and* scoundrill bout di place!', but a nice, cool shade of very light brown, with good hair and 'puss eye' is enough to ensure a bright future. By then the Jones boys had been shipped off to university and boarding school in Canada with no plans to return, and Sophie had a life of opportunity before her.

Gramma said she did not have the same luck the second time, having gotten herself in a situation with a dark-skinned man called Rexton, who was passing through from Spanish Town. 'Him did have a sweet mout, yuh see, Pumkin,' she explained, as she rubbed the flour between her hands to make spinners. Those long thin dumplings weren't my favourite but you couldn't make stew peas without them. 'Him did sweep me off mi feet, like dem seh in di filim dem.'

They had one night of passion, Gramma said, before he slunk off into the darkness, never to be seen or heard from again. She was annoyed when she found herself pregnant too late to do anything about it – and for a boy so dark 'if 'im neva smile inna di night time, yu cudden see him!' – so she popped my mother out and called her Paulette. It was clear to me, from the stories she told, that it was Auntie Sophie who was her priority. Auntie Sophie, who came from good stock, who would make us a respectable family, because that was what Gramma wanted more than anything: for us to be better, not have to work for other people as helpers, or live in cramped houses half covered with sad green paint.

Sophie needed the best cut of meat so she would be strong and healthy. Sophie needed quiet so she could study. Sophie needed good clothes because you couldn't have a pretty pretty girl like that running around looking like any old stregereggs. Driven by the constant fear of exposure, the Joneses made sure that Sophie's every need was met. She was sent to a prep school, which had a better student-to-teacher ratio and a higher quality of classmate than a primary school or the local all-age, where up to thirty children would be crammed into a noisy classroom. (My mother was sent to the local all-age.) Her uniforms and books were paid for, as well as her school lunches and any extra-curricular activities she did (swimming was not allowed because it would ruin her hair, but badminton was encouraged, as the ball reminded my grandmother of a very fancy church dress). Sophie did not drop her *h*s or add them where they were not wanted, no *haaxin fi harinjes* or *combin ar air*.

'What a way she speaky spoky,' Linnette, who owned the corner shop, would say, when Sophie came in, clean and bright and neatly pressed. My grandmother would simply smile. Sophie was like the little neighbourhood doll, an example of what they all could be if they only had a rich family to blackmail.

Auntie Sophie told me, years later, that once, when she was in her teens and on a rare shopping trip with my mother and grandmother, an older man insisted on buying her a ridiculously expensive pair of shoes that she'd been hankering after in the store. He wanted nothing in return, he was happy just to know he'd bought a beautiful young girl something she desperately wanted. He paid for the shoes and walked away with a spring in his step. My grandmother was only too happy to get something for nothing. He hadn't noticed my mother standing there, off to the side.

'Do you still have the shoes?' I'd asked her, as I'd sipped my cup of Milo.

No, she'd said. My mother had taken the shoes from her closet and stuck them under a tree to be battered by the rain.

*

At sixteen, Sophie was locked away in her room studying for her CXCs, aiming for sixth form, preparing to pull the family behind her as she ascended from the ashes, like a phoenix. My mother, at fourteen, preferred to go to the dance halls almost every night of the week.

'Your modda wasn't gwen pass no A level,' Gramma said, running a skirt through the sewing machine. 'She was lookin a man fi mine her.' My grandmother shook her head, disappointed that her younger daughter's only goal was to find a man to pay for everything. By then, Paulette had set her sights on Veteran, who was trying hard to become an area don. People said Veteran had scarred his own face so he would look hard and dangerous. He was very dark-skinned, but he bleached, leaving his face, neck and hands an ashy grey colour, pockmarked with spots, while the rest of his body was black as oil. Once, someone joked that he looked like a monkey. When it got back to Veteran, he drowned the boy in a barrel of sewage water, holding his head underwater, hooting like a baboon the whole time.

My mother was beautiful then, Gramma admitted, with deep umber skin and big almond-shaped eyes framed by naturally long lashes. As beautiful as her sister Sophie, only dark, so nobody really noticed unless it was to tell her, in a surprised kind of way, that she was very pretty for a black girl. But Veteran only dealt with brown-skinned girls, so when one of his crew, a light-skin bwoy with a crooked smile that showed off a gold canine tooth, took interest, my mother figured that was close enough.

Akil was barely six feet tall, wiry as a weasel, with small squinty eyes, high cheekbones, and an extremely inflated sense of his own self-worth. At least, that was how my grandmother described him. He had a thick swatch of wavy black hair and a smattering of acne on his cheeks that looked like someone threw a handful of pebbles at him and they got stuck there. He was of unknown provenance – it was rumoured that his mother had had a thing for Chinese men and didn't know which one was his father, which was maybe why his last name was Patterson (his mother's) and definitely why they called him Chinnas. He was an expert thief, able to squeeze his way through any set of grilles, unstick any window, slither under any door or worm his way past unsuspecting victims and clean the place out.

My grandmother was too wrapped up in making sure her older daughter was studying and getting enough rest and eating enough good food to take much notice of how her younger girl was spending her time, but she was still surprised when, just a few months shy of my mother's fifteenth birthday, her belly started to grow.

'At least she did ave the decency to tek up wid a Chiney man,' my grandmother said to me, as she parted my hair in two and rubbed grease aggressively onto my scalp.

Akil was not concerned about my mother's pregnancy because pregnancy was a woman's problem, although he wanted to know when his 'yoot' was born so he could proudly tell people how many boys he had created. Some men in Jamaica collect children like that, like playing cards they can take out and show off, safely wrapped in plastic, before returning them to storage. But since I came out a girl, I wasn't a very valuable card, and my mother was just a skettel who opened her legs too easy, so Akil drifted off quietly into the night leaving disaster in his wake, like a particularly ripe and noxious fart.

I guess my mother thought it was my fault he went away, since she left me at home while she tried to recapture his attention, to no avail. He kept waving her off, like she was a mosquito singing in his ears at night. It didn't help that Sophie fell deeply in love with me at first sight either, or that people often thought Sophie was my mother, since we're both light-skinned, or that, on the odd occasion my mother would reach for me, I would squirm away and turn to her sister instead.

Beyond the story of how I came to be, the topic of my father is never discussed, except to tell me that I take after him, with my light brown skin and my long loose curls that grow down my back, although I've been told I have my mother's best feature: her almond-shaped, dark brown eyes. *Be thankful for your skin colour*, my grandmother tells me. *The world will be an easier place for you.*

One stop, Driver

'Did you get detention?' Tamara asks.

She's stuffing the last of a greasy pizza slice into her mouth and I stare so hard at it I can see its imprint when I close my eyes. I look at my dry bulla stuffed with a square of cheese so orange it could only be made of plastic, the cheapest thing you can buy from the tuck shop, and sigh.

'No, but Auntie Sophie says I can't come over to your house for a while. I'm on social lockdown. Plus, now Miss Smith hates me more than ever, class will be even more unbearable. That taste good?'

'Meh, it can eat.' She licks the grease running down her arm. The smell of the pizza is driving me crazy and I'm relieved when she takes the last bite. I nibble at my bun. Dry as chip.

We are at school, sitting on a wooden bench under a huge jacaranda tree, and lunchtime is almost over. It is the best and worst time of the school day: our own hour of freedom when we can sit outside and be ourselves followed by an hour under strict observation in a classroom open to the outside. The sun is high and the breeze rustles through the leaves and over your skin, singing *shu-shu-shu-shu-shu-shu* until your eyes get heavy and your head feels like it's made from lead and you look like one of those babies who doesn't have any neck strength. Trying to learn maths in that environment is the worst form of torture.

I'm telling Tamara about my visit to the vice principal's office last week with Auntie Sophie and Miss Smith, my French teacher and arch nemesis. Tamara glances at the bandage over my eye and down the side of my face and looks away, licking the grease from her fingers. Her eye has wandered over to it every few minutes over lunchtime and each time I turn a little bit away from her, so that by now she's almost talking to my profile. I'm pretty sure she thinks the two things are related, my being called to the office and a busted eye. She looks at it again and opens her mouth to say something, but just at that moment the devil herself walks by and stops in front of us.

'Lunchtime is ho-ver, ladies,' Miss Smith says, looking directly at me.

'But, Miss, the bell don't ring yet!' Tamara says. 'We have . . . ten more minutes. See?'

She holds out her hand to show her watch, but Miss Smith is still glaring at me, which I can feel rather than see, since my nails have suddenly become very interesting. Miss Smith says. 'Tcha!' softly and walks off and Tamara says, 'Lawd, is whappen to her?' and I shrug in response. 'Why she hate you so bad?' and I look at Tamara and shrug again but I do kind of know why.

'For real, I thought you were going to ace French class, Pumkin, with that stoosh auntie weh yuh have,' she says, opening a bag of Cheese Trix and stuffing a big puff in her mouth.

'I know, me too,' I say sullenly. 'But that's what happen when you have a . . . when you have . . . a *country bumpkin* for a teacher.'

Tamara snorts and says, 'Mine she hear you!' looking exaggeratedly around to see if the teacher is lurking somewhere nearby, but the coast is clear. 'Why is she so obsessed with everything French anyway?'

'Auntie Sophie? I dunno, she just . . . *is*.'

Tamara sucks the Cheese Trix dust from her fingers and says, 'But . . . yuh don't think she will really move there? To Paris?'

I shrug again. The truth is, it is my aunt's greatest dream to go and live in France and so now it is mine, too. She was twelve, she'd told me, when her uptown friend's sister told them about her trip through Europe, and how, of all the places she'd visited, Paris had been the most cultured, the most romantic, the most other-worldly. She'd shown them pictures and videos, and Auntie Sophie had seen the Eiffel Tower and the Arc de Triomphe and heard her friend's sister speaking French at a quaint little café and that, she'd said, was that. She was obsessed. She learned all she could about France, borrowing books from the school library. She took French in high school and got the highest marks and won a bunch of prizes, majored in it at university and even got a job as local staff at the French Embassy, using the last of the Joneses' influence before they permanently closed that scandalous chapter of their lives, now that she was grown-up and enough time had passed. She was a secretary and didn't make much money but she could learn about the country and the culture, 'network' and make contacts; she had one foot in the door.

Sophie made it her mission to make her passion my passion. If she wasn't policing my English diction and pronunciation, she was teaching me the French names for bread and dumplings and fish as we cooked together in the tiny kitchen, for dresses and hats and bows when we were getting dressed for church.

'You look like a cupcake,' she'd told me once in French, when we were getting ready for church. I'd looked down at my frilly dress and started giggling, until my mother strode in and slapped me across my face.

'Stop talking foolishniss!' she'd yelled, before striding back out of the room. After that, Sophie and I were careful only to speak French in whispers or when my mother wasn't around. Which, to be fair, was often enough.

This was our dream: Sophie and I would move to Paris, start a new life, speak a new language, become new people. Sophie said my baking was so good that I could go to a fancy French cooking school and become a famous pastry chef. I'd open a bakery and call it Pumkin's Pâtisserie, she'd get a good job in a tall, sleek office and marry a rich man. No one would know that we'd lived in a pop-down house, had no money and were only passing for uptown: we'd start fresh and, this time, on the right foot. Sophie said not to talk about these plans with anyone but each other because talking about your business too loud incites jealousy in others, who will do all they can to block your dreams, so I try to wrap it up like fine pastry and tuck it into my heart and only take it out when we're alone. But if you'd asked me about it, I would have told you that it was really just a dream. I was trying to figure out where I belonged right here at home. Not rich or connected enough for uptown, not rootsy enough for downtown. Besides, Paris was so far away, you might as well have told me that we were going to live on the moon.

'HELLOOOO?'

'Huh?'

'Paris? Yuh auntie? Do you think she'll really move there?'

'I dunno,' I say eventually. 'Are there even Jamaicans there?'

'My girl, Jamaicans are everywhere. Like ants.'

I snort a laugh. 'That's true. I bet if you go to Timbuktu, yuh turn the corner and there's a pan chicken man.'

'"Two pung a chicken, three bills!"' Tamara shouts, startling a skinny little first-former walking by, holding a pile of books to her chest.

'What are you guys talking about?'

Tamara wipes the tears from her eyes and the laughter stops short in her throat. Mandy Chen is standing in front of us, a slightly confused smile on her face, as if she wants to join in on the joke but doesn't yet understand it.

'Oh, we were just wondering if there were any Jamaicans in Paris . . .' I say, glancing at Tamara. She is staring at Mandy with a look on her face like someone just farted in it.

'Oh, my uncle used to live there!'

'Really?' I say, at the same time I hear Tamara mocking Mandy under her breath.

'Yeah, he went on some kind of exchange thing one time. So I guess at least one Jamaican was living there once!'

Tamara belts out a big fake laugh and we both turn to look at her. She cocks her head and looks back at Mandy with her eyebrows raised, as if to say, 'What?'

'*Any*way, listen, a bunch of us going to Hellshire Beach for my birthday in a couple weeks. I want you to come. Not this Saturday, next Saturday. Can you make it?'

I glance nervously at Tamara, who is now looking at me expectantly.

'Just a really small group of us,' Mandy says, shooting Tamara an apologetic look.

'Of *course*,' Tamara says, her voice caustic with sarcasm.

'Ahm,' I say, twisting the curls sticking out at the end of my braid. Tamara will be mad if I say yes. She'd hated Mandy since I'd first met her last year at a birthday party for the little sister of one of Auntie Sophie's university friends. My aunt had insisted I attend to meet 'the right kind of people'. I'd stood out like a sore thumb, and a girl named Candida, smelling fear, came in for the kill, teasing me mercilessly about my obviously home-made dress when everyone else was in the latest styles from Miami. Mandy had saved me, pulling me towards the bouncy castle sitting on the massive lawn. The castle was for the smaller kids but Mandy didn't care: she wanted to bounce anyway, even though it wasn't such a cool thing for eleven-year-olds to do. She didn't care that she'd never heard my last name or seen me at her posh prep school. She didn't care that I didn't know any-body else at the party. And once she found out we were both going to Aggie's, she'd decided we would be friends.

Auntie Sophie was thrilled. She told me later that Mandy's family owned a ton of wholesale goods and haberdasheries – or *Chiney man shops* – downtown and that Mandy and her broth-ers practically grew up there. I wondered if that was why she didn't care about status, even though she was very rich.

After the party I'd breathlessly told Tamara about Mandy, how I'd never met anybody who seemed so sure of herself, and that must have been the wrong thing to say because she'd screwed up her face and said we had enough friends, we didn't need to add some rich little princess to our crew. She made that same screw face if I so much as mentioned Mandy, so I feel awkward sitting between the two of them now, with Mandy waiting for me to accept her invitation and Tamara ready to murder me with her eyes if I do. But Auntie Sophie will kill me even deader if she finds out I passed up this opportunity.

'Commmme, man!' Mandy whines at me. 'It will be fun!'

'I . . . yeah, yes, ahm . . . I'll ask my aunt?' I said, glancing at Tamara again.

'Do that – actually do you want my mum to call her?'

'No! No, no, that's okay. I'll ask her.'

'Good, tell me tomorrow. Trust me, it's gonna be so much fun! Bye, Tamika!' she says, as she flounces off.

'*Tamara*,' says Tamara, to her retreating back.

I look at my friend and give her an apologetic smile, although I'm not entirely sure what I'm apologetic about.

'I thought you auntie put you on social lockdown?' she says.

'Yeah, with you,' I say sheepishly. 'She'll kill me if she finds out Mandy invited me and I don't go.'

I shrug and shake my head, roll my eyes, *Can you believe that?* I want to convey, but she just looks at me blankly and says, 'Well, at least your *auntie* will be happy,' before she turns around and flounces off too, just as the school bell rings.

★

St Agatha's School for Girls – Aggie's – sits at the top of Half Way Tree Road, which cuts through the city. Head upwards from Half Way Tree and you're going uptown; head down from Half Way Tree, you're going downtown. Aggie's has a 'stellar reputation' and is 'proud to educate young ladies from all walks of life', which means there are girls from downtown areas so bad not even Jamaica Power & Light will send staff down there to read the meters, rich girls, who have never set foot inside a public bus, and girls like me and Tamara, who sit right in the middle like the pivot point on a seesaw. But some schools attracted more uptown students than anything else, and Aggie's was one of them. I was intimidated by the various shades of brown and cream and white I'd encountered for the first time, the way they all seemed already to know each other, the way they laughed and yelled and pawed at one another, sitting on the wooden benches around the largest, oldest tree until their parents drove down the circular drive in their Benzes and their Bimmas. I would watch them snatch up their Jansport backpacks, pink and red and blue, which never seemed to get dirty despite being kicked about on the ground, wave goodbye and bounce off to their rides, jumping into the front seat and giving their mothers or fathers a kiss hello or sitting in the back while their drivers drove sombrely out through the imposing gates.

Sometimes Tamara's father drops us off to school in one of the cars he's servicing, but most of the time we take the bus, although I'm usually alone since Tamara is always late. I am neatly combed and pressed in my blue and white uniform when I leave home, my shoes slick with polish to try to hide how old and despondent they really are, but the way the buses work is this: you squeeze into the smallest space you can find, the pressure of all the bodies keeping you upright. You stand there for a good half-hour or so while the driver piles more and more passengers inside. The sweat starts seeping through your clothes. Your head starts pounding in time to the dance-hall music the driver is trying to deafen you with, while some ancient woman in the back yells loudly about the Devil trying to sway the people with this unholy music and why can't we find Jesus, who has saved her in her time of need? You do not look this woman in the eye, unless you want a private sermon the whole way to school. You keep your backpack on, even when people push and shove past you and shout that you're taking up extra space, because it's the only thing that keeps your butt from being squeezed and pinched and rubbed in ways you do not appreciate or ask for. When the bus has so many passengers that it lists to one side like a sinking ship, half the people hanging out of the windows, it trundles wearily off.

To stop the bus, you squeeze your arm through the throng of passengers and bang on the side of it with a coin and yell, 'One stop! One stop, Driver!' and the bus will pull over. This happens so often that a five-minute journey takes roughly forty-five minutes. Sometimes I think it would be faster if we all got out, hoisted the bus onto our shoulders and carried it the whole way.

If you're a schooler like me, you just have to get off wherever the driver feels like stopping and run the rest of the way. By the time I make it to Assembly, I'm a sticky, sweaty, rumpled mess, wild curls pulling out of my bun, the polish on my shoes a faint memory lost under the dust of other people's footprints. The sixth-form girls hiss and peck at me to get myself in order before Mrs Dickens, our fearsome principal who stands five foot two (but whose aura is six foot three), picks you out of the crowd with the one lazy eye she has that makes every girl feel she is staring right at them. But it is the vice principal, Mrs Roberts, with her stiff hair sprayed into a helmet over her tiny head and her propensity to o v e r-e n u n c i a t e each and every syllable who is responsible for disciplining wayward, dishevelled, perpetually tardy or, in my case, insubordinate girls.

It was in Mrs Roberts's office that I found myself last week, her tiny head barely poking over her massive desk, Auntie

Sophie sitting beside me with her nerves balled up like a knot of yarn being worried by a puss, and Miss Smith standing to the side, murder etched into the lines on her face.

'What exactly are we to do with you, Miss Patterson?'

I glanced over at my aunt and then back to Vice Principal Roberts. She was staring at me over the top of her glasses, waiting for an answer. I shrugged, keeping my eyes averted from Miss Smith, whose death glare I could feel burning the side of my face.

'You'll have to do better than that, Miss Patterson,' said Mrs Roberts.

'Pumkin.' Sophie looked at me, hard.

'But, Auntie Sophie,' I whined, 'she can't even speak proper *English*, how she muss teach me French?'

Sophie pursed her mouth together and glanced at Miss Smith, who was beet red.

'That is hexackly what I'm talking about, Mrs Roberts!' the French teacher said. I saw both my aunt and the vice principal wince at the addition of that extra *h* and tried to catch Sophie's eye to give her the look, the one that said 'See?' but she wouldn't look at me.

'She is *rude*! She is *disruptive*! It is *himpossible* to teach her!'

'What do you have to say for yourself, Miss Patterson?' Mrs Roberts said.

'Miss, she pronounces everything wrong and when I –'

'*Who is the teacher 'ere? Eeh?*' Miss Smith yelled, lunging forward towards me.

'Miss *Smith*! Please get a hold of yourself!'

'I have to be honest, Mrs Roberts,' Sophie said, in her most cut-glass accent, 'if this is any indication of how my niece is treated in class, it's no wonder there's an issue, and I'm starting to think it is not entirely with her.'

I looked at Miss Smith, who was still staring at me with murder in her eyes. She had a very freckled face that was round like the moon and wide spaces between all her teeth through which little pieces of her gum hung down. She was trembling with so much rage that the small plaits around her head were quivering like little worms writhing over each other. We'd hated each other from the first day she'd walked into class and introduced herself as 'Miss Simmit'. Some of the girls had tittered and I had looked on in disbelief: I hadn't expected a teacher at a school like this to mangle her own name.

Sophie had drilled me about my diction, my accent, my pronunciation and, most of all, about the dropping of *h*s from where they should be and putting them back in places they didn't belong. 'People will hear that, Pumkin, and they will put you in a box from which you will never get out,' she'd said.

I cringed whenever my mother told me to ''urry up' or my grandmother told me to 'Peel di harinj fi mi nuh.' Sophie said we shouldn't be like those uptown people who treat people from below Half Way Tree as if they were 'less than' (even though *we* live below Half Way Tree). She *said* that, but I saw the way she startled when my grandmother made those slips of the tongue, pronounced the *h* in Thompson, for example; I saw the way she curled her lip when my mother said anything at all; I noted how she always, *always* corrected me if I spoke anything less than the Queen's English. When I started at St Agatha's, I heard those uptown girls switch from English to patois and back again and I asked Sophie why they could

35

do it and I could not. She'd said their pedigree was beyond reproach so they could do what they wanted, but we, coming from where we did, did not have that luxury.

'We will always have to prove we belong, Pumkin, because in truth, we do not. We're just passing. We need to pass.'

'But . . . why?' I'd asked her, and watched as a river of red flowed upwards from her neck into her cheeks, but she just told me to finish my homework, although I was already done.

When I heard the girls snicker at 'Miss Simmit' and saw the way they glanced at each other, I'd snorted loudly. Miss Smith spun around from the blackboard, on which she was writing her name, and stared at me. 'You need a tissue?' she said drily.

'No, Miss,' I muttered, then made eye contact with a green-eyed girl and sniggered.

From that day onwards we were mortal enemies, Miss Smith and I. I wasn't fluent in French, like Sophie, but years of being read French books and listening to her tapes from the embassy meant I wasn't completely useless: I knew mangled pronunciation when I heard it. Miss Smith was chewing the French up in her mouth, grinding it down with her molars and expelling the powdered dust of its remains. I would ask her, endlessly, to repeat herself. Was she *sure* that was how that was supposed to sound? Could she please enunciate, speak more clearly, sound it out a little more slowly because it didn't sound quite right to me. She would counter with 'I'm the teacher here!' and I would parry with 'But my aunt speaks French and that's not how that sounds!' She would lunge with 'I cannot 'elp your aunt's poor pronunciation!' and I would jab with 'The irony!' It was the 'Vous etch' that did me in, though. The 'Vous *etch*', which had had me slamming my book down on the desk and kissing my teeth, that landed us all here with Miss Smith looking at me so hard I was surprised I didn't melt on my seat like ice cream and drain away into the gutter.

'Miss Patterson, I'm going to give you a warning here,' said the VP. 'You have one o p p o r t u n i t y to pull your socks up. We will not tolerate students dis-res-pect-ing our teachers, no matter how strongly you feel about the subject matter. Any further dis-*tur*-ban-ces and you will be pulled out of class and forced to take a lesser elective, which, as you well know, may affect your chances of staying on for sixth form and going to university. Are we clear, Miss Patterson?'

I looked up at Sophie, who cocked her eyebrow. I was so sure she would be on my side, sure she would roll her eyes and give Miss Smith the stink eye and tell Mrs Roberts to stuff it, that I was right and she was wrong. But her eyebrow just stayed there, mid-air, until I grumbled, 'Yes, Miss.'

'One thing, Mrs Roberts,' my aunt said, as she pulled her handbag strap onto her shoulder. 'I'd like your assurances that there will be no *aggression*', and here she glanced at Miss Smith, 'towards my niece, moving forward. I appreciate she has not displayed the manners we've tried to instil in her at home, and we will address that, Mrs Roberts, but at the end of the day, my niece is the child here. Someone needs to act like an adult in this situation.'

Miss Smith started to sputter but the vice principal held up a hand. 'We ensure an environment of m u t u a l respect, Miss Jones. M u t u a l res-pec-t.'

With that we gathered our things, said our goodbyes and turned to leave, the heat from Miss Smith's eyes searing into my back.

'High seat kill Miss Thomas Puss'

'Trying to elevate yourself too high can lead to your embarrassment'

Boots

I almost fall out of my chair the day Boots comes in carrying Sophie in his arms. I'm in second form at Aggie's now, twelve years old, and in my usual position huddled over the dining table, conjugating French verbs. My grandmother is sewing at the dining table. My mother is God knows where.

Boots isn't tall and he isn't short, but he fills up the doorway just with his presence, a man in a space where men were not. Like a fox in a henhouse. My grandmother did not allow men in the house unless something needed fixing. As far as she was concerned, they brought nothing but trouble.

'But see yah my lawd,' my grandmother mutters, as I gawp at the doorway.

'Mama, this is – oh, just put me down on the couch, Boots – Mama, this is Boots,' Sophie says nervously, as the alien sets her on the couch. My grandmother raises her eyebrow and waits.

'This is Boots, Mama,' Sophie says again, that tell-tale red creeping up her throat.

'Hee-vlin, Missus Jones,' Boots says, striding confidently over to my grandmother – whose last name is MacNally – to shake her hand. He is medium-toned and good-looking, with a squarish head, a broad nose and close-cropped hair. His face is split open in a wide and friendly smile that shows straight white teeth with a little gap between the two front ones.

My grandmother takes his hand gingerly, her arm flailing as he pumps it enthusiastically. 'Boots?' she says.

'Yes, ma'am.'

She looks down at his sneakers. Boots lets out a loud, booming laugh and shakes his head. 'Nutten to do with my shoes, ma'am.'

'Den is why dem call you Boots?'

'Truthfully, Missus Jones, I don't remember now yu nuh. Is juss suh dem call me from time.'

'Boots works at the embassy, Mama,' Sophie pipes up, from the couch.

'Oh?'

'Yes, ma'am. I'm the bearer,' he says.

'Oh.' My grandmother could not have made it plainer that she was not impressed by the man whose job was to make deliveries and pick up packages and wait in the lines to pay the company's bills.

'Boots saved me today, Mama. I twisted my ankle,' says Sophie. It's only then that I notice her foot, swollen to the size of the pomegranates that grow on Miss Bertha's tree up the road. 'Pumkin, bring me some ice nuh?'

I look from her ankle to Boots, and when he catches my eye, he winks, which makes my face heat up as I run the few steps to the kitchen.

'Well, tank you, Mista Boots, for tekkin my daughter home,' I hear my grandmother say. I can tell from the tone of her voice that Boots has overstayed his welcome, having stood in our living room for more than two minutes at one time. I start frantically popping cubes out of the ice tray into a kitchen cloth, not wanting him to leave before I get another good look at him.

'Not a problem, Missus Jones! I was glad to help,' he says, with another booming laugh.

I fling the last of the cubes into the cloth and run back out into the living room, staring at Boots a moment before walking over to Sophie. He smiles at me and pulls his keys out of his pocket, jiggling them three times before putting them back in.

'Wishin you a good heev-lin, sar,' says my grandmother, pointedly.

'Oh! Yes, yes, ma'am, a good hee-vlin to you, very good hee-vlin to you, ma'am. Miss Sophie! If yuh want I can pick yuh up in the mawnin? Tek yuh into work?'

Sophie looks from Boots to her mother, then to her swollen ankle, and sighs. I will her to say yes, not entirely sure why, beyond the fact that I want him to come back to our house.

'It's no problem yuh nuh, Miss Sophie. It's not out of my way.'

'You sure it won't put you out, Boots?'

'Yeah, man!' He laughs that laugh again and does his thing with the keys: taking them out of his pocket, jiggling them three times, then putting them back.

Sophie glances at her mother again. My grandmother's mouth is turned down in a deep scowl, her arms crossed and that one eyebrow cutting a sharp angle on her forehead. But I know Sophie is thinking about how she's going to navigate the buses with a lame foot. She's always so careful on the bus, trying her best to squeeze into a small space and staying still so she doesn't get rumpled, getting off one stop early even though the bus stops right outside the embassy, so people won't see her. I know she won't give up a chance to be driven to work.

43

'Well, all right then, if you're sure.'

'Awrite awrite!' he says, as if he has won a prize. 'Eight o'clock, okay?'

'Eight o'clock is perfect, thanks so much, Boots.'

'Good, good. Then good hee-vlin to you all, Missus Jones, Pumkin,' he says, 'and till tomorrow, Miss Soph.'

I follow him to the door, a weird feeling in my tummy as I watch him go. By eight o'clock tomorrow I'll already be on my way to school and I will miss him. I wonder, for a moment, if I could ask him to take me there, so we could all be together, the three of us. I could be like those other girls who get driven to school, arriving fresh and cool from the A/C, not wrinkled and harassed from the bus. With one hand on the doorknob he turns towards me, drawing his other hand out of his pocket. I expect to see that bundle of keys again but instead he draws out a piece of candy and hands it to me. I want to tell him that I'm not six years old, but my brain still hasn't recovered from the shock of the Man in Our House. And truthfully it thrills me that he's giving me something, even a thing as small as this. People didn't, in general, just give me things. I manage to whisper, 'Thank you,' and he winks at me again and walks out of the door.

'A *bearer*, Sophie?'

I've barely closed the door on Boots before my grand-mother starts in on my aunt.

'Mama, please, he's just a friend from work who did me a favour.'

'Is dem kinda fren yuh keeping now? A *bearer*?'

'Why you keep saying it like that? There's nothing wrong with being a bearer!'

'Nutten don't wrong wid it but if yuh tink I go tru all this

44

trouble fi get yuh a good heducation an big big job at di hembassy fi yuh end up wid a *bearer*, is lick yuh lick yu head!'

'Oh, my God, he is a *co-worker* who did me a *favour*, Mama, not my – my *boyfriend*! I barely even talk to him at work.'

'Better not! Set yu sight dem higher dan dat!'

Sophie rolls her eyes and shakes her head, flopping back on the couch. My grandmother wanders into the kitchen, muttering under her breath about sacrifices made and the efforts it took to raise children to a better station than oneself, only to watch them slide right back down. I sit beside Sophie, resting my head on her shoulder as she puts her arm around me.

'You do your homework yet, Pumkin?'

'Yes, Auntie Sophie,' I say, unwrapping Boots's sweet and popping it into my mouth.

*

Boots picks Sophie up for work the next day, the day after that, and every day for over a month, well after her ankle has healed. He also drives her home every evening. With every visit he brings something: Danishes from Sugar & Spice that I eat in a circular motion until I get to the yellow cream in the middle; glazed doughnuts that melt as soon as they touch my tongue; apple turnovers, crispy with sugar crystals on the outside and smooshed with cinnamony apple inside.

I decide to make him gizzada, that crisp butter pastry filled with shredded, sweet and spicy coconut. I've never baked for anyone outside my family before, except Tamara, and I watch as he bites into it, so nervous it feels like I've swallowed ants. But then I see his face do that thing faces do when they bite into something delicious for the first time: pinch in on itself like someone just stepped on his foot.

'*You* mek this?' he says. 'Is lie yuh tellin. Is buy yuh buy it.'

'No, I made it!' I say, a big smile on my face.

'Is *buy* yuh buy it, man! Tell me is where yuh buy it, come, man, tell me.' And I giggle and insist that it was made by my own two hands until my grandmother tuts and pointedly tells him, 'Good *hee-vlin*, Mista Boots!' No matter what he brings for us, it can't melt her icy heart. She does not like Boots, but I fall more and more in love with every visit.

And so does Sophie.

I see the goose bumps spread across her arms if she even hears his name, the light in her eyes when he toots the horn outside in the mornings, toot toot! I tease her about it endlessly.

'Boots *and* Sophie sittin-inna-*tree!* K-I-S-S-I—'

'For God's sake, Pumkin!' she yips at me, but I see her smile as she turns away.

'Will you and Boots get married, Auntie Sophie?'

'*What?* Pumkin, is where you get that from? No, nobody's getting married around here. Not to Boots.'

'But why? I like him. Don't you like him?'

She stares out of the back window, out onto our little yard of crab grass, while I stir melted butter into a tub to make a cake.

'He's not . . .' she says, shaking her head. 'I do like him, Pumkin. But he's not . . . the right . . . *person* for me.'

I give her a look. Who could be more 'right' than Boots? But I'm confident that if he keeps bringing her little treats, keeps making her laugh that tinkly laugh she does around him, keeps making her neck go bright red, she'll come around. And then we'll live together, in a house somewhere in a nice neighbourhood. That's a dream that makes more sense to me than going to France, a place we will never reach.

*

One time Boots delivers Sophie home with three bags of the best jerk pork I have ever tasted in my life. The meat is cut into chunks, a crackling layer of skin covering thick, juicy fat that clings to the firm meat. I eat a whole bag with my fingers, the spice so intense that I have to soak my swollen, tingling lips in a glass of ice water for twenty minutes afterwards, the greasy brown paper lying like a shed skin on my lap. Since Boots has brought us a feast – the pork, fried dumplings and bottles of coconut water – my grandmother couldn't justify sending him right back out of the door, so he is allowed to eat with us this time. She tucks into her pork with relish, licking the spice off her fingers and making satisfied noises in her throat. It still doesn't warm her to Boots, though: my grandmother just likes getting nice things for free.

'Bwoy you waps off that pork, Pumkin,' he says, laughing that booming laugh as I look up guiltily, my hands and lips covered with spicy oil.

'I should take you two to Boston.'

'In America?' I say, confused.

He laughs for a good long minute before he says, 'I don't have that kind of money yet, Pumkin, but I can take you to Boston Jerk, in Portland. If yuh tink *this* pork good, Lawd have mercy, yuh gwen *dead* when yuh taste Boston jerk.'

Sophie laughs nervously and glances towards the bathroom, where my grandmother has excused herself but from which she is now returning, ostensibly to run Boots off the property now that her belly is full.

47

Frankie

There's a rooster in my neighbour's yard called Frankie. A big
ol' bird with gold and black feathers, a huge black comb
bursting out of the top of his head like a fountain of oil, those
weird wrinkly balls hanging low under his neck, and a piss-
poor attitude. Frankie guards his chicken coop of hens
aggressively. I'm pretty sure he thinks the entire house is a
coop and that Alma, the neighbour, is just a really big chicken
because any attempt to enter the yard will leave you with
weeping bloody gouges in your legs. Alma's house has never
been burgled.

Sometimes I watch people come to visit her, tapping as
quietly as possible on the gate and stage-whispering, 'Alma!
Alma!' while they glance nervously around for Frankie. They
open the gate and wince as it creaks, pausing for a moment to
see if the noise has attracted the beast, before sprinting up
towards the house. This is usually when Frankie dashes out
from wherever he's hiding and races after them. They scream
blue murder as they run up to the front door and fling themselves inside while Alma cackles from the window where
she's been watching it all. I personally think Frankie got his
bad attitude from Alma, who is as crotchety as they come.
'Nutten but crosses, dat ooman,' my grandmother says, but it
doesn't stop her taking eggs and chickens from Alma's coop
in exchange for sewing her curtains and cushion covers.

I'm standing at Alma's gate now, sent over to collect eggs

for a coconut cake I'm baking for my aunt's office. Ever since Boots's reaction to my pastries, I'd felt more confident baking for other people. I'd volunteered to bake pastries for Sophie's office a few weeks ago for a colleague's birthday and since then they've asked for banana bread, corn pone, carrot muffins and gizzadas. Every week a few batches of something else. Now they'd requested a coconut cake and I'm here at Alma's on the hunt for eggs. I watch Frankie and his girls trip their way across the yard, scratching at the ground, unearthing whatever delectable treats chickens find in the dirt. My face scroonches up on itself when I think of how people love eating chicken-foot soup on Saturdays, even though they know what chickens do with their feet all day.

'You 'fraid fi come in, Pumkin? Him not gwen trouble you, you nuh,' Alma calls out of her front window.

Liar. I can see him eyeing my calves from the corners of his beady little chicken eyes.

'I don't know, Miss Alma . . .' I stand at the gate still, nervous. I have a small scar on my right leg from an encounter with Frankie and I'm not looking to add another. Alma sighs and says, 'Awrite, awrite, hol' on deh.' She hoists her body up from the easy chair set by the front window where she watches the world go by. After a few moments I see small beads of grain raining down the side of the house, hear Alma calling, 'Come 'ere, Frankie! Come 'ere!' until the birds rush over, peck peck pecking at the ground. As soon as they're distracted I unlatch the gate and run for it.

Alma's place is about as big as ours but she has it all to herself now that her four children are grown and gone. There are pictures of them all over the walls, her three sons Len, Kirk and Dalston, her daughter Odessa, who all live in

Kingston but never, ever come to visit. If there weren't pictures I'd never know that they exist. The living room is filled with glass figurines, snow globes and kitsch set on every available surface, bought with the money they send her. I think they send money so they don't have to come home.

'What you making this time, Pumkin?'

'Coconut cake for the embassy again. Gramma says she'll add some pillowcases to the bedspread she's making for you for this batch of eggs.'

'Yes, yes. Coconut cake. I *do* love a good coconut cake . . .'

Alma pats her ample stomach as she says this, staring wistfully out of the front window. There's an old radio beside the easy chair tuned in to Bitty Crawford, a talk-show host prone to screaming fits of outrage at the plight of poor people in Jamaica. Bitty's six-bedroom Stony Hill mansion was featured in an architecture magazine I found in the embassy's waiting room when I went to Sophie's office once. I wondered: if one of the poor people he's always shouting for turned up at his door, would he let them in?

'Oh, Miss Alma, if you give me ten eggs instead of six, I could make an extra cake for you? A small one.'

'Is true, yuh would do dat? Well, if you haw-fferin I won't say no, mi dear!' She turns away from the window and moves towards the chicken coop in the yard but then she turns back to me and says, 'I still wouldn't mind those pillowcases, though.'

I roll my eyes at her back while she goes to collect the eggs. I wonder why she bothers with a chicken coop when she lets the birds run free around the whole yard, if she uses them like uptown people use guard dogs. I pick up and put down hideous glass figurines of dogs and pigs and chickens until she comes back and hands me a basket of cloth-wrapped eggs.

'Well, you muss be very proud of you hanty, don't it?'

'Proud of Auntie Sophie, Miss Alma? Well, yes, I guess?'

'Yes yes. Imagine somebaddy from Potter's Lane gawn a France! Well, I never thought I would see the day.'

'. . . France . . . ?'

'You grandmodda couldn't *wait* fi tell me,' Alma says, with a sneer.

I feel my heart leap up into my throat, then plummet to my gut. Sophie's going to France? Like, *actually* going? That can't be right. 'What yuh mean, Miss Alma?'

'Den dem don't tell yuh yet? Yuh hanty get tru, mi dear. Har job sending har go a France. I would tink dem wudda tell you long time . . .'

Nobody's said a word. Not a word. What does that mean? She's going to France . . . without me?

'But you know, *I* know what it's like to have successful pickney, you nuh! My children, far hexample, all a dem have big, big job in −'

'Sorry, Miss Alma! Sorry, I have to go, I have to . . . I have to start the . . . I have to go!'

And I race out of Miss Alma's house and across the yard, Frankie nipping at my heels but unable to catch me this time. Not this time.

★

I burst through my front door, the eggs rattling in the cloth, but I don't care about them any more. My grandmother is bent over her sewing at the dining table; my mother, as usual, is nowhere to be found.

'Where is Auntie Sophie?' I shout.

'Ex*cuse me*?' my grandmother says, with her eyebrow held aloft. But her expression changes when she spies the basket of eggs hung carelessly over my arm. She shakes her head. 'I know I shoulda *never* tell Alma nutten. Dat ooman juss love *chat* people business!'

I stand there looking at my grandmother. There is a man who lives in my chest and he is wide awake now, and he's drumming drumming drumming. She shakes her head again and draws a great breath.

'She in di kitchen, dahlin, but hol' on –'

I don't hear the rest. I scramble into our tiny kitchen where Sophie is grating the coconut for the cake. Her neck is blazing red, the blush spreading upwards to her cheeks. Our house is too small for secrets: she knows I know. I look at her for a moment but she won't meet my eyes, so I take the basket of eggs to the counter. I crack four, separating the whites from two of them and putting them in a small bowl. Sophie is sifting flour into a big mixing bowl, adding baking powder and salt little by little. After a while, she puts her hand on top of mine. 'Pumkin . . . I was going to talk to you about it. I was going to tell you.'

'When?'

'Today. Now, while we were making the cake. I just found out a couple of days ago.'

I move my hand from underneath hers and start violently beating a mix of sugar, butter and oil. We don't have an electric mixer like at Tamara's so I have to do everything by hand.

'A couple of days . . .' I whisper.

'I told you . . . I told you I was working on a plan, right? There's this thing at work . . . a kind of programme where you can apply to transfer to an equivalent job in France. I applied, a long time ago actually, and I didn't really think anything would come of it but . . . but they finally approved it. I'm going to Marseille.'

I add the egg yolks to the beaten mixture, gingerly adding a few drops of vanilla extract. It was expensive. Sophie had just bought it for me with some cash her colleagues had given her for all the baked goods and I was determined to make it last. I beat and beat and beat the mixture, and then I beat it some more.

'Not Paris?'

'No, not Paris. I have to go where there's an opening. But France is France, right?'

I turn and look at her now, her features blurred by the hot, angry tears in my eyes. 'What about me? You're leaving me. Otherwise you would have told me already. You're leaving me here.'

I feel the tears spill over, burning tracks down my cheeks. She moves to wipe them but I swat at her hand and she pulls back, a hurt look passing over her face. I push away the salty tears and turn back to the lumpy bowl of batter, adding the flour and folding until it's combined.

'Yes, Pumkin, I'm leaving but I'm not leaving you behind. Not for ever. Look, I want to take you with me.'

I drop the spatula into the batter and look back at my aunt. She holds on to both my arms.

'I can't take you right now because you're not . . . you're not *officially* my daughter. But I have it all worked out. I'll go first and get settled in, then find you a school, and it will be easier to transfer you. If you get a place as a student, I can apply to be your official guardian, you see? I already spoke to them at work about it and they're working up a list of schools in the area I'll be in. So, you see, I'm just leaving you for a short while, and then we'll both be in France, Pumkin, in France! Just like we always dreamed of!'

Hope blooms in my chest and flutters. Sophie's face is all lit up.

'Can you imagine it?' she says, her hands squeezing into me. 'Maybe we'll meet the King after all! Pumkin's Pâtisserie, remember that? In *France*, Pumkin, me and you.'

Me and Sophie. I try to imagine it, me at school – in France! – far from here, from Potter's Lane. We played that game often, Sophie and I, *what we will do when we get to France*, but it was just a game, right? I never really thought we would actually go. Me and Auntie Sophie in France? What about my grandmother? What about –

'Mama?'

Sophie's face fell.

'She'll never let me go. You know she won't!'

'Pumkin, listen, you leave your mother to me. Don't worry about –'

'But you *know* she won't! She won't let me do *anything* with you unless you lie about it and tell her it's something else. How you going to lie about taking me all the way to France? She'll never let me go!'

'Pumkin!' She squeezes her hands tighter on my arms but I pull away. There are red marks where her fingers were but I can't feel anything. What was she thinking? My mother will never let me leave, out of sheer spite. She'll keep me here and there will be no more Sophie standing in her way.

'Pumkin, listen to me, *listen*! Do not worry about your mother. I will deal with her – me and Gramma will deal with her. You just focus on school and especially on your French lessons and we will work it out. Do you understand? I am not leaving you behind, Pumkin.'

Her eyes are wide. I want to tell her how scared I am that she'll go and she'll forget about me. She'll be having so much fun in her new French life, why would she remember me, all the way down here in Potter's Lane? I'd seen it, children at primary school whose mothers left for America or London, promising to send for them, but they just sat there year after year wearing the nice nice overseas clothes but never leaving, barely even hearing from them because phone calls were too expensive and letters took so long to reach you, you'd think the pigeons carrying them had lost their way.

I *know* my mother will not let me leave this place, not to go anywhere with her sister, not to go on to a better life with the one person she hates more than anything in this world, maybe even more than she hates me. But the words just twine themselves into a knot. The man in my chest bats away the flutter of hope and beats his drums even louder, the thump thump thump knocking me back and forth, squeezing the breath out of my lungs in short, sharp bursts. Thump thump *thump*!

I turn back to the coconut-cake batter, ready to pour it into our battered old baking tins that we found one time on the side of the road and scoured with bleach and a mesh wire until they looked like new. I think again that Sophie is leaving me, no matter what she says. I will be all alone. I take the batter off the counter and slowly spoon every drop of it into the garbage. Then I put the bowl carefully back down and walk out of the kitchen door.

I remember . . .

. . . I am lying in the bed I share with Auntie Sophie. I am scrunched up as close to the wall as possible, Sophie as close to the other edge as possible, the two of us trying to avoid the dip in the middle where the springs have given out. I am exhausted, but I cannot sleep. I see little coloured spots, red and purple and blue and yellow and green, floating in front of my eyes so I follow them and they dance in funny patterns. I'm trying not to move because it annoys Sophie when I toss and turn and the springs squeak and the whole bed flips and flops, like a wave trying to push us to shore.

But I cannot sleep. I think about the dip in the bed, so deep it's like a crater.

'Auntie Sophie?' I whisper.

There's silence for a long time, so I think maybe she's sleeping, but then she answers me, her voice thick with sleep. A mumbled 'Hmm?'

'Auntie Sophie, how come? How come we don't move from here?'

'What you mean, Pumkin?' But it sounds like one word because she's still half asleep – 'Whayemeenpenkin?'

'Well. Linnette says you have big big job at the embassy now. She says, if you really have a good job, why you still live here? In this house?'

'Who? Who is Linnette?'

'Linnette. She owns the shop on the corner.'

There's another long silence, and I think she's gone back to sleep, but then I hear her turn over and clear her throat. It's too dark to see anything but I turn my head towards her. I can sense that she's rubbing her eyes.

'Pumkin,' she says, and she sounds a little clearer now. More awake. 'That's not how it works. You don't just . . . start a job one day and move out the next. I don't have any money saved up. And it's not a big big job. I'm the lowest on the totem pole. I'm just a secretary.'

I don't know what a totem pole is but I make a note to look it up in the morning.

'But then what's the point?' I say, my voice rising before I remember myself and whisper again. 'I mean, why did you take that job? Couldn't you get a better job, since you went to university?'

'You know why I took that job, Pumkin.' She's really awake now. 'How often have we talked about getting out of here, moving to Paris? This job isn't about the money, it's about the connections. Opportunity. I have a plan.'

She shuffles beside me, changing her position, and I am silent for a moment.

'But Linnette —'

'Jesus . . .'

'— says that is foolishness, that nobody from here ever moved to Paris before and —'

'So that automatically means that nobody ever will? First of all, Linnette needs to mind her own damn business. Second, Pumkin, don't make people tell you what you can and cannot achieve. Some people, you know what, they think achievement and success are like — like crabs in a bucket, like, the only way to get to the top is to crawl over the others and push them further down. They don't want to put in the work, they just like to keep doing the same things they doing and just complain, or say that people lucky. If you're determined to do something, Pumkin, then find a way. And don't chat your business to other people, just put your head down and work at it. Or, by all means, listen to Linnette and stay here, in this house, in this neighbourhood, if that's what you want to do. Is that what you want to do?'

'. . . No, Auntie.'

'Good. Because I am going to Paris and I certainly want you to come with me. Now go to sleep. I have work in the morning.'

I turn back to the wall and run my hands over the cracks I know are there but cannot see. I try to think of Paris, but my mind draws a blank, so instead I watch the little coloured dots in front of my eyes until, eventually, I fall asleep.

Boston (but not that one)

The Sunday we go to Boston is bright and clear. The sun is deeply yellow, hanging heavy in the sky, like a perfectly ripe mango ready to drop off the tree. A light breeze brushes its fingertips across my face as I hold my head out of the window. There's a smell of heat and exhaust that blows itself away once we're on the road to Portland, a narrow, twisting thing that does not seem like it could hold one car, much less two side by side. When oncoming traffic approaches, we squeeze gingerly past each other, like lovers who have just had a fight and are too afraid to touch. I have never left Kingston in my life and I keep trying not to blink, not to miss anything. I did not know that my island was this beautiful. I did not know that there are trees so tall you can't see the tops; that bamboo grows like stately soldiers by the side of the road; that people stick their colourful little houses in the nooks and crannies of hills that burst out of the sides of the roads and stretch all the way up to Heaven. They look like a strong breeze would tip them right over into the rocky riverbeds below, or onto the road, directly in our path.

'It have alligators in that river,' Boots says, and I crane my head out of the window hoping to see one slithering its way over the rocks, but I don't catch even a glimpse of these old dinosaurs.

I think it's funny how the goats we pass wait patiently for a break in traffic to cross the road, while the packs of stray dogs just run helter-skelter among the cars.

'The goats are civilized but the dogs don't have no broughtupsey,' I say, which makes Boots boom with laughter and Sophie giggle.

I look from one of them to the other, then turn my gaze back out of the window. I'd been angry with Auntie Sophie since she'd told me she was moving to France, no matter how much she'd insisted that she wasn't leaving me behind, that she'd send for me as soon as she could. I think she finally agreed that Boots could take us to Boston just to butter me up, and I was too excited about it to keep sulking. Not a night goes by that she isn't talking about something Boots said on the drive home or did at work that had set her off laughing. And when Gramma asks her, every morning, if Boots is picking her up today, she turns a spectacular shade of red under her light brown skin, no matter how breezily she tries to say, 'Oh, yes, yes, he is.' So I know that Boots is the key to getting Auntie Sophie to stay.

We'll go to Boston and she'll see that she already has everything she needs right here. She and Boots will get married and buy a house and take me out of the noise and grit and dirt of our cramped little space. We'll live together in a nice house in a decent neighbourhood, away from my mother.

I watch Boots navigate the roads, which are overrun with taxis stuffed to the hilt with passengers. Pedestrians are forced to tuck themselves into the stony walls behind them so their toes don't get run over. The traffic going one way clings to the dun-coloured rocks – the traffic in our lane is right on the edge of a precipice. I peer over into it. If we fall into the river or wild jungle below, they'll never find us. We get stuck behind a huge, gassy truck for miles, the line of cars building and building, horns honking while a couple of daredevils decide to overtake around the corners, dance hall blaring from their windows.

'Clowns,' Boots says, shaking his head. 'They gonna get somebody killed.'

But the truck eventually takes a turn-off and we shoot forward again. The radio is on and Sophie and Boots are talking and laughing, laughing and talking, and the breeze is in my face and I almost don't want to reach to Boston, just want, instead, to keep driving like this. But the lull of the movement is too much for me, and the next thing I know, I'm waking up to a different scene.

The sea. This is my first time seeing that great expanse of water, and it makes my breath catch in my chest. That might sound crazy, since I live on an island, but lots of Jamaicans have never seen the sea. As we drive along the Portland coast I watch the water, awed. It is rough and angry and loud, smashing up against the sides of the low stone walls as if it's trying to break them down, to get at us in all its fury. It is not a happy sea. I imagine people trying to swim here and being broken against the rocks.

'It vex,' I say to myself, as I stare out at it from the window, but nobody hears me, so nobody responds.

*

The air at Boston Jerk smells like spiced smoke. We sit on wooden benches at wooden tables, one of many people at many huts, on this tiny strip of road, with dirt floors and zinc roofs. Men in loose shirts hang around the entrance of each, shouting at potential customers: 'Bess jerk right yah'so! Bess jerk pon di island!' The sound systems set up at each hut fight for attention, reggae music thrumming in our chests. To the right of the entrance is the kitchen – an open area with concrete blocks on which lie long, thick branches covered with cuts of meat, shrouded in smoke, corroded zinc hovering just above. Beside the makeshift kitchen, an ancient man with long grey dreadlocks wound loosely around his head sits smoking weed and staring into the sky, pointing at it every so often.

Boots orders jerk chicken, jerk pork, jerk sausage, hard dough bread, festival and Ting sodas. With him and Sophie deep in conversation, I wander over to the kitchen, curious about the smoke that stings my eyes but smells like spice and salt water.

'First time at Boston, likkle dahlin?'

I look up at the cook, a dark-skinned man with huge arms wearing a mesh marina, sweat glistening on his forehead. He is holding a long pair of tongs, which he uses to poke and prod the different types of meat, occasionally flipping them over. There's a woman beside him rolling dough for the festivals, those long, slightly sweet, crispy-on-the-outside, airy-on-the-inside fried dumplings that go so well with everything. I nod and look back at the meat, my stomach growling. The smoke is making my eyes water and I wonder how he can stand it, so close to the pit.

'You know bout jerk?'

I shrug. 'It's spicy,' I say lamely.

He laughs and flips a few pieces of chicken with his tongs.

'Yeh, *well* spicy!' he says. 'But real jerk is more than spice – you smell the smoke? How it don't smell like regular smoke?'

I inhale again, deeply, which is a mistake because it grabs

64

my throat and sets me to coughing – but he's right: it's the smell of the smoke that has drawn me closer.

'Awrite, you see this wood 'ere? Ah, pimento wood dis, it burn slow slow. And the smell weh you smellin? Yu gwen taste dat in the meat, mm-hmm.'

'But what if you don't have the pimento wood?' I ask.

'Den is not real jerk!' he says, in a huge voice, laughing like he's never heard anything so funny in his life. He sounds like he has a microphone in his chest. I look at him and can't help but grin.

'Dat is what yuh tell di people dem, when dem tell yuh seh summen jerk,' he continues. 'Yuh gwen ask dem, "Hexcuse me, dis cook pon pimento wood?" and when dem seh, "Naw," yuh tell dem seh is not real jerk, caw Bagga T down a Boston tell yuh bout real jerk. Don't it, Miss Mary?'

'That's right!' says the woman beside him, as she plops pieces of dough into a great wok full of sizzling oil.

The cook – Bagga T, I guess – slaps piles of meat onto a cutting board, chops them up and adds them to the plates. He looks at me, holds up his finger, then adds an extra sausage to the pile and gives me a wink. 'Order ready, big man!' he shouts, and Boots collects our lunch, and we sit down to eat.

I pop a piece of sausage – slathered in extra spice sauce – into my mouth. The flavour bursts onto my tongue, a mix of barbecue and smoke, pimento, thyme and garlic. It's so good I take a few more pieces and shove them into my mouth. It takes a while for the burn to start spreading over my tongue, like a slow-rolling wave, but when it comes, I think I'm going to die. My eyes tear up and my nose starts to run and the burn crawls all over my tongue and down into my throat. I grab for the bottle of Ting but Boots says,

'NO! Dat will just wash the pain round your mouth – eat the bread.'

So I stuff chunks of hard dough into my mouth, my cheeks puffed out like a chipmunk's. Sophie laughs and laughs. 'Tek it easy, Pumkin,' she says, and I just look at her and wonder how something so painful can be so delicious.

After we've eaten ourselves sick, Boots takes us to Frenchman's Cove. I can't believe this is the same sea that crashed and raged on the other side of the town – it's crystal clear here, quiet and calm and inviting. I sit looking out at the still, blue-green water, the men on the other side of the cove sailing tourists into the sea on bamboo rafts, the big bushy trees bowing down at the side, as if they're at the end of a performance. Boots is standing in the froth of water right at the shoreline, splashing Sophie, who is screaming about 'My hair, my hair!' but I notice she doesn't run too far away. I take a deep breath. I cannot remember ever being this happy.

*

I walk through our front door, sun-soaked and salted, pleasantly exhausted. There's no sign of my mother or grandmother, and I sit behind the door to make sure they won't surprise Sophie, who is just outside with Boots. I can see them through the crack in the door if I squint one eye. Boots is reaching for Sophie, but she moves away.

'Sophie . . .' he says, but she just shakes her head.

'I thought you did like me,' he says, pushing her playfully on the shoulder. He has a big grin on his face and I can see the glint of a gold tooth from here.

'I . . . yes, I do like you, Boots. Just . . . as a friend, though.'

'A friend.' The grin drops off his face and lands with a splat on the gravel drive. He looks out over our crooked front gate that won't close unless you lift it from the bottom. 'Oh.'

They both stand there looking at everything but each other for a moment. Something drops from my chest into my stomach.

'You know, I thought, when you walk past me at work like you don't know me, when you tell me to drop you off roun di back. When you only talk to me when nobody else cyaan see us. I thought that was because you didn't want people at work to know about us yet. You know, so they not up in our business till we were . . . official, you know? But . . . you juss don't want them to know that we talk at all, don't it?'

I switch my squinted eye, see Sophie wringing her hands.

'No, no, Boots. It's just . . . It's complicated.'

There is silence for a moment while Boots stares at Sophie. I realize I am holding my breath.

'I think . . .' he says, after a long while '. . . maybe it not so complicated. I think I understand. I see the people you run with at work. I hear the way you talk to them, careful careful like. You talk different with me, you know that? Like you don't have to think so much about what you going to say. Or how you going say it. I bet nobody don't know that is downtown you live, don't it?'

Sophie doesn't say anything but she is squirming, like something's crawling on her neck.

'We're not really downtown,' she mutters half-heartedly.

Boots reaches for her again but she moves even further away.

'Boots,' she says. 'I do like you. I *do* . . . but . . .'

Boots nods.

67

'But I just don't . . . fit. Right? Likkle too dark, likkle too downtown. Likkle too close to home. Don't it?'

'I – I don't know what you want me to say. I just . . . It's not . . . Look, I'm really focused on . . . I have plans . . . for France and . . .' She shakes her head and trails off.

There is another heavy moment of silence, but then Boots says, slowly, 'Awrite. Awrite.'

He walks towards the rickety gate and opens it. I switch eyes again. Just before he leaves, Sophie calls out again. 'Boots! Listen . . . you're right.'

Boots turns back, quick quick, and my spine straightens up, my stomach tight.

'Nobody knows I live here . . .' Sophie says, wringing her hands. Boots's shoulders sag, and my stomach deflates like a balloon.

'Don't worry, man, I not sayin nutten to nobody.'

He walks through the gate, closing it carefully behind him. Sophie stands there hugging herself and looking up into the sky. I watch her for a moment with my one squinted eye, but then I get up and go into our room before she comes in and catches me there.

The next day – and every day after – Sophie takes the bus to work.

'Beg waata kyaan bwile cow skin'

(You can't boil cow skin with borrowed water)

'You cannot depend on others to achieve your own goals'

And after that, a *macaron*

'Is drive we gwen drive the whole way to Henglan?'
That's really what the woman asked the flight attendant,
Pumkin. She was complaining that she didn't pay good
money to drive in a plane if she could have taken a taxi. I
wanted to laugh so hard — I mean, she didn't think about
the massive body of water between us and England? —
but I bit my lip, Pumkin, because it was my first time on
a plane too, so who was I to make fun?

I hold the letter to my chest and look out of the window.
That part always makes me giggle. I've never been on a plane
either and even *I* know it would be impossible to drive the
whole way. I stare at the tree in the back yard, at the patchy
crab grass lawn, and try to imagine the rolling green hills of
London as Sophie goes from Heathrow to Gatwick. I can't
wrap my head around a city so big that it takes an hour to drive
from one airport to another. I pick up the letter again, holding
it so close to my face that my breath makes it slightly wet.

Pumkin, I don't even know how to describe Paris to you, I
really don't. We dreamed so long about getting here, you
and I, and now I'm here and . . . That first day, walking
around, I was so overwhelmed I couldn't even speak, not a
word, the whole day. I walked past the Eiffel Tower, which
I have to tell you, Pumkin, is dusty and dirty and not as
impressive as all that. We got special tickets from the

71

embassy for the museums and I waited for two hours in a line at the Louvre just to see the Mona Lisa but then when I stood in front of it, I was so disappointed to see it is the size of a postage stamp! Maybe I thought I'd hear a choir of angels or get an electric thrill down my spine or something, anything, but nothing happened, it's just a picture of a girl that I'd already seen on TV.

And I am sorry to report that I didn't see one person ride by on their bicycle wearing a black and white striped shirt with a baguette sticking out of their basket, not one. But I ate a croissant, Pumkin, and I have never tasted anything so light and buttery in all my life, and after that a madeleine, and after that a macaron and I fear my hips will not survive living in this country. But it feels so odd to be here without you, my Pumkin, and I

I fold the letter and put it back in its protective slip with all the others. It's been three months since Sophie left, and I have five letters from her, each held safely in plastic.

There's the one where she tells me about sitting at the port in Marseille, watching the boats come in as she dips a biscuit in her hot chocolate. The one where she finally moves into the apartment they find for her that's too expensive for words but so tiny that she can barely open her arms and spin, although spin she does when she gets there and feels, finally, that She Has Arrived. The one where she talks about her first days at work when she feels so awkward and out of place that she and Gillian, the other woman who left with her from the embassy, huddle together for safety. She tells me how weirdly exhilarating it feels to walk on the streets and not be known by a single soul.

I was so mad when she left. I barely spoke to her in the weeks leading up to her flight. I didn't turn on the oven once, even though I knew she would have loved to take some bread pudding with her, or eat some sweet-potato pudding for the last time. On the day of her flight, my grandmother and I put on our Sunday best and piled into a taxi with Sophie and her one big suitcase that she borrowed from someone at the embassy. I remember thinking that if she hadn't messed things up with Boots, he'd be driving us to the airport now and we wouldn't have to pay all this money for a stupid taxi. And then I thought that if she hadn't messed things up with Boots, she wouldn't be leaving me at all. I tried to keep this anger in my heart the whole way to the airport, but when she reached over and held my hand I gripped it tight, the tears twisting themselves into a knot in my chest. Sophie was almost vibrating with excitement, but when she looked at me I could see it: she was scared.

When we said goodbye in the airport, the knot in my chest burst open and the tears flooded out, and it was that exact moment that I wished I hadn't spent all that time being mad, that I'd sent her off with even a few coconut gizzada to eat on the plane. My grandmother didn't shed a tear, just hugged her tight and said, 'Mi dawta, mi dawta,' over and over again until Sophie pulled her arms away and walked towards the gate.

Now I read her letters over and over and I think about Sophie roaming those strange French streets alone. I try to imagine myself beside her, one hand in hers, a chocolate eclair in the other, the breeze of Marseille blowing through my hair.

But I can't.

I only ever see Sophie, standing there on her own.

'What yuh auntie sayin?'

I startle and turn to my door, and there's my mother, filling up the doorway.

'Wh-wha . . . Mama?' I stutter.

Things changed after Sophie left. Without her favourite daughter to occupy her, my grandmother shifted all her focus to me. Her hard work had paid off with Sophie — she was living the life in 'forrin' with a big big job — so there was nothing stopping Gramma repeating her success. But it caused even more tension between her and my mother. They argued constantly, yelling at each other over the noise of the TV, my grandmother rubbing and rubbing her chest, screaming that my mother's bad attitude was going to be the death of her. I would move from the dining table to my room — my own room, now, since my grandmother refused to hand it over to my mother — my hands over my ears as I tried to do my homework.

'Is nuh my time now, Mama?' I heard my mother yell once. Something was wrong with her voice: it sounded like she had a frog in her throat. It took me a while to realize it was because her voice was thick with tears. 'When it gwen be my time?'

'Your time fi wha, Paulette?' my grandmother asked, sounding genuinely curious, but my mother just stuttered and spluttered before running out of the house.

'Is what she talkin bout, Pumkin?' my grandmother asked, and I shrugged and shook my head. But the truth is, I know what my mother meant but could not say, because I have also felt that way about her. Isn't it time for you to love me, Mama?

My grandmother had just turned away rubbing her chest, muttering about her 'eart' and 'ungrateful pickney' who obviously need 'likkle Jeesas'.

'Yuh *hanty*,' my mother repeats now, leaning against the door jamb. 'How ova-seas treating her?'

'Ahm.' I clear my throat. 'She's. Yeah, she's doing all right. She likes it.'

'Mm-hm.' My mother nods, looking through the door of my room leading out to the back yard.

You know when you want to pet a cat, and it's kind of working its way towards you, and you don't want to move because you know if you move at all, even a finger, even breathe too hard, it will startle and run away?

I feel like that now.

'She, ahm . . .' I start, glancing up at her face. She's still leaning on the door jamb, so that's promising. 'She says it's really expensive and her . . . ahm . . . her apartment is really small.'

'Ee-hee? Is how much of dem live there?'

'Just . . . just her. Just her alone.'

'She *one*? But den it cyaan too small. How much space yuh need fi one person, suh?'

She laughs and something unspools in my chest, something I didn't realize was tightly wound. I chuckle too. I try desperately to think of something else to say, but my thoughts get all jumbled together. I have an urge to say something negative about Sophie, but then I feel disloyal, and everything gets tied up on my tongue. But I don't want my mother to startle and run away, like those cats.

'Yuh hanty . . .' she begins, still staring out of the back door. 'She hall-ways get everyting she want. Every likkle ting . . . All the . . . all the tings maybe I woulda want . . .'

She clears her throat. She's still staring out of the door.

'An' now she tun big tings in forrin. Juss like Mama did want. Must be nice.'

A weird churning feeling climbs its way up my stomach. I look at my mother, really look at her. She always loomed so large over me, so big and angry, like a raging bull. But now she seems so small, like a child, her voice soft and breathy. So small, so sad, so left behind. She's not so different from me, I think.

'Maybe when I get to France, you can come and visit?'

I know immediately I've said the wrong thing. Her face hardens, her eyes move from the world outside the back door and lock onto mine, and now there's nothing left of the sad, small woman who stood here just two seconds ago. Now she's big again, expanded, her breath huffing loud in and out through her nose.

'Yuh not going nowhere, so dere will be nowhere to visit.'

She turns and walks away. I remain on the bed, surrounded by letters from Sophie, burning with disappointment that I startled the damn cat.

Miss Icy

Gramma makes me a pyjama set, white shorts with pink and purple polka dots and a matching top with spaghetti straps.

'An yuh muss wear dis,' she says, handing me a piece of fabric. I hold it up in my hands: it's a light, filmy fabric that buttons all the way down the front, with short, frilly cap sleeves and a high neck, just like she wears at night. It's hideous. She calls it a duster, I imagine because dusting the house with it should have been its only purpose in life. I stuff it into the back of my wardrobe, hoping a door will open to Narnia and take it away.

I pack my backpack on Saturday afternoon to take the bus up to Mandy's for a sleepover. I wave at Tamara as she sits on the lawn with her little brother, but she cuts her eye after me. I was supposed to be staying over at her place, but then Mandy came calling. Tamara doesn't understand how important it is to me, and Sophie, and my grandmother that I maintain friendships with people like Mandy. She doesn't understand that I'd rather be with her, where I can relax and just be, where I don't have to worry about my accent or saying the wrong thing, where I don't have to hold my breath waiting for the other shoe to drop, but I have no choice. Gramma has picked up right where Sophie left off.

'Dat Chiney one wid de tall hair,' she'd say, as she made me some outfit or another for one of the many sleepovers I'd been invited to. 'She yuh muss fren up. Good fi have dem kinda fren.'

When I knock on the door, I hear the unmistakable squawking of teenage girls and then it's flung wide, Mandy breathing heavily with a big grin on her face while two girls peer out from behind her.

'Pumkin!' they all yell, and fall to giggling, and she pulls me inside. A radio is playing tinnily somewhere off to the right, barely covering the sound of sizzling coming from the kitchen. It smells like plantain.

'I brought something,' I say, holding out a brown paper parcel in which I had wrapped the coconut drops I'd made. The paper is slightly greasy and crumpled from the bus ride over. It looks the way I feel, sullied and greasy, as if I'll leave a spot on the Chens' clean floors that can't be polished out.

'Thanks!' Mandy chirps, as she grabs the package and we make our way to the back yard, where three more girls are squished together in a swinging patio set. A plaid picnic blanket is laid out on the ground, crowded with beads and games and nail polish.

Candida, who'd hated me from the day we met at the birthday party where I'd worn my homemade dress, rolls her eyes deeply when she sees me and scowls. 'Why is *she* here again?' she says, as soon as I step onto the grass.

She'd called me a 'buttu' that first time we'd met three years ago, before Mandy had rescued me. 'What kind of a buttu name is *Pumkin*?' she'd said. I'd flinched at 'buttu': low class, uneducated, does not belong. I always felt Candida could smell my otherness on me, like she could sniff out the truth of who I was: an imposter.

Mandy ignores her now just like she did back then, flopping onto a massive orange cushion to the side of the blanket, pulling me down beside her. 'Pumkin brought treats!' she says, opening up the parcel and revealing the white and pink coconut drops that look like bubble gum on an ice crystal of snow.

'Pumpkin?' I hear one girl I've never met say to the other, quizzically.

'Sounds like a helper, don't it?' Candida says to her, loud enough for me to hear, but I pretend I didn't.

'Ohmahgaw,' Mandy says suddenly, her eyes closed around her coconut drop. 'Jeezam peas, Pumkin, is where yu get these?'

'I made them,' I say, and I can't help the big smile on my face. I look around at the other girls as each of them bites into the hard drops, which I know will melt on their tongues once they get past the crispy outer layer. This is the first time I have baked for these girls and I can't help the feeling of pride that blooms in my stomach.

'Whaa? No, you didn't.'

'I did!' I laugh, as they scarf down the drops. I can see Candida looking longingly at the pastries, then turning quickly back to her cuticles, a new-found source of interest for her. But her gaze keeps finding its way back to the drops, which are rapidly disappearing. There's a lot of exaggerated moaning from the girls. I know my drops are good. I take one and hold it out to Candida. A peace offering. She stares at me a moment, her lip curled up, before she relents, grabbing her own directly from the dwindling pile. I watch her take a bite and close her eyes for a moment before she takes hold of herself and says, with a shrug, 'Huh. They're all right.'

*

By the time night falls, we are all piled on top of each other in the den watching a VHS of *Clueless* on a big-screen TV and eating Shakey's pizza. This isn't my first night with these girls, who never met a sleepover they didn't like, but I always feel like an alien left to fend for myself among strange and unknown creatures. *Who has an extra room in their house just for watching movies?* I think, every time we pile into it, so full of cushions and pillows I have to walk with both my arms out so I won't fall.

'Ugh, I wish I had a closet like Cher's,' Mandy says, as the credits roll.

'As *if*!' says Natalie, and all the girls laugh.

Everyone starts talking and laughing over each other and I sit there, watching, until I notice Candida staring at me. Something kicks me inside my stomach. Probably the pizza.

'Where yuh live?' she asks me, her face screwed up tight, like she's been sucking lemons.

'What?' I ask, stalling for time.

'Where. Do you. Live?' she says again, slowly, cocking her head to either side with each word. The other girls, sensing . . . something, have stopped talking and are looking at us.

'How come I never see you anywhere?' she continues now. 'None of our other friends ever heard of a girl named *Pumkin*.' She spits my name out of her mouth, like a pumpkin seed.

The other girls are staring at me and I look at my knees, the thing that was kicking me in my stomach now in a frenzy, hot and chaotic. This is where it all goes sideways, I think. There's no way I can tell them I live on Potter's Lane: nobody in this circle lives on a Lane. They all live on Drives, and Roads and Closes, and Circles. So now they'll know I don't belong here at all. I start to think about how late the buses run, if I'll have time to change my clothes or if I'll have to make my way home in my polka-dot pyjamas. I glance at the clock on the VHS. It's already after ten. There's no going home now.

Just then, Mandy's housekeeper, Miss Icylin, shuffles in with a tray of cupcakes and the girls forget about me as they squeal in delight. I finally allow myself to exhale, even as I wonder how to answer Candida's question when she inevitably asks me again. But for now they seem to have forgotten about me as they hover over the cupcakes, like a flock of birds over breadcrumbs. *More food?* I think. It's unbelievable how much we've eaten today, and how much we've left behind. The girls have picked at the food and left mounds of it half eaten. I'd looked at the plates of chicken wings with heaps of meat still on them, almost whole burgers with two bites taken out of them, hot dogs and patties and pizza and and and. 'The dogs will eat well tonight!' Mandy said, when she caught me staring, and I laughed along with her but I felt that burning feeling in my stomach.

We're not starving at home. Sophie is still supporting us, and the money she sends, along with my grandmother's dressmaking money, is enough to keep us fed and clothed. But we never throw anything away. Stale old bread becomes bread pudding. We buy the affordable parts of the chicken: the neck, the back, the feet that are cooked in our Saturday Soup – but never the breast, because it's too expensive. We never have things like pizza and burgers and hot dogs. These are American things, luxuries. Our only luxuries are the things I bake. But Mandy gives these American luxuries to her dogs.

'Thank you, Miss Icy!' Mandy yells, as the girls grab at the tray of cakes.

'Yes, mi dahlin,' she says, in a soft voice, although the girls are already focused on the cupcakes, discussing which colour icing they want — blue or yellow or pink or white with sprinkles. I hang back, looking at Miss Icy. She is a stocky, sturdy, mahogany-skinned woman with a broad, smiley face. She looks back at me and smiles, gestures to the cupcake tray and then shuffles slowly back out of the door, humming something under her breath. She moves very slowly, like a big ship on the ocean, and I feel an overwhelming urge to follow her, to sit with her in her room at the back, out of sight out of mind from the rest of the house and these girls, with whom I do not belong.

Well and truly

'Do I *have* to hear about these people again?' Tamara asks me, rolling her eyes. We are on the little patch of lawn outside her house playing jacks, the crab grass scratching the backs of our thighs. Her little mongrel dog, Brownie (he's brown), is watching us nearby, his eyes fixated on the ball. He jumps up every time it bounces, his tail wagging furiously, then lies back down with disappointment in his eyes when we catch it ourselves.

'You're almost as bad as yuh auntie,' Tamara finishes.

She is popping guineps into her mouth and hurling the jacks ball so hard on the little slip of concrete by the lawn I keep having to get up and race Brownie to grab it first.

I clamp my mouth shut. I'd been telling her about almost being outed by Candida, but I guess she doesn't care.

'You always telling me how you don't feel right hanging out with them but you run quick time when they call you,' she continues, sucking the guinep out of the skin and into her mouth.

'That's not fair,' I say. 'You know I'd rather hang out with you, but Auntie So—'

'Yes yes, Auntie *Sophie* thinks I'm not *good enough*.'

'That's not true, Tamara!' I say, but my stomach squirms a little because, really, it kind of is. Sophie always scrunched up her face a little when I said I was going to Tamara's, while her face would light up like the moon when she knew I was going to Mandy's. And my grandmother was no different.

'It's not that she doesn't think you're good enough, she just wants better for us . . .'

'But what does that have to do with hanging out with these posh people all the time? Just because they rich don't mean they're *better*.'

'No, that's not what I meant –'

'Then what do you *mean*?'

But I don't really know how to answer because I don't really know what I mean. Sophie and my grandmother have drummed it into me that people like Mandy *are* better, and that to *be* better, we have to be part of their group. My grandmother would not be accepted, but if Sophie and I played our cards right, we could get 'in', turn things around. Just look at Sophie, already in France, half the battle won. But I didn't really understand it.

I think about Boots. He doesn't look like them, talk like them, isn't like them at all, but he's the best man I know. And Tamara isn't like them either, but she's my best friend. What does it mean, after all, to be better? So far it's been a lot of pretending . . . pretending to live somewhere else, sound like someone else, have things I don't really have. It makes me feel tired. So, no, I don't know what I mean, so I don't say anything to Tamara, just keep bouncing the ball and trying to pick up as many jacks as possible.

'Anyway, it's all *very* boring,' she says, with another great heave.

'What is?' I ask, when I sit down after collecting the ball for the hundredth time.

'All of it. The whole ting boring. Mandy is boring and you talking about her is boring and your aunt, jeezam peas. She so happy you have *stoosh* friends now. And she's not even here any more. And your grandmother all excited about all these stupid parties. *Pathetic.*'

She cracks another guinep in her mouth, sucking out the sticky ball of fruit inside. I never liked guinep. 'Half you life gawn!' people exclaim, whenever they learn this about me. 'Half yuh life!' when I say I don't like oxtail or stew peas or anything typically Jamaican that every Jamaican is duty-bound to enjoy.

'Oh. Sorry.'

I'm even more confused. Tamara wants to know everything about this group of girls, just like my grandmother and Sophie, but then she gets mean and snippy when I talk about them, saying she doesn't want to hear about my 'stoosh friends'.

I bounce the ball in silence and swipe up the jacks. Then it's her turn again. She hurls it with such maximum force that it bounces way off to the side, and this time, Brownie is quicker than me. Before I've even shifted my butt, the dog has grabbed the little ball in his mouth and run off with it, looking like he just won a prize. The two of us watch him for a moment.

'You think him gwen swallow it?' I ask.

But Tamara just flings the guinep peel on the ground and stomps off into her house, leaving me there with the crab grass itching at my skin.

*

I am trudging home from school, as slowly as I can. Tamara still isn't talking to me since the day Brownie almost ate the jacks ball, and my house feels hollow with Auntie Sophie gone. I am surprised to see my mother sitting on the couch as I walk through the door, even more surprised to find the TV off. I don't have time to take my schoolbag from my shoulders before she speaks to me.

85

'Yuh granmodda dead.'

I shake my head. I didn't hear her right. 'Sorry. What did you say, Mama?'

'Mi seh yu granmodda dead!'

I look slowly around the room. My grandmother's sewing is piled on the dining-room table where I left her hunched over it this morning. There's a plate left there, with crumbs from what looks like the back of a bread loaf, the butter-stained knife laid across it. She will be annoyed if it's still there when she comes home, I think. I turn back to my mother who is staring at the blank TV screen. 'What . . . what yu mean, Mama?'

She kisses her teeth. 'Is foo fool yuh foo fool? How yuh mean what I mean? Yuh granmodda dead! What else dat muss mean?'

The man in my chest starts up again. He's been playing every night since Sophie left, jerking my body back and forth with his rhythm.

'But. But how? When?'

She takes so long to answer that I think she will not say another word, but then she says, 'Dis afternoon. I did find her, when I come home.'

She glances towards the little narrow hallway that leads to our bathroom and then looks back at the TV. I look at the hallway too, still expecting Gramma to walk out through the graveyard of beads that used to hang there. Is she still in the room? If I go in there, will I see her dead body lying on the floor? I turn back towards my mother and wait for her to tell me what happened, but she just sits there staring at nothing.

'How, Mama? What happen –'

86

'Look 'ere nuh, stop axe me nuh whole heap a question! Yuh grandmodda. Is dead. Nutten more to seh dan dat.'

I look at her a moment longer. I wonder what to do next. Should I sit down? Should I make something, eat something? Is she sad, my mother? Should I try to call Sophie, long distance, take a bath, clean something? Instead I take up my schoolbag from the floor, where it has fallen off my shoulder, and I walk slowly towards my room.

'Is juss you and me now,' my mother says, and I stop short.

I turn to look at her and she is staring at me, looking right at me, seeing me as if for the first time. The drummer slamming a beat against my chest takes a break and squeezes my heart instead, squeezes it so hard I feel it will burst. Maybe that's what happened to my grandmother. Maybe something squeezed her heart until it burst.

I turn back around and head towards my grandmother's — no, my mother's room, now and my schoolbag slides down onto the floor. I stand there looking at the wall for a few moments before I climb up on the bed and, just before the drummer releases his hold on my heart, just before I bury my head in my grandmother's pillow and weep until my throat is raw, I think that now I am well and truly alone.

'Hungry mek monkey blow fire'

'People will be innovative and resourceful under harsh conditions'

The prodigal

I watch my mother move through the house, putting things away, tidying up, while my father relaxes on the couch. His feet are on the coffee-table, a toothpick in his mouth. Paulette has an extra swing in her step, an exaggerated roll of the hip when Akil is around. She sings and hums, like she's doing now, but her voice is so bad that every song sounds like a wailing revivalist piece. I wince when she hits a trembling high note and notice from the corner of my eye that my father winces too. I glance at him and he winks, but my eyes slide away from his.

'Is wa'ppen to you face?' he asks me, shifting his position on the couch to get a better look at the swelling over my eye. I glance up at my mother, who shoots me a look as she wipes down the cabinets filled with mismatched glasses in the corner of the dining room.

'Nothing,' I mumble, looking down at the French textbook I'm trying to read unsuccessfully in my lap, the presence of my father causing my brain to stick on one sentence over and over again.

'Dat don' look like nutten,' he says.

Paulette clears her throat. 'Dinna soon ready,' she says loudly and, I think, a little aggressively. A warning. I can feel Akil's eyes on my face a moment longer, the heat of his attention almost scorching my skin, before he turns back to the football match on TV.

Things have changed a lot since Sophie left and my grandmother died, the two events happening so close together I was convinced that watching her precious daughter fly away finally cracked my grandmother's heart in two. As soon as Sophie'd left, she'd had to come back for the funeral. A heart attack indeed, she'd explained. I don't remember too much from her short visit, just a feeling of nothingness all throughout my body. Plus, she was leaving me again, wasn't she? And this time really alone, with a woman who hated the look of my face.

'Why are you leaving me with her?' I'd pleaded. 'Don't leave me with her!'

'It's just for a little while longer,' she'd said, her face tacky with tears. 'I promise, Pumkin. It's taking more time than I thought, but Tamara's mum is still looking out for you until then and I *swear* it won't be for much longer.'

But I didn't want to hear her promises, so I'd just walked away and shut myself in my room, listening to the sound of her footsteps as she left me behind once again.

Akil turned up at the house before my grandmother was cold in her grave, blowing into my life like a gust of foul-smelling wind. I'd come home from school a few weeks after Gramma passed away and found him there. I'd come through the door, put down my bag and headed straight for the kitchen, expecting to be alone, as usual. Paulette couldn't touch the money Auntie Sophie sent to Tamara's mother for my upkeep, and now my grandmother was gone she'd got a job as a helper. I don't know where, although Linnette heard it was at a big house in Mona, but sometimes she came home late, and sometimes not at all, so I spent most of my time in the empty house by myself, cleaning up, doing homework, or making myself a simple dinner.

The day I met Akil, I'd heard the squealing of what sounded like pigs coming from my grandmother's old bedroom. I'd crept slowly to the wide-open door and seen my mother's legs splayed straight in the air, a man's butt pumping away between them. I'd stared for a second, horrified but intrigued, before turning away and retracing my steps to the kitchen, my stomach queasy. I slammed the cutlery into the dilapidated drawers, banged the pots onto our stove, clanked the plates together in the cupboard until the squealing stopped. A few moments later he was in the kitchen doorway, shirtless, zipping up his pants and leaning on the door jamb as if this was his house.

'Akisha,' he said, with a grin.

I stared at him for a second, this stranger standing in my kitchen, and cut my eyes away from him.

'Pumkin,' I said, looking back towards the dumplings I was forming for dinner.

'Yu cookin' pumkin?'

'My *name* is Pumkin.'

'Eeh? Is wha' kinda name dat?' He laughed, a strange, high-pitched giggle that sounded weird coming out of his mouth, like it belonged to a little girl. He was wiry but muscular, barely any fat on his body. Light-skinned and kind of Chinese-looking, with thick, straight black hair.

'It's *my* name,' I said shortly.

'Awrite, awrite.' He stuck his hands in his pockets. 'Well, my name is Akil.'

'That's nice for you.' I dropped the dumplings into the boiling water and started chopping onions.

'You don' get it?' he said.

'Get what?'

'Akil. Akisha.'

I turned and looked at him. Searched his face. Examined his features. The only thing I'd ever had to go on was Gramma's description of him. The longer I looked, the more I saw it: the nose we shared, the shape of his face, the same shape I saw when I looked in the mirror. So this was him. My stomach did a little wiggle, but I sucked in my breath, tamping it down. He was looking at me with one eyebrow raised, a smile on his face, like he was waiting on me to get the joke. *That's dumb*, I thought. *Doesn't 'Akila' make more sense?* Paulette wasn't even smart enough to get that right. I turned back to the onions and, after a moment's hesitation, began chopping them again. Chopping and chopping them, the tiny little squares getting smaller and smaller, the juice of them stinging my eyes, making me squeeze them shut and shake my head, trying to get the burning out.

'You can call me "Dada".'

I used the back of my hand to wipe the onion tears away and looked at him again. He was still grinning like a Cheshire puss. Who was this man? Did he think I was going to drop what I was doing and run into his arms? Where had he been, these thirteen years? If it wasn't for my grandmother, I wouldn't even have known his name. This was a house of women and there was no space for men here. I wondered when he and my mother had got back together. Had she been with him all those nights when she didn't come home, all those days she was nowhere to be found? So he didn't want to know me all that time, until now when my grandmother and Sophie were gone? Now he was standing in the kitchen asking me to call him

Dada. I wanted to fling the knife at him, but I just said, 'No, thanks,' and turned back to my now completely mashed onions. I would need to throw them away.

'Suit yusself,' he said, that annoying smile still in his voice.

He'd started coming around in random fits and bursts after that. Sometimes he'd be with Paulette in front of the TV while she fussed about him, but mostly I knew he was here by the squealing coming from my grandmother's old bedroom. I would bang and clank my way around the kitchen, trying to make something for dinner before parking myself at the dining-room table to do my homework, trying to block out the noise. The only positive was that Paulette made sure there was food in the house when he was there.

The first time he came on a Sunday my mother was in the kitchen. Seeing her in my space – looking for pots and pans and plates, opening and shutting drawers, rifling through the cutlery – felt like someone had thrown cold water over me.

'Come 'elp mi wid di dinna, me nuh know weh *nutten* is in dis ya place,' she'd said.

I stood there with my mouth gaping like a fish until she snapped me with the kitchen towel. *Get out, GET OUT!* I wanted to scream. She was moving everything, spoiling my system, spreading her dark grey energy all over the place.

Akil had sat at the dinner table like a king, leaning back over the chair with a toothpick sticking out of his mouth and his legs splayed out in front of him. Comfortable. I wanted to tell my grandmother. She'd make him to sit up straight, ask him who he thought he was, coming around here like he owned the place. She'd make him go away. But when I thought of her, I felt a big bubble of something hard and painful in my stomach, so I shook her out of my head.

That first Sunday, I'd speared a big, meaty chicken thigh and brought it, dripping gravy, over to my plate. Akil had raised his eyebrow at me, my mother shouted, 'But see yah!' before grabbing my fork and dropping the meat on his plate.

'But I want that piece,' I'd said, unsatisfied with the tiny leg she'd given me instead. Akil had chuckled to himself and Paulette had ignored me, drawing breath instead for the questions she'd eventually throw at him after he'd been here a while. *Where yu was last night?* she'd want to know. *None o' yuh business, woman*, he would answer. *Yuh was wid dat skettel Marsha, don't it?* she would hiss, and he would ignore her. Back and forth like a tennis match until their voices got louder and thicker, then silences so thick they stuck in my throat. There would be a fifteen-minute nap on the sofa after he ate, then he and my mother would go to my grandmother's room to grunt, there would be a few minutes of silence, and then the shrieking and shouting would start again while he put on his clothes and left us, the door slamming shut behind him. Then my face, my skin, my bones would feel the heat of her anger.

'Serve yourself,' my mother says to me now. My school books have been cleared away and Sunday dinner is on the table. Akil likes to come on Sundays most of all. The baddest of men cannot resist a good Jamaican Sunday dinner of rice and peas, plantain, coleslaw and chicken. My mother serves him with great care, digging through the dish for the biggest piece of chicken. I reach over and grab a chicken leg. I wonder what Sophie eats on Sundays, if the French also have Saturday Soup and Sunday roast chicken. Akil is already shovelling the food into his mouth like a man starved. He always eats like this, as if he's trying to kill himself with the food by lodging it in his throat, but like a snake it just keeps expanding and expanding until he swallows it down with a satisfied smirk. Maybe this is the only time he eats, he's so wiry. Maybe this is the only reason he comes around. Well, that and the squealing. I steal a glance at my mother. She's eating quietly but I can see the questions burning underneath her skin. I eat almost as quickly as Akil, wanting to get it over with so I can leave the table.

'Suh how yuh doin in school?'

I look up, startled, to find him looking at me. I stare at him a moment with my mouth open before I remember to chew, looking back down at my plate and spooning in a heap of rice.

'Yuh don' hear yuh fadda axe yuh a question?' my mother says.

'Good,' I say, around the mouthful of rice and peas.

'Awrite, awrite. I did good in school too, before mi did drop out. I did like geography, a did like history. Yuh did know seh di firs Jamaican did name "Arawak"?'

I roll my eyes. I'm pretty sure every Jamaican learns that in kindergarten. 'Everybody knows that,' I say.

My mother makes a noise and when I look at her, she is trying to hold back a laugh. I catch her eye and my lips curve up into a tentative smile. She smiles back and I feel like I have won a race.

'What subjeck yuh like den? I bet yuh, whole on, I bet is English yuh like, don't it? Cause yuh *well* speaky spoky.' He chuckles at this. This has been his favourite topic of conversation since he started coming around: how I talk so uptown, how he has 'a likkle stoosh dawta'. I cringe every time he calls me his daughter.

'English is okay. I like French.'

97

'*French!* What a way yuh stoosh! What yuh cyan do wid French?'

'I'm going to . . .' I stop and look at my mother, but she's busy chewing a chicken bone to dust. 'I'm going to move to France. To live with Auntie Sophie.'

My father starts laughing, that high-pitched giggle again. My mother starts as well, a deep, heavy laugh that comes from her stomach. There is a little pile of powder on her plate where the chicken bone used to be.

'Fi real? How yuh gwen do dat?'

I pause for a moment. I wish I hadn't said anything. 'I have to . . . ahm . . . I have to pass a test so I can get into the school there. Then . . . I can go and live there.'

'Awrite, awrite,' my father says, sticking a toothpick in his mouth and nodding slowly.

My mother starts laughing even harder.

'She not tekkin no tess and she not goin nowhere, yuh see mi?' she says, pointing her knife at me. 'Gwaan like seh a fi har pickney,' she mutters, under her breath. I try to catch her eye again but she studiously ignores me. Whatever little moment we shared earlier has flown out of the window, like a lost little butterfly.

'But – but you don't even want me here! Why won't you let me go?' I shout.

'Yuh NAT. GOING. NOWHERE,' she booms at me.

I can see her chest heaving and she's starting to sweat.

'But . . .' I start but she turns to me, very very slightly, in her chair and gives me a blood-boiling look, and I know this is the point where I should stop, be quiet, put my head down. I huff and look at the last few grains of rice on my plate, tears in my eyes. Akil is looking from one of us to the other, the toothpick moving around in his mouth, a smirk on his face.

'Awrite, awrite,' he says, and I want to hit him in the face. I curl my hand around my fork and squeeze it till I can feel my fingernails dig into my skin.

This is a circle we've both being going around for the past year, my mother and I. Whenever she sees me with my head in a book, she decides it's time for me to clean my room or wash the dishes or sweep the yard. Or else she blasts the TV so loud that I can barely concentrate. It's like she wants to condemn me to her own pathetic life. She's keeping me here out of spite and I hate her for it, and I feel like I hate Auntie Sophie too because I *told* her this would happen and now she's too far away to do anything about it.

'I'm sorry,' she'd said, when she'd called. It felt like Auntie Sophie'd spent the entire time apologizing and making soothing noises that only made me more annoyed. 'I'm so sorry you're going through this all alone, but just hold on to the plan.'

I think about the plan now as my head hangs over my dinner plate. It's not much of a plan to me: Auntie Sophie'd said I need to study for the French School Entrance Exam, take it, and pass it, and she will deal with my mother and the school. Auntie Sophie says she's saving up as much as she can to pay for all the things we'll need to get me to France, but it's a struggle since she's still paying for my school fees and uniforms and books as it is, and now her own rent and bills on top. At least the exam is free since I'll be taking it at Aggie's, but it's months and months away from now. I look up at Akil and Paulette, a stranger and a woman who hates the skin I'm in. They've forgotten me entirely, the first rumblings of tonight's arguments revving up like a tired old car. I don't want to be here with them for months and months. I don't want to be here one more *minute*! I hang my head back down over my empty plate and squeeze my eyes shut. At Aggie's they tell us to find an adult when we need help. But my adults don't help me.

So it looks like I'll need to help myself. I just wish I knew how.

Her own private earthquake

'I am d i s a p p o i n t e d to see you here again, Miss Patterson.'

I look up at the vice principal and my eyes slide away, back down to my hands, which are twisting themselves into knots in my lap. The last time I found myself in Mrs Roberts's office I'd had Sophie in my corner, but today I have only my mother. I sneak a quick look at her. She's wearing her best dress, her hair neatly combed and pinned as if she's going to church. She's taken time off from her cleaning job to be here and she's muttered and muttered about not being paid for the time, under her breath but loud enough for me to hear. I can feel the heat radiating from her as she shifts and shifts in her chair, constantly moving her hands, her legs, her feet, the handbag she's foraged out of my grandmother's cupboard with the leather worn away at the corners and on the handles. I know for a fact there is nothing in that bag but a bunch of stiff, balled-up tissues.

Miss Smith is standing in her usual spot beside the VP's desk, her wormy little braids quivering around her face, like she's standing in her own private earthquake. I try not to look directly at her: it's like looking at the sun – it burns. I don't know why I'm here and I have a ball in the pit of my stomach. My mother is staring at a fixed spot on the floor just to the right of the VP's wide desk, looking like she's the one in trouble, and I wish it was Sophie sitting here with me again, her back straight and her head high, her legs crossed delicately at the ankle and a sharp word poised on her tongue.

'Do you know why you're here today, Miss Patterson?' Mrs Roberts says, and I shake my head.

'No, Miss.'

Miss Smith snorts and my eyes jump up to meet hers for a moment before they return to the safety of my hands. My mind is racing, thinking back over the last few classes. Miss Smith and I are ever arch enemies; it is clear that she hates me, but after the last visit to the VP with Sophie, I've kept my head down and tried not to get in the teacher's way. It hasn't stopped her picking on me in class, accusing me of rolling my eyes and kissing my teeth even though my head is hunched as far as possible over my textbooks and my teeth remain stead-fastly unkissed. Sophie told me, 'Take the high road, Pumkin. Do what you need to do to get through the class and don't cause a fuss,' so that's what I do. I keep myself quiet.

'Miss Patterson, I'm sure you're aware that mid-year exams are extremely important, yes? I'm sure you're also aware that cheating is a grave offence here at St Agatha's.'

My head whips up. *Cheating?*

'Miss Smith has shared that you cheated on the mid-years, Miss Patterson. What do you have to say to that?'

'What? That's a lie, Miss! I didn't cheat!'

'She did cheat, I saw her,' Miss Smith chimes in.

'Saw me do *what*? It's a lie, Mrs Roberts, I swear I didn't –'

'She did have the paper from –'

'What *paper*? It's not *true* –'

'– outta my bag, she teef the paper –'

'It's a *lie*! I didn't steal *anything* and I *didn't cheat*! I *don't chea*–'

'Enough, *enough*, both of you!' the VP shouts, banging her hand on that great, big desk.

I fling myself back in my chair. This is worse than I could

possibly have imagined it to be. Miss Smith has her arms crossed over her chest, a look of disgust on her face. Does she really believe I stole the test out of her bag? Or is she purposely setting me up for . . . for what?

I look to my mother, her figure blurred and shimmery through the tears that have flung themselves into my eyes, but I don't see any movement from her, no outcry of indignation. Frustration blooms in my stomach and crawls up my throat. I did not cheat on that test, but teachers never take our side. Adults never believe us when we tell them the truth. If Gramma were here she would rail up in outrage on my behalf. If Sophie were here, she would refuse to accept this accusation. But Gramma's gone and Sophie isn't here. Instead it's just —

'Mrs Patterson?'

I look up again, wiping the tears from my face, but the VP is looking at my mother.

'This is a serious offence levelled at your daughter. We take cheating *very* seriously at this i n s t i t u t i o n. Is there anything you can share with us that may shed some light?'

My mother shrugs, one shoulder coming up slowly to her ear, then sliding back down. I can see the beads of sweat along her hairline, the defensiveness working its way over her skin like armour. She doesn't want to be here before these people of authority. But my breath catches in my chest when she says, 'I don't tink she woulda do dat, Miss. She nat dat type a person. Mm-mm.'

Her voice is soft and tentative, unsure. But, still, she has stood up for me. Maybe not how Sophie would, but it's something, right? I look and look and look at her, trying to get her to catch my eye, trying to let her know I'm grateful she's backing me up, but her eyes are still fixed to that one spot on the floor, as if she's lost something there and is waiting for it to reappear.

Miss Smith makes a choking noise in her throat but Mrs Roberts shoots her a look, then takes a deep breath and looks at me.

'Miss Patterson, Miss Smith claims that the 100 per cent you achieved on the test is not feasible without having prior knowledge of the test questions –'

'But that makes no *sense*, Miss, I just *studied* hard and –'

'– AND I ADMIT that it is highly unusual. However, I am loath to suspend a student so late in the year, particularly without hard evidence of a transgression.'

'*Suspend*, Miss?'

'She did *cheat*, I telling you!'

'HELLO!'

We fall silent at Mrs Roberts's booming voice, except for the breaths being kicked out of my chest by the man who lives there. *Kick! Kick! Kick!* He woke up in a fury and his pounding is so loud in my ears, I'm sure everyone else can hear it too.

'It's clear to me,' the VP continues, 'that this situation is untenable. Miss Patterson, I have no choice but to pull you out of French class. You will need to take another elective to pass the year.'

I don't hear the rest of what she says as my ears fill with cotton and my mouth goes dry. I can't be kicked out of French class: I need to take the prep course for the test. I need to pass this test to get to Sophie.

'Nutten don' go suh.'

I blink, not realizing I've actually spoken the words out loud. I'd barely heard them in my own head over the chest-man's kicking.

'Excuse me, Mrs Patterson?' Mrs Roberts says.

My mother sits up straighter under the VP's gaze. My mother's last name isn't Patterson but she hasn't corrected her the whole time we've been here. She clears her throat and tries again, doing her best to curl her words around themselves as if she's speaking in cursive.

'She tink she his movin' to ar haanty in France, but is nuthin don't go so, Miss. She his nat goin hennny-where.'

She pulls her handbag closer to her stomach, like it's a bullet-proof vest. The embarrassment that sloshed around my belly earlier crests into a great wave as I see Mrs Roberts raise her eyebrow for just a millisecond when my mother speaks.

'This is the . . . Miss Jones . . . who usually attends Miss Patterson's parent–teacher conferences?' she asks, looking down at a book lying open on her desk. I wonder what she's written about me in there.

'Yes'm, mi sista. But she his gawn now, gawn hova-seas.'

Mrs Roberts looks at me again, staring at me for a long moment before glancing back at my mother, whose gaze has returned to the floor.

'Well. Well, I'm sorry, Miss Patterson, but the decision is final.'

I feel like I have been punched in the gut. I feel like I'm going to pass out, slide out of the chair onto the floor, slide through the floor into the earth, slide through the earth straight through to Hell. I feel my mother shift and shift and shift again beside me. I hear, through the cotton that has grown in my ears, Mrs Roberts dismiss Miss Smith. I hear, as if from far away, Miss Smith protest. I hear, as if from underwater, Mrs Roberts tell her the issue has been resolved and she is no longer needed. I see, from the corner of my eyes, Miss Smith huff out of the room.

But who cares? Everything is ruined, now.

'Miss Patterson?'

I look up again at the VP. I wonder why my head feels so heavy, all of a sudden, like it's made out of lead. Her face looks a little softer, her tone a bit kinder. She hands me a pamphlet with a picture of the Eiffel Tower on it, smiling white teenagers with French flags in their hands crowded at the front, and beneath their grinning faces an address and phone number for a place in uptown Kingston.

'This is L'École française. They have a *wunnn-derful* after-school programme that may be better suited to you, Miss Patterson, as you are a little more advanced in the language. Perhaps you could continue your language studies there.'

I look up from the pamphlet to find her staring at me, her head cocked slightly to the side, like a curious dog's.

'We don't has any money for hextra lessons, ma'am,' my mother says, so quietly that we almost couldn't hear her, but with something rough in her voice. Her eyes are still fixed on the floor and I wonder, annoyed, what she's looking for there.

'Yes, well. Miss Patterson is an exceptionally good student in all other aspects and I am sure she will find a way to succeed. Right, Miss Patterson?'

I mumble, 'Yes, Miss,' more out of habit than in agreement. Because there's no way I can afford this place, and now there's no way I will pass the test, and there's no way to reach Auntie Sophie. Now all I can see in front of me is my dreams galloping further away, like a spooked horse.

★

When we get home, my mother invades my space in the kitchen again because she's in the mood for johnny cakes. I watch her rolling the dough between her rough hands, pushing and pulling and kneading it into submission, grinding the flour and salt and baking soda and water together. She pulls out big lumps and beats them into balls, which she flings into the waiting pan of hot oil, the drops splashing out and searing us both, although she seems not to feel it. She treats the balls of dough as if they've been rude, said something feisty, slapped her in the face and now she's teaching them a lesson. The balls crackle and glisten in the pan. My mother is too impatient to turn the fire down low, to prod the dumplings gently, making sure they don't burn. I can already smell them beginning to blacken. They will be hard.

Auntie Sophie's johnny cakes were perfect: fried golden and crispy on the outside, light and fluffy on the inside, just a pat of butter melting on top to finish them off. She was gentle with the dough, massaging it just right, coaxing it into its rightful shape. She'd told me the history of the johnny cakes, how they'd originally been called 'journey cakes' because eating a few, then drinking some water would cause the flour to swell in the stomach, keeping you full for hours. A necessity, she'd said, when very poor people had to travel a very long way. She used to joke about my mother's hard dumplings.

'We used to use them as door stops,' she'd said, 'or to stone mango thieves down from the trees.'

We would laugh until our eyes ran with tears at the thought of it.

'Is what yu laughin at suh?' my mother spits now, her eyes never leaving the aggressive kneading of the dough.

'Nothing,' I say quietly, turning away from the balls of flour now sitting, black, in the rancid oil.

I remember . . .

. . . *my mother and me on the way to the University at Mona, on the bus. It is the only time I remember being with my mother outside our house, without my grandmother or my aunt. We are bringing dinner for Auntie Sophie, who is studying late, dinner that my grandmother made: curry goat and rice. The food is in a big margarine container and wrapped several times over in plastic, but the whole bus can smell it, the sharp tang of the goat, the spice of the curry. My mouth is watering and I can't wait to get back home to eat my share. My grandmother's goat is the best, so juicy that the chunks of meat melt in your mouth like ice cream, but not sweet, of course. A very fat woman two seats up keeps glancing back at us, her eyes finding the source of the smell, and in my mind I tell her, 'Turn around Fatty Boom Boom,' which makes me laugh.*

The university gates are wide, like wings, and the road is long and smooth. I think I would like to take a skateboard and fly all the way down it, like Tamara's cousin Ricky tries to do on our street, whenever he comes to visit. He keeps falling over in the potholes, though. Ricky would love this street and I plan to tell him he can come here and skate. We stand and stare at the gates although I don't know why we don't go inside. I look up at my mother and she is just staring at the long, smooth road, her eyes kind of wide. I busy myself looking around and that's when I see Auntie Sophie, walking with a group of young women at the other side of the gate. I feel really happy when I see Auntie Sophie! I tug on my mother's hand and she flashes me off, but she looks anyway and she sees her sister with her friends. They are almost all light-skinned, with long straightened hair, or big bouncy curls, light eyes and small noses. They look like they are supposed to be here, like they fit in with the gate-wings. I think they are all so very pretty and I wonder if I look like them at all. I know I look like Auntie Sophie, so maybe I also fit with these girls.

Auntie Sophie is laughing and laughing, her hand at her throat. I stare at her. I don't think I have ever seen her look like this, like there is a light inside her face shining out. She doesn't look like this at home, but I don't know what it is that's different, other than the light. I look back at my mother and now she looks different too. Sweaty and rumpled and dark and sour. Her skin near mine feels hot, all of a sudden. Auntie Sophie and her shiny friends are getting into a shiny car, but I know if she sees us, she will come with us instead, so I shout, 'Auntie! Auntie!' and wave my hand.

I know she hears me because she stops with her hand on the door of the shiny car and looks back at us. She sees me and then she looks up at her sister. I wave again and I hold up the scandal bag of dinner that I was allowed to carry for her. One of her friends looks at my aunt and then back at me and my mother and says something, but Auntie Sophie shrugs her shoulders a little and says something that makes her friend laugh and gets in the car. I'm confused because didn't she see us? I'm sure I saw her see us — she looked right at me, didn't she? I call again, 'Auntie Sophie!' and I wave again, but the car drives off, the red of the taillights like two evil eyes. I look up at my mother and I am almost sure I can see steam rising from the top of her head like a cartoon. I start to ask her if she thinks Auntie Sophie didn't see us, but before I can say anything she rips the bag of food out of my hands, tears the plastic open and throws the contents right on that long, smooth road. Some of the meat gets on my arms and my shirt and my neck. It's still hot but not enough to burn, although I think of my grandmother and how she'll be mad because everyone knows if you get curry on your clothes that's it, you just have to throw them out or wear them as yaad clothes. I look at the road, full of delicious food that no one but a stray dog will eat now. The road looks like someone threw up on it. There's no way Ricky could skate through that. My mother throws the margarine tub on the side of the street hard enough to crack the plastic.

We turn around and go back home.

Croissants and coffee

The principal of the Lycée reviewed your transcripts and said she would be happy to accept you into the school, on the condition of your passing the language test. Once we have the acceptance letter we can get your student visa. And guess what, Pumkin, school here is free, can you believe it? I mean the good schools, too! See, Pumkin, I told you all that studying would pay off! And I also told you, my Pumkin, that I would not leave you behind. Now, I'm going to need you to do some footwork because I am too far away to take care of things and we both know ~~your mother is not capable~~ that you've got to do this on your own. You should be able to take the prep classes for the test at school — I remember doing it myself and you're going to have to really buckle down and study. Since you're taking French at Aggie's, you should be able to avoid the fee, which is good because it's pretty expensive and I can barely make ends meet right now — the pay is not that good and it is so expensive here. Please find out the test dates and let me know so I can start arrangements with the Lycée here.

Imagine it, Pumkin, you going to a French school! Us together in France! I can barely contain my excitement at our dreams coming true. But, first, you have to pass the test, which I have every confidence that you will do. I know you are worried about your mother, *but don't, Pumkin. You leave me to worry about that. We will find a way to get you to me.*

I put the letter aside and lean on my windowsill, my chest tight. How am I to tell Sophie that I've messed everything up? Been kicked out of French class, so now I can't take the test at school. I remember how I thought she was abandoning me when she left but, look, she really *is* planning to bring me over, and I've ruined the chance. I feel something crawl on my face and brush it frantically away, but it's only tears.

I'd been afraid to imagine the life my aunt was so excited for. There were so many steps in between – even if I find a way to sit this test, what if I don't pass it? What if it's all for nothing? And my mother . . . I know Sophie says she'll handle it, but when has she ever been able to handle my mother? I might have felt more confident if my grandmother was here but, well, she isn't.

Still, I can't help smiling at the idea of Auntie Sophie and me sitting at the Marseille port eating buttery croissants and drinking hot chocolate. I give myself ten more minutes to daydream and then I put the letter with all the others and get myself together. I have a mission to complete today, and it's time to go.

★

I take the bus up to Norbrook Road. I sit frozen still, my backpack in my lap so my clothes won't wrinkle. Now I look around me as I walk up the winding street. Massive bushy trees line the sidewalks. The street is wide and paved, although I notice it's riddled with almost as many potholes as Potter's Lane. An old woman passes with a basket balanced expertly on top of her head.

'Fruits, dahlin?' she asks. 'I have some lovely fruits for you here, guinep and banana? Hall type a mangoes, Julie Mango, Stringy?' I just smile at her and shake my head and she walks on. I look back at her, hips swaying wide from left to right, her left hand held straight out to the side to help her balance.

The houses are large and substantial, set far back from the road and a great distance from the neighbours on either side, with huge yards of smooth, smooth grass out front. *So much space*, I think. *How are they allowed to take up so much space?* I pass a massive gate painted so black that I touch it to see if it smudges my finger. As I touch it, I hear a click and it sweeps open slowly, like a very grand vampire sweeping his coat aside to let me in and drink me dry. I panic and run up the road, my heart in my stomach, but then I laugh when I look back and see a big, cream Volvo drive out, a woman so small at the wheel I can barely see her head over the top.

I keep walking. I'm on my way to L'École française, the after-school programme Mrs Roberts recommended, the pamphlet she gave me crushed in my fist. I don't know what I'm actually going to do when I get there, but I figure it won't hurt to go and see it, find out how much it all costs. Maybe it isn't that much . . . maybe I can find a way. I have to try something. I just can't bear to write the letter to Sophie that I know I'll have to write otherwise.

I love and hate walking along streets like these. Some of the houses here have high hedges and beautiful flowerbeds so you can't see inside the yards, or they're hidden behind wide gates with a little guardhouse beside it and a man sitting inside, listening to a tinny little radio. A lot of them have water fountains at the front and the names of the estate forged in cursive in the steel of the gate, names like The Fountains at Norbury.

I daydream that I live in one of these pink or peach houses, a house with lots of space and different rooms and big kitchens. A house of comfort and excess and full bellies and happiness. As I pass one of the gates I can just see a woman at the back, hanging laundry. She is small and dark, wearing a long red skirt, a black T-shirt and a colourful head wrap. The housekeeper, I figure. I don't think the people who live here hang their own laundry. Two massive, fluffy German shepherds sit like kings under the shade of a big tree, their tongues hanging out. They're relaxed now, but they'd rip you apart if you set foot in that yard uninvited. I stop and watch the woman, the pegs in her mouth as she pins the clothes onto the line. *This is as close as I'll get*, I think, as I stand there with the sun beating down on my neck. *Just standing here staring, or hanging the laundry.* I watch the woman until she catches sight of me, pausing in her laundry hanging to wave cheerfully. I raise my hand and smile.

Ten minutes later I stand in front of a two-storey pink townhouse with a balcony that looks more like a gingerbread house than a place of learning. I half expect a white woman to burst onto the balcony and release yards of straight blonde hair, beckoning me to climb up as birds sing cheerfully on her shoulders. There are huge bushes of wild roses at the gates and a short driveway that leads to a red front door. A small sign is attached to the column beside the gate:

> L'École française
> Mon – Thurs 4 p.m. – 6.30 p.m.
> Fri 3 p.m. – 4 p.m. (admin only)
> Sat 10 a.m. – 12 p.m./12.30 p.m. to 2.30 p.m.

I stare up at the house as I catch my breath and wait for the burning in my chest to dull. I really need to pee. Something catches my attention out of the corner of my eye and I see a stray dog staring up at me, black and skinny with a brown snout, his tail wagging uncertainly. He's out of place here and I feel a surge of emotion for him, because I'm out of place here too. 'Maybe you're a prince I'm supposed to kiss?' I ask him, and he steps forward hopefully, his tail now threatening to launch him into the air. I smile at him but look back at the house. I don't have time to play. As I put my hand on the gate I glance at him: he's watching me, but then he turns himself around and around and around on the grassy sidewalk, tucks his nose under his front leg and promptly falls asleep.

'Lazy prince,' I mumble.

I look towards the house. I hear a sound like the wind blowing hard in my ears, so hard it blocks out all other sounds except the frantic beating of my heart, which has now migrated up into my throat. I don't know what or who I'll find. I don't know what I'm going to say or what I'm going to do or why I'm even here. But I take a deep breath all the same, walk through the gate, push the red door open and step inside.

★

The outside of the house looks like a light, fluffy, two-layer cake, so I'm surprised when I find myself in a living room filled with very big, very dark furniture. *This isn't a school*, I think, because it's clearly someone's house. There's a red-velvet and mahogany couch, a television, two side tables with small crystal lamps, and porcelain ballerinas on every available shelf. Beyond the room is a short passageway, and if I lean way over to one side I can just see the edge of a very long mahogany dining table. Everything is big and dark and heavy and imposing, and I stand there, unsure of myself, until my gaze finds another small placard on the wall near the stairs with the words 'L'École française' and a small arrow pointing upwards.

I make my way up the stairs, which spiral upwards and upwards, the sound of clickety-clacking and shuffling getting louder the further up I go. When I get to the landing I see a small office where a sharp-looking woman is furiously typing away at an electric typewriter. She is sitting behind a broad mahogany desk and I think that the owner of this house *really* likes mahogany. There's a block of wood with a gold plate on it that has *Miss Keene* stencilled into it. She is small and bird-like, the desk so big she looks almost like a child sitting at her father's table, and her skin is almost as deep and dark as the furniture. She's wearing a silky burgundy three-quarter-sleeve blouse with a pussy-bow hanging down the front. Her natural hair is pressed straight and curled under and it reminds me of the Stormtroopers in *Star Wars*. Not a strand of it moves, despite the small jerks of her head as she bangs on the typewriter as if it has offended her. A pair of small rectangular glasses rimmed in gold perches at the end of her nose. She looks up over them now and I feel my whole body go rigid as she catches sight of me. I grip the straps of my backpack tighter, as if they can shield me from her glare. She looks above and behind me for the adult I should be with, and then her gaze lands back on me. A look of distaste ripples over her face before she says, '*Oui?*'

A tiny moth of panic flutters in my stomach: am I supposed to speak French?

'I . . . ahm . . .'

'What is it, child?' Miss Keene snaps, her fingers still poised over the keyboard, making it plain that I am seriously distracting her from some very serious typing. Her accent is cultured, almost British, the *t*s at the ends of her words popping like popcorn.

'I . . . ahm . . . I wanted to ask about the test, Miss.'

'What? Good Lord, come closer, child, speak up!'

I inch closer. 'I came about the test, Miss.'

'What *test*, child?' I can hear the exasperation in her voice. She's leaning forward over her desk now, peering down at me over her glasses, and I feel like a mouse that has been caught in the sights of a tremendous eagle, like I'll be eaten up in the most savage way possible, snick snack, nothing left but the end of my tail. My need to pee becomes a little more urgent.

'The . . . the language proficiency test for school placement, Miss?'

Miss Keene furrows her brow and looks me up and down. I become aware of how I must look: my old, faded shirt and shorts rumpled and crumpled from being squished in several buses and walking in the heat of the sun and racing to the front door. I reach my hand up to try to smooth down my hair, which has pulled itself out of its bun all over my head so I'm sure it looks like I stuck my finger in a socket. I'm here on my own, no parent in sight.

'And what,' Miss Keene says, 'would you like to ask about this test?'

I wonder how long she can keep her fingers hovering over the typewriter keys, as if she's been frozen in time.

'I . . . Well, my auntie, Miss? My auntie Sophie. She want me to come . . . I mean, she *wants* me to come and live with her in France. So I . . . ah, want to . . . I . . . I'd like to . . . take the course for the test here, Miss. So I can take it and . . . and meet . . . and go to school there. Miss?'

I feel like all the words were jumbled in a heap in my chest and I had to push them out, and now I'm out of breath. I feel the sweat starting to roll down the side of my face.

'*Your* aunt lives in France?' Miss Keene says. 'Where exactly does she live?'

'. . . Marseille, Miss.'

'Hmm. And what school do you attend, young lady?'

'Aggie's. I mean St Agatha's,' I say, then hurriedly add another 'Miss' when I see her eyebrow arch almost up into her hairline.

She leans her head back a little and I can see her thinking, although I have no idea what.

'Et tu parles déjà français? Quel est votre niveau?'

My mind blanks and I blink helplessly before I find my voice.

'Je sais parler un peu français, Madame. Ma tante m'a appris. J'ai bien peur de ne pas connaître mon niveau exact.'

'Well,' she says. She looks at me for a while and I feel myself get hotter and hotter. 'Well, the placement test is administered once a year on the last Saturday in June. It is a three-hour exam consisting of an oral, written and reading component. Registration is required at the latest one week prior to the examination and costs fifteen thousand dollars. Do you have fifteen thousand dollars for the registration fee?"

'I . . . I . . .'

'Our prep course is already under way, so you are very late. I am not entirely sure we would be able to fit you in. However, classes are twice a week, Tuesdays and Thursdays from four thirty p.m. to six thirty p.m. It is a very *intensive* course.' Her gaze sharpens. I nod silently, not knowing what else to do. 'Fees are ten thousand dollars per term, for two terms. We are almost halfway into this term so you would need to pay only for one and a half.'

The moth fluttering in my stomach explodes. I actually feel the heat of it, like a balloon of hot lava burst in my gut. That's thirty thousand dollars. It might as well be a million.

'Are your parents able to pay these fees?'

'I . . .' is all I manage to say before I shake my head.

'Will your *aunt* be able to send you the money from *Marseille*?'

I think back to Auntie Sophie's last letter. She's settling in, she'd said, but hadn't realized that France was so expensive. *I'm living off croissants and coffee*, she'd written. She was still paying my school fees and school supplies, and said she didn't have a *franc* to spare for anything else.

'I don't think so, Miss,' I say, so quietly I'm not sure the eagle behind the desk hears me.

'Well, then,' Miss Keene says, with a note of finality. She pushes her glasses up her nose with her pinky finger and resumes typing. I stand there looking at her, wondering . . . what, I'm not even sure. What does this mean? This was the only second chance I had. But what had I expected? Why had I come here? Why did I think anything that happened in a place like this would be available to someone like me? The man in my chest starts up with his foolishness and I feel my breath hitch. I am rooted to the spot, except for the slight swaying caused by the beating of my heart, which is climbing up my throat. It's climbing up my throat and expanding there, and soon it will cover my nose and I cannot breathe and I –

'Is there something else?'

I blink. Miss Keene is looking at me again over her glasses, her eyebrow raised. I shake my head and will my eyes to stop burning.

'No, Miss,' I mumble. I look at her for one more moment. It's like she's hypnotized me and I can't look away. When her image starts to blur, I turn to make my way down the stairs.

'Child!' I turn back towards Miss Keene, who is holding out a pamphlet. 'Take this.'

I shuffle towards her desk and take the booklet, which has a picture of a group of teenagers in front of the Eiffel Tower, just like the pamphlet for L'École, and the French Language Placement Test 1995 on the front.

'Thank you, Miss.' I am tempted to ask her if there's money inside, since I can't figure out why she wants me to have it, but I take it, dutifully, and make my way down the stairs and through the red front door, the sounds of the clickety-clacking echoing in my ears.

★

Prince the dog is still curled up on the sidewalk where I left him. When he hears me at the gate, he opens one eye, then the other. I watch him yawn and stretch, his tail thumping as he looks at me expectantly, as if we hadn't just met, as if he's known me all his life and is sure I'll have something nice to give him, a bone maybe, or just a pat on the head. He trots over to me, timidly, and squints his eyes and puts his nose on my leg. I reach down to rub his head, my tears making dark drops on his shiny black hair.

'Let's go, Prince,' I say, and he follows me back through the lushly lined streets, my tears leaving a trail on the deep black asphalt, like breadcrumbs showing the wrong way home.

Every dog have him day

Prince follows me all the way to the bus stop, sometimes running ahead of me, sometimes snuffling and digging somewhere behind, but always jogging back to walk beside me. I find a crumpled bag of saltine crackers in my bag and try to entice him with it but he just licks the salt off and looks up at me expectantly. *Dry crackers?* As I stand there waiting for the bus, he looks at me so sadly that I end up walking the whole way so I won't have to leave him behind.

'Wait here,' I tell him, when we get home, running inside to see what I can rustle him up to eat. I find some bread backs that I'd most likely use to make bread pudding and a battered tin of mackerel, which I open and dump out into an old dish. If my mother saw me wasting food like this she'd kill me but, as usual, she isn't here. The house is quiet. When I head out to give Prince his dinner, he is nowhere to be found and I feel like crying again. I call his name a few times before I realize how dumb that is, since he doesn't know it, and I don't know how to whistle, so I put the dish down at the back door off my bedroom and hope that he'll find his way to it.

Inside the house I find a rumpled piece of paper weighed down with notes and coins. It's a shopping list written in Paulette's childish scrawl, almost every word misspelled. On the rare occasions when my mother writes something, I have to say the words out loud before I can figure them out.

Wonyon, gyalik, swit pitayta.

I put my backpack on and head to the market. The day is still clear, blue, and hot with a muggy breeze, and my clothes feel like they've melted and become one with my skin. The streets are bustling with people on the sidewalks, cars blowing their horns impatiently, men leaning out of the windows to cuss each other, or to have long discussions, despite the line of traffic building behind them. Music blares from someone's car, the back seat dug out and upholstery removed to make way for a sound system that would wake the dead. I think of how still and quiet it was by L'École but then it makes me remember the meeting with Miss Keene, so I shake it out of my head.

There's a donkey tied up near the entrance to the market, placidly chewing a long stalk of grass and surveying his kingdom at the side of the road, and I wonder what he makes of all the noise and palaver. I pass a woman descaling fish by the entrance, her legs spread wide with her bright blue skirt tucked in, a big red bucket between her feet. She is singing as she cleans the fish, snick snick snick, a few passes with her little knife and it's gutted, ready for the frying pan. I watch her work for a few moments before I step into the market.

I love the market. I love to hear the market women sweet-talk their potential buyers, the way they describe the sweetness/bitterness/ripeness of the fruits and vegetables stacked like towers about to fall over on their low-slung tables. There are even a few uptown people here, gingerly picking up root vegetables and smelling mangoes, many of which had been stolen from their very own trees.

Tamara's cousin Donovan was one of the mango thieves who roamed the streets around Norbrook, Cherry Gardens and Jacks Hill, shimmying his way up the sprawling trees set in manicured lawns. He dropped the mangoes into the waiting hands of Rupert or Ackley, the two street boys he was always hanging out with. It took a while, sometimes, before the owner of the house or the housekeeper figured out why the leaves were rustling like crazy despite a complete and utter lack of breeze and came hurtling outside, yelling, 'GET OUTTA DERE, BWOY!' But by then they would have filled the whole box and Donovan would shimmy back down the tree, the boys running off to wherever they hid their stash of stolen fruit, laughing and swinging the box between them. They gorged themselves on the mangoes, sweet, sticky juice running down their fingers, the threads sticking between their teeth, before bringing the rest to their mothers to sell right back to the same people who, by rights, should have had those mangoes for free.

'Yuh tink dem uptown lady gwen climb de tree dereselves? They payin for the labour, Pumkin!' he told me once, when I asked him if he thought it was fair for people to buy the things they owned in the first place.

Now I pick up a mango and hold it to my nose, inhaling the sugary sweet scent. It was a Julie mango, the very best kind. The flesh would be almost orange, taut but soft, and sweeter than any candy. Gramma Cecille loved a Julie. She'd sit with a box of them between her legs, ripping at the skin of each one with her teeth so it was peeled down the sides like a banana, sucking every last bit of yellow so thoroughly that the seed looked polished, like a big white stone, by the end.

'Suh yuh fi eat it,' she'd say, grinning, when I looked on in wonder as she wapsed off five in a row and complained, later, that she should really watch her sugar. The memory makes me want to smile and cry at the same time.

'Twenty dollar a pound, or a dollar fi juss one, dahlin,' says the woman behind the stall. Even sitting I can see she is very small, like a tiny mouse. Her skin reminds me of bauxite, a deep reddish, earthy tone. She wears a yellow scarf on her head and her face is lined around the eyes and mouth, most likely because of grins like the one she is wearing now.

I try to smile back at her while I shake my head, slightly. I only have so much money in my pocket and it would barely cover the list my mother had scrawled. I put the mango down.

'Yu is Miss Sophie dawta?'

I turn back to her, surprised. She knew Auntie Sophie?

'Yu favour har. Miss Sophie, weh did live down Potter's Lane, gawn a farrin now?'

'Yes!' I say, too loudly. 'I mean, no, she's my auntie.'

The woman's head bobs up and down.

'I did see unnu togedda, weh time. She was a nice ooman, used to halways buy from me. Me know Miss Sophie long time! Yu favour har fi true. Gwaan, dahlin, tek dis one.'

She holds out a ripe, juicy mango, and I stare at her out-stretched hand a moment too long before I realize she is giving me one of her mangoes.

'I . . . I don't have enough money.' I am still staring at her outstretched hand.

'Den I neva haxe yuh fi any money, dahlin. Tek it, mi love, it sweet and nice.' She stretches her hand further towards me until I take it. The mango is heavy with juice. I can tell it will be sweet.

'Thank you.'

'Don' share it!' the woman says, leaning forward and wink-ing at me like we're two old friends up to some conspiracy.

I grin and tell her thank you once more. I look back at her

as I walk deeper into the market but she is already on to the next customer, an uptown woman with feathered silky hair and gold bangles that I can hear from here stacked up her arm. They clink like pebbles knocking against each other but soon the sound is lost in the noise of the market.

I decide to save the mango for when I'm home, but then I'm suddenly gripped by anxiety that my mother will take it from me. *Don't share it*, the woman had said. So I rip into the skin of it with my teeth and peel it away on both sides like a banana and bite into the firm flesh, my plastic bag of market goods banging into my arm. I stick my chest and arms out a little so the juice won't drip all over my clothes, but still it runs down my arm and I don't care at all, because the sweetness has filled my mouth and I can focus on nothing else. *Is there anything in the world*, I think, *better than a sweet, ripe mango?* Yes, I answer myself. A free one. I giggle and walk on, eating the mango as I go.

It's starting to get dark by the time I reach home, the house shrouded in shadows. There's still no one here. I put the bag of vegetables on the kitchen counter and walk through the tiny little space. I sit on the couch and wrap my arms around myself. I wonder what Sophie is doing now, what time it is in France, if she's walking along the port and eating *macarons*. I feel an ache in my tummy.

I get up and head into my room, feeling haunted, and it's then I hear a scratching at the back door. I freeze for a moment, my stomach flip-flopping. I hear it again, scritch scritch scratch. A frantic kind of sound. I creep up to the window and peer outside and I see a skinny little tail wagging back and forth.

'Prince!' I shout, which stops the scratching immediately.

I fling open the door and there he is, his mouth wide open in a smile, his tail wagging so hard his whole butt is moving. I can see he's eaten the mackerel and bread I left for him. I sit heavily on the ground and he runs up to me and steps all over my legs, his tongue lapping at the sugary streaks of mango on my arms.

'You came back, Prince,' I say, my hands patting at his stomach, and he snorts at me before walking around in circles and thumping to the ground, his head in my lap, the sticky juice of the mango growing tacky on my skin.

Sweet potato

'How are your stoosh friends?'

I snort and shake my head, laughing. It's Wednesday after school and Tamara and I are walking towards the bus stop on our way home. I've barely seen her the past few weeks since I'm so often with Mandy and her troupe. Those girls always have something going on, and Sophie might not be physically here, but she never fails to remind me, in her letters, that I should be 'developing these important friendships'. I'm not exactly sure what the point is since I'm supposed to be leaving eventually for France, but I do what she says all the same.

'What's happening with them? That girl, wha' she name, Amelia?'

I take a deep breath and exhale slowly.

'Mandy,' I say. I know Tamara knows her name, but ever since Mandy called her 'Tamika', she's made it a point to 'forget' Mandy's name.

'Are they coming to the barbecue?'

I shrug and say I don't know, but it's not quite true. They've been talking about the school barbecue for weeks – everyone has. It's the biggest school event of the year, with a major talent show open to students from high schools all over. A few popular singers and dancers were discovered at the Aggie's barbecue, so it's a big draw.

'Yu comin over?' Tamara asks, as we walk down our street, but I shake my head.

'I have to make a sweet-potato pudding for Linnette. Her sister is coming over.'

Tamara moans deep in her throat. 'Sweet-potato pudding?' she says, looking at me and waggling her eyebrows.

I laugh. 'If I have enough batter I'll make you a little one. But keep it quiet! Linnette will kill me if she finds out I gave away any of her pudding, especially since she gave me all the ingredients to make it.'

'For real,' she agrees, before giving me a wave at her gate.

I walk the few steps down to my own gate. The street is quiet, just three little kids playing jacks and the tinny sound of music coming from somewhere far enough away that I can't make out either the rhythm or the lyrics.

Once I'm inside and changed into my yaad clothes I tackle the sweet-potato pudding. I spend the next few hours cutting and grating sweet potatoes, adding dark sugar, flour and raisins and mixing everything with coconut milk. I melt some margarine and pour it with nutmeg, salt, cinnamon, vanilla, rum, lime juice and browning into the mix, churning and churning until my arm feels like it's burning. I scrape everything into two battered baking tins – a big one for Linnette and a tiny one for Tamara – and then I do my homework while it bakes. When I take the puddings out of the oven almost two hours later, they are a deep golden brown on the top and the air around them smells sweet and sugary. I leave them on the counter to cool and I get back to my books.

*

I jolt awake later, my books on my lap and a line of drool crusted onto the side of my mouth. 'Eww,' I say, wiping away the spit. I look outside my window and see the sun just starting to sink, the sky painted crimson and orange against a deep blue backdrop, and I hear movement outside my bedroom door. I stare at the scene in front of me a while longer before I sigh and turn away. My mother will be home now.

But when I walk into the kitchen it's not my mother I see, it's Akil, stuffing a large piece of sweet-potato pudding – Linnette's sweet-potato pudding – down his throat. The pan is on the counter and there's a big square cut out of the pudding, crumbs trailing over the peeling Formica. I see a line of ants already marching forward, ready to take their share. I'm stunned for a moment, more at finding him here than seeing him eat my food, but then something punches out of my chest and I shout, 'NO!' which makes him jump almost out of his skin, the whites of his eyes as big as car headlights. I push past him and grab the battered square pan, backing up with it tucked against my chest. I glance down at it. He's cut himself a thick, healthy chunk. I glare at him, feeling my face contort into a look of disgust. My grandmother always said I can't hide anything on my face.

'Dis potato puddin' *nice*, man!' he says, around a mouthful. He seems to have got over his fright. I watch him chew the pastry, his mouth clapping open and shut, bliss on his face. I feel a surge of pride before I remember that I hate this man. Remember that I don't care what he thinks. I tamp it down and wonder, instead, how he can just sweep in and create havoc and blow back out like a hurricane. He reaches for the pan but I take a few steps back, hugging the mangled bread pudding closer to me.

'It's not yours,' I huff. 'I made it for Linnette.'

'Linnette? Dat fat gyal from round de corner? She don't need no more potato pudding.' He laughs, reaching for the pastry again. I move even further out of his reach.

'You cyaan juss . . . you can't just come in here and – and just *tek* things that aren't yours,' I say, as menacingly as I can manage. He leans back and studies me, as if seeing me for the first time. Then he shakes his head and says, 'But see yah, lik-kle girl,' under his breath, looking out of the kitchen window and then back at me, his head cocked to one side, like a dog.

'Where yu modda deh?' he asks me, and I shrug. He pulls a toothpick out of his pocket and pops it into his mouth, starts to chew. We face each other like two cowboys in those black-and-white shows they play on JBC on Sunday afternoons.

'You look juss like yu auntie,' he says suddenly. 'You know dat?'

He chuckles, and it sounds like gravel dropped on concrete.

'Yu auntie, man. Sophie. *She* mi did want, you nuh? Couldn't believe seh Paulette did have such a . . . *beautiful* sista. But you know how it is . . . she did tink seh she too good for me. Sophie did tink she did too good for everybody round 'ere. Juss like you, don't it?'

I set my face as blank as I can make it, but I remember my mother staring out of my back door, looking so small and sad as she tells me her sister gets everything she wants, every little thing. A swirl of pity lashes through my stomach. And some-thing else, something like . . . guilt? Because Sophie wants me too . . .

My eyes focus back on Akil. He is leaning against the coun-ter, the toothpick jigging and jagging as he chews on it, shifting it from one side of his mouth to the other. Suddenly he lunges for the potato pudding again, but I'm quicker and I run out of the kitchen and lock myself into my bedroom. Eventually I hear him leave, his footsteps heavy on the gravel, although he is so skinny that I think it must be the weight of his soul.

When Linnette comes later to pick up the bread pudding, I have cut it into small squares, like those fancy brownies that Mandy's friend Natalie brought to school one time, and arranged it on a plate with flowers on the side so she won't notice that it's missing a big hunk out of the middle.

'What a way it look fancy!' she says, her chest heaving from the walk down the lane to our house, and I give her a shaky smile, glad she thinks I've done this on purpose and not to cover a mistake. I ask Linnette to please bring the plate back when she's finished, in case my mother notices it's missing, and she says she will. Then she reaches into her expansive bosom, hoisted up like a shelf holding two hams, and pulls out a crumpled wad of bills. She counts out eighty dollars and squeezes it into my palm and says, 'Tenk yu, mi dawlin – mi sista love a pitayta puddin but you know seh me juss cyaan mek it like you mek it.' She laughs a deep and throaty laugh and I join her but I'm still thinking about the cash she put into my hand.

'But, Linnette,' I say, 'you don't need to –'

But she just cuts me off with a smile and a pat on my cheek before she walks away.

'Mi wi bring back di plate later, awrite?' she calls over her shoulder and I just nod, which she can't even see. But my mind is racing. This money is all profit. I look at the sweaty, crumpled bills in my hand and a smile spreads slowly across my face.

I remember . . .

. . . I'm in our tiny little kitchen, hands deep in flour and batter and sugar. I spend hours here, measuring, beating, grating and folding, turning old bread backs into pudding, coconut shavings into sugary coconut drops, or gouttes de coco, *as I call them, giving all my creations fancy French names even though they're just typical Jamaican things. Auntie Sophie is with me. We are both covered with a light dusting of flour, our fingers sticky with honey and chocolate.*

'You're getting very good at this,' she says, spooning my version of crème brûlée *into her mouth. I've used condensed milk instead of cream and I didn't know what the cookbook meant by 'torching the sugar' so I just sprinkled cane sugar on top. It wasn't much to look at, but it made my aunt close her eyes for almost a full minute after she'd taken the first mouthful.*

'When we get to France, we'll open a pastry shop right in the middle of Paris. You'll bake French-Jamaican creations and I'll run the business. What do you think about that?'

I dip my spoon into the custard and lick it. 'Can we call it Pumkin's Pâtisserie?'

'That,' she says, 'is an excellent name. Pumkin's Pâtisserie, best brioche pudding in all of Paris!'

'What's brioche pudding?'

'It's Jamaican bread pudding made with brioche, which is something we're going to create.'

'I love it,' I say. 'We'll have sweet pomme de terre *pudding and macarons made with digestive biscuits and cocoa in the middle!'*

'Guava-filled crêpes and Otaheite tatin!'

'Crème brûlée with condensed milk!'

'Mille-feuille with . . . with . . . well, I'm not even sure what regular mille-feuille is made with . . .'

'Johnny cake with melted chocolate!'

'What? That's . . . No, where you get that idea from?'

'I saw them in the cookbook. Profit rolls. They look like johnny cakes.'

'Those, my sweet Pumkin, are called profiteroles and I don't think anybody will eat johnny cakes with chocolate on them, unless they're looking for a stomach-ache.'

'Well, we're making it up, right? And our pastries will be so creative that the King of France will hear about our pastry shop.'

'We'll make them for him exclusively.'

'And he'll make us princesses!'

'Well, duchesses, maybe. Let's be realistic.'

'Duchesses, then. And we'll be rich and famous . . .'

'And live in our own castle.'

'But . . . just me and you, right, Auntie Sophie?'

'Just you and me,' she says, touching her nose to my cheek. 'We'll have everything we want in this world, because Pumkin's Pâtisserie will be our success. Right, my little Pumkin?'

'That's right, Auntie Sophie,' I say, licking my spoon clean.

We are not frogs

A couple of weeks later I'm walking back up to L'École, a pile of gizzadas wrapped carefully in brown paper and stuffed into an old margarine tub, my heart stuffed haphazardly into my throat. I think of the wad of cash I've hidden in my bedroom and I pick up my step. In the past two weeks, I've made six hundred dollars. That same weekend Linnette paid me for the pudding, I'd gone back to her at her shop on the corner and told her my plan, my stomach a bundle of nerves. We worked out a deal: she would front me the supplies for pastries and, in return, she would sell some in the shop and keep a portion of the money. The rest I would sell at school. You weren't allowed to sell things at school, but people found ways to do it all the time. The teachers' eyes can't be everywhere at once.

I was too scared to bake at home, afraid my mother would discover my plan, afraid my father would take what wasn't his, so I'd spent the weekend baking in Tamara's kitchen, in exchange for leaving some sweet things for the family. I was prepared to suffer the consequences of spending the whole weekend away. Even though my mother acted like I was a particularly useless piece of furniture, she seemed to want me to be there whenever she was – which was rarely. But when I came back on Sunday evening, my backpack stuffed with things to sell, Paulette was sitting in front of the TV.

'Where yuh was?' she'd asked, as I shuffled past her, my hands on my backpack straps. She didn't look away from the TV.

'At . . . at Tamara's . . .'

I stood there watching her, waiting for a response, but she didn't say anything else, so I slunk off to my room, my heart pounding triple time.

The next day I brought my pastries to school: coconut drops, gizzadas, squares of bread pudding, apple turnovers, everything sticky sweet and wrapped in brown grease paper. I'd tied each one up with red string I'd found in my grandmother's sewing tin, the old tin of Danish cookies that would get my hopes up every time my grandmother opened it, only to bring them crashing down when I realized there were no cookies, just thread and scissors and thimbles.

I waited until 3 p.m., when everyone gets peckish and drowsy and the day starts to drag and the girls make their way over to the tuck shop to buy half-melted chocolates, and approached a set sitting under a tree. They were all talking over each other, laughing, squawking like chickens, until they noticed me standing there in front of them, my backpack open in front of me, like a shield.

I cleared my throat. 'I have these . . . ahm . . . I mean I'm selling some . . .'

I shift my weight from one foot to the other, something rolling and crashing in my tummy, like waves. The girls had all turned towards me, staring, waiting. I felt very hot, all of a sudden. But I thought about walking away, shame burning in my cheeks, and I knew I couldn't do that. I had to press forward. I had to get to Sophie, and this was the only way.

'Do you guys like pastry?' I said. 'Because I made some things, some different . . . like, coconut drops. And other things . . . ahm . . . and they're pretty good.'

As I spoke, I pulled the treats out of my bag and handed the samples around. Most of the girls took them but one said, no, thanks, so I put a few packages away in my backpack.

'Anyway, if you like them, I sell them, and . . . yeah, you can buy them from me. If you like them.'

I watched them for a moment as they opened the packages, broke off pieces of pastry and popped them into their mouths. I waited for that moment, the moment I always waited for, when I could see on their faces that they wanted one more bite, and another, and another, before I turned and walked away, a smile on my face. I didn't get very far before the girl who'd declined a package came running after me.

'I'll take one, actually!' she said, tapping me on my shoulder. I hefted my backpack down and opened it so she could reach in and grab one. She pulled out two and looked at me sheepishly. 'Awright if I take two?'

I smiled and watched as she ran back to her group, all of their hands now sticky with the things I'd made.

I repeated the process around the school, approaching groups of girls, pairs with their arms linked, loners straggling along to classes. The next day, girls approached me in steady streams, cash in their hands, specific requests on their lips. We carried out the transactions like those people on TV who bought drugs, them squeezing the money into my hands, me quickly passing them a brown square of grease paper, neither of us looking at the other, in case the sixth-formers or teachers caught wind of it.

Within an hour that second day I was sold out. By Wednesday I had to go back to Linnette for supplies to make up another school batch, and she told me she was all out as well.

'Dem waps dem off, Pumkin, cyaan keep dem on the

shelf!' she said, laughing and laughing until her heavy bosom shook like an earthquake.

I laughed with her and held the plastic bag full of flour and sugar and coconut against my chest, feeling lightheaded as I walked out of the door. But then I ran back to Linnette. 'Please. Don't tell Mama?'

She smiled at me and put her hand on my cheek. It was big and wide and warm, and I couldn't remember the last time someone had touched me like that. She put her finger to her lips and shook her head and sent me on my way. I headed straight to Tamara's, even though it was a week night, to bake more pastry for the shop and school.

'What is all this baking going on?' Miss Iona asked, when she found us in the kitchen for the second time that week. Tamara and I looked at each other, her eyes wide. She did not have the constitution to lie to her mother.

'It's for . . . ahm . . .' I shuffled under Miss Iona's glare as she stood over me, her hands on her hips. 'Miss Iona, it's for my new class. Ahm. Food and nutrition? You remember I got kic– I had to change from French class?'

She looked at me for a long moment, and then her face softened. She patted my cheek and I knew she was thinking about Sophie and our grand French plans, which seemed to have dissolved into nothing. Then she grabbed a square of bread pudding and winked at me before she swept out of the kitchen, leaving Tamara and me giggling on the floor.

Word had got around at school by then and so many girls came demanding treats that I had to set Tamara up as a delivery girl so we didn't draw a crowd and catch the attention of the prefects or teachers. I came home happy every day, my bag empty of pastries, a wad of bills pressed between the pages of my textbooks. At the end of the week, I went back to Linnette's shop and she gave me another wad of bills, minus her cut, and double the supplies from the week before.

★

Now, as I walk up to L'École, I'm hoping the magic will work one more time. This time, I have a plan. My hands shake a little as I hold on to my backpack straps. I'm scared of seeing Miss Keene again, of having her sharp, bird-like eyes look down on me, but I think about everything waiting for me on the other side of my fear: getting into the class, passing the test, going to France to be with Sophie, finally feeling like I belong somewhere.

I stand in front of the red door, staring up at it, still waiting for Rapunzel to fling down her hair. The door seems bigger this time, heavier. I take the brochure Miss Keene gave me out of my pocket. It is crushed and crumpled from the thousand times I have flipped through it. I rub my thumb over the faces of the happy teenagers on the front, the ones grinning and jumping in front of the Eiffel Tower, and I wonder, for the millionth time, if I make it over to Sophie, would I belong there? Would I fit in there any better than I fit in here? These people don't even look like me.

The door bangs open, startling me out of my thoughts, and a herd of students pours out. I realize with growing horror that I've timed this all wrong, coming after school instead of at closing time on the weekend, and I try to make myself as small as possible, curling in towards the column by the gate. I try to look like I belong here, even though it's obvious that I didn't exit the school with all the other kids. *I'm just waiting for my mother to pick me up*, I think. *I'm not a . . . not a vagrant or anything . . .*

I watch the students out of the corner of my eye. They have fancy backpacks and cultured accents, even when they speak patois to each other. Their uniforms, although creased and dirty at the end of the day, are crisper than mine, no buttons missing, no threadbare hems, although many of the girls start rolling up the waists of their skirts as soon as they step out of the gates, to make them shorter. And there are boys! Boys of all sizes: tall ones and short ones, skinny ones and fat ones. They don't look like the boys who live on my street. One of them has a mischievous expression on his face. He's wearing a Trinity High uniform, a prestigious school that is, unusually, co-ed. He says something to a girl in a full white uniform, an Indian-looking girl with a long thick braid hanging down her back, and she takes her backpack and hits him with it. Everyone laughs, including the boy and the girl and me, and I wonder what it would be like to be in that group.

It makes me think of Mandy and her friends. They're nice to me — well, except for Candida, who always looks like she's just caught a whiff of rotting fish when she sees me. They invite me places, to eat lunch with them, to sleepovers. I go every time, Sophie's voice in my head reminding me: *These are the kind of friends you should be making, Pumkin.* But I'm always trying to find the reason why they want me around. The stress of hiding where I live and what my mother does for a living, of speaking so properly that my jaw starts to ache, of pretending I already ate so, no, no, I don't want any KFC or Burger King, of getting everywhere early so they don't know I take the bus is exhausting.

Parents start driving up to L'École and one by one — sometimes in twos and threes — they get into their cars, most of them shiny and sleek and new, some of them huge

140

monstrosities. *No one here has ever been on a bus*, I think. A few of them glance at me and I set my face, as if to say, 'Jeezam peas, where *is* my mother?' and sigh, annoyed that she is late. They don't pay me any mind. I duck down and rifle through my bag as if I'm searching for something, just to give myself something to do. I stay crouched as I watch the last of the teens drive off in their air-conditioned luxury, thinking of how I'd hoped to be a student here, and I shake my head. It was hard enough to fit in at St Agatha's. How had I expected to fit in here?

'Young lady, do you need me to call someone for you?'

I yelp and pull myself up to my feet. Miss Keene is standing in the doorway, peering out at me expectantly, but I can't open my mouth. She screws up her forehead and steps further out onto the front step, looking at me quizzically. 'Are you a student here, young lady?'

'N-n-no, Miss. Ahm. Not yet. I . . . ahm . . . I wanted to ask about joining the classes, Miss?'

'At *this* late stage! It's the middle of the term. Why didn't you sign up earlier?'

'I . . . I . . .'

'Wait . . . You came in here the other day, asking about the placement test, *non*?'

'Yes, Miss.'

'To join your aunt in Bordeaux, you said,'

'Yes, Miss,' I say again. 'I mean, no, Miss, in Marseille.'

'And you're here again.'

'Yes, Miss.'

'And are you here to *register* for the preparatory course, or are you just here to loiter at my front gate?'

I want to tell her that I left last time because I couldn't

afford the class or the test. I want to tell her that I was inspired to find my own way, and that I'd thought I had absolutely nothing of value to anyone else until someone paid me for my pastries. I want to tell her that I've been baking and that people like the things I make, and that I can pay for everything if she'll allow me to do it likkle likkle, because I don't have all of it all at once. I want to give her the gizzada I brought so she can see for herself that my pastries are good, that people will keep buying them, that I promise I'll pay for everything if she gives me the chance, because if she doesn't then I don't know what else to do. I want to tell her that another year or two or three with my mother, in this place, in that house, would just kill me, that my aunt might really forget me by then, and I'll be stuck. But I don't know how to explain all this to the woman peering down at me from her heavy red front door. I don't know where to start.

'Miss . . .' I manage to get out before my eyes well over with the familiar burning and the tears tip onto my cheeks. I wipe them away, embarrassed that I can't hold it together. Miss Keene just looks at me for a long moment, her eyes roving from the top of my head to my feet. I can feel her gaze halting on the stains on my shirt, the loose threads poking from my sleeves, the hem of my skirt that has come undone on one side so it looks asymmetrical, my socks that have lost their elasticity and are slouching down in my beat-up, battered school shoes that are worn down to flip-flops on one side each. Her arms are crossed over her flat chest. Now that she isn't hidden behind that monstrous desk, I can see she is all limbs and angles, covered almost head to foot in a silky grey long-sleeved blouse tucked into a pleated burgundy skirt that hovers a few inches above a pair of unexpectedly fashionable grey shoes with a big shiny buckle on each side. Her hair is still formed into a battle helmet. *There is nothing soft about her*, I think, until my eyes catch on a delicate gold chain around her neck with a ballet-slipper pendant, almost hidden in the folds of her blouse. It doesn't seem to fit this woman at all. A battleaxe pendant, maybe, but a delicate pair of ballet slippers seems out of place on a woman who seems so hard.

I'm surprised when she takes a shallow breath and says, 'Come inside,' before she turns and walks away, disappearing through the red door, which she has left ajar.

*

I sniff and stand there for a moment, confused, before grabbing my backpack and shuffling cautiously after her. I see Miss Keene disappearing up the stairs and I race towards her. By the time I catch up, she is settled behind her mahogany desk. *It's like armour*, I think. She picks up a box of Kleenex tissues and slaps it down in front of me, watching as I wipe at my face and blow my nose.

'Let us start from the beginning,' she says eventually. 'What is your name, young lady?'

I clear my throat. 'P-p-pumkin, Miss.'

'*Pumpkin?*' Her head draws back and her lips purse, as if she's just bitten into a lemon. 'That is your actual name?'

'N-no, Miss.'

Miss Keene looks at me, that eyebrow raised high and pointy, the world's sharpest question mark.

'Everybody . . . everybody calls me Pumkin, Miss.'

'And do you have a last name? I certainly hope it is not *Patch*.'

It takes me a moment to get it but, by the set of her face,

I don't think she's making a joke, so I stutter, 'P-p-patterson. Miss.'

'Well, Miss Patterson, what is your situation?'

'My . . . my situation?'

'You have said your aunt is in France, you need to take the placement test, you obviously attend St Agatha's. Your French, if I remember correctly, is fairly competent. And you cannot afford the fees. Why aren't you taking the course at St Agatha's?'

I try to think quickly of some legitimate excuse I can give about why I can't do French at school, but I have a feeling those hawk-like eyes will see right through me. So I take a deep breath and tell her.

'I was . . . removed from class, Miss.'

'*Removed?* Whatever for?'

'The teacher. My teacher, Miss. She.' I sigh and then it all comes out. How she'd said I cheated on the mid-years but that *I did not*, and the meeting with the vice principal.

'Who is your French teacher?'

'Miss Smith. Except she says it "Simmit",' I can't help but add.

'Miss *Joan* Smith? Well. No wonder . . .'

'Do – do you know her, Miss?'

'Unfortunately. It is a travesty that she is allowed to teach the language,' she mutters, before remembering that she's talking to a student and putting on her teacher face again.

'And what of your parents, Miss Patterson? Who takes care of you?'

I hesitate a moment before answering, 'I take care of myself. Miss.'

The eyebrow shoots up again. 'Explain yourself.'

So I tell her about my grandmother and my aunt, how it used to be, and I tell her about my mother, how it is now. That I cook for myself, that I clean for myself, that the most I see of my mother is some cash in a bowl, and the times that I do see her it is as though I am the one who disappears. I don't know why I tell her all of this or why I'm being so truthful to this hard, bird-like woman, but once I start I can't stop, until I get to the part where I'm selling pastry and hoping I can have a place in her school. I take the grease paper of gizzadas out of my backpack and put them on the desk, like an offering. She immediately takes it up and puts a coaster underneath the package before leaning back in her chair and looking at me. I feel exposed and uncomfortable but also, somehow, lighter.

Suddenly Miss Keene pushes back her chair and stands up, walking briskly around the desk. 'Follow me, please,' she says, and I scramble out of my own chair and fall into step beside her.

'The placement prep classes take place in this classroom every Tuesday and Thursday from four thirty p.m. for two hours,' she says, indicating a door through which I can see a small room bathed in light with a white ceiling fan whirring slowly. It has a small number of desks, and walls painted cream, with framed posters of people who I will later come to learn are French people like Napoleon and Edith Piaf.

'Punctuality is of the utmost importance, Miss Patterson. If you are late once, you will not be allowed into class. Twice, and you may not return at all. Is that clear?'

'Y-yes.'

She cocks her head and opens her eyes wide.

'Yes, Miss,' I say quickly, although I'm still confused about what's happening.

'The common room is through there,' she says, walking down the hall and pointing to a bigger room with a couch and an overstuffed armchair, shelves overflowing with books, and a few desks with chairs. 'You may use it to study and do homework until six p.m. each day except Mondays, Saturdays and Sundays. On Saturdays students can use it only until four p.m. – but on Saturdays, I will require your assistance in the administration room.'

She stops then and looks down at me. 'Miss Patterson, please close your mouth. We are not frogs.'

I snap my mouth shut so hard it makes a loud clap, at which Miss Keene's eyebrows shoot up and she rolls her eyes.

'Are you able to make it here on Saturdays between ten a.m. and twelve p.m. to assist, Miss Patterson?'

'Ahm, assist, Miss?'

'Yes, Miss Patterson,' she says impatiently. 'To help with filing and such each week, in exchange for which you may attend the preparatory courses.'

I feel my mouth drop open again. Was she saying that I could . . . come here? As a student?

'Frogs, Miss Patterson.'

I inhale sharply and say, 'Yes, Miss! I can help you, Miss!' nodding so hard my head feels like it will fall off and roll down the length of the corridor. I was sure if it did, Miss Keene would simply roll her eyes and kick it delicately away until it bounced down the stairs and out of the door.

'And do you think you'll be able to raise the money for the test fee through your,' here she waves her arms around, 'baking endeavours, Miss Patterson? I'm happy to waive your fee here but there can be no such arrangement with the testing facility.'

'Yes, Miss! You'll see, when you taste my gizzada.'

She looks at me for a moment, then gestures for me to follow her back to the office.

'You have unfortunately missed one month of classes, so you will need to do quite a bit of catching up. Please take those books from that third shelf – no, the other set, *s'il te plaît*. Open the big one to page three and do the exercises in the first chapter.'

'Now, Miss?'

'There is no time like the present, Miss Patterson,' she says, taking a seat at the monstrous desk. 'You may use the telephone to call your parent, if need be?'

But I shake my head and tell her that no one is expecting me home. There's no one to call. She nods once, turns to her typewriter, and furiously begins to type, banging on the keys so hard I wonder what they've done to offend her.

I stand there with the textbooks in my hand. They are slightly bruised and worse for wear but still whole. I'm in a daze. *What just happened?* Is she really allowing me to join the class? Does she really intend me to sit here and start right now, under her eagle eye and her apoplectic clattering?

'Do you have a pen, Miss Patterson? An exercise book?'

I jump at her question. 'Ahm, I have a pen, Miss . . .'

She pulls open a drawer and gets out a fresh exercise book, the one that looks like it has black and white static all over the front of it. I take it, gingerly.

'You may sit there, Miss Patterson, and begin,' she says, indicating the chair I was sitting in before. 'Oh, and, Miss Patterson? You will leave the textbooks here – you may use them only in L'École française. Is that clear?'

'Yes, Miss,' I murmur.

I open the textbook – filled with writing and scribbles from former students, and I stare at the first page. Could it be this easy? Why would Miss Keene allow me to sit here and take her class for free? But I remember my grandmother always said, 'Horse say, when you see water, you must drink.' Take the opportunity when it comes, so I do. I focus my eyes, uncap my pen, and I get to work.

★

An hour later I bid Miss Keene *adieu*. I could have stayed there all evening, working with the sound of her typing in my ears, but it is already late. I am so excited about the events of the evening that I almost fly down the stairs, which prompts Miss Keene to call out to me, 'Please do not *barrel* down the stairs, Miss Patterson. We are not elephants!'

I smile and slow down, glad I do as I hear a crinkle of wax paper – Miss Keene is opening my gift of gizzadas. I stop and wait on the stairs until I hear it: that little sound of pleasure, and then I run, quietly and grinning, out of the door.

★

When I get home later, I sneak quietly inside the house, practising the excuses I'll give my mother if she asks. Some activity I have to do after school, or maybe detention. But there's no one at home. I change my clothes and make myself some dinner in the kitchen, eating it alone at the dining table. *See?* I tell Miss Keene in my mind. *No one is waiting for me. No one at all.*

Belly full

I spend the next few weeks in a loop of school, homework, French lessons, baking, selling and working in L'École's office. For once I am grateful for my neglectful mother, who doesn't notice and doesn't care what I might be doing, leaving her little misspelled shopping lists for the market and barely giving me a glance if she happens to be around while I do my homework at the dining table. Once, on my way home from school, I spotted her and Akil shouting at each other in front of Linnette's shop. Well, Akil was shouting. My mother was just standing there, her eyes glassy and staring, like a puppet's. I stood there for a moment wondering if I should go and . . . what? Rescue her? But then Linnette came out, waving her arms and yelling at Akil to 'tek yuh stregeregs behaviour else-where'. So I made my way home.

There is such a demand for my pastries that I cannot keep up, making bigger and bigger batches to sell in Linnette's shop, and at school.

'What a way you tun Big Tings,' Tamara says drily, watching me shred coconut one evening in her kitchen. My arm is burning as the pile grows. Tamara used to help me, measuring ingredients, folding butter into flour, but she never did it quite right and it ended up being more work for me to fix her mistakes or tell her exactly what I needed, so now she just looks on, bored. I glance at her now and smile, but she doesn't return it.

'How much you selling now?'

I take a break from grating and wipe my hand across my forehead. Some of my hair is plastered there.

'Last week I made eight hundred dollars altogether.'

I'm still a little in shock that people are paying me for the things I create with my own hands. I calculate that if I keep on like this, I'll have around three thousand dollars by the end of the term. It will be more money than I've ever had in my life.

'It's still not enough, though,' I add now. Even though I don't have to pay for the classes at L'École, I'll still be way short of the test fees by the registration deadline. I'll have to make a hell of a lot for it to be enough, but I don't know what else to do. I'm already baking and selling as much as I can. Tamara only shrugs one shoulder, so I push away the thought and turn back to the coconut. Soon after, I watch her walk out of the kitchen. I think maybe she's just going to the bathroom, or to get something from her bedroom, but she doesn't come back.

*

It's Mandy who gives me the idea. When I turned up at that first class at L'École, there she was, grinning like a Cheshire puss and waving me over to sit beside her.

'What are you doing here?' I'd asked, surprised.

'Hello, did I not sit right beside you in Miss Smith's class? You think any of us passing French without outside help? Come, sit next to me!'

I'd glanced at the seat, which was filled with boy, and back at her, shrugging. She'd turned to the boy and said, ever so sweetly, 'Braaaandonnn, can you move to another seat so my friend can sit here?' while batting her eyelashes so hard I could almost feel the breeze from where I was standing. Brandon had screwed up his face and looked at me. I tried to bat my eyelashes too but I must have looked like I was having a seizure, based on the expression that came over his face.

'Pleeeaaaase, Brandoooon.' Mandy poked him playfully in his arm until he rolled his eyes and huffed a 'Fine' under his breath, moving a few desks over. Mandy squealed as I sat down beside her. 'I didn't know you came here! Why yuh neva tell me?'

'I just started,' I say. 'I kind of got kicked out of French at school.'

'Oh, my gawd, I *heard*! But don't worry, nobody believes you cheated on that test. Miss Smith hated you from day *one*.'

'Yeah,' I said quietly, not really trusting that *no one* thinks I cheated. I can imagine Candida believed it wholeheartedly.

We always sit together after that. After class, we wait by the gates for her mother to pick her up and talk about our classmates: which girl had already kissed a boy (she had, it tasted like bun and cheese); which boys we'd kiss, marry, kill. Her mother drives up in her big SUV and she waves and flounces off, and only then do I make my way to the bus.

'You need a ride, Pumkin?' she asked me once. 'Your mum is always so late!'

'I . . . ahm . . . yeah,' I said, laughing nervously. 'But no, no, thanks, I'll just wait . . .'

It's one of these times, waiting at the gate, that I take out a tiny bundle of grease paper filled with my tamarind balls that I'd resisted selling, saving them for the end of class when I usually feel like I'm going to fall over from hunger. They're sticky sweet, the flesh of the sour fruit rolled into mounds and mounds of sugar.

'Jeezam peas, those are my favourite! Gimme one nuh?'

I hold the package out to Mandy and she grabs two, plopping one into her mouth with a sigh of pleasure.

'You muss be making *nuff* money, Pumkin. I see everybody with this brown-paper pastry.'

She bends her head way back and drops the second ball in from a great height. I worry it will fall all the way into her throat but she chews and chews, her head swivelling from side to side with satisfaction. Mandy is one of my best customers, but she thinks I'm selling pastry for pocket money. I want to tell her, then, about the whole plan: how what I'm making isn't 'nuff', but that means explaining why I need it in the first place, and then she might find out I'm here at L'École out of the goodness of Miss Keene's heart, not because my parents have money to burn on extra lessons. And then it might all come out, how much I need the money, where I actually live, how different I am from her. So instead I just say, 'Yeah it's okay,' and shrug my shoulders.

'Oh! You know what? You should sell your stuff at the school barbecue. Then you'd make a whole heap of money.'

My body goes still. The school barbecue. The biggest event in the school year. Hundreds of people come to it: parents and siblings and friends of friends. The school grounds are turned into a kind of fair, with stalls full of food and drinks and crafts for sale. There's a DJ and music, and a huge talent show. If I could sell my pastries there, I'm sure I could make enough for the registration.

'That's . . . a really good idea,' I say slowly.

'I know,' says Mandy, still chewing the tamarind ball. 'But mind the prefects or the teachers don't catch you selling at school, though. Last year my friend Shayla? She was making

152

these friendship bracelets and selling them? And the Bull found out and she got in *so* much trouble.'

The Bull is a sixth-former who everyone is convinced is actually a forty-year-old woman who cannot graduate, and makes life miserable for the rest of us as a result. She has massive nostrils and likes to stand real close and breathe aggressively on smaller students.

'Yeah, I know. I'm trying to keep a low profile,' I say, with a grin.

'Well, I'm still going to be your best customer! Lawks, *finally* my mum is here, I gawn. See you at school tomorrow, bring plenty pastry for me!'

She grabs me up in a hug before running over to jump into the SUV. Her mum smiles at me and gives me a wave before driving off. The car is so big I think of a whale trying to change course in the ocean. Once it's out of sight, I make my way down the sloping road towards the bus stop. The grease paper that was full of tamarind balls is now empty: Mandy ate them all. But I don't feel hungry any more. For once, my belly feels full.

*

When I get home from Miss Keene's, the phone is ringing. I rush over and grab the handset.

'Hello?'

'Pumkin! Lawd have mercy, man!'

'Aunt . . . Auntie Sophie?'

'I've been calling the house like crazy!'

For a moment I can't speak. I haven't heard Sophie's voice in ages.

'I got your letter, Pumkin, and I *had* to call. I just can't believe everything that's been, I mean my *gosh*, Pumkin, that

153

awful, horrible woman kicking you out of class. I mean, *cheating*? As *if* you would, and then all this baking and selling, at school! What is going *on*?'

I grimace, thinking about the letter I'd written to her weeks ago, when I'd been in despair about being kicked out of class. I wish I hadn't sent it. Now my shoulders tense as I wonder what the fallout will be.

'No, no, Auntie Sophie.' I laugh nervously. 'You don't have to worry! It's okay —'

'How is it okay, Pumkin? Listen, this selling-at-school business, this should not be your focus right now. You need to be studying, not *baking* and selling and — and running a *business*! No no no no no . . .'

'But, Auntie Sophie, it's not a business, it's just a few things for a few girls, just, like, one and two things,' I say, crossing my fingers behind my back. There's a moment of silence while she mulls this over, a silence in which I can hear doubt and scepticism as loud as a drumbeat. My gaze wanders to the ceiling where I see a daddy-long-legs perched in the corner. I watch him, but he just sits there, not moving, not doing anything. Finally Auntie Sophie heaves a big sigh.

'Listen, Pumkin,' she says, 'if you're not taking the test through Aggie's, we'll have to pay the registration fee. Everybody thinks the minute you leave JA, you earning tons of money but nothing is further from the truth. I have to pay back all my travel and accommodation fees for coming over here, I'm in an apartment I can barely afford, I'm still paying your school fees and your uniforms and clothes you keep growing out of, the bills for the house . . . Honestly, Pumkin, I just don't have an extra dollar to spare. How much is it? Like, twenty thousand?'

It's fifteen, but I don't answer because I'm holding my breath. It seems she wasn't waiting for a response anyway since she continues.

'Pumkin, if we can't pay it this year we may . . . we may have to postpone for a year, hope you can get back into French at Aggie's in fourth form or, I don't know . . .'

There's a pause where all I hear is breathing. I wrap the long telephone cord around my wrist like a bracelet, then let it untwist. I have no idea what to say.

'I know it's not what you want to hear, Pumkin, but –'

A click. Dial tone.

'Hello?' I say. 'Hello?'

She's gone. I look at the handset and hang it up. Stare at it for a second, then pick it back up, but there's still just dial tone. I hang it up again and glance back at the daddy-long-legs in the corner, as if he's responsible for the bad connection. I think about what Auntie Sophie just said. One more year. One more year without her, without my grandmother. One more year with Akil breezing in and out of the house like he owns the place. One more year with my mother.

I wasn't sure, before, if I really wanted to go to France. I've been working at Auntie Sophie's plan because it's what she wanted, but now that it might not happen it's so clear to me: I don't want to be here. There's nothing to stay for. But in France there's Auntie Sophie. There's everything she said we could do and be. Why would I want to stay behind, alone and lonely, in a house where tension sits like a guest who just won't leave even after you've given them all the signs? France isn't just Auntie Sophie's dream, it's my dream too.

Suddenly the phone rings again, the sound startling me so much I jump back. I grab the headset.

'Hello?'

'Pumkin! I'm so sorry, the phone card ran out. But listen, please try not to be disappointed at how things have turned out, I know –'

'But you're wrong, Auntie Sophie!' I blurt out, surprising even myself.

'About what?'

'We don't have to wait till next year,' I say breathlessly. Because I know I can make this work. I have my own plan, but if she knows the full details, she'll derail it. So I'll just have to . . . blur some of the truth.

'Auntie Sophie, I was going to write you another letter, because guess what?' I continue. 'I'm going to L'École française! And . . . and . . . L'École students don't have to pay the fee either, it's included, just like at Aggie's. So everything works out!'

My armpits are sweaty with the strain of willing Auntie Sophie to believe this brazen lie about the fee, my heart thumping around my chest like a trapped bug.

'What? How on earth – how you mean you're at L'École? Who is paying for that?'

'Nobody!' I chirp, convinced that if I remain upbeat, she won't hear the untruths in my voice. 'They're letting me take the classes for free!'

'That's ridiculous. Doesn't Beverley Keene run L'École? You mean to tell me that *Beverley Keene* is letting you go to her how-much-thousand-dollar-a-term school for *free*?'

'Oh, you know her?' I ask, my heart sinking. I don't want Auntie Sophie calling Miss Keene. But if she learns that I'm selling pastries to pay for the registration she'll shut it down for sure, tell me to focus on my studies, especially since selling at school is categorically not allowed. But I won't survive one more year.

'I know *of* her, and from what I know, she's not inclined to take on poor students out of the goodness of her heart.'

I take a deep breath and steady myself. I have to convince Auntie Sophie I've got this sorted.

'Well, what it is, Auntie Sophie, they have some, ahm, scholarships for low-income students, right? And Mrs Roberts told me to apply for one when she kicked me out of class. So I went straight there and I explained my situation, and I took the test and I got a space!'

I strain my ears to hear if she believes me, if there's a hint of scepticism in her voice, but she isn't saying anything, so I barrel on.

'I might also have bribed Miss Keene with some gizzada.'

'Ha! That would work.' She laughs, and I feel my shoulders creep slightly away from my ears.

'Well. I have to say it was good of Mrs Roberts to steer you in that direction, although if she could manage to do that I don't know why she kicked you out in the first place. That woman —'

'It's okay, though, Auntie Sophie, because L'École is way better, so it all worked out, you see? I'll take classes there, work so hard to pass the exam and then . . . and then I can come to you. You still . . . you still want me to come, right, Auntie Sophie?'

'Pumkin! There is nothing I want more than you to join me over here, nothing!'

My sinuses start to burn, but I don't want to cry so I blink and blink and blink. I shake my head, switch the phone to the other ear.

'Pumkin, I am so in awe of how you've found a way to stay on course. I know it's not easy doing this on your own. I'm so very proud of you.'

I smile into the phone, losing the battle to keep the tears in my eyes. But it's going to be okay. I'm back on track. I'm sure, now, about my goal. I have my plan in place. I'm going to make it to Auntie Sophie.

It's a gah-toe

I hold my cake to my chest, like a shield. It's dark in the auditorium, the only light coming from the small windows that line the top of the room, all the way around. The barbecue planning committee is sitting at a long table, sixth-formers with heads bent together in discussion, Miss Solomon, the school librarian and one of the most intimidating teachers at our school, at the end. She raises her head and says impatiently, 'Come, come, child!' In my mind's eye I see myself tripping and falling forward, the cake flying out of its carrier and smashing to bits on the floor.

'What are you auditioning for?' one of the sixth-formers asks. Her voice is very small, like a child's, which doesn't fit her body at all but makes her feel safe to me.

'Ahm,' I say, 'I'm not really here to aud–'

'Speak up!' Miss Solomon barks, startling me and at least one of the sixth-formers, who turns to another girl and opens her eyes wide while they both try to stifle their giggles.

I clear my throat and speak a little louder. 'I'm not really here to audition for, like, a part in the show, I . . . ahm, I want to know if I can have a stall. At the barbecue?'

'A stall for what?' says Miss Solomon. She pronounces the *h* in 'what' so that it sounds like a lot of wind blowing at the beginning of the word.

'Cakes. And . . . and pastries and things.' I hold the cake

carrier out in front of me. 'I'm really good at . . . at baking. I brought one. You can try it.'

'That is highly unusual,' Miss Solomon says, dipping her chin and giving me a laser beam stare over her glasses. I wonder why she wears glasses if she always looks over the top of them, but then I decide they must be to focus the laser beams for maximum damage.

'Yes, Miss,' I say, which makes no sense at all.

The girls look at one another while Miss Solomon continues to peer at me, until one says, 'Well, maybe we can taste the cake and then decide what to do?'

'Come, bring it here,' Miss Solomon says, holding out her hand with her elbow on the table, as if she can't be bothered to make the effort to lift it.

I shuffle forward and put the carrier carefully on the desk, unclipping the top and pulling it off. It is three layers of chocolate cake with a chocolate butter-cream icing. It looks plump and moist and juicy, the icing glistening and smooth. I pulled out all the stops for this one, dusting off one of Auntie Sophie's old French cookbooks she'd brought home from the embassy, spending quite a bit of my money on fancy icing sugar and bitter chocolate, but it will have been worth it if I can get a stall at the barbecue. It would solve all my problems.

'It's a *gâteau*,' I say. '*Au chocolat*,' I add, so quietly that no one could possibly have heard it.

'*Oh*,' says one of the girls. 'It's notta cake it's a *gah-toe*.'

'Lawks, Shelley-Ann, how yuh stay suh?' another says. She turns to me. 'It looks good.'

I give her a wobbly smile until Miss Solomon yips, 'Plates? Forks?'

160

Oh. I didn't think about how they would actually *eat* the cake. I look helplessly at Miss Solomon, who sighs as if much aggrieved and hoists herself up from the table. 'Wait here!' she barks, doing her angry-duck walk across the floor and out of the door.

As soon as she's gone, the girls huddle together and start chatting loudly, laughing and screeching, while I stand there, wondering if wishing hard enough could make me disappear. I don't know where to look so I keep my eyes on the cake, although they can't help but roam to the girls every few seconds. After a hundred years goes by, in which I grow old and withered and die and am reborn into this exact same awkward position, the door slams open and Miss Solomon waddles back to the table carrying paper plates, plastic forks, napkins and a big knife with dents in the blade. She deals the paper plates like cards and cuts aggressively into the cake. I want to tell her to be careful, to be gentle with it, but I don't trust myself to speak.

The man in my chest starts warming up his drums as they pick up their forks. Then they take their first bites and my right ear clogs with a high, whining pitch, like a mosquito stuck on one note has flown in there and stopped it up.

'Oh dear,' Miss Solomon says.

What does that mean?

I shift from foot to foot, the man in my chest drumming a light, feathery beat as the girls eat the cake with their eyes closed, making little noises of satisfaction every now and then.

'Well,' Miss Solomon says. She presses her fingers into the crumbs on her plate and puts them into her mouth.

One of the girls keeps nodding, as if she's answering a question.

'Well. It's not customary for students in your age group to have stalls, you know,' Miss Solomon says. 'The food stalls are typically run by parents and sponsors, the occasional sixth former . . .'

'I don't just do chocolate cake, though!' I almost shout, which makes Miss Solomon's eyes snap wide open at the audacity of it. 'I also do, ahm . . . Coconut? It has coconut cream in between the layers and then coconut shavings all over it.'

'Mmmm,' say the girls.

'Coconut?'

'Yes, Miss.'

The committee members look at each other and then, as one, their heads bow together. All I can hear are whispers, no matter how hard I strain to hear what's being said. I wring my hands together. They look like the girls on *Schools' Challenge Quiz*. I hope they give me the right answer.

'Okay, Miss . . . ?'

'Patterson.'

'Miss Patterson. As I said, it is not customary for students in your year to sell at the stalls. However – *however, before you protest*, Miss Patterson – in this instance we might be able to work something out. You would be able to *share* a stall with an adult or sixth-former, but before you get excited, Miss Patterson, there will be some *rules*.'

'Yes, Miss!' I nod my head so hard I can feel my brain bounce against my skull. There's a ball of electricity in my stomach that I want to shoot out of my mouth. Instead, I hop from foot to foot.

'One, you will have a time limit on how long you can sell at the stall, we will not have . . . What year are you in?'

162

'Third form, Miss.'

'Right, we cannot have third-formers selling all night. You'll need to close up by eight p.m., latest.'

'Yes, Miss!'

'Please bear in mind that the aim of the St Agatha's barbecue is to raise funds for the school, so a percentage of all sales must be donated to the school. I can't remember the . . . Claudine? You remember the percentage?'

'I think it's fifteen per cent, Miss Solomon,' one of the girls says.

'So your stall partner can help you with the sales and the – the accounting and all of that.'

I've been keeping my own books for weeks as I sell my pastries, but of course they don't know that. I'm a little disappointed that I won't get to keep my whole profit, but I know how much things sell for at these barbecues. Even after the donation, I'll have more than enough for the registration.

'And third, we'll need to get a signed permission slip from your parent or guardian allowing you to do this.'

The man in my chest lets out a huge belly laugh. HA! he shouts.

There's no way my mother will sign a form allowing me to do anything, but there's also no way I'm getting this far only to turn around now, defeated. So I tell the man in my chest to *shut up* and out loud I say, 'No, Miss Solomon. It won't be a problem at all.'

Baby powder

My hours at L'École are my favourite times of the week, especially when I'm working alongside Miss Keene. The tasks themselves are tedious: filing, bringing some order to the library of textbooks and reading material, addressing the envelopes for her never-ending stream of typed letters, but I love going through the French books, and the little snippets of conversation I have with Miss Keene, often in French. I love the order of it, the structure. Miss Keene isn't as hard as she appeared the first few times I met her.

Sometimes I catch her staring out of the window, her fingers playing with the little ballet-slipper pendant that always hangs around her neck, an odd expression on her face.

'That's pretty,' I said to her once.

She'd turned so slowly from gazing out of the window, like she was coming out of a dream. She glanced down at her chest, then let go of the pendant, giving me a tight smile and asking me if I'd reorganized the books R through V.

Today it's the end of class and I'm lingering at the gate with Mandy, waiting for her mother to pick her up, pretending that mine is on the way, as usual. Mandy's mother is late today and, besides a couple of other stragglers from class huddled at the opposite side of the gate, it's just the two of us together, her humming breezily under her breath, me with my hands on my backpack straps, constantly adjusting and readjusting them.

'Hey, what are you doing this weekend?' she asks suddenly. She pushes on before I have a chance to respond. 'We should do another sleepover!' she says, her eyes bright. 'This weekend?'

I hesitate. Another sleepover. Another night contorting my body to dodge all the questions, nodding and smiling when I don't understand things, curving my accent into round curlicues, pretending pretending pretending so they won't find out I don't live anywhere good, I've never left the island, I can't afford to buy trendy new clothes from Miami. I am not like them at all.

They'd drop me like a hot stone if they found out my mother was a housekeeper. They'd laugh if they knew I was selling pastry not for fun, not to have my own allowance to go shopping, like Mandy thinks, but to take this exam to try to get out of my life. They don't know I work in Miss Keene's office in exchange for extra lessons that they take for granted. That's what they would do, if they knew the real me. It all made me feel so tired.

'Just me and you, though. That would be fun, right?' Mandy continues, breaking into my thoughts.

I blink at her, and she must see the confusion on my face, because she says, 'I know it can be a bit much of a muchness when we're all together, especially if Candida's there.'

'Why does she hate me so much?' I ask, surprised that the words even come out my mouth.

Mandy shrugs. 'I think she's just jealous. She's a little weird, Candida, but our mums have been friends for ages and we've literally known each other since birth so . . .'

'Jealous? Of what?'

'I dunno. You're so sure of yourself, and confident. Candida is *very* insecure. I think she feels threatened by you. I mean, I'm just speculating, but I know her pretty well so . . .'

I am stunned into silence at the thought that a girl who has everything could be jealous of me. I want to bust out with a deep belly laugh. Sure of myself? Confident? I must be a better actress than I thought.

'Anyway, how about it? We could just chill and watch a movie or something.'

I think, then, about our time here at L'École without her gaggle of girls, how much easier it is. A sleepover with just us two might not be so bad. And, anyway, I don't know how to say no to this invitation.

'Sure. Yeah! That sounds like fun,' I say, trying to inject some enthusiasm into my voice.

'Let's do it at your house this time, though. My parents are having some stuffy dinner-party thing, and if we're there, we're gonna be roped into attending and, trust me, it will be *so dry and boring.*'

Ah. I feel the smile slip off my face and land in my stomach where the first shred of panic is beginning to bloom.

'My . . . my house?'

'Yeah, why not?'

I scramble to think of a reason why she can't come over to my house but my mind remains frustratingly blank. I've never had a friend over to my house, not even Tamara. With my aunt, my grandmother, my mother and me squished up into two rooms there was nowhere to sleep or huddle together, whisper and giggle. Even now that my grandmother and Sophie are gone, my mother's anger takes up so much space, there isn't room for anyone else. And the idea of Mandy, this uptown princess who lives in a big, sprawling house and drives in big, fancy cars setting foot in my shambles of a house, on my shambles of a road, in my shambles of an area makes my lunch start travelling back up my throat. I imagine Mandy there while my mother is in one of her rages, cowering with me in the corner as we're both beaten by whatever she has to hand. A panicked giggle escapes my lips at the thought of it and Mandy must think that means 'yes' because her smile widens and she says, 'This Friday, then?' and once again I open my mouth to try to say something, anything, but her gaze shifts and she breathes out a '*Finally!*' and rolls her eyes as her mother drives up.

'Wait, I – Hold on,' I try to say, but she's already flouncing towards the SUV.

'We'll sort it at school tomorrow, awright?' she calls back to me, as I stand there, stuttering, until she hops into the car and drives away, leaving me staring after her.

*

The next two days seem both to rush past me and crawl painfully upon their bellies. I am consumed with nightmarish thoughts of Mandy at my house, in my neighbourhood, and what will happen when I'm outed. I try to come up with some excuses – my mother's sick, the house will be a mess – but she just talks over me and laughs and says how fun it will all be. She is hell bent on coming over and I wonder if she really wants to hang out with me or just needs to escape her own home. I wish I could talk to Tamara about it, but our friendship has become so tentative lately, there's no way I can tell her Mandy's planning to come over. And my mother, well, I have no idea how to ask her things like this.

I tried to get her attention last night. I'd come home from school to an empty house, as usual, staring around the cramped little space, wondering how it would look to Mandy and trying to ignore the squirming in my stomach. Paulette had burst through the front door, startling me. She pulled up short when she saw me standing there.

'Evening, Mama,' I'd said.

She'd shaken her head and made her way to her room, mumbling, 'Eve-lin' as she passed me by. I followed her to her bedroom door where I watched her fling open her chest of drawers and start pulling clothes out of it, throwing them on the bed. My stomach rolled and roiled as I practised the words in my head: can I have a friend sleep over this weekend? Simple, straightforward. But when I opened my mouth, my throat was so dry that my words turned to dust before they reached my lips. She picked up a red dress and put it to the side, shoving the rest of her clothes back into the drawer. She turned to come out through the bedroom door and noticed me standing there. She looked at me, her eyebrow raised in a question.

'I just wanted t-t-to ask you something, Mama.'

'I don't have no time fi no question right yah now,' she said, as she barrelled past me into the bathroom, where I heard our meagre shower start up, the water pressure so low it sounded like a trickling little stream. I went and sat at the dining table, my homework spread out in front of me. My mother eventually emerged from her room, heading for the front door. She was in a short tight red dress and a long dark wig of straight black hair. Her face was painted. She was beautiful, even through the permanent scowl etched on her face. I wondered if the people, whoever they were, wherever she went made her smile. I wondered if there was any joy in her life at all. I watched her as she walked to the door; she hadn't said a word to me. Before she put her hand on the knob, I shouted out, 'Where you going, Mama?'

Her head whipped around at me, her scowl burrowing a little deeper into her face. 'Your fadda mussi tink seh him cyan just tek up wid some skettel gyal and juss leff me suh, but nutten don' go suh!'

I could see the baby powder all over her chest, a sign to others that she's fresh and clean. The stoosh girls at school make fun of women who do that. They pat their chests with their hands and pretend to be ghetto girls, dropping into thick patois that sounds ridiculous on their tongues.

'Oh,' I say, because what else could I say about that?

'Yes!' she yelled, like a battle cry, before walking out of the front door. She didn't even close it properly.

I sighed and got up to close and lock it, deciding that Mandy would just have to take no for an answer. My mother probably wouldn't be here tomorrow anyway, but it didn't matter. I just . . . couldn't have her come here. I couldn't have her know.

★

But now it's Friday morning and at the school drop-off I see Mandy hop out of her mother's car with a slouchy overnight bag that looks brand new. I imagine it on my mangy bedroom carpet and feel a little lightheaded. Mandy waves and bounces over to me, her hair in one long braid over her shoulder and tied at the end with a bow, like a child in a fairy tale.

'Hi!' she chirps at me. 'Are you as –'

'You can't come over!' I shout at her, making a girl walking by jump and give us a quizzical look.

'What? *Why?*'

I look at her for a moment and realize there's nothing for

it. I'll just have to tell her the truth: she won't accept any other excuse. My shoulders feel heavy.

'Mandy . . . my house . . . my house is . . .'

I clear my throat. Then I take a deep breath and let it out slowly. The man in my chest doesn't even give me a warning, just one big thump that jolts me forward and makes me feel like I'll topple over, right on top of Mandy.

'I live in a . . . in a really, really small house in . . . not . . . the best neighbourhood. You won't know the area.'

I shift from one leg to the other. I take off one strap of my backpack, then slip my arm back through it and put it on again. I pull the end of my bun, then pat it back down. I don't know what to do with all this nervous energy building up in my limbs. Mandy looks at me for a long moment and then she says, 'Are you embarrassed about where you live, Pumkin?'

There's a tone to her voice, a hint of pity, and suddenly I cannot look her in her face, and my skin feels like it's burning up, like it's caught fire and it's burning all the way down into my stomach. I need to pee. She puts a hand on my shoulder and I glance at it, sure it will burst into flame.

'Pumkin, I don't care where you live! I don't care about your neighbourhood. It doesn't matter to me.'

'It doesn't?'

She shrugs. 'Nah. You're my friend. I just . . . want to hang out with you.'

I stare into space for a moment, until she nudges me with her shoulder and smiles. 'Pumkin, for real, I don't care what kind of house you live in. You don't need to feel shame.'

I take a deep breath and hold it and let it out slowly. 'I don't . . . I don't have a VCR or anything. I mean, to watch movies and stuff like that. I don't have all that stuff you have.'

171

'So? I brought some board games anyway – you like Ludo? Plus I have *gossip*! I really don't care about watching movies or whatever. It will be fun, Pumkin, plus I already have my bag and I don't want to have to ask someone to take me home, after I already told my parents I'm going to yours . . .'

By now I was fidgeting so much I had worked up a light sheen of sweat on my forehead, although the fire in my skin was dying down.

'What about the bus? We'd have to take the bus home. That's how I get home.'

'Huh? Your mum can't pick us up?'

I shake my head and smoosh my lips together. 'She doesn't have a car,' I say.

'Oh. Okay. Well, then, we take the bus! I mean, I'll be with you, right? It will be part of the adventure,' she says, smiling wide. I feel the tiniest little stab somewhere in my side at the idea that my poverty is an adventure for her, but eventually I smile back. Maybe, I think, it won't be so bad. Maybe she'll see me for who I really am and I can stop pretending. Maybe this will be a good thing.

The sleepover

Mandy is her usual chatty self on the way to the bus, nattering on about who likes whom, which girl did which embarrassing thing, giving me a preview of the gossip she said she had to share, but I'm too busy trying not to throw up to pay much attention. Now that I'm on the way to my half-dead house in my bruk-down neighbourhood with a girl who has never seen the inside of a bus, I regret giving in, am kicking myself for not putting up more resistance. I pray that my mother doesn't decide to stay home tonight, mouthing the words silently because the universe might not hear me if I only say them inside my head: *Pleasedon'tbetherepleasedon'tbethere pleasedon'tbethere* . . .

Mandy's constant babble starts to sputter and drip and dribble until it comes to a complete stop once we get to the mass of people at the bus stop. I watch her from the side of my eye as she looks around her, like a foreigner who doesn't understand the street signs in a new place . . . which I guess, in a way, she is. I randomly remember Sophie laughing at Boots one time, calling him a 'dry-land tourist' because he'd never left the island but would adopt a twang every time he spoke to someone with an American accent. People glance at us and do a double-take, looking Mandy up and down, their eyebrows cocked, before shifting their gaze over to me. I feel self-conscious: this isn't the usual anonymous commute I'm used to, where no one spares me a second glance unless it's to yell at me for taking up an old person's seat or to stare at me lasciviously while they waggle their eyebrows. I wonder, for a moment, if there has ever been a woman who responds positively to that stupid eyebrow waggle that men do.

Mandy shrugs her overnight bag higher onto her shoulder as she glances around and I wish she would stop being so obvious.

Our bus rumbles up, the black smoke wafting from its behind as it leans precariously to one side and Mandy starts to look distressed as people jostle us about. The bus hasn't even pulled in and everyone's fighting for a prime position to embark, as if it will leave them behind if they don't get on with immediate haste – to be fair, it probably will. I can see that Mandy's not used to being pushed and pulled and rumpled and rumbled, so I grab her arm and pull her closer to me, using my body as a shield while I press us forward.

'It's this one,' I say, as the bus comes to a halt, but she doesn't register. The throng of people pushes us into the bus, like a wave pushing seaweed to shore, and we receive a small miracle in the form of two seats at the back – which we have to give up two seconds later for a wiry woman with a large basket full of something that evidently requires its own seat. The bus isn't so full today but we still need to stand, our arms stretched way over our heads as we hold on. Mandy's nose crinkles as she catches wind of someone who is not familiar with soap and water. I can see she's having a hard time, her hair already pasted to her head with sweat, only two fingers around the bus rail, like she doesn't really want to touch it but also really doesn't want to tip over onto another passenger, and I start thinking she's already regretting asking to come to my house. I imagine her telling her friends about the bus, how it belches out black smoke, how it smells like BO, how loud it is, not like their nice, clean, quiet, spacious fancy cars. And then I feel a wave of anger. Who asked her to do this anyway? Why did she have to be so pushy about coming over? How can she live in this place and never, ever have taken a public bus?

I engage in a heated argument with her inside my head: I have to do this every day, and you can't manage *one* bus ride? You think everybody lives like you, in your big house with your fancy cars and someone to cook for you and clean for you and mow your lawn and do all the things you don't want to do yourself, I say. In this imaginary argument, she stares at me, chastened, and I feel vindicated by the fact that I'm winning. I glance at her now. She looks like she's discovered shit all over the sole of her favourite shoe, and I toss my head and stand up a little straighter. *Serve her right*, I think. *Dat she want, dat she fi get*.

When we get out at my stop, Mandy looks slightly shell-shocked, like she's been wrung through a washing-machine. She looks down at herself and seems surprised to find herself in a state of disarray.

'You all right?' I ask, a little roughly, and she nods but doesn't say anything. She's still looking around like she's found herself on another planet and I'm getting more annoyed. She said she didn't care but we haven't even reached anywhere yet and it looks like she cares very much indeed. I roll my eyes and start walking.

'It's just up here,' I say, and she follows me like a meek little mouse. I look at the streets and everything seems different to me now, as I see them through her eyes. It all looks so . . . poor. I see the graffiti on the crumbling walls as if for the first time, how the paint peels on people's houses, and some aren't painted at all; I see how deep the potholes in the road are, deep enough to swim in when it rains.

'Where are we?' she asks suddenly, startling me out of my observations.

'Ahm, Waltham Crescent? We soon reach my house.'

'Okay.'

'Guess you never been around here before,' I say, laughing.

'Nooo,' she says, drawing out the word. 'Everything looks so different.'

'Different from what?'

'I dunno, juss different . . .' She shrugs her bag higher on her shoulder again and I roll my eyes.

We walk in silence for a moment and then she says, 'So, you have to come all the way up to Norbrook for L'École, then? It's so far.'

I roll my eyes again and wonder if it's possible to roll them until I sprain a muscle. 'I have to come all the way uptown to go to school every day. We can't all live in Mona or Jackshill.'

Her face goes red at that and she doesn't say anything more.

We hear music in the distance, getting louder as we turn onto the top of my road. Freddie McGregor's 'Big Ship', the music clear and crisp, the bass thumping in our chests in time with our steps. There's a throng of people at Linnette's shop on the corner, buying bread and cigarettes and sweets, maybe even my pastries, I think, and I turn to tell Mandy that my baked stuff is so good that I sell it here at this shop, and it sells out every week, but I take a look at her face and change my mind. It's not as though she'll care.

The anger leaks out of me as we walk towards my house, and I start to get nervous again. Once we're there, it's all over. I might have been able to redeem myself with a nice house on a bad street, like Tamara's, but taking her inside my house will make this all worse. I wish I could have taken her to Tamara's instead, and I glance at my friend's house as we approach it. The curtains are drawn and there's no movement outside the front, not even Brownie, the dog. I wonder if anyone's inside. I wonder if I could ring the bell and take Mandy there and just pretend, pretend, pretend. The sweat that had cooled on my skin after leaving the bus runs down the back of my neck.

As we near Tamara's house, I spot two boys sitting on the low wall in front of Miss Bertha's place. Miss Bertha is an old woman who spends her days in floral housedresses, sweeping the path from her front door to the gate with a yard broom, handing out sweets to teenage boys and fluttering her dry old eyelashes at them. Her hands always linger on theirs as she passes them the sweets, her shoulders shimmying up and down like the female version of that eyebrow waggle. She has the best wall for sitting, low and wide, so there are lots of boys for her to try her antics on, bribing them, uselessly, with her boiled sweets.

The two boys watch as we approach, the one turning to whisper to the other before staring at us again. I feel the moment that Mandy clocks them because she moves closer to me, until our hot, sticky arms rub against each other. I know the two boys as Robbie and Junior – Junior lives on the street with his grandmother, Miss Pearl, and no one knows where Robbie lives but he's always at Junior's house. It's rare to see one without the other. Robbie is shirtless, his jean shorts – tattered at the bottoms but whether from decay or style I don't know – hanging low on his thin, muscular frame. He's only a couple of years older than me, fifteen, I think, but he looks hard, like he's packed the life experiences of a forty-year-old man into his skinny body. Junior is in long khaki pants, part of his school uniform, with a collared white shirt sticking halfway out of the waistband, drumming his feet on the wall. They wait until we're in earshot and then Robbie says, with a lazy grin, 'Pumkin, you have a new friend.'

He rubs his bare stomach and I feel Mandy tense beside me.

'You not gwen introduce yuh new friend, Pumkin?'

Junior just looks on, expressionless, his feet thump-thump, thump-thumping on the wall.

'Don't you have homework to do or something like that?' I say, as we walk past.

'*Homework?*' he jeers at me. 'Is what yuh tek dis ting for? Bad man don' do *homework*.'

I glance at Junior, who I know for a fact will scramble to get his homework done rather than face the wrath of his grandmother, who once beat his ass with a rolling pin in front of the whole neighbourhood because he failed a maths test.

'Well, gwan go teef someting then,' I huff, grabbing Mandy's hand and walking a little more purposefully towards my gate. The two boys break into laughter and I look back at them when we reach my gate. They're still chuckling, facing us, staring, Robbie still rubbing his stomach in a way that makes my skin want to peel slowly off my bones. Mandy keeps her head down during the whole exchange and, for a moment, I think how different she is from the girl holding court at school, the babbling brook of gossip, the confident, wide-smiling girl in her element.

I look up at my house as I open the gate and I feel like I'm also seeing it for the first time. It is devastating in its sadness. The yard is small and inconsequential, the grass brown and patchy in some areas, long and weedy in others. There's a few shrubs at the front of the house leading up to three concrete steps that head up to the front door. The paint starts out at the top, a sea-foam green, but then gives up halfway through, revealing rust-coloured streaks and splotches, and everything is bunched up under a flat, ugly roof. There's a set of windows at the front with a couple of the boards missing. I look longingly back down the road to Tamara's house. I take a deep breath and open the gate, afraid to look at Mandy's face, afraid of what I'll see there.

*

When we get inside the television is blaring and my heart drops like a stone into my stomach: my mother is home. I glance around and thank the heavens that, at the very least, the house is tidy. I watch through the side of my eye as Mandy takes in our lumpy old couch, our shiny mahogany dining set cramped right beside it, the mismatched lamps and the old carpet and the ratty strings of beads hanging from the ceiling in place of a door. I try to decipher her expression but her face is carefully constructed into a mask revealing nothing. Just then, my mother barrels her way out of the kitchen and I am momentarily confused by the expression on her face, which I slowly realize is joy. She stops short when she sees Mandy and the smile drops from her face, just as my heart, which was previously churning in my stomach, drops down further into my bowels as Akil steps out behind her. This is why my mother's face looks the way it does. We are all four standing there, staring like predator and prey bucking up each other at the watering hole and wondering who will make the first move. They take in Mandy from head to toe and I see Akil's eyes hook on her expensive overnight bag before they flip back to the rest of her.

Mandy breaks the silence, startling all of us when she lunges forward towards my mother and says, 'Hi, Mrs Patterson . . . Mr Patterson, I'm Mandy,' waving a hand jauntily. I see my mother take in her accent and she glances at me, a wave of surprise moving quickly over her face before it settles into an expression I don't understand. It's not until later that I recognize the ridiculousness of Mandy calling Paulette and Akil 'Mr and Mrs'. I don't realize these things till later because the shock of my mother's response wipes everything right out of my brain.

'Hello, dahlin,' she says, in her very best English. She doesn't correct Mandy about her marital status. 'Akisha neva tell me she was having a friend over, I wudda clean up likkle bit,' she says, gesturing to the living room, which is spotless because I spent all yesterday evening cleaning.

'Oh! I hope it's okay that I'm here, then?' Mandy says, glancing at me quizzically, but I'm too shocked by my mother's response to acknowledge her.

'Yes, yes, dahlin,' my mother says, with a broad smile.

Akil has said nothing this entire time. He is leaning against the door jamb, picking at his fingernails, which are all slightly too long for a man, I think, and still staring at Mandy, absorbing her, consuming her somehow as his eyes crawl over her from toe to head and back again. From the corner of my eye I see Mandy cross her arms over her chest. I clear my throat.

'Yuh want someting to eat, dahlin?' my mother asks, and I wonder if she would be so pleasant if she could see the way Akil is looking at my friend, I wonder where she's pulled this weird little accent from, and I wonder why I flinch every time she calls her 'dahlin'.

Mandy says, 'Ahm . . .' and looks at me. I snap out of my reverie.

'No. No, thanks, Mama, we not hungry yet.'

'Awrite. Layta den.'

I push Mandy towards my room. She smiles at Akil and Paulette as she scurries past and I notice she gives Akil a wide berth. Before we turn the corner I look back and they are still standing there gazing at me, the smile wiped clean from my mother's face. Akil's lips curl upwards, like a wolf's, as he picks picks picks under his nails.

I pull my backpack off my shoulders in my room and drop it onto the floor, finally able to let out the breath I didn't know I'd been holding. I flop down on the bed, which makes a loud squeak from its overburdened springs. Mandy is looking around warily. She still has her overnight bag in her hand, like she's afraid to put it down. I glance around my room, with its peeling paint and that big brown stain on the ceiling that I stare at sometimes, the rusty brown carpet that I'm pretty sure caught mange and never recovered, the shiny dark chest of drawers from Courts.

'You can just, I dunno, put your stuff down anywhere,' I say, sweeping my hand around like we're on a game show. *This can all be yours!* I think randomly, and giggle. Mandy gives me a weird look and puts her bags on the floor, then perches beside me on the bed. And now I don't know what to do.

I try to think about what we did at her house or at her friends' sleepovers, but my mind is stubbornly blank and anyways I don't have a 'TV room' and a drawer full of board games or a state-of-the-art Nintendo or even an older sister with a closet full of cool clothes to raid. I think briefly about Sophie and what she would do in this situation, but then I remember how careful she was never to have any of her friends come to our house. In fact, I'm pretty sure she would be so mad to know that I've spoiled everything, ruined my chances.

'Ahm. So, I brought Ludo and Uno, if you want to play something?' Mandy says, and I think, *Thank God*, and say, 'Yeah, let's do Ludo,' and she takes the board game out of her bag. We play a few rounds in relative silence, and just when my shoulders start slowly to peel themselves away from my ears, she suddenly says, 'How come? Well. How come you're at L'École? I mean, it's kind of expensive . . .'

She is still looking down at the board and a burning feeling spreads up from my stomach. I don't like the way this question makes me feel but I don't know what else to do but answer it.

'I do some work for Miss Keene and she lets me take the classes. And remember I sell my pastries? I'm saving up for the placement test. And I get to sell at the barbecue. I'm the only third-former who does. My pastries are *that* good,' I say defiantly, as if it can make up for my lack of . . . anything else, as if it can wash out the wave of embarrassment crashing against my gut.

'I know, especially your coconut drops,' she says, and smiles, glancing up at me. 'But . . . why didn't you live with your auntie Sophie?'

'Auntie Sophie used to live here.'

Her eyebrows make a break for it, running towards her hairline. I can see her trying – and failing – to place my pretty brown cut-glass-accented aunt here in this house, in this neighbourhood.

'She wanted to move out but my mum wouldn't allow me to go with her so she just stayed. And . . . then she moved to France. And, that's why I'm at L'École. I'm trying to get to her.'

'Oh,' she says, in a small voice. 'Well, I guess she kind of felt sorry for you, Miss Keene.'

And I don't know what to say to that because it makes me feel like crying and slapping her at the same time, so we sit in silence for a while, moving the Ludo pieces aimlessly across the board. Suddenly I realize I'm thirsty and I haven't even offered her something to drink. I start to wonder if there's any Pepsi or soda or even a box of juice, and I think back to when we were at her house, how her housekeeper just kept bringing us food and drinks, like there was a restaurant set up in the back, like her own little personal catering company, and I feel tired, all of a sudden, of thinking about how this experience stacks up to the way she lives her life.

'Are you thirsty?' I ask her, and she nods. I leave her in the bedroom and head to the kitchen, hoping I won't see Akil and Paulette and that there's something I can offer besides tap water. I pass Akil on the couch; he smiles at me with that wolf smile and I cut my eyes away from him. *Why*, I ask myself frustratingly, *is he here?* Every day I come home and I'm on my own, fending for myself, cooking for myself, listening to the noise coming from the neighbours as I do my homework by myself, and today, of all days, they are both here.

My mother is in the kitchen. I pull down two glasses from

the cupboard, the two Coca-Cola glasses Boots won for Sophie at Kentucky Fried Chicken, because they are the only two that match, and I open the fridge door and peer into its gaping maw, hoping beyond hope that a bottle of soda will have grown in there.

'Is who da gyal deh?' my mother asks, as she leans her broad back against the edge of the sink.

'Just a friend from school, Mama.' I don't look up from my search of the fridge, afraid to look her directly in her face. She makes a weird noise in the back of her throat.

'You and you antie is one an' di same,' she says, with a chuckle, and then I can't help but look at her. 'De two a unnu tink seh unnu too good fi yuh station.'

I turn back to the fridge.

'Is what yu lookin for in dere?' she says sharply.

'I need to give her something to drink, Mama.'

She looks at me for a moment, then points with her chin at the cupboard behind me. 'It have cream soda in dere, yu gwen need ice.'

I turn slowly, for some reason afraid to turn my back to her. It's like I can feel her all coiled up, ready to spring. I grab the two-litre bottle of cream soda out of the cupboard and snap back towards her, but she hasn't moved: she's just standing there watching me, her face expressionless. I open the fridge again and glance at her, take out the ice tray from the freezer.

'So, what yuh likkle stoosh friend tink bout where yuh live, eeh?'

I clink the ice into the glasses and try to ignore the burning feeling that's started growing in my stomach again. My stomach has burned so much today that I wonder how I don't spontaneously combust.

'Eeeh?' my mother presses. 'Yu brave fi true, fi tek her down here. She look like she never pass Half Way Tree in har life . . .'

'I . . . It was her first time on a bus,' I say, because I don't know what else to say. My mother seems to find this fact hilarious, throwing back her head and letting out two sharp barks of laughter. I glance at her and find myself smiling, and then I catch her eye and we're both laughing at the absurdity of it.

'Aaaaah, bwoy,' she says, wiping the tears from her eyes. 'Some people very lucky inna life . . .'

She turns to open the cupboard above her, takes out condensed milk and a tin of Milo, and I feel that whatever the moment was that we just shared with each other, it's over now. I want to stretch it out, to say something that will make her laugh again, but my mind is resolutely blank. So I pour the cream soda into the two glasses and walk with them out of the kitchen, glancing back at my mother as I leave, but she doesn't notice I've gone. I step past the couch, ready to cut my eyes at Akil once again, but there's only empty space where he was sitting, the TV blaring at nothing and no one. I hear the low timbre of his voice as I near my room and something makes me speed up, the cream soda sloshing over onto my hands.

I barrel in and he's there, sitting on the bed beside Mandy, who has backed herself into the wall as if she's trying to push her way through to the other side. Her mouth is curled up in disgust and her eyes are wide with alarm. They turn sharply to look at me as I walk in.

'Awrite, Akisha?' he says, that sharp, wolf-like smile playing over his lips. 'Was juss talkin to yu fren here.'

He turns the smile back to Mandy. I can see her still trying to inch away from him, even though there's nowhere else to go with the wall at her back.

'Why?' I ask.

'Why? Den don' I want to know your fren dem? Especially when dem so pretty.'

I glance over at Mandy and see something shudder over her face and it makes me angry. I am angry that this man is here in this house, that he is here in my life when I was perfectly fine without him, that he is making a bad situation even worse with . . . whatever it is he is doing in here, in my room, which feels dirtier now that he's been in it. I'm angry at my mother because it's her fault he's here, and at Auntie Sophie because he wouldn't be if she had just taken me with her right away. Inexplicably I'm also angry at Mandy for exposing me like this, because that's how I feel: exposed. As if I'm showing her my belly.

'Can you get out!' The words burst out of my mouth and slam into his face, surprising all three of us. 'We're having a girls' night. We're playing games,' I say.

He looks at me for a long time and then that smile slithers back into place and he chuckles.

'Awrite, awrite,' he says, and he takes his time getting up off the bed, giving Mandy a lingering look, licking his lips before he moves towards the door. 'Awrite, girls' night.' I hear him chuckle to himself as he oozes out of my bedroom door. I put the two glasses of cream soda down on my dresser and close the door, then sit on the bed beside Mandy. The anger has bled out of me and left only the embers of embarrassment in its wake. This whole night has been a disaster and

I am wishing I could turn back time and tell Mandy no, no no no, you can't come over. You just can't.

'Pumkin, you know what?' Mandy says, rubbing her arm. I notice she won't look me in my eyes and I wonder what Akil was in here saying to her. What was he trying to do? 'I forgot that I told Mummy I would call her when we got to your house. Can I use your phone?'

'Ahm, yeah, all right. It's outside.'

We head into the living room. Akil and Paulette are back on the couch. My mother watches us walk past, Akil acting like he's absorbed in an ad for some bank that involves a lot of singing and dancing, but I notice his eyes follow us from the side as we pass by. I show Mandy the phone, which is stuck to the wall behind the dining table and has an extra long cord so you can walk around the corner and pretend like you have some privacy in this house. I sit at the dining table while Mandy wanders with the receiver into the kitchen.

'Mum?' I hear her say, her voice low and trembling. She is trying to be quiet, to speak softly, but I hear her as well as if she is shouting in my ear. 'Mummy, I don't want to stay here. Can you pick me up?'

There's a beat of silence, and then the channel changes on the TV and there's another ad playing at top decibel, more singing, more dancing, and I wonder why almost every ad we have on this island sounds like the beginnings of a dance-hall party, regardless of whether it's for food, car parts or insurance. The singing drowns out Mandy's voice for a moment, even though she has to raise her own voice for her mother to hear her. I catch the words 'awful' and 'scared' and 'Tell you when you get here, just please' and the man in my chest wakes up all of a sudden and just starts one piece of banging against my breastbone, making me short of breath. Mandy comes out of the kitchen and hangs up the phone gently. Now I'm the one pretending to be absorbed in the TV.

'Pumkin, my mum says I have to come home. She's coming for me.'

I look back at her but she is avoiding my eyes, looking somewhere just to the left of my face. I can see her hoping I don't ask why, as clearly as if it's written in bold letters above her head, like a thought bubble in a comic book, and I want to tell her it's okay, I won't ask, I already know why. So I just say, 'Okay,' and I see the breath escape her, like from a balloon. She runs to my room to get her bags and brings them back to the dining table, where we sit in silence watching a whole section of the news plus weather before the phone rings, startling all of us.

'Hello? Hello?' I hear a man say, the smooth, curvy sounds of his accent evident in just those two syllables. His voice is gruff and heavy, the kind of voice that will not be contradicted, the kind of voice that doesn't have time to waste. 'Chen here, I can't find the house, what's the address?'

I glance at Mandy as I give her father directions from the Half Way Tree clock and hang up the phone.

'That was your dad,' I say to her, and feel a burst of annoyance at the hope that blazes in her eyes. *You're not being freed from prison*, I think. We turn back to the TV before I say out loud, 'I wonder where he was calling from, though, if he was lost?'

'He has a cellular phone,' Mandy says matter-of-factly, and I just say, 'Oh.'

A few minutes later we hear two small beeps at the gate. Mandy grabs her bags and jumps off her chair.

'Goodbye, Mr and Mrs Patterson. It was nice to meet you,' she says, as she walks quickly towards the door.

'Yuh leaving hall-ready?' my mother says, as she and Akil turn towards Mandy, whose hand is already on the doorknob.

'Yes, sorry. My mum said I had to come home. Sorry!'

I walk with her out to the gate where a big black SUV is waiting. As she opens the car door I catch sight of her father, his face gruff, clearly displeased that he has had to drive all the way to this side of the world to pick up his daughter. Or maybe he's just mad that she was in such an area in the first place.

'I'm so sorry I have to go, Pumkin,' Mandy says, although she doesn't look sorry at all. She looks back to her old self, relaxed and smiling, now that she has been rescued. 'See you at school, though!' she says cheerily, and hoists herself into the behemoth of a vehicle. I watch them drive off and see Robbie and Junior still there on the wall, watching the huge car drive away, then turning to look back at me. I cut my eyes after them and walk into the house, closing the door softly behind me.

'She cudden manage it, eeh?' Akil says, with that infuriating smile. 'Too ghetto fi di likkle princess.'

My mother looks at me and starts to laugh, and he joins her, until they are both laughing at me. My eyes begin to burn but I make myself walk slowly to my room, casually, unbothered, unaffected. The man beats the inside of my chest in time with my steps, and the burning in my eyes threatens to melt over onto my face like wax, but I make it to my room where I stand in front of the two glasses of cream soda, sitting there covered with condensation, the ice long melted. I wonder what this means now, because I know it means something, this whole event, this exposé. I know that something will change now, and I know it's out of my control.

I knock the glasses off my dresser and watch as the soda spreads across the threadbare carpet, like blood.

'Bad pasture mek sheep shabby'

'If you don't provide the best support, don't expect the best result'

Contraband

'It has come to my attention that someone is selling baked goods at school,' Mrs Roberts, the vice principal, says at Assembly one week later. 'Let me remind you that the sale of items on school property is expressly forbidden. This is a place of learning. This is *not* a place for you to run a business! If you are found to be the seller, there will be consequences.'

She pauses for a moment to let her words settle in. I can feel Tamara, beside me, straining not to turn her head to look at me, but a few other girls can't resist glancing over. I keep my eyes straight ahead for the rest of Assembly, until we are released back into the wild and I can let go of the breath I was holding.

'What you going do?' Tamara asks me quietly, as we file out into the sunshine, but before I can answer a couple of girls walk by and whisper, 'Pumkin, you have the stuff?' and I whisper back that I'll meet them after lunch. I feel like a drug-dealer.

I look at Tamara and shrug helplessly before we separate and head in different directions for classes. We're a week out from the barbecue, and I think, for a moment, that I should stop selling at school until it's over. If they find out it's me, they'll pull me from the stall, I'm sure of it. But I'm so close, *so close*, to my goal . . .

The Monday after the disastrous sleepover, I came home with more than half of my pastries. A lot of my regular customers ignored me, or walked by in clumps of girls, giggling when they saw me. I don't know what gossip Mandy was spreading. I was desperate to know and equally desperate not to. I thought of her telling her friends about my father, about . . . whatever had happened in my room. What had he said to her? What had he done? The thought sent a shiver from the crown of my head all the way down to the base of my spine as I sat under the lunch tree, alone, picking at the edge of a square of Toto. The sun was high and hot, the sky blue. Like every day. Every day was the same, except not today.

Tamara came to sit beside me. I'd been at her house the day before, as usual, gone to church with her family. As soon as we'd got back, we'd changed into our yaad clothes and she claimed she had homework to do, or singing lessons, or something vague, and left me to bake alone in her kitchen. I'd wanted to talk to her about Mandy. It was like a bubble stuck in my throat, wanting to burst out, but there's no time to talk at church and the pastries weren't interested in hearing my sob story.

'What is happening?' Tamara asks me now, and I told her the story. Of Mandy coming over, her first bus ride, her rising discomfort the deeper she got into our neighbourhood. Akil, trying God knows what in my bedroom while I wasn't there. Just two minutes, I wasn't there. Mandy's father, coming to the rescue.

'Ah, that's why,' she says.

'That's why what?'

'Why the girls are saying they not buying from you any more because it's dirty.'

'What? Which girls? What's dirty?'

'All of them. And the place where you cook the food. It's *unhygienic*, one said. But I did pinch her so hard you see?'

'But . . . my house is *clean*!'

'Then is why you telling *me* that?'

'I'm not *dirty,* just because I don't live in a nice house,' I say, under my breath. It sounds like I'm trying to convince myself. A memory pops into my head of Sophie giving a homeless man money, desperately trying, but failing, not to touch his skin with her fingers. I remember the way she wiped and wiped and wiped her hand against her jeans afterwards, even though she'd given him such a lovely smile.

'Well, listen. Mrs Roberts is on to you now, which mean the whole of the teacher dem going be looking for you, so you might as well stop this selling business now.'

I think about the stash of cash in my room. I think about how much I still need to earn to make the registration fee. I think about Sophie in Marseille, all the letters she's written, all the promises she's made about how amazing things will be when I get there. I think about how much I could make at the barbecue. I think about Mr Murray, who has a pan-chicken stall at the corner of Liguanea. I think about all the uptown people who buy barbecue chicken cooked in a dirty old oil drum sold by a man they don't know on the side of the street at four o'clock in the morning, coming back from their parties; how they stand there and wolf the chicken down, soaking up the juices with hard dough bread, licking the sauce off their fingers. Mr Murray, who comes from the same place I come from. How come *he's* not dirty?

And then I see Mandy walk by, Candida at her side. Candida sees me, too, and she loops her arm through Mandy's, whispers into her ear, tips her head back and laughs. But Mandy doesn't laugh. She just looks at me, and her eyes are sad, like she's going to cry, until she turns her head and they walk away.

★

By the end of the week, the trickle of girls who are still buying my pastries despite the *dirty* rumours becomes a steadier stream, although a few girls still screw up their noses and make gagging sounds when I walk past. It turns out that a lot of my customers can't do without my sweets when 3 p.m. rolls around and their only choice is the tuck shop, where that ancient troll, Miss Irene, sells bulla cake so rock hard that one girl famously broke a tooth on it. I see a few of them pull the cakes from my brown grease paper and put them in their lunchboxes, so it looks like they came from home. I don't care, as long as they're still giving me their cash.

Tamara and I were also slowly back on track. She'd rolled her eyes when I came over on Sunday to bake, but she'd sat with me in the kitchen this time.

'You and this baking,' she'd said, shaking her head. 'Baking baking every minute.'

I smile and glance over at her. Her eyes are wandering over all the pots and pans and muffin forms.

'Hold on, is where you get all these new things?'

'Miss Solomon gave me permission to use the stuff from Home Ec to make cakes for the barbecue.'

'Riiiight. But this is not for the barbecue . . .'

'Well.'

She sighs and shakes her head. 'You must really want to get in trouble.'

'I *don't*. T, you know I just need to do this until I have enough for the test. And, anyway, I like it. I like making my own money. I like having something that . . . I dunno, that people want that only I give them. Why does it bug you so much?'

'It don't *bug* me! I'm just saying . . .'

'You gwaan like I selling crack at school.'

'Maybe that would be better. You'd only have to sell a little and you'd have all the money you need, instead of having to do this foolishness every week.'

'Well, I don't know how to bake crack.'

We look at each other until I see the corner of her mouth twitch, and then we burst out laughing. We laugh and laugh, until tears stream from our eyes and my tummy hurts. Then we slowly run out of laugh, like a train slowing down, and Tamara sticks her finger into a mixing bowl and scoops up some cake batter, popping it into her still-smiling mouth, and I feel like everything is okay in the world again.

★

When I get home that afternoon, my backpack full of carefully wrapped pastries, my mother and Akil are sitting on the couch watching TV. They'd pulled one of their disappearing acts for a few days after the sleepover-that-wasn't, but then my mother showed up alone and we circled each other warily for a few days more. Now my stomach draws tight when I see the back of his head. I hold on tighter to my backpack straps as I shuffle past the couch, mumbling hello.

'Oy! Den yuh cyaan say "hello"?' my mother snaps.

'I did –' I start to say as I turn to them, but then I see the brown grease paper in their hands, the red string trailing between their fingers. Akil's mouth is full, his cheeks puffed out like a nut-filled squirrel's, my mother's fingers sticky. She sees me looking at the little package and says, 'Linnette shop mi get dis, sweet pitayta pudding. It nice, man. Better than yours!'

She laughs, and Akil says, 'Fi real?'

'Yeah, man,' my mother says. 'Dis one *nice* man.

'If yours did dis good, you cudda sell it,' she adds, pointing towards me.

'Eeh-hee,' Akil says, in agreement, licking his fingers as he finishes his thick slice of pudding.

He reaches over and tries to steal a piece of my mother's, but she slaps his hand away and shouts, 'No!' shifting away so he can't reach.

I want to shout, too. I want to tell her that I *did* make it, it *is* mine, I *am* selling it. I want to tell her, See, *see*? I can look after myself. I don't actually need you at all. But, of course, I can't. I imagine her and Akil finding out that I'm making money. They would never let me keep it, especially if she knew what I'm planning to do with it. 'Dat dyam tess!' she always says. 'Yuh not tekkin no *tess* fi nuh go nowhere.'

I'm still looking at the grease paper in her hands when she finally glances at me. 'Stop stare pon mi food, man!' she yelps.

'I'm glad you like it, Mama,' I mumble, before I turn towards my bedroom.

'Is wha she say?' I hear Akil ask.

'Me nuh know,' my mother answers, then I hear another slap. 'What a seh, NO!'

I close my door against the sound of the TV and Akil and Paulette fighting over the last piece of sweet-potato pudding. I feel a little sour until I think that they spent their money on the sweets that I made and they don't even know it. And that, at least, makes me smile.

*

That night I cannot sleep. The bed is too big without Auntie Sophie in it. I toss one way and then the other, stare at the cracks on the wall through the light peeking in at the edges of the doors and windows. My palms are itching. People say that means money is coming but it's never been true for me. I think I just need to do something with them, bake something maybe. I finally get out of bed, fighting with the threadbare sheets twisted this way and that around my legs, like they're trying to hold me back. I head to the kitchen and stand there in the dark. There is a streetlight on the corner outside, kind of far away but it's enough light for me. I know where everything is. I take out a tin of condensed milk I hid in the back of the cupboard, trying to be as quiet as a mouse, even though I can still hear the muffled sound of the neighbour's TV, the voices of people arguing on the road. It is never quiet around here. Then the light flips on suddenly and burns my eyes. My mother is standing there, looking rumpled and sleepy, her face creased from the pillow, her hair sticking up in tufts.

'Is what yuh doin in ere dis time a night?' she says, and I stammer out that I can't sleep and I'm making warm milk. She asks me if I think we have condensed milk to waste.

'No, Mama,' I say, reaching to put the tin back in the cupboard, making a mental note to come and move it tomorrow so my mother can't find it.

But then she says, 'Mek some fi mi nuh.'

She leans against the counter with her arms folded, watching me. The kitchen is so small that she is right behind me. I can almost feel her breath on my neck. She is only ever this close when she wants to hurt me. My whole body is tense. But all she does is watch as I mix the condensed milk with water and put it in our little pot, as I grate the nutmeg into it, as I measure out just a pinch of the cinnamon I usually ration carefully for baking. I feel the need to impress her, to make the best warm milk I've ever made. I'm annoyed at myself for feeling like this, but I can't help it. Auntie Sophie used to tell me that warm milk was magic, that it would bring me to the Land of Sleep, where I would have sweet, sweet dreams, dreams sweet like the milk, and I can't help but hope that there really is some magic in this pot that will make my mother sweet sweet sweet like the milk.

She watches as I stir and stir and stir the milk and every time the spoon makes a lap around the pot, I expect the blow or the pinch or the flick of her fingers on my skin.

I glance back at her as I reach for two mugs and she is just standing there still, watching. I pour the milk into two cups equally and give her one, my hand shaking just a little. Then I hold mine in two hands. My stomach is so tense that I don't think I can drink it any more.

She puts her nose to the mug and inhales, makes a satisfied sound in her throat, blows on it a little, then takes a sip. She takes another, then another, tiny little sips that surprise me, then closes her eyes and nods her head once and says, 'Mm-hmm.'

Then she leaves the kitchen without another word.

I take my own mug back to my bedroom. She liked it, I could tell, and that makes me feel a little strange. I hope the magic works, I think. I hope it makes her sweet. I hold that hope in my heart as I sit on my bed and drink my own cup of magic in the dark.

Cake

Nine thousand dollars. That's how much I counted this morning. I keep the cash divided and stored in different places: sticking between the pages of a big, hardcover mathematics book in my hard-to-open drawer, tucked away in a folder of papers for English class, stuck underneath my mattress, folded carefully inside individually wrapped maxi pads in a big pink box. I'm careful to put those on the back of the pads, where the sticky part is, because they're expensive and I have to get the big, bulky ones they give out at school and they start asking questions if you take too many. I already know how much money I have: I keep everything written down in my maths exercise book so it looks like homework if anyone finds it, but I take it out obsessively to count it, over and over again.

The sky outside my classroom window is blue blue, the sun hanging heavy. The breeze blows the few wisps of cloud and my eyes follow them, my mind full of plans for the school barbecue and my shared baking stall next week instead of on the tectonic plates Mr Thompson, our geography teacher, is trying to get us interested in. I'm thinking about which cakes and pastries I'll bake, how many, what sizes and how much I'll charge for each. Tamara's father has agreed to drive us there so we can carry everything.

A few days ago I'd practised scribbling *Paulette MacNally* over and over until it looked adult enough before giving my forged permission slip to Miss Solomon for the barbecue. I'd held my breath so tight my chest burned, but the librarian barely glanced at it before sticking it into a box full of other papers, making me feel all the stress was for nothing.

I need to make six thousand dollars from the bake sale at the barbecue to pay for the exam registration, due in two weeks' time, or else I'm stuck until next year. Which is why I'm thinking about sales and pricing instead of listening to Mr Thompson's soporific voice in class right now. The bell rings, knocking me out of my thoughts. I close my geography book and stick it carefully in my backpack behind the stash of pastries I'll sell this afternoon. I realize I have no idea if we have homework or not so I tap another girl on the shoulder.

'We have homework?' I ask.

Chrisanne shakes her head. 'Test next week,' she says, as we step out of the classroom.

I groan. I don't have time to study.

'On what?' I ask, but Chrisanne doesn't have time to answer because someone yells my name.

'Miss *Patterson*!'

It's Miss Smith. Chrisanne gives me a sad look and walks away. I sigh and turn towards my old French teacher. We've mostly been able to avoid each other since that fateful day in the VP's office. If we pass each other, she gives me looks that would peel my skin off if they could, and she never talks to me unless it's a reprimand. I try to keep my eyes down because I'm too afraid they'll roll themselves if we make eye contact, like they're trying to do now.

'Yes, Miss?'

'You are *wanted* in Mrs Roberts's office.'

My stomach flips. I don't like the way she said *wanted*, all gleeful like. There's never a good reason to be called to the vice principal's office, a fact I know all too well. I want to ask Miss Smith what for, but I don't want to give her the satisfaction of telling me, so I thread my arms through my backpack straps and follow her. The bag feels heavier and heavier with every step, like I'm carrying rocks in it, and my mind is racing. *She knows*, I think, the panic starting to fill my body, all the way up to my eyes.

She knows.

*

Mandy walks out of Mrs Roberts's office just as we get there. She rushes past me, not even sparing me a glance, and I look back at her as she hurries away. I wonder what she did to be called to the VP. We don't talk any more, not since the sleepover-that-wasn't, so I can't ask her. Inside the office Miss Booth, the VP's secretary, pauses in her filing to peer at me over the top of her glasses. She gives me a look that says, *You're in trouble, and it's your fault, and I have no sympathy for you*, and watches me walk into the lion's den. I wonder if they hand out glasses to every woman who works in a school, just so they can look at you over the top of them. I wonder if that's a class at Teacher's College: Peering (A Look Over the Top of Your Glasses). A giggle wiggles out of my tummy and makes its way towards my throat but it's blocked by the man in my chest, who is excited for today's performance. He's warming up.

''Ere she is,' Miss Smith says, triumphantly.

I catch Mrs Roberts's flinch at the lack of *h* and I ask myself, again, why it is that Miss Smith is at this school, this school full of uptown people, teaching a foreign language when she cannot master her own.

'Thank you, Miss Smith.'

'Mm-hm!' Miss Smith says, folding her hands in front of her.

There's a moment of silence until Mrs Roberts says, 'That will be all, Miss Smith.'

I glance at the French teacher and clock her disappointment. I guess she thought she had front seats to this show. Now it's my turn to feel triumphant, even though it's a tiny feeling, flitting quickly through my stomach. She shoots me a look full of daggers as she turns and walks out of the door, closing it firmly behind her.

'Miss Patterson. You certainly like it here in this office.'

The VP is seated behind her huge desk, as usual. I realize I have never seen her anywhere else but behind this desk. *She's permanently attached*, I think. *She has no legs. The desk is her legs. That's why she's here all the time. She sleeps here, upright. But how does she pee? I need to pee. I really, really need to pee.*

Her hands are steepled in front of her. She does not offer me a seat. She sighs very deeply. 'Miss Patterson, do you know why I've called you here today?'

My backpack doubles in weight. I'm suddenly afraid it will pull me backwards and I'll land on it, waving my arms and legs like a turtle. I shake my head. 'No, Miss.'

'It has come to my attention that you are selling baked goods at the school. Is this true?'

I freeze. My knees feel weak. I let out a little croak, neither a yes nor a no. The VP sighs again. It sounds like her soul is so heavy. *It's all the wood she's attached to*, I think, and then wonder why I can't stop thinking foolishness when everything is crashing down around me.

'Your backpack, Miss Patterson, open it, please.'

My whole body starts to shake. I want to throw up.

'*Now*, Miss Patterson!'

I startle. I pull my arms slowly through its straps: first the left arm, then the right. I pull on the zip and only when I see that it's blurry do I realize that there are tears in my eyes. I slowly open the backpack and look inside it, hoping that somehow I'd left all my sweets at home today, even though I saw them there a few minutes ago. But there they are, squares and squares of brown grease paper tied up with red string. I hold the backpack out to Mrs Roberts and she leans over and peers into it.

'How many classes do you have today, Miss Patterson?'

I'm confused for a moment with the change in direction, so it takes me a minute to think of my class schedule. Geography, history, English lit, physics and maths. I sniff the snot that's starting to run down my nose and say, 'Five, Miss?'

'Mm-hmm. And yet there is only — Let me see inside that bag again? Ah-huh, only one textbook in that bag. What are those items taking up all the space that should be for your textbooks, your exercise books, your pens and your pencils?'

'It's. Miss. It's . . . cake and . . . different . . .'

'Cake.'

'Yes, Miss. Mostly. Some . . . pastry.' My voice is so small I can barely hear myself. My chest is starting to hitch. I'm trying to push the words out but my throat is choking up with tears, my nose is starting to run, my eyes leaking. This is so dumb. This is all so stupid.

Mrs Roberts stares at me for a long moment while I collect myself. The room is deadly silent except for the sound of my impending meltdown.

'Miss Patterson, you are aware this is a school and not a mar-ket-place?'

I don't trust myself to speak so I nod, up and down, up and down.

'Does your . . .' she glances down at a paper '. . . aunt know that you're selling items at the school, like a common market woman?'

'Muh . . . my aunt S-s-sophie is . . . is . . . gone . . . Miss,' I snivel out.

Mrs Roberts looks back at her paper, her head cocked slightly to the side. I try taking some deep breaths to get myself under control.

'Ach, yes, to Marseille,' Mrs Roberts mutters to herself. She looks at me again, her eyes squinting. I think she's remembering the last time I was here, with my mother. I can almost see her brain churning.

'Sit down, Miss Patterson.'

I shuffle to the chairs and flop into one, my legs giving way under me. There's a thin cushion covering the hard wood of the seat. It does nothing to cushion my fall. I feel my insides jump up and land again. I glance at Mrs Roberts, waiting for her to reprimand me about being unladylike, but she's busy pulling tissues out of a Kleenex box, handing them to me. I take them and blow my nose.

'Miss Patterson, did your mother put you up to selling things at school?'

I sniffle and shake my head. 'N-n-no, Miss. She doesn't know.'

'*Why* doesn't she know?'

'She would . . . she would take the money from me, Miss.'

Her brow furrows. '*Why* are you selling baked goods on school property, Miss Patterson?'

I want to tell her the whole story but it all seems so big now, like a huge ball of yarn, and I can't find the beginning of it. Everything just sticks in my head and won't unravel in the right sequence.

'The last time you were in this office, Miss Patterson, you told me you were trying to get to your aunt. Is this related to that goal?'

'Y-yes, Miss.'

She looks off to the side and a small spark of hope ignites way down deep in my stomach. I remember the look she gave me when she met my mother, how she gave me the brochure for L'École. Maybe she understands that this is what I have to do, that this is the only way. Maybe she'll give me her blessing, make an exception, allow me to carry on, just until I make it through.

'M-m-miss? It was only . . . it'sonlyuntilImakeenoughfor-theexamIwasn'tgoingto —'

'Stop stop stop, Miss Patterson. I cannot make out one word of that. But I think I understand.'

The spark of hope flares . . .

'Unfortunately, Miss Patterson, I cannot allow this to continue.'

. . . and extinguishes. I can actually hear the sizzle of a doused fire in my ears.

'I get what it is you're trying to do. But we have rules in place for a reason. This is a place of *learning*, Miss Patterson, not a place of *b u s i n e s s*. Your focus needs to be on your education. And not to mention, if I make an exception for you, I'll have to do so for other girls. You are not the only one in a tough situation at this school. You will relinquish the packages you have with you today and you will bring no more items for sale. Is that understood?'

My head feels heavy and slow, but I manage a nod.

'And, Miss Patterson, I understand from the barbecue committee that you've been given permission to sell at the event. This permission is r e v o k e d.'

Black starts to bleed into the edges of my vision. There's sweat all over my face suddenly, but it's cold, cold, even though my body feels hot, a heat burning me up from my stomach. There's a pain in my chest and I feel like I can't breathe. I grip the arms of the chair to keep myself upright, grateful that I'm already sitting down.

'Miss Patterson, I am truly sorry it has to be like this. But I cannot make exceptions. Now, typically, there would be detention on top but . . . I think this is punishment enough. And, Miss Patterson, I don't know what's going on at home, but might I suggest you visit the school's guidance counsellor? She may be able to help.'

★

' "She may be able to help," ' Tamara mimics. 'How? Is she going to pay for your exam?'

We are walking home from the bus stop, our uniforms crumpled and rumpled from the ride. I catch a glimpse of myself in a shop window: most of my hair has escaped from my bun. It's in a fuzzy halo around my head. For the second time in a week, my eyes are puffy and swollen. My backpack, with its one lonely geography book, looks deflated.

Tamara is furious. I'm a little surprised, because I'd always had a feeling that she hated my baking, hated how much time it was taking up, hated that I was doing something for myself. But I'm so tired and sad right now that her anger is like a balm.

'You know, I did hear all the teachers was eating everything in the staffroom,' she says. 'All the things that you made, that they "confiscated", they nyam off all of it. Is juss craven them craven!'

I don't say anything as I walk beside her. All the fight has drained out of me. If I can't sell at school, and I can't sell at the barbecue, I won't make enough money to register for the exam. Selling at Linnette's corner shop isn't enough: she only has so many customers. Everything I've done so far has been for nothing. I pull my backpack straps up on my shoulders. I can feel the edges of my geography book hit me each time. I want to fling it into the gutter but even the idea of throwing it away is laughable. Where would I get another backpack? But then I think about the stash of cash I have hidden all over my room. I could use that. I could buy another backpack. I could buy a lot of things, actually. Since it's nowhere near enough to take the test, to get to Sophie, I might as well spend it on whatever I want, right?

'Who you think buss pon you?'

The question snaps me out of my thoughts.

'I guess a prefect? Muss be . . .'

'Nah, I heard from – you know Althea Barnes? Her sister is a prefect and she told her that the prefects didn't know anything and dem did get cuss out because they should have been payin attention.'

'For real?' I say listlessly. *Does it really matter now?* I want to say it, but I just don't have the energy. Tamara's off again,

209

trying to play detective, but her voice sounds like background noise. I tune it out, my thoughts moving like sludge, until they snag on a memory. Someone hustling out of Mrs Roberts's office, just before I get there, brushing past me, not even looking my way, like . . . like she can't look me in the eye? Maybe because she just revealed my secret? Maybe because she just ruined my whole life?

Mandy.

Boonoonoonoos

The week leading up to the barbecue, after Mrs Roberts took the last of my sweets, felt grey and heavy. I missed my delivery to Linnette's shop because I couldn't find the energy to make anything. It all seemed so pointless. She'd come to find me, knocking on our warped gate with a coin, banging banging until I came out of the front door.

'Pumkin! Is where mi cake dem deh? Is wa'ppan, yuh sick?'

Sick. Yes, I was sick. Sure.

She reached over and put her hand on my forehead, then on my neck. I leaned into it but it was gone as quick as it was there.

'Mm-hmm, yuh hot, man. Gwaan guh lie down but, Pumkin, listen, you have anything mek already inside?'

I shook my head.

'Lawd have mercy . . . awrite. Well, if yuh sick yuh sick but the customer dem asking fi di ting dem, corn pone, bread pudding, coconut drop. Yuh should see how dem vex, Pumkin, when nutten not dere! Dat muss mek yuh feel likkle better, don't it?'

Sure. Much better. I looked at Linnette, her great big smile above her great big bosom. She had a body made for hugging.

'Gwaan guh lie down, Pumkin. But urry up and get betta, di customer dem waiting, yuh hear dahlin?'

I nodded and went inside. I curled up on my bed, burrowing into the dip in the middle, staring up at the ceiling.

*

At school, I went to my classes, my backpack now full of books instead of pastries. I tried to focus on the teachers, on the lessons, on taking notes, but everything felt so heavy, like I was swimming in molasses. Girls still sidled up to me, asking for pastries under their breath. They didn't care about me being *dirty* any more, their hunger for my treats more powerful than the urge to shame me. I'd shake my head. *I'm not allowed*, I'd said. But could I maybe just make something for them, something small? Could I sell it to them outside the school gates? Could I just . . . not sell it to them at all? It was okay to bake things for your friends, right? I shook and shook and shook my head. *I'm not allowed*, I'd said. The girls huffed and puffed and went back to buying tough rock cake and soggy, half-melted chocolate bars from Miss Irene at the tuck shop.

But the worst thing of all was that I'd stopped going to L'École. I didn't see the point, since I couldn't afford to pay the registration fee anyway. Miss Keene had done enough, letting me take classes in exchange for a little admin help. How could I go back and tell her it was all for nothing? How could I tell her I'd wasted her time?

*

The day of the Aggie's barbecue rolls around, a Saturday. I'd viciously hoped it would get rained out, big black thunderclouds rolling through, the kind of rain that feels like the heavens are just pouring out buckets of laundry water that fills up the gullies and washes the cars away and brings the buses to a halt and keeps people at home.

But it was a perfect day for a barbecue.

We'd watched the deliveries coming into school the day before, the stalls getting set up on the hockey field. I had no intention of going, even though I'd bought my ticket – out of my own bakery money – ages ago, when I'd thought this was going to be a life-changing event. But Tamara had harassed and cajoled and pleaded and begged me to go with her all week, ramping up yesterday, all the way to school, every class we had together, and all the way home, until I'd given in. We'd arranged for me to go over to her house in the afternoon to get ready.

It's still morning now, and I'm lying in bed staring up at the cracks. Now that I'm not baking I have all this time, this slow, sludge-moving time. I think that this is how it will be now. Nothing will change for me, I'll just carry on like this, staring up at these same cracks in this same ceiling, while my aunt has so many adventures in France that she forgets about me entirely, while my mother treats me like a lizard you don't notice at all until it moves and then you attack it with a broom, yelling and beating it to get it out of the house.

I hear a scrabbling at the door of my room, the one that leads into the yard, and my stomach does a little leap. I sit up and peer out of the window, hoping it's Prince, the little dog that followed me home a hundred years ago. He comes and goes of his own accord, disappearing for weeks and turning up again all of a sudden. I always leave some turn cornmeal outside for him, but most of the time it's the ants that enjoy it, so much so that a great heap of them have taken up residence. But today I see the whip of his tail snapping back and forth and my heart does a little leap and I smile and call his name. His butt goes crazy when he sees me, and I start to wiggle my way out of the bed to let him lick my fingers even though I don't like how it feels.

'Oy, is what yu tink dis is, a hotel?'

My entire body jerks as my mother slams into my room. I'm so stunned for a moment that I'm frozen. I'd thought I was alone at home, as usual. I glance back at the doorway but Prince is long gone. They say dogs and children can sense evil, so I'm not surprised he took off. My stomach lurches when I think of what my mother would do if she found him at my door.

'Big big Satdeh mawnin and yuh still in yuh bed? *Get up, man!* Yuh fadda soon come and him want plantain wid him breakfast.'

She ducks back out of the door, leaving it wide open, but I'm still stuck to the edge of the bed, my mouth open. Akil is coming and what . . . ? I'm staring at the empty doorway when my mother fills the space again.

'I say fi *get up!*'

She barrels towards me like a bull, her hand outstretched, and I have a very strong feeling that she's going for my hair, that she'll drag me out of bed by the roots of it, so I jump out before she's close enough to touch me. She stares at me for a moment, then shouts, 'Yu tink di plantain going cook itself? Yu tink yu juss going lie down here like some kinda princess and me muss be cooking and cleaning, after me done cook and clean for other people all week? *Eeh?*'

'No, Mama.' I shake my head. *As if you're here long enough to cook*, I think but don't say. *I'm the one who cleans, not you*, I want to add. But I keep my mouth shut. I know this mood.

She storms out of the room again and I follow her into the kitchen, as she discusses with the Lord God how it is that

I could be wrapped up in bed while she is out here labouring, and what do I take this for, some kind of hotel service?

When she gets to the little kitchen she proceeds to bang the pots and pans around as if she's trying to beat the devil out, flinging the cupboard doors open and shut. *If you're always here cooking, why don't you know where anything is?* I burn to say.

'Fry up the plantain, mek yusself useful,' she barks at me.

I see a heap of plastic bags strewn across the counter top, full of groceries, and I feel a pang of resentment. For Akil she goes shopping. I wash my hands in the sink and find the two big plantains. I want to squish them between my hands but instead I peel back the skins and cut them diagonally, pour a heap of oil into our misshapen frying pan and wait for it to get hot. My mother is chopping scallions by the sink and I watch her for a moment out of the corner of my eye. I think she's mad because, no matter how she tries, she cannot cook plantain. It's just like the johnny cakes: she's too impatient, too rough. Back when we were four people in this house, she would cut the plantain slices too thick, and then she would leave them in the pot and go off and do other things, then curse blue murder when she came back to find them blackened and sticking to the pot.

'You need to baby the plantain, Pumkin,' Auntie Sophie used to say. 'It needs a lot of attention, just the right amount of heat, just the right amount of oil.'

She told me never to take my eye off the slices, not even for a second, not even to look at the time on my watch, because they were very sensitive and they would burn, immediately, just to spite you. At just the right moment – and there was no indication when this was, it was just something you had to know – you had to turn them very gingerly onto their backs, like tiny little babies, and go through the process on the other side.

I stare at the plantain now, although I can't help but glance up at my mother every now and then. I realize Akil must be on his way – nobody eats cold plantain – so she won't care if I'm over at Tamara's. And then I think, *When has she* ever *cared?* and I huff out a little laugh. Paulette looks at me and then turns back to the scallions. *Is how much scallion she need suh?* I clear my throat and say, 'Mama. I'm . . . ah . . . going over to Tamara. To spend the night? And . . . go to church. In the morning?'

I turn the plantain over. I almost want her to tell me no. Then I can tell Tamara that I really can't go. But she doesn't say anything to me for a very long time, just scoops all the cut-up scallion into a bowl and puts it to the side, picks up the bunch of ackee and starts pulling out the black seeds.

After a while she says, 'Mm-hm. Betta yuh mek yusself scarce.'

I use the spatula to scoop the plantain gently onto a plate with a paper towel on it to soak up the extra oil. I stare at the slices for a moment.

They're perfect.

*

Mr Wilson, Tamara's father, still drives us to the barbecue even though there are no piles of cakes to bring. Tamara is hyper and overexcited but I have a sour feeling in my stomach that only gets worse the closer we get to the school. Miss Iona has allowed us to wear lip gloss, and I've taken my hair out of its usual braid, letting the curls hang down my back.

'It's so weird being here on a Saturday, don't it?' Tamara

says, as we walk inside, giving our tickets to the guard at the gate. We each get a band made of orange paper stuck around our wrists. Tamara hides hers under the row of bangles on her arm she keeps playing with, twisting them around and around, crashing them against each other. Her hair has been carefully curled and I can see a little raised line on her neck where she burned herself with the curling iron.

'Yeah,' I say. It *is* weird. We can see the outline of the front row of classrooms, the trees we usually sit under to take breaks, everything barely silhouetted against a thick, inky blackness. We scurry towards the music, towards the hockey field, towards the light. There are stalls all around the perimeter, some with food, some with clothes and bags and toys for sale. There's smoke from a few big steel drums and the smell of the barbecue is everywhere. It's packed full of people: clumps of girls together, groups of guys together, each looking at the other; adults milling around. I don't know what to do with myself.

'Should. Should we –'

'Let's go that way,' Tamara cuts in, dragging me by the arm. I slow down by the pastry stalls, curious to see what's for sale, hoping everything looks tough and dry, but Tamara pulls me onwards. We pass a man in a stained white apron stirring a huge pot of what smells like mannish water, a long line of adults waiting as he spoons the soup into styrofoam cups. I wrinkle my nose. Who wants to drink a cup of soup and get hit in the face with a pair of goat's balls? I never understood why adults go crazy for it.

Tamara keeps pulling me until we get to the stage, a big black raised platform with a runway at the front for the fashion show. The DJ booth is to the right of it, a monstrosity

217

connected to two massive speakers. It's so loud here that I feel every cell in my body jump in time with the beat.

She stares up at the stage, then looks around the sides, her head swivelling. It seems like she's looking for somebody but I can't imagine who, and before I can ask, she glances at her watch and says, 'Come, let's get something to eat.'

We get plates heaped with barbecued chicken, rice and peas and fried dumplings, everything covered with a thick sauce, and find an isolated little corner on a ledge by a tree.

'Who do you think is here?'

'Aiunno,' Tamara grunts, her mouth full of food.

'You see anybody from school?'

She shakes her head. Glances at her watch.

I turn back towards the crowd. The place is filling up, but I still haven't seen one girl I recognize. I realize I'm looking for Mandy and her friends so I can steer clear of them. My eyes snag on a boy; he's already looking at me. His curly hair is cut low to his head, his cheeks slightly round, one with a dimple that deepens when he smiles at me. Something hot shoots down into my stomach and burns up everything inside my body. I feel the steam evaporating from my cheeks. I look away sharply, but I can feel my eyes straining to look back at him. Eventually I lose the battle and I glance his way, but his head is down in a scrum with his other friends. I feel a deep sense of loss. I look at my sticky-with-barbecue fingers and wonder if there's sauce all over my face. I wipe and wipe and wipe with a napkin but it just destroys the napkin and my fingers still feel sticky. I reapply my lip gloss and look back at The Boy and *ohmyGodhe'slookingatmeagain*.

'Let's walk around!' Tamara says suddenly, grabbing me up before I can answer. We dump our plates in a garbage can that's already starting to overflow. We're heading right towards The Boy and I've forgotten how to walk. Is it right leg then left, or left leg then right? I wobble.

'Hi,' he whispers, when I walk past him. He touches my arm.

'Hi,' I whisper back at him, feeling the spot where he touched me tingle and cribble and crabble and heat up. But Tamara glances back, kisses her teeth and yanks me forward. He waves at me, and I wave back. Tamara pulls me towards the stage area, where lights have come on and more people are gathering. I'm looking back, looking for him, but I've already lost him in the crowd. Tamara whips me around, grabs me by the shoulders and says, 'Stay here. Don't! Move!'

'Wha . . . ?' I start to ask but then she's gone, and I'm standing all alone in a crowd full of people. Suddenly I feel very stupid, just standing there with my 'two long han''. Everyone around me is in groups or clusters or pairs. I look back towards The Boy, but I still can't see him. What if he comes over to talk to me? *What if he doesn't?* I look around to see if I can spot Tamara. I have no idea where she's gone or what she's up to, but the longer I stand there alone, looking into space, the dumber I feel, so I decide to go and buy something to drink so at least I have something to hold on to. *I'll come right back*, I think. *She won't even notice.*

I'm standing in the drinks line, peering over to the stage in case Tamara comes back, when Mandy, Candida and their friend Natalie walk up with another girl I don't recognize. My stomach clenches and the man in my chest opens one eye, not sure yet if this is worth a performance. They're all wearing makeup, cute tops and short skirts, like a uniform. I suddenly feel plain in just my lip gloss and my old dress. I take a deep breath.

'Oh, *hello*, Miss Ghetto Jamaica!' Candida says, a horrible smirk on her face. Mandy shoves her in the ribs and stage-whispers her name; Natalie rolls her eyes; the other girl looks confused.

'What? But that's where she come from, don't it? *Downtown?*'

Mandy shakes her head and joins the line behind me, the other three girls following. I can feel them there, like a wall of heat.

'So how come you not selling your market goods here?' Candida says loudly. 'You see this girl here, Lisa? She's a big big higgler! She sells all over school like a market woman. But you know, a lot of these ghetto girls? They have to do what they have to do to *survive*, you know? To pull themselves out of poverty. That's how you pay for school, don't it, ghetto girl?'

I feel hot all over, standing in the barely moving line, my back to these girls. My eyes start to burn and my stomach churns. I feel rooted to the spot, unable to move except for the tiny little forwards shuffle we all make as the next person is served, and the next.

'What?' Candida continues, over the fevered shushing of her friends. 'But it's nothing to be ashamed of, right, *Punkie?* That's what they call her, Lisa, *Punkie*. Buttu name. You ever notice those ghetto girls always have those weird names?'

I wish, for the millionth time in my life, that I'm one of those girls who are always ready with a sharp retort. Those girls you never mess with because they'll cut you down to size, just with their tongues. But my mind is blank, all the words gone, just a swirling cloud of shame filling it instead. My tongue is not razor sharp: it is a hot, heavy, useless lump in my mouth. I hear Candida take a breath. She isn't done, but suddenly I am, I can't hear one more word, so I just walk away. Like a coward.

'Pumkin!'

I walk faster towards the place where Tamara left me. She's still not back. Why did she leave me there? Why did I leave that spot? The DJ lowers the music by half a decibel, starts mumbling into the microphone.

'Pumkin!'

I glance behind me. It's Mandy. I pick up the pace but she grabs my arm.

'Hold on nuh, Pumkin, man!'

I whip around.

'What? What is it, *Mandy*?'

'I just . . . Look, I'm sorry about Candida. She's just. She's just . . . like that.'

'Like what? Like a bitch?'

Oh. *Now* my tongue works. Great.

Mandy sighs. 'Yes. She's a real bitch sometimes. I don't know what's her problem with you. I think she's jealous —'

'Yeah, you said that already but obviously we both know she has nothing to be jealous about. You see where I come from. You made sure everybody else knows it too. Poor little ghetto girl, right?'

Mandy blinks a few times. At least she looks embarrassed. The DJ mumbles something else and the crowd whoops and cheers. The noise fills my ears.

'Listen,' she says. 'I didn't mean . . . I wasn't trying to, like, *shame* you or anything. I was just surprised, you know? And . . . and I was a little scared, for real. I know I'm a big wuss, right? It was just . . . so different.'

I huff and turn away. I don't need to hear this little princess talk about where I live like it's some sort of jungle she got lost in. Like she was scared she almost got eaten. But she grabs my arm again.

'No, hold on nuh, man. I'm trying to say sorry, Pumkin! I'm sorry. I . . . I told Natalie about it and I *told* her not to tell anybody but Nats can't hold her mouth and she told Candida and she just, ugh. She spread it around and made it sound even worse. I really feel bad, Pumkin.'

I notice then that the music has stopped and the crowd has quieted. No more mumbling from the DJ. From the side of my eye I can see the lights on the stage go on. I guess the show is starting, but I'm still looking at Mandy. At least, I'm looking over her left shoulder, carefully watching groups of people walk around the stalls, since I can't seem to meet her eyes. She's fidgeting with the hem of her tank top. I don't know what to do with this apology. It makes me feel worse. It makes me feel pitiful. But I don't want to feel pitiful, so I decide to feel angry instead.

'If you're so sorry, why did you tell on me?' I say, finally looking in her eyes.

'I just *said* I only talked to Nats about it and she –'

'No, not about *that*,' I break in, my breath ragged and hitching. 'Why did you tell Mrs Roberts on me, about selling my pastry? Why did you do that, if you didn't mean for, for *whatever*?'

Mandy looks genuinely confused and I have a moment of doubt. The crowd cheers and whoops again, then falls silent as a backing track starts. I'd rather be looking at whatever they're looking at than having this stupid argument.

'Pumkin, I don't know what you're talking about. I didn't tell Mrs Roberts anything about you.'

'You *did*, I saw —'

'I *didn't*!'

'I *saw* you coming out of her office, just when I went in there!'

'That wasn't about *you*. I didn't tell her anything about you!'

'Then why were you there? *Just* before I get called in?'

'I got in trouble, okay?'

'For what?'

'For! Mannnn, it's so *schoopid*, I kinda . . . cussed. In front of Mr Bailey.'

I can't help the laugh that barks its way out my mouth. Mr Bailey is a timid little mouse of a man who's deathly afraid of all the girls at school. We can't understand how he ended up teaching PE at a girls' school.

Mandy grins. 'Just oooone little cussword slipped out and Mr B went into conniptions and I had to go to Mrs Roberts and "explain myself". It didn't have anything to do with you. Why would I tell on you? I used to buy your coconut drops every day!'

'You stopped buying from me after you came to my house.'

Her cheeks go pink and she has the decency to look sheepish. 'Well. That's true. Kind of. I mean, it was a little weird after that and . . . I just kinda felt a way about how I left your house, and then people started saying those things after I opened my big mouth and I thought you'd be mad at me.'

I'm so surprised Mandy felt embarrassed that I just stand there with my mouth open like a goldfish.

'But anyways!' she continues. 'Shani didn't stop buying from you, right?'

Shani Pereira, a tiny little girl who always wore her hair in a big puffy bun at the base of her head. She bought heaps of my stuff every day, drops and puddings and pone. At one point I'd wondered if she was reselling them.

'You see how small she is, you think she was eating all them sweets every day all by herself? We have break at the same time, we give her our money and she just buys everything one time for all of us, me, Natalie, Tanya D, Jessica Lee and, yes, Candida. If you think Candida wasn't wolfing down your tings, even though she gwaan like she don't like you, ha! And now we have to go back and buy Miss Irene's dry-up bulla cake and *excuse me* but I'm not eating that. So why would I go and tell on you to Mrs R? We're the ones suffering!'

I look at her for a long moment. She's not playing with her tank-top hem any more, she's standing with her arms akimbo, staring me down. I'm very, very confused. If she didn't tell on me, then who did?

I can hear a group of boys singing that Shai song, the one that's a few years old but still drives all the girls crazy. I try to focus on the voices telling me who they'll fall in love with, if it ever happens again, but I can feel Mandy waiting for something and I don't know what to do next.

'Listen, Pumkin,' Mandy says, after a moment. 'Can we be friends again?'

I'm so surprised at the question that I take a step back. I can almost feel my eyebrows touch my hairline. 'For real?' I say.

'Yes!' Mandy says. She has a big grin on her face.

'But . . . why?'

'Because . . . I dunno, you're a nice person, I like hanging out with you. I mean, Natalie and the girls, we think you're really cool. And I swear I didn't tell on you about the pastries.'

I feel something weird flop around in my stomach but I'm trying to keep still. *The cool girls think* I'm *cool?*

'But I'm a *ghetto girl*, right? I mean, I still don't live in some fancy uptown place. I don't know all the fancy people you know.'

Mandy tuts. 'Look, we don't care about all that foolishness, right. Like, I know it's my fault, I shouldn't have said anything, but I was just, I was just really surprised and I made a mistake, but truly, I don't care about where you live. None of us do. Except maybe Candida but, you know, she's just . . . whatever.'

I look at her for another moment. She caused me a lot of grief, this girl. But even though I always felt weird around her friends, like I didn't quite belong, I also had fun too. The hardest part was trying to hide who I was, where I come from, the fear of being discovered. But now they know, right? Now I don't have to hide: it's all out. And they still want to be friends. I smile at Mandy. 'So, you want to come for another sleepover at my place?'

Mandy's face freezes. I understand, for the first time, what it means when someone looks stricken.

'I think . . . maybe . . . ahm . . .' she starts, but I giggle and slap her gently on her arm.

'I'm just joking. I think we can keep the sleepovers at your place. I don't think downtown is the place for you.'

'Right, right,' she says, exhaling a laugh. She looks very embarrassed and I feel a little bit good about it. But mostly I feel good that we can still be friends, and I don't have to pretend any more to be something I'm not.

'Friends,' I say.

'Friends!' she says, and she gives me a big bear hug.

'All right! Let's go and find the rest of them now. They're probably still in that drinks line. It was sooooo long.'

'That's okay, you gwaan. I need to find Tamara. But we'll hang out again soon. I promise.'

I watch Mandy walk away and I feel lighter, somehow, a big smile plastered on my face. A swell of applause and cheering bubbles up around me and I turn back to the stage, where the boys have finished singing. I decide to retrace my steps, pushing through the crowd to get to the front to see if I can find Tamara. When I spot her, I stop dead in my tracks: she's wrapped up tight in the arms of a boy, their faces attached at the mouth. My jaw drops open. *What the . . .*

I feel like I shouldn't be watching but I'm too fascinated to look away. Tamara is *French-kissing* a boy! Right out in the open! So *this* is why she was dragging me from place to place, her head swivelling from one side to the other, like a pendulum. After what seems like an eternity, they pull away from each other. He leans in and whispers something in her ear and she covers her mouth and laughs. I watch her watch him saunter to his three friends and form a huddle, their heads bent together. Then I run towards my friend.

Ay, red gyal

'Tamaraaaaaaa!' I scream right in her face, startling her.

'AAAAAAAAAH!' she screams back in mine, giggling.

'Who was *that?*' I ask, hitting her shoulder.

She is giddy with excitement, fidgeting and moving from foot to foot and laughing. I have never seen her so happy. We start walking further into the crowd – well, I walk. Tamara does this little hop-skippety thing, like there's fizzy energy built up inside her and she doesn't know how to let it out. I imagine that if we were alone on this big field, she'd run and run and run.

'Kevin,' she says, with a grin.

'Kevin *who?* Where did you meet him? Was he just singing on stage? OH, MY GOD, was he singing the Shai song to *you?*'

'Kevin from church.' She giggles, she skips. 'He's in the choir, and, well, you know how Mama is, I almost never get to see him cuz she always muss know where I going and if she knew I was meeting a boy, jeezam peas.'

'She would kill you.'

'Kill me dead! But I knew he was singing here tonight so we agreed to meet up and, you know . . .'

Her eyes are huge and glassy, like she's replaying the kiss in her mind and can't believe it happened to her. *I* can't believe it happened! She hops and skips again. I think about the boy who waved at me and made me weak in the knees, and how

Tamara's gone so much further ahead of me. I feel a little worm of jealousy sliding down my throat, so I squash it into bits, smile wide and push against her with my shoulder.

'So Kevin is your boonoonoonoos?'

'Oh, wow, are you seventy years old? You can just say "boyfriend", you know,' she says, laughing.

'*Boyfriend!*' I yip, and she holds her head high, a cat-that-got-the-cream expression on her face.

Another, bigger, worm slides down my throat and joins the first. They wiggle there, churning the jealousy around and around in my belly. It's not just that she'd had her first kiss and I hadn't. It's that I didn't even know all this was happening. I keep my tone as light as I can when I ask, 'So why didn't I know about Kevin?'

'Well. You wouldn't.'

What does *that* mean? She finally stops hopping and skipping, and we're just walking normally through the crowd, going nowhere. The mood has shifted slightly between us, the giddy excitement evaporating, like vapour, into the air. I decide to leave it alone for now. I watch the crowd. The groups of boys and groups of girls are mingling, the boys showing off for the girls, the girls screeching and laughing. The lines for food and drink are getting longer. I glance at the stalls, crowds of people bundled together in front of them, and I think again about how much money I could have made if I'd been allowed to sell my pastries here, how it was my last hope for getting to Sophie, how all of it ended up being for nothing.

'Oh, I spoke to Mandy,' I say, to distract myself from following that train of thought. 'She actually apologized to me, if you can believe it.' I force out a little laugh, trying to lighten the mood again.

Tamara stops in her tracks and stares at me, her forehead scrunched together. 'Wait. She apologize for bussin on you to Mrs Roberts?'

'No, no, she says it wasn't her who did that. No, she apologized for treating me bad. For, like, telling people where I live and all that. So, yeah, we kinda made up, I guess. But it don't —'

'And you believe her?' Tamara scoffs.

'I mean, yeah, I guess.'

Tamara kisses her teeth and starts walking again. 'Whatever,' she says.

I scramble a bit to catch up with her. I know she doesn't like Mandy and my 'stoosh friends' but I don't know what to say. I can be friends with them both. Plus it seems like she has this whole life I've been missing out on. *Kevin*. I tut to myself. But I don't know what to say so we just walk in silence, weaving through the crowd, the sound of the a cappella group on the stage echoing after us.

'So, hol' on.' Tamara starts up again. 'You juss forgive her like that? After she tell everybody how you're a ghetto girl and —'

'She didn't say that. She only told this one girl, Natalie, because she was . . . I . . . I guess she was scared of Akil, he was there and —'

'Who *cares*? After all of that, you just turn big fren again?'

'I mean . . . she's nice, they're nice. Except, okay, except that Candida girl, I don't know is what I did do to her but —'

'They're *nice*? The girl couldn't even manage one night in your house because she so scared of . . . of what even? She think is really the ghetto we live in? She even know what *real* ghetto look like?'

She stares at me, slowly shaking her head. 'You're so *desperate*,' she spits.

'What? Desperate for *what*?'

'Desperate to be somebody else! Desperate to live somewhere else! Like who you are and where we live not *good enough*! You desperate to be one of them uptown girls, juss like yuh auntie!'

I stop walking and gape at Tamara. *What is this? What is happening?*

She turns back to me. Her face, so lit with joy a few moments before, is dark and smouldering, everything screwed up towards the middle. Her fists are clenched, and she's breathing like a bull. She reminds me of my mother, and I take a step back.

'You *so* busy trying *so* hard to be better than all of us that you don't know who your real friends are. You don't even know what . . . you . . . you didn't know Kevin and I was "good fren"? How yuh muss know when you don't even talk to me any more? All you do is hang out with yuh uptown fren dem, or go to you stupid French class, or bake bake bake, everything so you can *go to you auntie in France*. You really think you better than me now, don't it? You really think because you auntie in forrin and you hang out with all these brown girls who never touch foot below Half Way Tree, that you *reach*, don't it?'

I take another step back. My face stings, just as if she's slapped me. She's stabbed me right in a very tender place. I feel my sinuses start to burn.

'All you can talk about is getting to France. It's so *boring*!

And you never stop and think, never *one time,* that you leaving me here. Yuh leaving me! Like, where we live is the gutter and yuh leaving me here in it, going somewhere better, somewhere nicer. But what is wrong with where we live? What is wrong with who we are?'

She turns her back to me again, her hands on top of her head, then whirls around. I think of the top spinning round and round when we play jacks, how we frantically try to pick up as many as possible before it falls over.

'*That's* why I told Mrs Roberts about your selling, awrite?' she shouts. 'It was *me,* and that is *why.*'

The air puffs out of me like I've been punched in the gut. I have a moment to wonder how Tamara, my best friend, is beating me so badly without laying a finger on my body before her image starts to blur. There's a pressure in my ears, like they've been stuffed with cotton. The crowd is muffled and the lights strung up between the stalls are blurred and blinding all at once.

When the burning in my sinus melts over onto my cheeks, I turn and run away, the muffled sound of Tamara shouting my name trailing behind me.

★

I rush towards the front gates, barrelling through the crowd, feeling my shoulders brush hard against other bodies. Someone grabs my arm as I walk past but I shake it off and run to the front of the school and out of the gates. It feels like a hive of bees have been let loose in my head, buzzing angrily about, knocking up against the walls of my skull.

It was Tamara! Bzzz bzz bzz!
I thought she was my friend! Bzzz bzz bzz!
I thought she was helping me! Bzzz bzz bzz!

I walk angrily, shaking my head to try to get the buzzing out, huffing and puffing, so many thoughts whipping around my head that I can't seem to snag one of them. After a few minutes I look up and around me. My feet have taken me on my normal route home, towards the bus stop. I glance at my little plastic watch: 9:23. I blow out a puff of breath. The buses run on their own schedules on Saturdays, and trying to catch one after 8 p.m. is a lost cause. You could wait ten minutes or an hour at the stop. Mr Wilson was supposed to pick us up at 10 p.m. but there's no way I'm going back to school now. No way I'm going to sit in the same car with Tamara after what she did, everything she just said to me. I decide to walk home along the bus route. Maybe I'll get lucky and it will drive past, pick me up on the way.

There's a sound system blasting music somewhere nearby – always music playing, somewhere – but very few people straggling along on the streets. There's newspaper blowing everywhere on the road, garbage in the gutters, the detritus of a busy square emptied out at night. A car passes by me but there's no other traffic on the road. I cross my arms in front of my stomach and walk; my feet are heavy, like concrete blocks.

Although the buzzing in my head has calmed down, Tamara's words still pulse in my head. *What is wrong with where we live? What is wrong with who we are?*

Nothing! I think. *Everything!*

I think about Sophie at the university gates with her friends, her hand at her throat, her head thrown back, laughing laughing, while my mother and I stand on the road just watching her. Watching from outside. I think about how she's so careful about setting her mouth the right way so her accent comes out perfectly, even though all the uptown girls lapse into patois whenever they want.

'Their pedigree is beyond reproach,' she'd said to me. 'We will always have to prove we belong.'

But she'd never answered me when I'd asked her why. Why do we need to fit in with this particular group of people? What was so wrong with the type of people we are? I think about Mandy, how she said they didn't care where I lived. She saw my house, my road, and she still wants to be friends with me. The rest of them too.

See? I tell Sophie in my head. *They know, and they don't care.*

Mandy still wants to be my friend. She's not coming back to my house, though. Was Tamara right?

I pass under a streetlight. This one catches my attention because it's one of the few that work on this road. I heave out another breath. It's too much. It's too confusing. I don't know what to do. I've been so busy pretending, hiding myself, squeezing myself into a tight little ball and shoving myself down into the deepest parts of me that I don't know how to be myself. I think about Sophie. About all our dreams of being somewhere else, of being some*one* else. But were those my dreams? Do I want that? To live in a place where I don't know a soul my own age, where I'll have to live in a different language, where it *snows*? But then I remember Sophie's arms around me, us baking in the kitchen, the way she held my hand at night as we lay in our bed, trying to avoid rolling into the dip, and I feel an ache twisting in my chest. I don't know who I want to be. I just know I want to be with Sophie. Without her I feel so desperately alone. But now I'll never get to her. Because of Tamara. And just like that, I'm mad again.

'Waa gwaan likkle brownin?'

The voice comes from somewhere in the darkness beside me, so all-of-a-sudden that my heart leaps to my throat and back down again. I see the man leaning against a chain-link fence set back from the road, his hands hanging from the fence to either side of him, like Jesus on the cross. My whole body tenses. I try to pretend like I haven't heard him. I speed up. He pushes off the fence and starts to walk, slowly, beside me.

'Yuh naah ansa mi? Eeh likkle brownin? Yuh look good inna da dress deh.'

Only now do I realize how stupid I've been, walking by myself on a dark road, hardly any people about. I tug my dress down and glance around. This area, which is bustling in the daytime with school kids and people changing buses to and from work, shopping at the stalls and stores nearby, is deserted. There's no one around, but far in the distance, ahead of me, I see a skinny woman in dress clothes, like she's coming from work even though it's Saturday, walking with a little boy. I focus in on the woman and speed up again. The man beside me speeds up too.

'Den yuh naah ansa mi? Is wa'ppen, yuh too good fi di I, likkle brownin?'

He chuckles to himself. If I walk any faster, I'll be running, but I'm afraid if I run, he'll run after me. I'm afraid of what will happen if he catches me. Maybe, if I just keep calm, maybe he'll go away. The man in my chest perks up. Now *this* deserves a beat, I imagine him saying, as he takes a seat before his drums and starts banging. Not even a warm-up rhythm this time, just straight into the heat of the thing.

'Coo pon dis ya . . . ay, red gyal! Yu too good fi chat to big man? Ay! Yuh nuh see seh mi a try talk to yuh?'

Everything I've ever heard about the girls goes through my head at warp speed: the girls at school who get felt up in the bus, who come to school with ejaculate on their skirts and have to borrow new ones from the school office so they can go to class; the girl who drops out of school because she gets pregnant, and you find out the father is some fifty-year-old pastor from her church who forced himself on her; the girls who walk alone on the road and get taken, held down, violated . . .

Please, I whisper.

'*Ay gyal*,' the man hisses, closing the distance between us, reaching out to me. I am so scared my stomach feels like it's melting. It's going to drain through my legs. His fingers graze my arm, he's about to grab me, but the minute he touches my arm it ignites a rage inside me. I am so afraid that I'm angry about it. Enraged about it. I just want to go home. I just want to go home and this man is making me scared and I don't want to be scared. I'm tired of being scared, tired of making myself small. I just want to – to scream. I want to scream at everyone and then maybe this man in my chest will stop playing his stupid drums and just get out get out get *out of my chest*. So I do it.

'NO!' I scream, long and loud, the loudest I've ever yelled, ever in my life, as I wrench my arm away from this man who thinks he has the right to touch me. Then I take a deep breath and I do it again.

'LEAVE ME ALONE!' I scream, the last word long and extended, rumbling like a lion's roar, scraping my throat as it bursts out of me. 'GET AWAY FROM ME!'

The man is so startled that he stands there, his eyes so wide that he looks like a frightened owl, his mouth open in surprise. I am so angry now that I could tear him to pieces, slash him with my claws, rip at him with my teeth. My hands are clenched into fists and my teeth are grinding together and I'm ready.

'Ay, is what going on over there?' I look around, even though I want to keep my eyes on this man who seems to have been turned to stone by my yelling. It's the woman who was far in the distance. She's turned around. She's making her way towards me, pulling her son beside her.

I look back at the man, but he's shaken off his shock. He glances at the woman on the way to me and then back to me. This must be the first time a girl has ever yelled at him, because he looks like he doesn't know what to do with himself. He looks at the woman approaching again, she's closer now, and he shakes his head and waves me off, like he's tired of the argument, like it's not worth the bother, and he saunters away.

My whole body is vibrating when the woman reaches me. My throat hurts from the screaming. I think I scared the man in my chest too, because he's gone completely quiet, still as a mouse.

'Yuh awrite, dahlin? What you doing outta road this time of night?'

'I . . .' I shake my head. I don't even know where to start. I look at the little boy. His hair is shaved very close to his head, and the barber has shaved a part into it. He's cute, hiding behind his mother's skirt and looking up at me with big big eyes.

'Come, mek we walk up to the next road, the buses runnin up there.'

We walk, and I feel like I'm melting again, the anger draining out of me, reverting back to fear.

I move a little closer to the woman, glad for the company. She's even smaller than I thought she was when I saw her from so far away, but she has that kind of aura, the one that says, 'Don't mess with me.' That must be why she's walking alone too. She looks neat and tidy in a brown pencil skirt and a cream blouse. Her hair is in thin dreadlocks pulled back into a bun, and her face is very tired. She hums as we walk, holding hands with her son, who keeps straining his head forward to look at me. He is a very quiet little boy. I wave at him but he gets shy and retreats out of sight until I see his head slowly move forward again, turned to peek at me. He can't be more than six. I look at the woman's profile. I want to ask her something, tell her something, but I don't know what to say, and I feel so tired, so I just walk close to her.

A car drives past as we walk under another working streetlight, and it stops a few feet away, the brake lights glowing like red eyes in the dark. I don't know if I have the strength for another confrontation, but at least I'm with the woman now. We both glance through the window as we pass the car, wondering why it's stopped.

'Pumkin? Is you that?'

I stop in my tracks and peer into the dark car, but I can't see who it is. I don't know anybody who drives a car. The woman stops beside me too, pulling her son up short beside her.

'Hold on,' the man in the car says, and I see him fiddling with something on the roof until suddenly the light comes on and I can see him clearly: his squarish head, broad nose and close-cropped hair, his face split open in a wide and friendly smile that shows even, straight white teeth with a little gap between the two front ones. And this time I really feel myself melt, a weight lift from my shoulders, a spark of joy wiggle up from my toes to the top of my head. My own face splits into a smile, because the man in the car is Boots.

Right in the dip

'You know this man?' the woman beside me says, and I nod enthusiastically.

'He's my . . . he's my uncle,' I tell her.

I skip up to the car and peer into the window.

'Boots!' I say. I have never been so happy to see someone in my life. I peer into his face. I haven't seen him since the day he dropped us off and never came back. I didn't realize, until seeing him now, how much I missed him.

'What yuh doing out here this time of night, man?'

Again, I don't know where to start, so I just shrug and shake my head.

He peers around me to look at the woman and her son, who are both standing there gazing sceptically at him.

'Who dat?' he asks, in a whisper, and I shrug again. I've lost my tongue.

'Come, Pumkin, let me give you a ride home.' He unlocks the doors, then peers around my head again. 'I can give you a ride home, Mama?'

I look back at the woman and smile. Her son pushes against her leg. 'Yes, Mama,' he whispers, clearly tired of walking.

'Well, I wouldn't mind a ride, tell truth,' she says.

I turn to go in the back seat but she tells me to sit in front with my uncle and gets in the back with her son, who scrambles joyfully inside. I sit in the front and Boots says, 'Seatbelt!' and I buckle up, remembering how he wouldn't move the car until

239

our seatbelts were buckled, back when he took me and Sophie places. He asks the woman where she lives; she says not too far but it's fine if he drops her at a corner where the buses run; he insists he'll drive her home; she says she doesn't want him to go out of his way; he says it's no trouble, no trouble at all, and finally she accepts. Her son's head is already heavy on her lap.

'Pumkin! Pumkin, how you doin, man?' Boots shouts, before he laughs deep from his belly. I remember now how he was always laughing, how it always made me think of Santa Claus.

'Awrite,' I say, with yet another shrug. I can't seem to control my shoulders now.

'*Awrite?* Juss *awrite?*'

I glance at the back seat but the woman is staring out of the window, her son fast asleep now. 'Well . . .' I start. I twist my hands in my lap. Where is the beginning of this story?

Boots keeps glancing at me and then back at the road. He's starting to look like an owl, his head swivelling back and forth on his neck like that.

'Yuh miss yuh auntie, don't it?' he says, in a voice so gentle it brings tears to my eyes. I gaze up at the roof of the car. I don't want the tears to fall over.

'I was at the barbecue,' I say. 'I was supposed to sell my sweets there, so I could pay for the exam and go to France, to Auntie Sophie. But I didn't . . . I didn't get to do it. So.'

'Oh, lawks.' Boots shakes his head, his hand on the gear stick. It smells like Pine-Sol in here and I notice the little Christmas-tree thing hanging from the rear-view mirror. This is not the car we went to Boston in.

'I remember she used to always talk about it, you nuh. How she going go to France and take you with her.'

240

He falls quiet and the silence feels too oppressive, so I end up telling him the whole story anyway, in fits and starts, like a really old car trying to drive after a long time parked up. How Sophie left, how she thinks I can take the test at school but I got thrown out of French class for something I didn't do, how Miss Keene took pity on me and gave me free classes but I had to find the money for the exam, how the barbecue was my last hope to make enough to do it, how Tamara sabotaged me. I can feel the woman listening in.

'And yuh wudda mek *nuff* money! This likkle girl you see, Miss?' He glances in the rear-view mirror at the woman in the back. 'When I tell you she mek the best bread pudding you *ever* eat in yuh *life!*'

'Is true?' the woman says. She's staring at me now. It makes me squirm.

'Yeah, man! I seh she mek a bread pudding one time? *Man!* It mek you toe dem curl up! Don't it, Pumkin? *Bread* pudding, *potato* pudding, *coconut* cake, *coconut* drop, *tamarind* ball, everyting nice nice, man!'

'Ee-hee?' the woman says. 'And is sell you sell dem?'

I look back at her and smile. I know she was listening in when I told Boots the story — we're in a car, there's nothing else for her to do — but I say, 'Yes,' anyway.

'Bwoy, dat rough, man, dat rough, dat rough,' Boots says, shaking his head.

We fall silent again, only the whispering sound of the radio turned down low.

We pass the area with the buses that the woman and I were walking towards. It's busier here, more lights, people waiting at the stops, but not a bus in sight. I lean on the window and look up at the stars and whisper, *Thank you.*

'Ay, but hold on, Pumkin. I feel like we coulda sell your cake at the embassy you nuh?'

I whip around from the window to Boots. Something flips in my stomach.

'Oh, you work at the embassy?' the woman in the back says.

'Yes, Mama, the French one, down on Holborn Avenue.'

'Oh, I don't know that one, just the US one I know, and . . . ah . . . and Canada, I think.'

'Yes, the French one small, not so much people going to France from here,' he says, and laughs his booming laugh until he catches my eye. The smile drops from his face then. He clears his throat.

'I'm a bearer there. Bring tings, tek tings, pay the bills, yuh nuh?'

The woman is nodding, up and down, up and down. 'That's a good job,' she says finally.

'Yes, man. Yes, yes. Good employer.'

Boots keeps glancing back at her in the rear-view mirror.

'I work at the building society, JBS,' the woman says. 'I'm a secretary there.'

'Then that is also a good job, man!'

'Yes.' She nods again, her head bobbing and bobbing and bobbing.

'But you think I can sell at the embassy?' I burst in.

Boots glances at me, like he'd forgotten about me for a second, but then he grins a big grin. 'Listen, man, when yuh auntie used to bring in your sweet dem, people used to *fight* over it! She would have to hide it till after lunchtime, and the whole mawnin, people would come whisper whisper, "Save me a piece, Sophie, before you put it in the kitchen, put one aside for me, yuh hear," and by the time everybody do that, there wasn't nothing left to put in the kitchen. And then one time she seh, "No, man, it have to be more fair," she put every-ting in de kitchen one time and argument bruk out!'

He tips his head back a bit and laughs and laughs. The car swerves slightly while his eyes are off the road.

'All now I hear people talk about the tings Sophie used to bring, *your* tings. Trust me, dem will buy it. You can make them, I will pick them up and sell them for you, and then you will have enough money for your test. Don't it can go suh?'

I stare straight ahead of me. I'm too afraid to be hopeful again. I don't know if I even want to try.

'What yuh tink, Mama?' Boots says, looking in the rear-view mirror.

'That sounds like a good plan,' she says, her head bobbing up and down again. 'And you know, we could do with some tings like that at JBS. We down on Hope Road and everyting around there –'

'*Expensive*, man!' Boots bursts in.

'*Expensive!*' she agrees, her head dipping even lower down and higher up. 'If you see how the tings round there dear! Dem have a little canteen at the office but that food not saying nutten. And they don't have nothing nice, you know, come three o'clock when you want –'

'You need a likkle someting *sweet*, don't it? Round bout three o'clock,' Boots springs in.

'You want something *sweet*!' she agrees. 'Nothing at all round there.'

'Den see it deh, Pumkin, two clients you have, right here!'

He laughs his big belly laugh and I can't help but smile. Two clients. My stomach starts to cribble and crabble. If I can sell to the embassy and the JBS, plus Linnette's corner shop, I'll have more than enough.

'I will have to taste someting first, though. Get a sample.'

Boots looks at me and lifts his eyebrows. 'What you seh, Pumkin? You cyan make Miss . . . You know, I neva catch yuh name.'

'Grace,' she says, from the back seat. A little smile plays around her lips.

'Miss Grace,' Boots says, with a flourish. 'Dem call me Boots.'

She laughs and they glance at each other in the rear-view mirror. Boots remembers I'm still in the car and says to me, 'So wha yuh seh, Pumkin? You can make Miss Grace a likkle someting?'

I look back at Grace and smile. She smiles back at me. I notice for the first time that she's really pretty. I glance down at her son, who is dead to the world, his head heavy on her lap. Her arm is resting on him, protectively. I glance at Boots's big wide grin before I look back out of the window. I can see the moon, big and round and glowing, *Just like Boots's face*, I think, and I smile.

*

When Boots drops me home, I sneak quietly into the house. It's not yet 11 p.m., but the whole place is dark. My mother believes I'm sleeping over at Tamara's and I don't want her to think someone's breaking in. I sneak up to her bedroom door and peek inside: there's a big lump of duvet breathing heavily in and out. She's home. Alone, it seems. For a moment, I stand and watch her sleeping. I think about Boots and Grace, and their new plan to help me get to Sophie. I think about my mother saying Sophie gets everything she wants, about it never being her turn. I don't know how to feel in this moment.

So I turn away from her.

I head to my room, take off my dress, put my hair into a braid and look out of the back door window, hoping to see Prince curled up there, but there's only the silhouette of the cherry tree. I think of how fickle the friendship of stray dogs is, but then I think of Tamara, and that makes me feel sour.

I crawl into bed. This time, I sleep right in the dip.

'If yuh bawn fi heng, yuh cyaan drown'

'Your destiny will be fulfilled'

Rough

I peel myself from my sweaty sheets. The sun is blazing down outside and the little half-dead fan propped on my dresser is doing its best to move the air around, and failing mightily. I head to the bathroom, wash my face and peek into my mother's room. It's empty now. I go and stand in the tiny kitchen.

By the time Boots dropped Grace at her house last night, her son heavy and hoisted on her shoulder, we'd agreed that I would make some samples, enough for her and Boots to take to work to see if people would buy them. Boots is convinced they'll sell out before lunchtime . . . but I'll have to make them first.

Sophie and me, we used to whip up some creations in this little space, but after baking in Tamara's relatively spacious kitchen, using her good good oven, my kitchen just looks even more tired and defeated. Besides, all my supplies are over at hers now: my tins and trays and moulds, bags of coconut and cane sugar.

I change out of my sleeping clothes and walk over to Tamara's, my chest tightening and tightening the closer I get. *Don't let it be Tamara, don't let her answer the door, don't answer the door,* I say, with each step. I open her gate and her little dog, Brownie, goes crazy with barking, which sets off all the dogs in the other houses, the ones roaming the streets, every dog in the vicinity, all the dogs in all of Kingston.

'Is juss me, man!' I snip at him.

'OY!' I hear Miss Iona's voice from the window, yelling at the dog. 'Big big Sunday mawnin! Stop yuh noise!'

Somehow I don't think Brownie cares what day it is.

'Miss Iona?' I shout, over the din. I want her to open the door. I don't want to talk to Tamara.

'Hold on, Pumkin,' she says.

Brownie finally realizes I'm not here to rob the place, even though if I were, I'm sure he would tuck tail and run. He is a humungous coward. I have seen him run like crazy from a ground lizard that wasn't even chasing him. He trots over to me, licks my hand, and I think about Prince, wonder if I'll ever see him again. *She has a dog*, I think. *She has a dog and I don't have one. One more thing she has that I don't have, and still she wants to take the only thing I have that —*

'But yuh not dressed for church!' Miss Iona says, as she opens the door, slapping me out of my train of thought.

'N-no, Miss Iona. I'm not coming today. I just . . . I just came to pick up my, ahm, my baking things.'

Miss Iona stares at me for a moment, leans against the door jamb, one arm akimbo. She's wearing a church dress in a very shiny yellow fabric, her legs wrapped up tight in stockings, her face covered in powder two shades too light. Just looking at her makes me feel even sweatier. Miss Iona insists that we wear tights to church and today I'm glad I don't have to stuff myself into them. It should be illegal to wear tights in the Caribbean.

'Is what happen with you and Tamara, really?' she asks finally.

I look away. I watch Brownie shuffle and snuffle in the flowerbeds around the grass, biting at God knows what. Miss Iona's waiting for an answer but what am I supposed to tell her? I was doing something I wasn't supposed to and your daughter told on me? That I'd thought, of all the people in the world, she was the one who had my back, but she was the one who stabbed me in it? That I thought I was alone before when everyone left – Sophie gone to France, my grandmother gone to the great beyond, my mother who doesn't even notice me enough to beat me any more – but now I really know what loneliness is? That wouldn't go down well for me. Miss Iona would focus on the 'wasn't supposed to be doing' part and that is not the part that matters here. I look back in her direction but my eyes find the floor. I look at the seam of her tights along her toes, which have weird lumps and bumps on them. *Closed-toe shoes should also be illegal in Jamaica*, I think.

'Miss Iona,' I say, and my voice sounds so small, even to me. 'Is it okay if I get my baking things?'

She looks at me a moment longer, then sighs. 'Cyaan keep up with unnu,' she mutters, as she moves aside to let me in. I walk quickly towards the kitchen, my heart thumping in my chest. I glance at Tamara's door, which I can see as I cross the living room, and it is, blessedly, closed. Her little brother, Trevor, is sitting on the ratty old carpet in front of their couch, playing with a toy car, making vroom-vroom noises. 'Hi, Trevor,' I say, as I walk past.

'Hi, Pumkin,' he says, between vrooms, without looking up.

He's going to get in trouble for sitting on the floor in his church clothes, and sure enough, by the time I reach the kitchen Miss Iona is screaming bloody murder about him creasing up his pants and getting fuzz all over everything. I can hear him roll his eyes from here.

I gather up my baking things, the trays and moulds banging together. I heap the bags of flour and sugar and coconut and nuts on top, and only then do I wonder how I'm going to walk with everything. I don't want to ask Miss Iona for a plastic bag while she's in the middle of cussing off poor Trevor, so I quietly start opening all the cupboard doors, looking for the one that has the big plastic bag with all the other, smaller, plastic bags stuffed into it.

'It's that one.'

I whip around. Tamara's standing by the door, leaning against it like her mother did at the front door, her hands twisting together in front of her. She points to a cupboard on the far left, under the sink.

'You looking for a scandal bag, don't it? They in there.'

I cut my eyes after her and stick my lower lip out in a pout, like I'm ten years old. I grudgingly open the cupboard door, annoyed that she's helped me, and rifle through the plastic bags till I find a big red one that looks sturdy enough to hold all my carouches. I can feel a Tamara-shaped heat to the left of me, hyper-aware of her presence.

'But where you going to bake?'

I ignore her, busying myself with stuffing everything into the bag. I put the baking goods in first, the trays on top, and realize that everything will spill if I walk with it that way, so I have to take everything out and start over.

'You don't have to . . . You can stay here, yuh nuh? You can still use the kitchen,' she tries again.

'Why? So you can . . . so you can . . . come . . . like . . . mash everyting up?' I yelp, moving my arms about so wildly that the baking trays clang together like cymbals, my back still turned towards her.

'No! I won't do that. I wouldn't do that!'

'Right!' I say. 'Like you wouldn't tell the school on me so they would throw me out of the barbecue? Like you wouldn't do that?'

She's silent. I finish repacking the bag. Then she makes a noise in her throat and mutters, 'You know what . . .' and I feel the heat of her leave the doorway.

I take the bag and stomp through the living room. Trevor's still on the floor and I want to yell at him, *Didn't your mother tell you to GET UP FROM THERE?* But I don't even tell him goodbye as I walk out of the door, the bag swinging from my hand, bouncing against my leg, the plastic so see-through that everyone can see my scandal.

*

Boots was right: everything sells out before lunchtime that Monday. Apparently the ambassador himself missed out on buying one of the wedges of potato pudding and made Boots swear he would get first pick the next day. Grace has similar success with the samples she gives out at JBS.

'They will buy them,' she says. 'You really have a talent, likkle girl!'

I'm back in business.

I'd turned up at Linnette's door that Sunday after that weird little non-fight with Tamara and told her that Miss Iona's oven wasn't working. She was surprised, but she's too invested in my little bakery business to turn me away. She was just happy I was back at it because her customers keep harassing her for the pastry that she promises them every day will be there tomorrow.

I'd never been inside Linnette's house. It's definitely bigger than ours but not as nice as Tamara's: the living room is very chuck up with big, oversize couches and chairs in that deep, burgundy colour that so many people think is regal but just makes every room look heavy and dark. There's a TV on, loud and blazing with the shouts of a very sweaty television pastor. I suppose this is Linnette's version of church. My grandmother always muttered that she was a heathen.

Her man, Fitzroy, is sprawled in a lumpy old Laz-E-Boy in front of the TV. I can smell the eye-watering tang of white rum coming off him in waves, like when you see the heat hovering on top of the road. *Big big Sunday mawnin*, I think, looking at him, but Linnette shuffles me quickly past and into the kitchen. It's a small space, but clean and neat, a cut-up chicken and some spices for Sunday lunch already laid out on one counter. The oven door creaks loudly when I pull it open, and it breathes out a weird sour smell. The numbers for the temperature have rubbed off the buttons. I scour the insides first with Ajax and a scrub brush, but it doesn't do much for the state of the thing. I hope my pastries won't take on that weird smell.

I get to work on my signature coconut drops and a sweet-potato pudding: grating the sweet potato, adding dark sugar, flour, raisins and coconut milk, melting the margarine I find in Linnette's fridge, and carefully adding nutmeg, salt, cinnamon, vanilla and browning. I rustle around in her cupboard until I find a lime to add the juice. I leave the kitchen to find Linnette and ask her for some dark rum to add. She glances at Fitzroy, who's snoring loudly over the blare of the TV, his mouth wide open, and says, 'Mek me see if I have any.' *Right*, I think, resisting the urge to look towards rum-soaked Fitzroy.

I add the rum, mix everything together and pour it into a deep baking tray, pop it into the oven that I pray is the right temperature and start on the drops. While the water and diced coconut boil, I mark the time on my watch and creep outside again to stand against the wall, my eyes on the TV and the backs of Linnette's and Fitzroy's heads. Normally I'd be chatting and laughing with Tamara now, or we'd be doing our homework and studying together as we waited for things to rise and things to turn syrupy and things to fold and things to mix. I feel too awkward standing behind Linnette and Fitzroy so I go back into the kitchen and stare into space until it's time to add the sugar and ginger, then stare into space some more until the drops stick together and it's time to cool them.

When that's ready a couple of hours later, I start all over again. By the time I leave Linnette's it is evening. There's enough bread pudding and coconut drops for the shop, for Grace and for Boots, and a few extra pieces for Linnette and Fitzroy, who is still laid back, snoring, when I leave the house. If it wasn't for the rasps coming out of his throat, I would have thought he was dead.

*

A week after I start selling at the embassy and JBS, I'm back at L'École with a box of my tamarind balls in hand, my backpack slumped over onto my feet. The exam is just a few weeks away and I'm hoping Miss Keene will forgive me for missing all my classes. I'm hoping my tamarind balls will be sweet enough to get me back in. I'm standing in front of her while she sits behind her big mahogany desk, peering down at me over her glasses, like the very first time I met her, when I thought she would eat me up like a little mouse.

'And where have you been, Miss Patterson?'

I shuffle from one foot to the other. I contemplate telling

her I was sick but I'm afraid her sharp eyes will see right through me. Something somersaults in my stomach. I open my mouth but she barrels on before my voice has time to collect itself and climb up my throat.

'Miss Patterson, did I not tell you that if you missed even one class, you were not to return?'

'Yes, Miss, but –'

'And how many classes have you missed? By my record it's been . . .' she checks a big book on her big desk '. . . six. *Six* classes, Miss Patterson.'

'Yes, I know, Miss, but I can –'

'The placement exam is in . . .' she checks the calendar on her wall '. . . ah, *six* again, six weeks' time. And you have missed more than a handful of *critical* classes, dropping off the map without a word, and now you've sauntered in here again, expecting to just *drop* back in at your leisure?'

'No, no, Miss, it's not that—'

'Miss Patterson, I gave you an opportunity and you have squandered it. An opportunity, I might add, that I have never before bestowed upon a student. I really don't see why I should give you another. You have *completely* wasted –'

'*Please* just let me *TALK* !'

Miss Keene bounces back in her chair as if the force of my voice shoved her in the chest. Her eyes are open wide and I think, for a moment, about the man on the road in the dark, how stunned he was that I yelled at him. I wonder what is happening to me, that I'm shouting at people now, but I know I have only a half a second before Miss Keene recovers and banishes me from her property for ever, so I start talking as fast as possible.

I tell her everything. About my mother and Sophie, the

baking, selling at school, saving my money, the 'audition' for the barbecue. I tell her how I study while the cakes are rising in the oven, how I sit at my dining table doing homework in an empty house, go to sleep in an empty house, wake up to an empty house. I tell her about Mrs Roberts and all the times I've found myself in trouble, about Tamara and how I was dropped from the barbecue stall, how I'd given up hope until Boots picked me up. I tell her about him and Grace, about him and Sophie, which has absolutely no bearing on this conversation but it's like I just can't stop pouring out the story of my life. I tell her that I'm baking again, selling again, and that I think I'll make it this time, even though I have to do it at Linnette's house, which is almost as small and cramped as mine and it takes twice as long as at Tamara's house. I tell her everything completely out of order, jumping around from one part to another, no idea if she's following, and then for my big finish, I plop my little box of tamarind balls on her desk and step back, completely out of breath.

Miss Keene doesn't say a word throughout my monologue, just sits, like she's pinned to the chair, her mouth closed in a tight line. She picks up the box of tamarind balls as soon as I plunk them down, stretches behind her for a paper cloth, wipes the spot where it sat for all of three seconds, folds the paper a few times and then places the box on top of it.

'Sit down, Miss Patterson. Please.'

I perch at the end of the chair, my wobbly knees grateful.

'How old are you again, Miss Patterson?'

'Fourteen.'

'Hmm.' She turns and looks out her window. The sun is streaming through it. I can see the dust motes dancing in a shaft of the light beaming down on the typewriter. Her hand digs out the chain she always wears half hidden under her blouses, her fingers playing with the little ballet-slipper pendant.

'I had a mother like yours,' she says, and I look at her sharply. *No one has a mother like mine*, I think. Miss Keene doesn't see my face, though: she's still looking out of the window.

'Uninterested. Hard. Unloving. Never a kind word. It's like that often, you know, where we come from.'

Where we *come from?*

'Not that every mother in a poor family is mean and unloving, that's not what I'm saying, you understand? But very often . . . You know, your mother is just a child herself before she has her own child, she's not so . . . not so educated, didn't have love and . . . you know . . . there's other things to worry about. Putting food on the table. For example. No time to really . . . to really *raise* a child, to love her, really. Where we lived, it was rough, *rough*. We-had-to-collect-water-from-a-standpipe rough. Gunshots-in-the-nighttime rough. Rough is the only thing some people know, you understand? They don't know how to be tender. My mother . . .'

I'm so confused. My eyes wander around the room, this room in this house in the nice part of town. Miss Keene is still staring out of the window, still playing with the ballet-slipper pendant.

'And then, you know, you have a talent, maybe, and maybe a way out of the cycle. That cycle of poverty, I mean. And sometimes they feel . . . they feel *threatened* by it. By you.'

She turns to me and smiles. The first time I have ever seen her smile. It changes her face completely. She looks young.

'I was a dancer,' she says, before turning back to the window.

'I got a scholarship to Agnes Bishop, and then a scholarship to the Académie des Arts and I moved to Paris. I was sixteen, just a couple of years older than you.'

My eyebrows shoot up at that. Agnes Bishop is the school of dance, art and culture in Jamaica, founded by a British-born Jamaican who married a future prime minister and gave birth to another. Try as I might, I *cannot* imagine Miss Keene's stiff body bending and swaying in dance, but it's the second part of that statement that really makes my heart flutter.

'Paris?' I say, incredulous.

'Yes, Paris,' she says slowly as she stares out of the window. I look out of the window too, sure that I'll see the Eiffel Tower, the glittering water of the Seine, the Arc de Triomphe. But it's just a big Julie mango tree swaying in the breeze. I look back at Miss Keene. I try to reconcile what she's just told me with what I can see in front of me – with her cultured accent, with this house that she's turned into a school for uptown children.

'I was a good dancer!' She laughs. 'I was a really good dancer.'

She goes quiet, stays quiet so long that I think she's forgotten me entirely. I clear my throat. 'But, Miss, if you lived in Paris, why did you come back here?'

She keeps staring out of the window a few moments longer and I'm just about to repeat my question, but she says, 'It's quite a long story, Pumkin. Suffice it to say, I spent many years there and then . . . then I decided to come back, and I set up this school and I've done quite well for myself.'

'But how come you didn't teach dance, Miss?'

Abruptly, she turns to me. She's lost the dreamy look in her eyes. The bird is back.

'Anyways,' she says, her voice firm and loud again, 'you see I'm not so different from you, Miss Patterson. Not so different at all. I see a lot of myself in you. I see a lot of strength in you. You will make it, I can see it.'

I feel a hitch in my throat.

Miss Keene glances at the clock on her desk. It is also mahogany. 'Class is about to begin, Miss Patterson. I suggest you go and find a seat.'

I stare at Miss Keene, stuck to my seat in disbelief.

'*Vite*, Miss Patterson!'

'Yes, Miss!' I'm grinning as I hop off the chair. There's a fizziness in my stomach. I grab my backpack, hoist it onto my shoulder and walk-run to the door.

'Miss Patterson?'

I turn back. 'Yes, Miss?'

'I have . . .' she takes a deep breath '. . . I have a rather large kitchen here that doesn't get much use. I'm not much of a cook.'

I blink at her. 'Okay?'

'Well, as you're here for classes, you may feel free to use it. For your little business. As you've lost the use of your friend's.'

I feel my eyes widening as I stare at her.

'There's no time to waste, Miss Patterson, and if you're taking twice as long to bake at your neighbour's, you're taking only half the time to study. You can use my kitchen and we can use that time to do extra prep work if you'd like, Miss Patterson. It is not a requi—'

'YES! Yes, Miss. I'd like . . . I can do that, Miss. Yes.'

She nods once, a sharp movement, like a full stop at the end of a sentence. She takes some papers from the desk and shuffles them together. 'Good,' she says. 'I suggest you come straight after school so you can get it done before classes, or you'll be here all night. I know your mother . . . well . . . keeps her own *schedule*, but she may very well miss you if it's late and you're not at home.'

I doubt it, I think, but I'm so excited about this new development that I don't spare a second thought for my mother. It's not like she ever thinks of me. If Miss Keene had told me to be here at three in the morning, I'd be here. I feel energy whizzing through my body. I want to run or turn somersaults or scream and beat my chest. But instead I just grin till my cheeks hurt and run out of the door to class before Miss Keene can change her mind.

When I look back, just before I head out of the door, she's staring through the window again, her hand on her pendant, dreaming, I think, of the city lights of Paris.

When yuh mek it big, yuh see?

Miss Keene is a liar. She said she rarely uses her kitchen, she's not much of a cook, but that was all just deception. Miss Keene is a brilliant cook.

I come to L'École every day now, right after school. The first time I walk into that kitchen, I swear you could hear the choir of angels you always hear in the movies. It is beautiful. Big enough to hold my kitchen, Tamara's, and about a half of Linnette's all together. And the appliances! A big shiny stove, a glorious working oven big enough to bake *two* cakes at a time, mixers and blenders and sieves in different sizes, ceramic mixing bowls that fit inside each other. It's heaven. I swear my pastries come out lighter and sweeter.

She'd cooked pork chops that first day I came over, a thing I'd never had because that kind of meat was always too dear for our house. I could smell the seasoning on the smoke coming out of the pan, which was on a low, low fire, throwing my concentration as I tried to ignore the gnawing in my stomach. I tried to remember the last time I'd had a full meal: the barbecue, I think, and before that it was Sundays at Tamara's, where I ate the roast chicken and rice and peas with the family before I baked. Mr Wilson wasn't too happy about suddenly having an extra mouth to feed until I started leaving a big coconut cake behind every week, his favourite. My mother only cooks in fits and starts, whenever Akil is expected to drop by the house – and when he does, I try to make myself scarce.

Miss Keene's pork chops are the best thing I've ever tasted. She seasons the meat from the night before with salt and pepper and sugar and cinnamon and a 'dash of this and that', then simmers it for a couple of hours on a low fire. By the time it comes out, smothered in juices, the meat falls right off the bone. Miss Keene had put out two plates, two sets of knives and forks on her big mahogany dining table. I'd assumed she was expecting company. I wondered what kind of friends Miss Keene had, if she had a boyfriend.

'Dinner's ready,' she'd said on that first night, and I had stared at her retreating back as if she'd just spoken Japanese. My hands were still dusted with flour and I looked at them too, as if they could help me.

'It will get cold, Miss Patterson!' she shouted, from the next room, and I quickly washed my hands, patted them dry on the kitchen towel and shuffled towards the dining room. I stood in the kitchen's door jamb, watching as Miss Keene got herself settled, until she gestured to the seat next to her, where a plate – my plate? – was waiting, the steam from the chops and rice twisting and turning above it.

'This . . . this is for me, Miss?'

'Well, do you see anyone else here, Miss Patterson?'

I shook my head.

'Are you not hungry? You must be hungry, after a full day of school. I was always *ravenous* after school. I used to have to make johnny cakes so they would –'

'Swell up in your stomach!' I finished, and a ghost of a smile flitted across her face. 'Sometimes I just boil a yam and eat it. That's dinner,' I added. I'm not sure why.

The ghost of a smile disappeared and she gestured to the plate again. 'It will get cold.'

And so I sat down and ate the best thing I've ever tasted, the perfect ratio of fat to juicy meat. I ate very slowly, very very slowly, because I didn't want it to end. I felt a little sad when I took the last bite, even though I was full, more full than I'd been in a long time, proper full, not just with a belly full of swollen flour and water.

Miss Keene cooks for us every single day. She plays music in the background, a lot of French music I don't know. Once she played music from a woman who sounded like a warbly old goat and she told me it was Edith Piaf, who was very popular and much-loved all over the world, which I found a little astonishing. While she cooks, I bake and we practise for my exam: conjugating verbs, stringing sentences together, elocution, enunciation. It feels like the times I baked with Sophie, like the time when I was happiest. I don't think about paying for the exam; I don't think about Tamara; I don't think about my mother or how I will get to Sophie. I just listen to the warbly old goat and run my fingers through heaps of flour and butter and coconut and make sweet things and feel all right.

★

'You look good, man, Pumkin!' Mandy's friend Natalie says one day, as we sit under the tree at lunchtime. It's slightly overcast and all the girls are outside, enjoying the rare cool breeze.

'What? Me?'

'Is true,' Mandy says. 'You look different.'

'Different how?'

'I dunno . . .'

They peer at me, their heads cocked to the side, like puppies. Candida is shovelling her lunch into her mouth, cutting her eyes after me as she does whenever I get the slightest amount of attention.

'Healthy!' Mandy proclaims.

I look down at myself, as if I can find a clue. Candida glances over and says, 'She get fat, that's all.'

True, my uniform is a little tighter after all the meals at Miss Keene's.

'Oh, *please*,' Natalie says. 'She was so mawga before, *as if* she could be fat. But, yeah, you gain some weight. It looks good!'

Candida grumbles and rolls her eyes again. I'm starting to find her digs at me comical, especially since the other girls ignore her.

'And your skin. Your skin looking good. I wish I had skin like that.' Mandy sighs, rubbing a finger along her jawline, where a line of acne marches up to her ear. Candida glances at me and tuts, but I see her fingers trail over her face too.

I don't know what to do with all these compliments. I look at my hands and mumble, 'Thanks!' in as perky a voice as I can manage. I want to change the subject but my mind has gone blank.

'Wait, wait. Whyyyy you looking so good?' Natalie asks, leaning back and peering at me, her eyes squinted together. 'Is it . . . for a boy? You have a boyfriend, Pumkin?'

'What?' I say, startled.

'Whaaa, Pumkin you have man and don't even tell us?' Mandy shrieks. 'Who is he?'

'Wh-what? No, I don't!'

'Tell ussssss, Pumkin,' they whine.

'As if anybody would want —'

'Oh, give it a *rest,* Candida!'

I feel a wave of triumph crash into my chest at the look on Candida's face and I press my lips together so I don't giggle.

'What*ever*, I have to go to class,' she says, jumping up and stalking off in a huff. I see her look back once, wondering, I suppose, if her friends will tell her, no, don't be like that, we didn't mean it, don't leave, but they're pressing closer into me, nudging me with their shoulders, singing about *booooooooyy-frieeeeeends* and making me dissolve into laughter.

'I *swear* I *don't* have a boyfriend. Where would I even meet a boy? All I do is come to school, bake and study for the exam.'

'Hmm,' Mandy says, clearly unsatisfied with my answer. 'Well, do you *waaant* a boyfriend?'

I think about the boy at the barbecue, the one who was staring at me, the one who said, 'Hi,' and made something fizzy whizz through my tummy.

'What would I do with one?' I wonder out loud, which makes Mandy and Natalie burst out laughing. I laugh and shake my head, reaching into my backpack to pull out the coconut drops I've brought for them. Mandy yips and grabs hers out of my hands, unwrapping it right away. Natalie shows more restraint.

'Ah caa even tah you ow muh ah lav dees,' Mandy says, around a mouthful of drops.

'How much?' Natalie asks.

'I'm not *selling* them to you,' I say. 'You're my . . . They're just for you. Not *selling* them.'

'Mm-mm.' Mandy shakes her head, swallowing. 'We want to help you. There's not much time until the exam, Pumkin. You need to register ASAP.'

I feel a bit emotional as I look at the two of them watching me expectantly. Like I want to cry, even though I'm not sad. I think about Tamara then. I glance over to the tree where we used to eat together, but there's only a group of first-formers sitting there, looking warily around in case some older girls come to chase them away from that prime lunch spot.

I smile at Mandy and Natalie, and say, 'Don't worry, guys. I'm doing all right.'

They frown at me sceptically.

'Trust me,' I say.

★

The truth is, I've already registered for the exam.

Having a big working kitchen with the right tools and baking help from Miss Keene means I've doubled my supply to Boots, Grace, and Linnette's shop. Boots picks me up at Miss Keene's in the evening and I give him the orders for the next day; he drops me at home with the cash from that day's sales, and Grace's sales from the day before, which I tuck away in all the various hiding places in my room. Then Boots delivers Grace's stash to her. Every day, I try to give Boots some money for selling my sweets, for delivering to Grace, for driving me home, but every day he refuses.

'When you mek it big, you see? When you turn big big baker? Just don't forget the little people!' he says, throwing and catching his keys in his hands as he sits in the car at my gate, laughing his booming laugh.

It took a few weeks more on top, but eventually I had all the money I needed to register. I'd pulled it out from all the little hidey holes and counted it. Then I counted it again. Then I counted it again. I had enough. More than enough. Somebody did cartwheels in my stomach. I wanted to yell, to scream. I did it. *I did it!* I hid the money away again and spent the rest of the night panicking that someone would break in and steal it, the panic permeating my dreams. In those dreams, the robber had Akil's face. And then my mother's.

The next day I bundled it into a big envelope and stuck it between the pages of my geography book. I carried my backpack the wrong way around, in the front, like the belly of a pregnant woman, petrified that someone would snatch it. By the end of the school day I had a cold, clammy backpack-shaped sweat stain at the front of my uniform.

I took the bus to the registration centre, not far from school. I walked past the guard at the door, who was sitting there bored, staring at me, and I wondered why an examination centre needed a guard. Then I thought about all the people coming to register with their cash, and I knew someone would rob the place right there and then, with me in it, just before I could write my name down. I ran into the centre so fast, determined to beat the imaginary burglar who had followed me all night and all day, I was completely out of breath as I stood in front of the woman at the front desk. Her eyebrows were very high, and she looked me up and down very slowly.

'*I'mheretoregisterforthetest!*' I huffed out in one breath, dropping the envelope on the desk. She frowned at me, then moved her head to the side to look behind me. I brushed up my accent.

'Sorry,' I said. 'My mum's in a rush. She's waiting in the car outside. Sorry.'

I didn't think her eyebrows could go any higher, but one climbed up to her hairline. Only then did I notice that they were drawn on, thin thin, like with a fine-tip pencil. She pulled out her ledger with the speed of a sloth making its way up a muddy hill.

'Name,' she said out loud, but her tone said: *I'm bored*.

'Pum— Akisha Patterson.'

'School.' She sighed. *I've made the wrong career choice.*

'St Agatha's.'

'Date of birth,' she reluctantly let drop out of her mouth. *I don't want to be here.*

'October twenty-first, 1981.'

She hunched over her ledger and wrote very carefully. I watched her face, concerned that it would crack and turn to dust before she was done, she was so dry.

'Address.'

I hesitated.

'Ad*dress*.'

'Twelve Norbrook Road, Kingston 6,' I said, giving her the address for L'École.

Her eyes flicked up to me, then back to the ledger. 'Cash or cheque.'

'Excuse me?'

'Are you *paying* with *cash* or a *cheque*?' she said, exasperated, as if my mere presence was a huge inconvenience, even though I'd found her just sitting and staring into space two minutes ago.

'Cash,' I said, taking the envelope off the desk and putting it back down again.

She heaved a heavy sigh and slowly opened the envelope, removed the bills, counted them, lost her place and had to start again from the top. She wrapped the bundle in an elastic band and sat it on the desk, then wrote me a receipt.

'Information is over there.' She pointed with her chin to a

corner of the room with a flat piece of wood bolted to the wall, pamphlets and papers stuck in plastic holders along the length of it. I found the pamphlet with the exam date in large red letters on the front: 28 June 1995.

'Is there . . . do I need to bring anything? Or is there something I should –'

'Everyting is in *there!*' she yipped, irritated.

'Okay, Jeez,' I muttered, under my breath. I carefully folded the papers and receipt together and stuck them into my geography book. I glanced at the woman again but she'd already forgotten me, engrossed in whatever was going on with her fingernails. I hoisted my backpack over my shoulders, held on to the straps at the bottom, and walked out of the door, past the security guard, who was now busy watching a tree.

I'd done it. But it all seemed so . . . anti-climactic. Where were the drums, the people shouting in the streets, the fireworks? A year ago it had been hopeless: kicked out of class, no money for extra lessons, no money to pay this exorbitant registration fee. Now it was done, and *I*'d done it, *I*'d found a way, *I*'d done the work. I was registered. I could almost see the finish line. But everything looked like it had before. No one was celebrating. I felt a bubble of satisfaction in my gut, but I tamped it down. I'd passed the first hurdle, yes.

But now I have to pass the test.

Winter is the *worst*

I haven't told a soul that I've done what I set out to do.

Because maybe if I tell Miss Keene she won't let me come to her house any more. And maybe if I tell Boots he won't pick me up from Miss Keene's and laugh his booming laugh as he tells me silly jokes. Maybe they'll say, 'Oh, that's great, goal achieved, we've done enough now, you can go home.' Maybe they don't know that at home I feel like I'm drowning, and being with them is like being thrown a lifesaver. Maybe they don't know that being with them *is* home.

So when Miss Keene asks how I'm getting on, I tell her I'm almost there. And when Boots asks worriedly if he's selling enough, I say yes, just a little bit more. I bake my coconut and chocolate cakes, my bread and sweet-potato puddings, my coconut drops and rock cakes, and I collect the cash and I store it in my hidey holes, alongside my papers for the exam. I get more and more requests from the embassy, people asking for cakes for birthdays and graduations. I want to do it all but Miss Keene doesn't allow too many: the exam is my focus, she says. And it's fine, since I don't need the money like I used to. Since I don't feel so heavy with desperation.

I spend all my evenings with her and with Boots, my weekends with Mandy and her friends. We do a rotation of sleepovers at all the girls', even Candida, who had to invite me to hers since the other girls threatened to boycott if she left me out.

No one asks to sleep at mine, but it doesn't make me feel bad like it would have before. They already know where I come from. But I make sure to bring elaborate cakes and pastries to every gathering, tiers and tiers of chocolate, piles of square brownies, bricks and bricks of drops. I give them all French names. Their parents love me.

I try not to think about Tamara. I keep my head straight when I walk past her house, roll my eyes when Brownie the dog yap-yap-yaps at me through the gate, like he has no idea who I am. I come home and turn the TV on, low, so it feels like someone's there, and I do my homework and go to bed.

And I don't know if this is happiness, but I know that, for the first time, I don't feel quite so alone, or quite so scared. And now I'm not sure if I want anything to change.

'It's two more weeks till the exam,' Auntie Sophie says excitedly, when she calls me one evening. 'And you'll take it, and you'll pass, and we'll register you at the school, and you'll get the visa, and by spring you'll be here. You'll see, it's all going to work out.'

'Spring?'

She laughs.

'Yes, spring, when everything is newborn after winter, when everything grows up green and colourful again and the sun comes out and people go crazy because it's warm.'

'There's only summer here,' I say, as if she wasn't also born and raised here, right in this very house.

'Ha, yes, but here there are seasons, winter being the *worst*! Oh, Pumkin, it's cold like you can't even *believe*! Ah sorry for you!'

She laughs again, her regular big laugh that I know, and that makes me laugh too.

'And, oh, then you have autumn, that's when summer's ending, and the leaves turn into these flaming colours on the trees. There is so much waiting for you here, Pumkin. It's all . . . I mean it's so new. It's still new for me too, you know. It will take a while to – to get used to everything, but we'll do it together. There's so much I want to show you.'

And I smile, because crazy people and flaming trees are things I also want to see, things I also want to discover with Sophie. When she talks like this I can almost feel myself there with her. It all makes me so confused because things are so different now. I'm not the same lonely little girl who panicked at the thought of staying here one more year. But won't everyone go back to their lives once I've achieved my goal of getting to this test? Can I really count on them to keep rallying around me?

Before she hangs up, Sophie tells me to hold on a little longer, to keep the faith: it will all work out in the end. I put a smile in my voice and tell her I will, I will, and I know it will.

Try not to breathe

'I need to tell you something.'

'Mm,' Miss Keene murmurs, as she wraps the last of my gizzadas in my signature brown paper, tying it with red string.

'I've . . . I've registered for the exam. I made enough money.'

I'm still scared to death that Miss Keene will send me home for good now, but the secret is burning a hole in my chest.

'Ah,' she says, with a chuckle. 'I was wondering when you were going to tell me.'

'When I . . . You mean you already knew, Miss?'

'Yes. The exam centre lets me know when students from L'École have registered.'

'Oh.'

I wait for her to chastise me for using the address when I'm not officially a student here, but she doesn't say a word.

'I thought,' I begin, after a moment, 'I thought maybe you'd tell me not to come to your house any more.'

'Why would I do that?'

'Because I paid for the exam? So I don't really need to bake any more, I guess.'

She sighs. 'Well, you still need to practise for the exam, Miss Patterson. It is a very challenging test and you need to be as well prepared as possible. Correct?'

'Yes, Miss, that's true.'

'And you said yourself your aunt is still getting her feet wet over there, financially. She's still paying for school here, and there will be fees to pay to move you over, plane tickets to buy, visa fees – you'll need winter clothes. I'm sure she'll take care of all that but, if you have a way to help her a little by doing something you love, *while you practise for the exam and get your school work done*, then you should continue to do it. Don't you think?'

I hadn't thought of all that, and suddenly I was glad I hadn't given in to the temptation to spend my hard-earned money buying box lunch at school. 'That's also true, Miss!'

'Yes. And also, Miss Patterson . . . well, I quite enjoy having you here, baking with me in the kitchen. You're very good company.'

I almost die. I feel my soul trying to leave my body. I have to pull it back in through my belly button. The grin on my face threatens to snap my head right in half. 'Me, too, Miss!'

'Good. So I will see you on Monday after school, as usual, yes?'

'Yes, Miss. Definitely, for sure.'

I run outside where Boots is waiting for me, leaning against his car and jiggling his keys in his hand. He lets out that laugh when he sees me, and I can't help but laugh too. He and Miss Keene help me pack the pastry into the trunk and she waves as we drive off, Boots tooting his horn twice, toot toot! The evening is cool and I lean my head on the side window, the breeze whipping strands of hair loose from my braid. I'm thinking about Miss Keene enjoying my company, I'm thinking about the call I had with Sophie, her life in France obviously good enough for her in a way that a life with Boots was not . . .

'Auntie Sophie called me.'

I glance at Boots to see what effect her name has on him, but his face is joyful as ever, his smile wide, his eyes twinkly.

'Ee-hee? Is wha she sayin?'

I shrug. 'Nothing. I mean, she said a lot, but . . .'

Boots nods as if what I said made even a lick of sense. I look at him a moment longer, then sit up straight in my seat. I take a breath. 'Boots, can I ask you something?'

'Yeah, man! Anyting.'

'How come . . . how come you help me so much, even though . . . even though Auntie Sophie . . . like . . . she didn't . . .'

'How yuh mean? Then why I wouldn't help you, Pumkin?'

I take a deep breath. I'll just have to spit it out. 'You wanted to be with Auntie Sophie, like – like be her boy-friend, right? But she . . . she said no. Even though, Boots, I could *see* she liked you too! I could see it. And I wanted you to be together. I thought we would all live together. I used to dream about it. And I saw you that evening, when you were talking – I didn't mean to eavesdrop!' Which is a lie, since I was eavesdropping on purpose. 'But I heard what she said, and it . . . it kind of made me mad. So maybe it made you feel mad too and it made me just wonder why you would help me anyway. That's all.'

Boots is quiet for a moment, and that makes a little knob of panic twist in my stomach. Boots is never quiet. I glance at his face and the smile has fallen off it. I want to pluck the words out of the air and stuff them back down my throat.

'You know, Pumkin, I did want that too. Me, you and yuh auntie . . . it woulda nice, don't it?' He throws me that wide

Boots smile and a wink, and my stomach relaxes. 'But, you know, I wasn't mad. Just . . . disappointed. But I did understand, still.'

'But *I* don't understand, Boots. How come it was okay for her to tell you that? I mean she basically said you weren't good enough! Right?'

And I feel mad on Boots's behalf because isn't that the fear that always drives me? That I'm not good enough? Not good enough to fit in with the right crowd, not good enough to pass this test, not good enough to get to my aunt? Not good enough for my mother?

Boots nods slowly, up and down, up and down. 'Yes, yes . . . that's . . . yes. But, Pumkin, yuh have to see it from yuh auntie point of view. Dis place where we live, bwoy, sometime is still like slavery days, yuh nuh? Everybody have dem place and dat is de place dem have: field slave, house slave, master. And when yuh in de middle, and yuh have a chance to move up, yuh don't wanna do nutten to fall down in the other direction. You don't wanna give anyboddy a reason to question your place. Fi real, often times I think these uptown people more enslaved than we are, yuh nuh? Living behind the grilles all over their doors and windows, 'fraid to talk the language of our own people, 'fraid to be too *rootsy*.'

A taximan drives past, toots his horn and waves his hand at Boots. Boots taps his horn twice and throws a wide smile before turning back to the road.

'But life *seems* easier for some people,' he continues. 'Yuh granmodda, she did work hard to make sure yuh auntie was moving in the right direction, yuh see me? So she would have a better life.'

'But couldn't she have had a better life with you?'

'Maybe, maybe . . . but her whole life, Sophie had it drum in her head that she must be a certain way, talk a certain way, have a certain type of friend, a certain type of life, that only one type of life is a good life, and that is not something I could give her. And, for real, Pumkin, sometime yuh cyaan fault people for being products of their environments. What kinda choice she could make, when she did tink she did have no choice at all?'

I lean my head back against the window and think about Tamara and Mandy and Candida, about Sophie's grand plans, about Miss Smith and how I make fun of the way she says her own name. Is this what I am, a product of my environment? A person who thinks I have no choices because my aunt and my grandmother already made my choices for me?

Sophie always talked about going to France where 'Nobody knows how far we had to drag ourselves up.' She made it sound like we'd be making an escape. But what were we escaping? The wrong postal code?

'An de ting is, Pumkin,' Boots says suddenly, startling me out of my thoughts, 'de ting is, I feel sorry for people like yuh auntie. They must be well tired, always trying to be someboddy else.'

I put my head back against the windowsill. He's right. It's exhausting.

*

The house is quiet. I walk to my room, my head still full of the things Boots said in the car. I go through my open door and my heart drops, literally drops out of the bottom of my stomach. My mother is in my room and so is Akil. He's leaning against my dresser, its drawers all open, my clothes rumpled and crumpled inside, like an animal's been running around in them. My mother's on my bed, a wad of bills spread out in front of her. My secret stash of money. The box of maxi pads I'd hidden them in is strewn on the mattress. I stand in the doorway, frozen, absolutely frozen, my mind stuttering through questions and exclamations. The man in my chest springs awake and gives me one big thump, then another, and another, and each time I cough just once, and then he stills. Waiting.

'Is what you really say you doin in this house?' my mother says, her voice low, her hand on the cash. Akil is picking at his long fingernails, not looking at either of us, but his eyebrow jumps up just a little higher.

'Wh-what you mean, Mam—'

'Where alla this money come from?'

I glance at Akil. I haven't seen him here in months. I'd almost forgotten he existed. I look back at Paulette, staring me down, her hand still on the money on my bed, her bottom sliding into the dip in the middle.

'I – I just –'

'Is whore you whoring out yusself, likkle girl?'

Akil snorts a laugh, his eyebrow inching just a little higher.

'What? No! No, Mama, I just—'

'Then is *where* alla dis money come from? How yuh have suh much money in here?'

'I just – I bake things! And then I . . . I sell them some-times. That's all, Mama.'

She leans back a little, still looking at me. There's a moment of silence when all I can hear is the click click click of Akil working on his nails and the beat of my heart pounding in my ears, like the ocean.

'Huh!' My mother says. 'Huh! So you here selling . . . hol on, up at Linnette shop you sellin?'

I nod.

'Dat likkle . . .'

'Mi did tell yuh, man!' Akil says finally. 'Dat fat gyal. Mi did tell yuh!'

But he doesn't say what it is he told her. He still doesn't look up from his stupid fingernails.

'So is sell yuh selling tings, making a bag of money, and yuh don't give yuh modda nutten? I here runnin this house, payin for everytin, and yuh here makin money and don't give me none?'

At this I feel the first thread of anger start to weave itself through my shock. *Running the house?*

'Wha— how you mean, Mama? How you mean "runnin this house"?'

'How yuh mean what I mean?' Her voice is rising now, getting louder and deeper and heavier. Akil is chuckling to himself and I feel an urge to walk over and thump him in his face, just to see the shock on it.

'Is who yuh tink yuh talkin to?' she yells.

'I don't know! I don't know! *You* tell *me* who I'm talking to! Auntie Sophie pays the bills around here! And for my school! And I've been paying for my own food. I cook here, I clean here, *I* take care of the house! So who *am* I talking to? My mother? You're no kind of mother! I don't know what you *mean,* running the house. How? How are you running this house?'

My chest is heaving. I feel like I can't catch my breath – the anger is roiling up inside me. Somewhere outside me I can't believe I've said all this to my mother. And apparently neither can she. Her eyes and her mouth are wide open, like a big bullfrog's. We stare at each other, and from the corner of my eye I see Akil's other eyebrow rise to join the first. I see him clap his hands in delight.

'What a way she feisty . . .' he says, chuckling and chuckling and picking his nails, *click click click*.

That seems to spark a fire under Paulette and she starts to heave herself up off the bed, ready, from the look on her face, to kill me. But she was sitting in the dip and she can't get herself out. She pushes and pushes with her butt, trying to wiggle her way off the mattress, but she keeps sinking back down into it. She looks so comical, with her wide bug eyes and her mouth twisted into a snarl, completely unable to get up, that I snort out a laugh. Finally she takes off one of her shoes and flings it at me, followed immediately by the other. My arms rise instinctively to protect my face; the impact of the shoes stings my arms, the buckle of one scratching me.

'Den you don't have a roof over yuh head!' Paulette screams at me. She's given up trying to stand, acting like she'd always planned to stay sitting there, rearing up like a cobra getting ready to strike. 'Why you tink yuh so special? Yuh know how much pickney your age *workin*, puttin food on the table? Is what you sellin all dem tings for, if you here bawlin bout how you *have to by yuh owna food*? Eeh?'

'Den yuh forget she going to her auntie in France, man!' Akil says, chuckling, still chuckling, throwing my paperwork for the exam on the bed beside the cash.

My mother doesn't even look at the papers, just grabs them and holds them out like a machete she wants to chop me up with. I guess Akil filled her in on the contents because she says, 'All dis money weh yuh mek, yuh spend it on some *eed-iat* examination! Is suh yuh *schoopid?*'

She pushes off the bed again, pushes and pushes until this time she manages to slide off, stumbling as she stands. I take a step back. I'm still angry, so angry, but the shoes seem to have knocked all the bravado out of me.

'Yuh is a dyam *eediat.* Don't I tell yuh seh yuh not taking no *hexam?* Don't I tell yuh seh yuh not goin *nowhere?*'

'But – but I just don't understand! I don't understand *why* you won't let me go! You don't even *want* me. You don't even . . . you don't love me, you don't even *like* me, you never, *ever* took care of me. Why won't you just let me leave?'

'Look ere nuh, stop axe me nuh whole heap a ques—'

'Is it just out of *spite?*'

'YES! YES!' she yells. 'Auntie Sophie, Auntie Sophie, Sophie Sophie Sophie. Everybody give Sophie everyting she want. Everybody go out of dem way to make Sophie happy, give Sophie what she need, mek sure Sophie have dis and dat. What about Paulette? Eeh? Nobody don't business bout what *I* want, what *I* need! Nobody never business bout me! Well, is one ting I have dat Sophie want, one ting! And she not. Gwen. Get it.'

She rips my exam paperwork in two.

'No!' I lunge forward, grabbing for it, but she rips it again, and then again, and then again.

'Yuh cyan gwaan bake yuh tings dem,' she says, the fire gone out of her completely. She's calm again. 'I gwen talk to dat bitch Linnette, she gwen give me the money direct, yuh see me? And is time yuh finish wid dis school business, earn yuh livin.'

My vision is blurry but I can see Akil nodding, nodding, like he's pleased with this outcome.

'What . . .?'

'Well, don't yuh have big big job now?' Akil says. 'Yuh cyan gwaan focus on that. Yuh have enough schoolin. Waste a time.'

I don't look at him, focusing instead on my mother.

'But – but you can't just do that. I can't just – You want me to drop out of school? You can't just do that.'

'Ee-hee? Mek we see. Mek we see bout dat,' she says, scooping up all the money from the bed before flinging the pieces of paper on top of the box of pads. I'd thought I was so clever, hiding cash in there. I notice, for the first time, that all my textbooks are open and flung around the room – they'd found that stash as well. But the mattress on the bed is undisturbed. They don't know there's more money under there, right under the dip. But that's little comfort now.

My mother moves towards the door, Akil pushes himself off the dresser. I sidle along the wall so I'm out of the way. One more spike of anger crashes through me as they pass, pushes the words out of my mouth before I've even had a chance to finish thinking them,

'I wish Auntie Sophie was my mother! I wish I was her daughter!'

'Well,' Paulette says, shrugging one shoulder nonchalantly as she walks out of the door, Akil chuckling behind her. I hear the clunk of a key turning in the lock and I stare at the door. I only now realize that the key that's usually sticking out this end – the key I never really notice because I never use it – is missing. It's on the other side of the door. I grab the handle and pull and pull but the door doesn't budge. I whip

286

around to the back door – the key is missing from the inside as well. I run over and do the same, pull and pull, with the same result: solid, unyielding, locked.

I feel like an animal's been let loose in my head, wild, trapped, trying to get out, beating itself against my skull. I want to call Sophie, Tamara, Boots, Miss Keene, Mandy, Linnette. My brain cycles through all the people who can help me until it settles on the truth: there's no way for me to call them. There's no way for me to let them know. I don't even know what's happening. Are they planning to keep me locked in here for ever? What if I have to use the bathroom? I look at the ripped-up pieces of my exam paperwork lying on my bed, like snowflakes. The test is next week, and I'm certain that Akil saw the date and told my mother, and I'm also certain that, whether or not this confinement is meant to be for ever, it will be long enough for me to miss the exam.

My breathing gets even shallower and the man in my chest takes this as his cue. Except this time he must be really angry, because instead of thumping on his drums and taking my breath away, he's stabbing and stabbing me. I inhale, he jabs, I exhale, he stabs, over and over, until I crawl to my bed and try not to breathe at all.

I remember . . .

. . . *a few months after my grandmother died, I hear a strange sound coming from the back rooms. A crying and a wailing and a gnashing of teeth. I tiptoe across the tattered old carpet, the sound louder, and louder, and louder still until I get to my grandmother's room and see my mother on her knees beside my grandmother's bed. She is wringing an old cloth in her hands. It is my grandmother's headscarf, her favourite, the red one with the white flowers all over it.*

I can just see the side of my mother's face. It is slick with tears, scrunched in on itself as if she's in a terrible pain. She moves her upper body back and forth, back and forth, mewling like a cat. I have never seen my mother like this and the shock of it has me frozen in place, afraid to move, afraid to breathe.

'Whyyyyyy? Whywhywhywhywhywhy? Why I couldn't good enough for you? Why, Mama, whyyyyyyy? Why I couldn't good enough for you?'

Her words start in whispers and end in wails, like a siren. I put my hand to my stomach. I don't know what to do.

'Why I couldn't GOOD ENOUGH! *What more I coulda do, Mama, whyyyyyyyyyy?'*

I am being punched in the gut, quick sharp jabs, punch punch punch! I cannot bear to see my mother like this. I put one foot into the room. I take it back out. I try again, one foot in front of the other, toe to heel so I stay as quiet as possible. I am approaching a sleeping bear and I'm afraid it will bite, but her sobbing is drawing me closer and closer, like a magnet. My mother is swaddled in her grief. She does not see me.

'*AAAAAAAAAAAAAAAHHHHHHHHH,*' she wails, flinging her head onto the bed. The cheap, shiny duvet stifles the sounds of her murmurs and mutters. She sounds like she's underwater, or in a tin can far away.

Slowly, carefully, I reach out my hand. Slowly, gently, I rest my hand on her shoulder. My mother jumps up, shock written in her wide-open eyes, her open mouth. I can feel that my face mirrors hers. We're both startled, both surprised to find ourselves here, both unsure of what to do. She looks at me, and looks and looks, and slowly, tentatively, I shuffle closer, reach my hand back out, touch her shoulder again.

She flinches. I snap my hand back as if it's been bitten. I've made a mistake. She'll be mad that I saw her this way. I'll pay for it.

I turn to leave, but quick, quick, she snatches my hand and it's my turn to flinch. I wait for her to twist it hard, to bend my wrist back, to hurt me, but she pulls me closer, puts my hand to her chest, and begins, again, to weep. I put my other hand on her shoulder and when she leans into me — though I cannot bear to see her like this, cannot bear this new knowledge that my grandmother is the source of her pain — I lean back into her, and my heart sprouts wings, and soars.

Rapunzel, Rapunzel . . .

The sun's rays streaming through my window wake me up the next morning. I'm still wearing the clothes I had on yesterday. I turn to look at my bedroom door and jump up and out of bed when I see it's ajar. I want to check if the front door is locked but I need to pee so bad that I run to the bathroom first. After I wash my hands, I head back down the short hallway and check the lock on my bedroom door, hoping the key will still be sticking out of it but it's empty, and I feel a little silly thinking it would be that easy. Something burns on my arm and I run my hands along it until I find a cut crusted with blood from where the buckle on my mother's shoe caught me. I stand at the doorway to the living room, what's left of the beaded curtain draped over my shoulders.

There's no one here.

I walk to the front door and pull it. It opens, but the grille outside it is locked with the two heavy padlocks that always sit there, and I know they took my keys when they left my room yesterday. I stand staring outside for a moment before I remember the phone. I'm not even surprised when I lift the handset and hear nothing. I check for dial tone but there's nothing, not even that weird, empty space you hear in phones sometimes. I check the bottom and there's no telephone cord. I put the handset back down, gently.

I walk to the kitchen. There's a side door that leads outside. We never use it but that, too, is enclosed with a padlocked grille. I search the cupboards, and find a few tins of mackerel, a breadfruit, some flour. A half-empty tub of margarine in the fridge. I remember the three patties I have in my backpack. *At least I won't starve.* I could roast the breadfruit on the stove, but I start thinking of the spark from the flame jumping onto a kitchen cloth, the flames from the cloth catching on the curtains, the flames from the curtains spreading on the walls, until the whole house is burning with me in it, screaming and screaming and screaming, trapped in the house, the smell of my skin burning like the breadfr–

'Stop it!' I say to myself, shaking the thought out of my head. 'Stop!'

The thought sticks its tongue out at me and keeps on going, not listening to me, so I leave the kitchen and go back to my room. I eat a cold patty, which I don't taste at all, and I pick up one of my battered books, but my eyes keep slipping over the words. I think about the fairy tales Sophie used to read to me: Cinderella, trapped in service to her wicked stepmother and stepsisters; Rapunzel, stuck in her tower; Sleeping Beauty, imprisoned by a curse in a deep sleep. I wonder how come boys never seem to get trapped in fairy tales. I wonder if anyone will rescue me. I wonder what's going to happen next.

*

A few hours later I hear the heavy clunk of the padlocks and I dash out to the living room, but Paulette just glances at me with a sour expression before she locks everything again. She has plastic bags full of flour, butter, coconut shavings, soft brown sugar, raisins, bread and sweet potatoes.

'See de ting dem here,' she says, as she plonks everything

down on the kitchen counter. 'Now yuh have plenty time fi mek de ting dem, yuh cyan mek more.'

'So you're just going to keep me locked up here for ever?' I ask, from the kitchen doorway.

She doesn't say anything, just pushes past me from the kitchen back into the living room.

'People will come looking for me!'

'Peo— who? *Who* gwen come fi yuh?'

She's staring at me now, genuinely curious. But I'm afraid I've said too much. It's Monday, and Miss Keene is expecting me after school. Boots will drive up there to collect me and give me the orders for the embassy and for Grace's office. If she tells him I didn't turn up, he'll come for me. Right? That's what he'll do? I mean, it only makes sense . . . I hope with every fibre of my being that Boots will come by, and that my mother will be gone when he does. But I can't tell her that or she won't leave. So I try something else.

'Mama, look. Can I just take the test? I mean, I know you won't let me go to Auntie Sophie, but I just . . . I just want to know I can do it. I studied so hard for it all year and I already paid for it! It's not like I can get the money back. So just . . . maybe just let me do it and I'll come right back here, I promise!'

And of course I'm thinking that, if I can just get out, I'd do the test and run straight to Miss Keene and beg her to let me stay there, beg her to call Sophie, beg her to fix everything. But my mother just laughs and asks me if I think she was born yesterday.

So I switch tactics.

'If I don't go to school, they'll . . . they'll . . .'

'Yes? What dem gwen do? Dem gwen call *me*, yuh modda, and I gwen tell dem seh yuh not coming back. Dat is all.'

I'm so angry my whole body shakes, just quivers and quivers, my shoulders up by my ears, my fists clenched, my jaw tight. I fling myself onto the couch, lean on the arms facing the world outside, determined to stay there until I see the wash of Boots's headlights. Boots will come for me, I'm sure. My mother turns on the TV and drops on the other side of the couch. I feel the weight shift, pushing me higher on my side. I don't think we've ever sat on this couch together. I can feel her presence burning at my back, but I'm going to sit here all day! I'm going to sit here and wait for Boots. I can feel her shifting and shifting on her side of the couch and I feel a thrill at the fact that she's as uncomfortable as I am.

All day! I think defiantly.

Except . . . my stomach starts to growl and gurgle eventually. And I can't take the burning at my back, the burning of my mother so close to me. And my throat is parched, I'm so thirsty. And my one leg's gone to sleep. So I huff, push myself off the couch and limp past Paulette, who shifts and shifts again, and go to my room where I eat another cold patty. It scratches its way down my dry throat. I sit on my bed for a moment and fight the burning in my nose and behind my eyes. I pick up my French exam book out of habit, but then I throw it back down. *What is the point of that?* People on TV argue and chat and laugh and sing to each other. I don't know if I can go back to the couch again with my mother there. I get up. I try the back door once more, but the grille hasn't suddenly freed itself of its locks. I feel haunted. I don't know what to do with myself. I sit back on the bed and I cover my face with my hands and I try to breathe and I realize that there's only one thing I can do right now.

I go to the kitchen to bake.

I beat the batter so hard it begs for mercy. I crush the eggs in my hands so bits of shell end up in the bowl. I mix and pummel and whip and pour in such a fury that I know these puddings will come out hard and bitter, but I don't care. Maybe it will be so bad that Linnette comes to complain. Maybe the customers will stop buying the tough-as-rock sweets and there'll be no money for my mother. I pour a heap of batter into a tin so sloppily it spills over the edges. I'm so mad I don't even notice the sun dipping down in the sky, the streetlights popping on, the sound of the crickets getting louder. When I hear the familiar toot-too-too-toot of a horn outside the gate, I startle and check my watch. It's just after 7 p.m.

Boots!

I scurry to the kitchen doorway, my hands crusted with dried egg and flour and sugar, flecks of batter all over my clothes. Paulette is already at the front windows, peering out.

'Is who dat?' I hear her mutter to herself. She turns and sees me standing there.

'Is who dat?' she asks me, louder, but I can't bring myself to answer. I just stare at her with my mouth open, my heart beating all the way down in my stomach.

We hear the plink-plank-plonk of a stone banging against the gate, then Boots calls out, 'Pumkin?'

Relief runs through me like water but my stomach clenches up again as my mother runs towards me, grabs my arm.

'*Is who out dere?*' she demands, shaking me, but I still don't answer. She starts pushing me towards my room and I try to resist, pushing back against her. I take a breath to call for Boots but she clamps her hand over my mouth while she pushes me further towards my room.

Plink-plank-plonk. 'Pumkin, you in there?'

I hear the scrape of the gate on the ground, the side where one is lower than the other and has worked a groove into the dirt.

The neighbourhood dogs start barking, barking. *You know this person? No, you?* And down the line until they're all calling out *who is it, who's there, what you doing here, lemme bite you.*

My mother is wrestling me towards the room and I am pushing, pushing back against her. She twists my skin so hard, right on the fresh scab from her shoe buckle, that it burns and burns, both sharp and dull at the same time. Little whimpers are escaping my throat and I hate hearing it, how pathetic I sound, but I can't seem to stop.

Plink-plank-plonk. 'Hello?'

Boots is closer now, almost at the door.

I try to breathe with my mother's hand over my mouth, try to shake my head so she loses her grip so I can shout for Boots, tell him I'm here, tell him to rescue me, but my mother's hand is like a vice. My breath is trapped in my throat and now I need to cough. I sputter into her hand and she gives me one big push, then runs up, grabs me and pushes me one more time into my room. I hear the thunk of the key in the lock.

'Nononono . . .'

I pull on the door, pull and pull and pull, but it's heavy and unmoving. I bang on it, I kick it. I yell for Boots. I shout and scream and call for him. This house is so small. He must hear me. He'll hear me. The TV gets louder. I call and call and shout and bang and kick until I get tired, until my hands hurt and my toes feel sore. I put my ear to the door and listen but it's just those same people on TV, chatting and laughing and singing. I wonder what they have to be so happy about.

★

Every day after is the same. It feels like I've been locked up in here for ever but it's only Friday, just a week gone by. I don't know what happened with Boots on Monday: by the time my bedroom door swung open again he was long gone. I spent the whole week in the same routine: furiously baking, because I had nothing else to do, or sitting in my room trying not to cry. Paulette is home every single day. I remember when I felt alone because she was never here, how I wished she would come home and be my mother. Now I wish we could go back to the time where she didn't know I was alive. She left only to get more baking stuff or to deliver my angry-baked pastries to Linnette.

Once while she was gone I decided I would MacGyver the locks, pick my way to freedom by sticking a bobby pin in the padlock and fiddle it around like I saw in the movies. All it did was warp and bend the bobby pin so bad that it got stuck in the lock and I had ten minutes of pure panic just trying to pull it out. Akil came by a couple of times. I stayed in my room then, but he didn't even come inside the house, just fought with Paulette at the front door, screaming at her about money.

Now I lie on my bed, the back door open (the grille still securely locked), looking up into the sun, wondering if I'll go blind if I just sit here and stare at it all day. My stomach is cribbling and crabbling: it's the day of the exam. I did everything right for one whole year, jumped over every hurdle so I could take this exam, and after all of it, here I sit, staring up at the sun instead of making my way to the exam centre.

I'm burning up with the unfairness of it. Hot tears squeeze out of the sides of my eyes and I brush them away, hard, annoyed that I still feel this way. What's the point of bawling about this now? I wonder if Auntie Sophie's in a panic: she would have called and called and got no answer. Is Miss Keene mad at me, thinking I just couldn't be bothered to come to her house any more to practise? What did Paulette tell Boots? Does Mandy notice I'm not at school? What does Tamara – Well, she'd probably be happy about all this, the traitor.

I hear a commotion at the front door. Someone's shouting my mother's name. It takes a moment for me to recognize the voice: Miss Iona. *Well, that's weird.* I slink off the bed and lean in the living-room doorway. My mother is sitting on the couch, watching Tamara's mother bang and call at the gate.

'Is what *she* coulda want here now?' she asks the living room. She turns to me. 'Is call yuh call her?'

'How?' I sputter, and she grumbles under her breath.

'Paulette!' Miss Iona yells from outside, banging and banging on the gate with a stone. 'Paulette, it's important, you in there?'

My mother heaves a sigh and pulls herself up from the couch. She doesn't like Miss Iona. Too 'churchy and self-righteous' she calls her, but I think she just hates that Sophie sends her the money to take care of me.

'Come, go in yuh room,' she says, walking towards me with a bunch of keys out.

'You don't have to lock me in there.'

'GO in yuh ROOM!'

'Yes, I'm going, I'm going, but you don't have to lock me in there. I won't make any noise, I promise!'

I take a few steps back, but she pushes me and pushes me

and pushes me into my room, and I hear the thunk of the key in the lock. I sigh and flop myself down on the bed. The TV is off, thank God, so I can still hear Miss Iona banging and calling and I wonder what could be so important. My mother calls back that she's coming, she's coming, that Miss Iona should hold her horses. I hear my mother walk down the little driveway. I wonder if I should try calling out, since the TV isn't blaring as usual. But I just don't have the energy. What would be the point, anyway? I lie there staring at the watermarks on the ceiling, my mind blank, the breeze blowing through the open back door. I don't know how much time goes by, but I can feel myself start to drift off, everything taking on a blurry quality, and I'm happy to be falling asleep because I can't bear to be awake.

'PUMKIN!'

'AAAAGH!' I scream and jolt up, my hand to my chest. I can actually feel my heart trying to beat its way out. I stare at my back door and I think I'm dreaming, I must be dreaming, because there are Tamara and Mandy, together, hanging off the grille, two big grins on their faces.

You never eat a patty in a cocoa bread?

'Come, come, Pumkin, hurry up,' Tamara says, but I can't seem to move or to answer, only stare open-mouthed as I watch Mandy fitting the keys in the padlocks, trying to find the right one.

'But . . . how you get the –'

'Don't worry about that right now. Hurry up, put on your clothes, let's go.'

'Which one is it, man? So many . . . stupid . . .' Mandy mutters, as she tries key after key. I slide off the bed, still not sure if I'm dreaming.

'It's this one,' I say, reaching through the grille, touching the key to my freedom.

Tamara pushes me back. 'Go. And. Put awn. Yuh clothes!'

'*Which* clothes? Where are we going?'

'Which? Is foo-fool you foo-fool? You're going to take the exam! If you're late they won't let you in, so *hurry up*, change *out of your yaad clothes*, put on something decent, and LET'S GO!'

'Finally!' Mandy says triumphantly, as she swings open the grille. They flow inside my room, like a rush of water, Mandy grabbing my arms, Tamara whirling around my room, pulling out drawers, looking for clothes. I don't know if I'm more stunned that I'm being rescued by my friends, or that it's these two friends together.

'Pumkin, listen,' Mandy says, shaking me a little with each

word. 'We don't have time. We'll explain everything on the way but if you stand here any longer with your mouth open like a snapper, your mother will come back before we can leave. Do you want that? You want your mother to come back and find you still here? Or you want to come with us and take the test and go to Auntie Sophie? Which is it?'

I'm so confused my head is spinning. I don't even have a chance to answer Mandy — *Of course, of course*, I want to say, *yes, I want to go* — before Tamara shoves my school uniform at me.

'I don't know where anything is in here, just wear this,' she says, already pulling the T-shirt I'm wearing over my head.

The excitement of it all catches up to me. I wiggle out of my yaad clothes and into my school uniform, scurry around the room scooping up my backpack, then I stop in my tracks.

'The papers! My receipt — she tore everything up,' I cry, but Tamara waves her hand impatiently in front of my face.

'You don't *need* that, man, just *come!*'

We run out of my room, although Mandy turns around to lock the top padlock. Tamara stops to give her a funny look.

'I can't just leave it open like that!' Mandy says, and Tamara rolls her eyes and we run around the corner, down my little dirt driveway and through the rickety gate. Each of them holds my hand as we run down the street, like three little girls skipping, and they don't let go until we're almost at the bus stop. I hear a familiar *toot-too-too-toot* and Boots waves from across the road. We run over and leap into the car, all three of us squeezed up in the back, giggling and giggling from the thrill of whatever this is we're doing.

'Pumkin!' Boots bellows, then laughs and laughs as he peels away from the kerb.

'Boots! How did you . . . I don't even know . . .' but I'm out of breath and there's a stitch in my side, so I give up and lean back on the seat, looking from my friends to Boots and back again.

Tamara and Mandy can't talk either. They're breathing heavy but laughing so hard in between they can't catch their breath.

'Bwoy, Pumkin,' Boots says, glancing at me in the rear-view mirror. 'Bwoy, I tell you. First things first! We going to the exam centre now, so get your mind ready! And here, eat this.'

He takes one hand off the wheel to hand me a patty wedged into a cocoa bread. I take it but my stomach is too busy holding a carnival to bother about food, so I just hold it, enjoying the warmth of it.

'Oh, you have any more?' Tamara says, and Boots hands over another two.

'Why you put the patty in this bread?'

The car goes silent, all of us staring at Mandy, like she's an alien just suddenly beamed into the car.

'What?' she says.

'Yuh . . . yuh never have a patty in a cocoa bread yet?' Tamara asks.

Mandy shakes her head. 'No. Never. Why would I put an already bready thing in more bread?'

Tamara just stares and stares at Mandy, shaking her head slightly in disgust. Boots bursts out laughing, and I giggle because I'm completely freaked out to be having this conversation with these three people right now.

'Just try it, man!' Boots shouts.

Mandy shrugs and takes a bite. Everyone is silent as she

stretches her mouth over the patty and cocoa bread, as she chews and chews, moving her head slowly from side to side.

'It's just . . . so much bread,' she says, once she's swallowed, and both Tamara and Boots shout out in indignation and talk over each other, trying to explain why a patty in a cocoa bread is the greatest invention since the aeroplane, how it's the cheapest food that will fill your belly, how the slight sweetness of the cocoa bread pairs perfectly with the patty, as if they're talking about gourmet food. I watch them for a moment but then it really hits me: I'm free. I'm on my way to take the exam. I'm in the car with Boots and Tamara and *Mandy*.

'What is going on?' I yell, and everybody falls silent for a moment before they all start talking over each other again, but it sounds like chickens squawking and I can't make out a thing.

'What? What?' I keep saying, until Boots shouts, 'Awrite, *awrite*!' and bangs on the roof of the car, like a judge calling order.

'You eat, I will explain.'

So we all sit back and eat (Mandy pulls her patty out of the cocoa bread, causing Tamara to roll her eyes deeply and mutter about rich people wasting food) while Boots explains how he went to pick me up at Miss Keene's on Monday as always, how she'd told him I never turned up and she'd tried to call but the phone was disconnected, how he'd turned up at my house –

'I saw you! I tried to call out, but my mother . . . she . . .'

He reaches back for my hand and squeezes it before putting his on the steering wheel again. We're stuck in traffic, the windows down and the car so hot that my skin sticks to

Mandy's whenever our arms touch. I can smell the exhaust and it makes me feel lightheaded. I ask Boots if he can turn on the AC and he closes all the windows automatically. There's a blast of lukewarm air that feels as hot and heavy as outside, but eventually it starts to cool.

'I did think someting was off,' Boots continues. 'She told me you were sick, yuh modda, that you were staying home. I ask her if I can bring something for you but she say you don't need me for anything, and I mustn't come back around there. Something juss . . . never feel right, you know dem way deh?'

So Boots went back to Miss Keene to tell her he thought something was wrong. Then Mandy picks up the thread of the story. On Tuesday, when she went to L'École for class, Miss Keene asked her if I'd been at school. Of course she'd told her I hadn't, and that our homeroom teacher had asked the class if anyone knew where I was because I hadn't called in sick to school. So on Wednesday Mandy asked Tamara if she'd heard from me –

'And that was *very* weird,' Tamara jumps in, her mouth full of food.

'Yeah,' Mandy says, and they look at each other for a moment, something passing between them.

Anyways, Mandy convinced Tamara to check on me, so she came to the house –

'Wait, you came to the house?' I say, lunging forward in my seat to look at her.

'Yeah, and I asked for you and your mother told me the same thing she told Boots, that you were sick. And that's what she told Linnette too –'

'Hold on, *Linnette* came to the house?' Where was I, when all these people were at my door looking for me?

'*Yesss*, because she said something wasn't right with your pastry. She said they were all . . . burned up and, I dunno, weird, like, they never taste good any more, and people were complaining, and she knew something was wrong. So me and Linnette went to my mother.'

By then they'd all conferred and figured out that whatever it was that was going on was most likely designed to keep me from taking the exam.

'I mean, your mother is *never* at home, she never business before bout you – sorry to say it like that but you know it's true,' Tamara says, 'And then all of a sudden she's there every day, looking after you when you're sick? Right in the week when you have to take this test she don't want you to take? But you not sick enough to take a break from bakin? Riiiight . . .'

Miss Iona spent Thursday morning trying to figure out how to help me get out and, when she figured out a way, spent Thursday afternoon praying for forgiveness for what she was about to do. She told Linnette what to do, then she told Tamara to tell Mandy to tell Miss Keene to tell Boots. My mind spins when I think of this chain of people banding together to help me, like a weird kind of Telephone or those lines of people moving a bucket of water down the line to put out a house fire.

'But how did she get Paulette to leave?' I ask, when I think of this morning, Miss Iona coming to the house and calling my mother out.

'*Weeell*, she wouldn't tell us the details,' Tamara says,' but it was something about how Linnette just saw your fa– Akil with some woman, and that Linnette knew where they were and if she went right now she could catch him, or something like that.'

'That's it? *That*'s what got her to leave? She believed that?'

Tamara shrugs. 'Looks like.'

I lean back against the seat. That seems like a really weak story. I can't believe she fell for it. Didn't she wonder why Miss Iona, of all people, was telling her this? She must really be obsessed with Akil to just hear his name and take off like that.

'Wait, but how did Miss Iona get the keys?'

Tamara grins. 'Trevor.'

It takes me a moment, staring into her grinning face, to figure it out. And when I do, I laugh and laugh.

'That's your little brother, right?' Mandy says.

'Yup, my likkle teefin brodda!'

Miss Iona took Trevor with her, and while she explained to my mother that Akil was traipsing around town with some light-skin girl, Tamara's brother was quietly filching a set of keys out of her pocket.

'No *wonder* Miss Iona had to pray – she lied to my mother and then got her son to *steal*?' I squeal.

'Yes, and all of us have to do double time at church because of it so you better pass this test!'

The test. In all the excitement of being broken out, I'd forgotten that the test was the goal. I check the little plastic watch that's always on my wrist: it's just past one o'clock. The exam begins at 2:15 p.m., and if you get there one minute after 2 p.m., they won't let you in. Miss Keene had drummed that into me. *Make sure you're on time*, she'd said. *It would be tremendously foolish to miss this opportunity because of tardiness*. But we're still stuck in traffic and we're not even close to the centre.

My stomach does a little flip-flop thing and I squeeze into the space between the two front seats and ask Boots if he can drive any faster, but there's nowhere for him to go. We're pretty much parked. I lean back in my seat. *Why didn't they rescue me earlier?* I think, and then I feel bad for being so ungrateful. I'd just be sitting in my room staring up at the watermarks on my ceiling if it weren't for my friends. I look at them. Tamara is taking over-dramatic bites of her patty and cocoa bread and making little moans of pleasure while Mandy watches, her lips curled in disgust. It's surreal to see them together. Something fills up in my chest when I think of them working together, making plans with Boots and Miss Keene and Miss Iona just to help me.

'How come you —'

They both turn to me, but I'm looking straight at Tamara.

'I thought you — How come you're helping me now?'

She looks down at her hands, greasy with oil and full of patty flakes. Then she looks out of the window. The car lurches forward, then screeches back to a stop, the traffic moving like sludge. She glances at Mandy, who looks back at her, then shuffles forward in her seat to ask Boots what he does for a living.

'I'm a bearer,' Boots says, and Mandy asks him what that is and Tamara and I lock our eyes and roll them at this girl who doesn't seem to know anything.

'Is where she really come from?' Tamara asks, but she's smiling. 'Is the same Jamaica we live in?'

We giggle, then fall silent, rocking back and forth as the car moves and stops, moves and stops. Tamara takes a deep breath and says, 'I made a mistake. When I . . . when I told on you. At school. I shouldn't have done that. I'm really sorry, Pumkin. I'm really sorry I did that. But what I said to you at the barbecue, that was true. I just felt like, like . . . I dunno.'

She stops for a moment, takes another deep breath. 'Like, when we were smaller, we used to make fun of your auntie Sophie, how she was so stoosh and hoity-toity. But you just turned into another version of her. All you could talk about what was getting to France, France France France, all the time. And you were hanging out with . . .' she glances at Mandy, still talking to Boots, and lowers her voice '. . . all these stoosh people. Is like. I dunno. Like, you only remembered me when you had to use my house to bake. You didn't have time for me any more and you were planning to just — just leave me. And I was mad. I was mad that I wasn't good enough to be your friend any more. I was mad that I wasn't good enough to make you want to stay.'

I don't know what to say at first, when Tamara finishes. I can hear Mandy and Boots chatting but it's just background noise. I realize, for the first time, how selfish I've been. How much I complained about being alone, when all these people were going out of their way to help me.

'I guess I got a little obsessed,' I say, with a laugh, trying to ease the tension. Tamara gives me a look, her eyes wide, as if to say, 'You *think*!'

'I'm sorry too, T,' I continue. 'I didn't know you felt like that. It's just that you have Miss Iona and your dad and Trevor, right? You always have somebody who cares where you are, who makes sure you eat something, makes sure you do your homework. And I was . . . I mean, for real, I'm jealous. If we going to talk the truth. Sometimes it hurt to leave your house and come home to mine, after Auntie Sophie and Gramma were gone, when it was just me one there.'

The car lurches forward, throwing us all against the seats. Boots leans on his horn and yells, 'CLOWN!' at the taximan who decided to drive on the sidewalk to bypass the line of traffic. The entire lane of cars and half of the pedestrians are cussing the taximan, who waves them off with a flick of his hand as he careens down the sidewalk.

'Yuh gwaan til yuh kill smaddy!' a woman yells.

I turn back to Tamara. 'The truth is, T, I feel really confused. I want to go to Auntie Sophie – I do – but now that I have Boots and Miss Keene and Mandy and Linnette helping me, and I . . . I have you back again . . . I'm just . . . I'm just not so sure. You don't know what it's like to live in that house with my mother never there, or when she's there she treats me like a piece of furniture, to be all alone all the time and suddenly all these people come into my life and it feels like I have, like, some kind of family. But the thing is, all of it has this expiry date, right? If I don't pass this exam, if I don't go to Auntie Sophie, then . . . it won't stay like this. It will go back to how it was before and that's even worse, because now I know how nice it is to have people. So, it's not that I want to leave you behind, T. You're more than good enough to be my friend. Auntie Sophie, she taught me to focus on the wrong things, I think, but that's not really her fault either. But still I just . . . I just want to make it to her because she's all I have, really.'

She reaches across the seat and grabs my hand, squeezes it. 'She's not. Obviously,' she says, waving around the car. 'But I get it. Mandy . . . she called me a selfish cow.'

'What?'

'Yeah.' She laughs. 'She said a lot of things. But she was rallying everybody to help you and I thought, Man, I thought, *that should be me*. It should be me fighting to help my friend. So, yeah. She's all right, I guess, this stoosh gyal.'

'I can hear you, you know,' Mandy says.

Tamara pushes her playfully on the arm and says, 'Mind yuh business, man! Big people talkin.'

I smile at them ribbing each other, my heart full and heavy, and then the traffic opens up and we zoom away.

*

We peel into the exam centre on two wheels, all of us holding on to each other and squealing in the back seat. It's eight minutes to two when we arrive. We lost five minutes to the guard at the gate who wanted to see ID, exam registration papers, blood type, family history dating back to slavery. He took his sweet time looking up my name on a ratty piece of paper and finally waved us through when he found it there. I bolt out of the car, Tamara, Mandy and Boots cheering me on, and there is Miss Keene, staring out over the driveway, wringing her hands, a soft-looking satchel sitting at her feet. She starts waving me over immediately, *comecomecomecome*, and I am so happy to see her, the last in this chain of people propping me up, that I forget to be nervous about the exam until I get to the door.

There are around thirty children in the room, all seated and composed, some whispering to each other, some staring into space. Everyone's in their school uniforms, all from different schools, and I say a silent thanks to Tamara that I'm wearing mine too. The invigilator is a thin, wiry man with very round glasses and a moustache that looks like a fuzzy worm has fallen asleep on his top lip. Beside him is a woman with light brown hair swept up in some kind of fancy bun. She looks so polished she almost shines. I think she's the one who will do the verbal part of the test.

My nerves catch up with me. My stomach starts to cribble

and crabble and I can feel my hands shake. All this work to get here, all this effort . . . What if I fail? What if all of this was for nothing? What will I tell everyone, Tamara and Boots and Mandy? Miss Keene. Sophie! What will I tell them if I don't get through. I feel a little dizzy and my breath comes out in shallow little bursts. Dark clouds move in from the outside corners of my eyes and everything starts to look a little blurry. The man in my chest perks up. He's feeling neglected, I can tell, and now he's ready to thump thump THUMP!

Suddenly Miss Keene grabs me by the shoulders and turns me towards her. She's so short that we're pretty much eye to eye.

'All right, Miss Patterson. There's been a lot of excitement and palaver to get you here, but you're here now. So be *here, now.* I need you to breathe. A long breath in, and hold it. A long breath out. Come on, in and out. That's it.'

I keep my eyes on hers as I breathe like she tells me. Slowly the clouds around my eyes move away, my stomach calms down. The man in my chest is annoyed: he wants to do his drumming but the breathing won't let him, so he just presses against my chest instead, which isn't quite as bad. I breathe in. I hold it. I breathe out.

'We've been working towards this for a long time, Pumkin,' says Miss Keene. 'You are well-prepared, you are ready. You know what you have to do. You're one of my best students, you know? If anyone is going to pass this exam, it's you.'

She called me Pumkin.

'If you feel overwhelmed, just remember to breathe. We'll be right outside, waiting for you. You're not alone. Okay?'

I nod. Nod and nod and nod, like a bobble head. Miss

Keene reaches for the satchel and hands it to me, then pushes me gently through the door. I rush inside and find a seat, get settled. The wiry man looks pointedly at his watch and then at me, clearing his throat. The woman beside him is too involved in whatever she's reading to notice me. I open the satchel: there are notepads and different-coloured pens, pencils and erasers. I arrange everything on my desk and take more deep breaths. The boy sitting beside me catches my eye, gives me a big grin and a thumbs-up, which makes me smile.

I can do this, I think. *I'm ready.*

Don't put goat mout

'I failed. I know it.'

'What*ever*,' Tamara says.

'You did *not* fail,' Mandy says, around a mouthful of my coconut cake.

I push her shoulder and some of the cake crumbles to the ground.

'AAAH! Look what you doing! This thing is precious, man!' She stuffs the rest of the cake into her mouth, crumbs falling everywhere.

We're at school, under the tree as usual at lunchtime. It's been two weeks since my daring rescue, since I took the French exam.

It wasn't how I'd imagined it. I'd thought I'd breeze through the written part, babble on fluently in the verbal part. I'd thought the examiners would be so impressed with my skills that they'd tell me right there, on the spot: You're through! You've passed!

Instead, the polished lady was stone-faced, giving nothing away as she told me we were done and I could leave.

I packed my things back into the satchel Miss Keene had brought for me, slowly, slowly, my whole body feeling like a leg that had fallen asleep.

I was so numb, I barely reacted when she told me I could stay with her for a while, that we were heading to my house to pick up my stuff, that she'd clear things with my mother.

I thought Miss Keene probably didn't understand whom she was dealing with if she planned to just 'clear things' with my mother so I could stay at her house, but when we got to Potter's Lane it was dark and empty. Boots stayed in the car as Miss Keene and I cautiously let ourselves in, as I packed my schoolbooks into my backpack, grabbed up some clothes and squashed them against my chest. I saw Miss Keene looking around and wondered what she was thinking, if the house where she had grown up looked anything like this one, if it made her sad to be here, or happy that she'd made it out.

'She'll be so mad,' I'd said to her, my clothes bunched up in my arms.

She'd been staring at the dip in the middle of the mattress, but she looked at me and said, 'Don't you worry about that.'

Since then I've been staying in her guest room, which is upstairs and has its own little balcony and a big four-poster bed and a wide closet and a little kind of hassock thing that I can sit on when the panic that lives deep down in my stomach bubbles over and spreads throughout my body. When I feel like I'm falling and can't stop myself, that feeling just as you tip over, arms flailing, eyes wide. And to make matters worse, the man in my chest came with me. He punches and punches and punches me in the nighttime, shouting that I've failed, failed the exam, disappointed everyone, that I'll never see Sophie again, that Miss Keene will tell me to go home, that Boots will disappear. That I'll be stuck here with my mother, who doesn't want me but likes to have me, just out of malice, who hasn't called or looked for me since the day I disappeared from the house, even though we left word with Miss Iona to let her know where I am — I didn't want to do that, but Miss

Keene said she didn't want to get arrested for kidnapping so we had to.

There's three things holding me together. One: Boots and Grace come over for dinner a lot. They're officially together now, and I'm happy when I see Boots's wide smile when he looks at her, even though it hurts a little bit when I think about what could have been with me and him and Sophie. Miss Keene cooks and we all sit together and I stay mostly quiet and listen to them chat and it feels . . . good.

Two: Sophie and I talk more often now. She couldn't believe her sister went 'to such lengths' to keep me from taking the exam and I wonder how she could already have forgotten who her sister really is. She calls every few days on those phone cards. She and Miss Keene talk a lot now too, but Miss Keene always sends me upstairs so I can't hear what they're discussing.

Three: I'm baking again – like, properly baking, not the angry pastry I was making while my mother locked me up but my usual sweet, soft, fluffy, tasty puddings and cakes. Miss Keene won't allow me to bake for sale right now because I have to study for end-of-year exams – which she had to explain to Linnette, who was not best pleased about the hit her shop would take – but I can bake for fun, for my friends. Boots says my customers at the embassy are going through withdrawal, and Grace says her colleagues at the building society ask her every day if there's anything, anything at all?

'Listen, you need to stop stressing,' Tamara says, as she rips open a bag of Cheese Trix. 'We still have end-of-years to get through and you have to pass those too. You don't have time to stress about a French test that we all know you passed.'

'No, but don't put goat mout on me!' I say, knocking on the wood of the tree, which makes Tamara roll her eyes.

'I don't understand,' Mandy says, now that she's swallowed the cake, 'why you can't just go to your aunt. I mean, even if you failed – *which you didn't!* but let's just pretend for a minute you did – why does it matter? Why can't you just move?'

'I have to pass the exam to show my French proficiency so I can be accepted into a school,' I say, like a robot, reciting what Sophie's told me a million times already. 'But my mother still has to sign over legal guardianship or something like that. Or else, I dunno, people could just kidnap children and take them to France, I guess.'

'What *I* don't understand is why your mother won't just do that,' Tamara says. 'I mean, no disrespect, right? But she obviously don't want to be your mother. She's like . . . I mean, wouldn't she prefer if you were gone? No disrespect.'

'My mother would cut off her nose to spite her face. That's why.'

There isn't anything to say after that so we all fall silent, looking at the other students wandering around the school, leaning our heads back and enjoying the breeze, listening to Tamara crunch away at her Cheese Trix. Eventually the bell for class rings. We start packing up our things, but not two seconds later Miss Smith materializes in front of us like a particularly nasty fart and shouts, 'It's time for class! Get up from under this tree!'

'We're *going*, Miss – Jeez,' Mandy says, as we stand up, pulling on our backpacks. I notice Miss Smith doesn't say anything about her tone, doesn't glare at her or tell her to check her attitude. She only glares at me, her face in a sneer. I want to stare her down but I don't have the energy today. I look at the ground as I walk away, feeling her gaze on my neck.

'Wow, she really does not like you,' Mandy says.

'I can't wait till you pass that test and she finds out you're moving to France and you can just *shove it in her face*,' Tamara says, glancing back at the teacher. She's standing there watching us, watching me, even though other girls are taking their sweet time getting to class.

'Don't put goat mout, Tamara!' I say, looking around for some wood to knock, settling for my own head when I don't find anything else.

★

When I get home, Miss Keene is sitting at the dining table, nervously chewing her ballet-slipper pendant. I've never seen Miss Keene look nervous, so I get nervous.

'I failed!' I huff out, my backpack sliding off my arm and falling weakly to the floor. My stomach is churning. I need to use the bathroom.

Miss Keene looks up at me, startled. 'What?'

'I failed the test. Don't it?'

'What . . . Why would you say that?'

'Because you look worried.'

'Oh. Oh, Lord, no, no, it's not about your exam results. Those haven't arrived.'

She's taken the pendant out of her mouth but she's rubbing it between her fingers, looking off into the distance.

'Well, what is it, then?'

'What?'

'Miss Keene!'

She glances at her watch and gives her head a little shake. 'Sorry, sorry, it's . . . They're a little late, that's all.'

Now it's my turn to say, 'What? Who's late, Miss Keene?'

But before she can answer I hear the *toot-too-too-toot* and I let out the breath I was holding. It's only Boots, and maybe Grace. I look confusedly at Miss Keene – why is she in such a tizzy about Boots and Grace being late? – but she's jumped out of her seat and flung the front door open, leaning half her body outside. I shake my head and roll my eyes. Adults are weird sometimes. I hoist my backpack higher on my shoulder and start making my way up the stairs to change my clothes. I check my watch: Boots and Grace are a little too early for dinner but, whatever, I'll come back down and find out what all the fuss is about.

I'm halfway up the stairs when I hear it.

'You wouldn't *believe* the traffic, Bev. It's like every striking soul on this island has a car!'

The voice stops me in my tracks. My stomach lurches up into my throat and sticks there, so for a minute I think I'm choking. I'm completely frozen, my limbs stuck in place, my backpack sliding uselessly down my shoulder and falling to the floor with a thwack.

'Oh, my gosh!' the voice says, closer now, inside the door. 'Oh, my gosh, Pumkin!'

I don't want to turn around because I know it can't really be. It'll be a ghost. Or a figment of my imagination. I'm having an auditory hallucination and I don't want my eyes to confirm that she's not really there. But I hear it again, the voice.

'Pumkin,' it says, so softly it pierces my heart, which starts to bleed. Finally I turn around and there she is, Sophie, standing in the doorway, her eyes wide and liquidy, staring at me, gripping the handle of a small wheely suitcase. She looks the same but different. I wait for her to disappear, to dissolve into

320

the atmosphere, but she remains resolutely, solidly there. We stand like that for what feels like an eternity until all the energy that got pulled out of me comes crashing down over me, like a tidal wave. I push a weird kind of shrieky yelp out of my blocked throat and run to my aunt, tackling her in a hug that pushes her backwards.

'Pumkin!' she says, squeezing me into her.

'Pumkin,' she says, kissing the top of my head.

'My Pumkin,' she says, wiping my tears away with her thumb.

'I'm here,' she says.

'I'm here.'

*

We bake a cake. After we put all her bags in the guest room – 'I hope you won't mind sharing with me again,' she laughed – and I change out of my school uniform, we go straight to the kitchen.

'You have no idea how much I've missed your baking, Pumkin – although I obviously don't need to be eating any more sweets!'

She moves her hand down her figure, which is still trim. I've been staring at her since she came in, looking her up and down, taking all of her in, and she's exactly the same as the last time I saw her two years ago. Exactly the same but drastically different. She's wearing her hair differently, in a cinnamon-bun thing at the back of her head that I immediately want to copy, and her clothes are different but it's not that: it's some-thing in her face that's changed. But her eyes are still big and bright, her smile when she looks at me just as wide.

Miss Keene insists that she take a nap to get the edge off

the jet lag but Sophie says she wants to try to make it through until bedtime, to regulate her body clock.

'You'll need a clear head, Sophie, for later . . .'

But Miss Keene trails off when Sophie glances at me and shakes her head slightly. I pretend I don't see it because I'm too excited about having my aunt right here beside me in the kitchen, baking like we used to. At least, I bake and Sophie sits on the kitchen stool and peppers me with questions, tells me about her life in Marseille, dips her finger into the mixing bowl to get at the batter. By the time I get the cake tins into the oven, Sophie's head is dipping forward and she grudgingly accepts that Miss Keene is right: she has to take a nap. She heads upstairs and I finish the cakes, then go up and sit on the hassock thing, try to study while Sophie sleeps, but I'm too distracted by her presence.

The sun is still high in the sky when Miss Keene knocks gently on the door and wakes Sophie. 'Sleep too long and you'll feel worse,' she says, as Sophie rubs her eyes. Her hair has pulled out of the cinnamon bun and it's so much longer now than when she left.

'It's almost time to go,' Miss Keene whispers to Sophie, but not low enough that I miss it. Sophie, still half asleep, mumbles something I don't understand, drags herself out of the bed and into the bathroom. I hear the spray of the shower. I wonder what it's almost time for. Only now that the fizz of the excitement has melted away do I start to wonder what my aunt is doing here, suddenly, after two years away.

When she comes out she's all put together again, her hair back in the cinnamon bun, a sleeveless, silky-looking blouse tucked into loose red pedal-pushers, a slim brown belt at her waist. *Will I look like that*, I wonder, *when I live in —*

'Why are you here, Auntie Sophie?' I blurt out, startling her as she twists a small earring into her lobe.

'What a question!' She laughs, screwing the earring's partner into the other.

She looks at me in the mirror and laughs, but I set my face in stone and stare back. I know something's happening. I want to know what it is. She must see the resolve on my face because she sighs and her shoulders drop. She turns and walks towards me, crouches, holds my hands in hers, looks me straight in my eyes. 'I'm here for you, Pumkin.'

'For . . . for me?'

'Yes. I'm here to take you home. With me, to Marseille.'

My heart soars up, a giddy sense of elation whirling around until it crashes right into a big rock of reality.

'But the test, Auntie Sophie . . . I didn't . . .'

'I'm not worried about that test. I know you've passed it —'

'*Don't put goat mout* —'

'No goat mout, Pumkin! Listen, I know what you're capable of. I feel it in my soul that you got through with this exam, and you have to believe it too.'

'And Mama? You said . . . you said I couldn't go unless she let me. Is she letting me go?'

Sophie drops her hands, looks away, heaves a heavy sigh. She sets her jaw. 'She will. She's going to.'

But it sounds like she's talking to herself. She has a look on her face like she's going hunting, determined this time to take down the beast. My chin sinks into my chest. Does she think it will be any better now? Now that she's come back in her fancy clothes and her cinnamon-bun hair, with her new air of experience, does she think my mother's going to say, 'I was wrong before, I've changed my mind, *now* you can have her!'

I shake my head. Sophie thinks the power of thinking positive is enough, but she wasn't in that exam centre as I stuttered and stumbled my way through. And her wishes aren't strong enough to break down the hardened walls of my mother's heart.

A rap on the door makes me jump.

'We should go, Sophie. Boots is here,' says Miss Keene.

'Go where?' I ask, as Sophie stands up, goes searching for her handbag.

'We shouldn't be too long. Can you manage on your own?' Miss Keene continues, as if I didn't just ask her a question.

Can I manage on my own? I want to laugh at the question, but instead I try desperately not to roll my eyes.

'But where you going?'

Sophie clears her throat. 'We're going to see your mother,' she says.

I stare at her while I try to grab on to one of the thoughts whizzing through my head.

'Listen,' Sophie says. She's looped her bag across her body, come back over and put her hands on my shoulders. 'I don't want you to worry about all this, Pumkin. We're going to take care of everything.'

Miss Keene is nodding along, her back stiff and straight as always, shoulders back.

'I expect you to get some studying done, yes?' she says, and they leave without waiting for my response. They get halfway down the stairs before I burst out of the room.

'I want to come!' I blurt out.

'I don't think that's wise,' Miss Keene says, shaking her head. She continues down the stairs, grabs the keys from the little nook underneath.

'Please, Miss Keene, Auntie Sophie? I'm not going to study – I won't be able to concentrate!'

'No, no, this is not a situation where you –'

'PLEASE! It's . . . This is about my life! I need to know . . . It's not fair. I had to do it all by myself. It's not fair that I can't see what's going on now – it's not fair! Please.'

Miss Keene and Sophie look at each other. I hear the slam of Boots's car door, the crunch of his shoes on the short driveway. The thought of everyone deciding my fate without me makes me want to throw up.

'Please. If you don't take me with you I'll – I'll get the bus! I'll turn up there anyway! I need to know what's happening.'

Miss Keene huffs out a breath and waves a hand at Sophie. *It's your choice* that wave says. She opens the door for Boots before he can knock, nods at him. I can't see him, just hear the jangle of his keys and his booming voice as he says, 'Eevlin, eevlin. You ready, Miss Keene?'

Sophie looks back at me. I'm still standing at the top of the stairs, one hand wrapped around the banister.

'Yes, we're ready,' she calls. 'Come on, then,' she says to me, and a thrill of electricity blasts through my body as I run down the stairs. We get into the car, Miss Keene in the front, Sophie and I in the back. We strap ourselves in. We're off to see my mother.

Jones!

The sun is still bright in the sky as we drive down to Potter's Lane and, in no time at all, we're turning onto the narrow little street. Boots has to slow as the car dips low in the deep potholes and makes its way back up, like the world's least exciting roller-coaster. We pass Robbie and Junior sitting on the wall as usual, the two boys peering curiously into the car as we drive by. I wonder what Robbie does when Junior is in school. Ten minutes into the ride, Sophie had unstrapped her seatbelt and pushed herself forward to whisper whisper whisper to Boots and Miss Keene in the front. I strained my ears so hard I got a headache but I didn't catch anything. Now, as we dip and tumble down the Lane, Boots turns down the radio and says in a low low voice, 'Yuh tink him gwen come?'

Sophie glances at me and I pretend to be absorbed in watching two little kids playing hopscotch on the sidewalk, but if I were a dog you'd be able to see my ears turned towards Miss Keene, who is talking so softly softly that her voice is like a little murmur of water flowing in a wild overgrown wood full of screeching beasts.

'He said he would,' she says. '*Grudgingly*,' she adds.

I want to ask who 'he' is but I obviously can't do that if I've been pretending not to listen and, anyway, we've just pulled up in front of the house. I was half hoping we'd find it dark and empty but the living-room lights are on and I can see the flickering of the TV. Boots kills the engine and I shuffle over

in the back seat, ready to open the door, but nobody moves
except to take off their seatbelts. I look first at Sophie, then at
Miss Keene, then at Boots, but they just sit there without saying anything, so I lean back against my seat, thoroughly
confused. The silence in the car is thick and tense, like wet
concrete slowly slowly hardening. I think Miss Keene must
feel it too because all of a sudden she gives her head a little
shake and mutters something and opens her door.

'Sophie, a word.'

I lean back over to open my door too, but she looks at me
and tells me to stay in the car for now. They have things to
discuss before we get started. *Get started with what?* I want to
ask but I know I'm not going to get anything out of her, so I
just roll my eyes and flop back against the seat as the women
leave the car. They walk far enough away that I can't eavesdrop. I lean my arm on the window, then my chin on my
arm, and look back up the street. Robbie and Junior are staring at us from their wall. The two kids who were trying to
play hopscotch have abandoned the game and are tearing up
and down the street, yelling. A stray dog, brown and black
and scrawny, is staring after them with its tongue out, looking like it can't decide whether to join in or give chase or lie
down.

'Is it weird?' I ask Boots, suddenly.

'Ay?'

I turn my cheek flat onto my arm.

'Is it weird . . . seeing Auntie Sophie again?'

I hear him shuffle shuffle in his seat.

'Naw,' he says, a little unconvincingly, I think. 'Naw, man.
Everyting criss.'

I don't say anything. I want to know what it is we're doing

here. I want to know who is the mystery 'he' who might or might not come and what he's going to do when he gets here. I want to know how my mother's going to react when she sees us, especially Sophie. I want to know why adults don't just tell you what's going on instead of leaving your imagination to run wild and stress you out.

'Is a long time ago, yuh nuh?' Boots continues, even though I'd dropped the subject. 'I'm with Grace now, yuh nuh.'

'Who are we waiting on, Boots?'

'Ay?' he says, even though I know he's heard me, but before I can repeat the question, a big silver SUV turns the corner up the road and starts to make its way towards us. I lift my head to watch it as it navigates the potholes as slowly as Boots did, even though I'm sure the driver can't feel a thing in that car. It's as big as a boat. Robbie crosses his arms and leans back, watching the car as it drives past, Junior peering so far forward from his perch on the wall it makes me think of Humpty Dumpty. I can't see Robbie's face so clearly from here but just the way he's standing makes it clear he's planning to do something to this car if it stops here. Scratch it, steal it, mash up the windows, take off the tyres . . .

Miss Keene and Sophie are also watching the car as it pulls up to the house and stops. I scooch to the other side of the back seat for a better look. The door opens and I see an old white-looking man with close-cropped white hair in waves on his head. He's gathering something up from the passenger seat and his face is grim: his mouth is pressed into an almost straight line, his forehead drawn together so the skin between his eyes folds deeply over itself. He gets out of the car, some papers and a dark leather purse thing clutched to his chest. He slams the door and points the keys at it, which makes the car beep twice very loudly, the headlights blinking with each beep, and then he turns and looks straight at the two boys up the street.

Robbie is still staring with his arms crossed in front of his chest. Junior is peering over Robbie's shoulder. The man stares back at Robbie. He's old but his back is straight and I can feel the authority coming off him even from where I'm sitting, like the heat that wavers above the road sometimes. Robbie and the man stare at each other and some worldless conversation is happening between them. Miss Keene and Sophie look at each other, shrug and shake their heads, look back at this weird standoff. The man and Robbie stare at each other some more until, suddenly, Robbie kisses his teeth – I can't hear him but I can see that he's done it – and flings both his hands after the old man. *I can't be bothered with all this foolishness*, his hands say, as he turns around and walks away, slowly. Junior looks between the old man and Robbie a few times, clearly as confused about what just happened as I am. Then Robbie shouts something and Junior jumps off the wall and follows him, glancing back at the man every few seconds.

The old man watches the boys until they've left the street. Then he turns and assesses Sophie, who almost looks like she's wilting from the heat of his gaze. She puts her hands on her hips, crosses them in front of her chest, drops them by her sides, puts her hands together to pick at the cuticles, drops them down by her sides again.

'I'm . . . Sophie,' she says eventually, putting her hand to her chest in case he's not aware she's talking about herself. 'I'm . . . I don't know what to call –'

'Jones!' he barks, with one gruff nod.

Miss Keene steps forward, her hand outstretched. 'Mr Jones,' she says. 'I'm Beverley Keene, we spoke on the –'

'Yes, yes, let's just get this done with,' he interrupts, pushing past them both towards the gate of the house.

Miss Keene glances at Sophie and puts an arm gently round my aunt's shoulders. Boots, still in the car, chuckles to himself, shakes his head. I gawp at the old man. *Jones?*

'Are there dogs on the premises?' he asks. His accent is round and delicate, even though he is gruff and sour. Now that he's closer to me I can see it clearly, the shape of his face, his nose.

'No, no dogs. There are no dogs. Right, Pumkin?'

The old man's head whips around to me. His eyes pin me down. They are Sophie's eyes, hazel green, although hers are soft and liquidy and his are sharp like a hawk's, even though he's old.

'N-n-no,' I say, shaking my head.

'I assume this is the child in question?' Jones says, still staring at me. I want to look at Sophie but I can't peel my eyes away. What is he doing here? What would make Sophie call her grandfather, the man who was so scandalized by her existence that he paid to keep her away? And why did he answer her call? Is she less scandalous now, with her light brown skin and her cut-glass accent, her education, her job in France? If his face is anything to go by, I'd say no: he looks like he's bitten into a mouldy lemon. For the first time ever I feel a pang of pity for Sophie. I don't think she's used to people looking at her like that, taking her measure and finding her wanting. But, still, he's here, this man who never was here for her before.

'Yes, this is Pumkin. I . . . This is Akisha. I call her Pumkin.'

331

She laughs a little, a nervous little tinkle, but Jones just stares at me a moment longer, then glances into the car at Boots, looks at Sophie, and says, 'Let's get this over with, then. I don't have all night.'

He pushes open the gate, which promptly sticks fast in the ground. He pushes and pushes it savagely, like that gate was the one who seduced his teenage son and threw his family into turmoil. The noise of it screeching and rubbing against the concrete sets off the dogs next door, which sets off the rest of them around the whole neighbourhood.

'You have to lift it,' I shout, over the noise of his aggravated assault. He pauses, lifts the gate and opens it the whole way. Miss Keene and Sophie share a hidden little laugh and follow Jones onto the driveway. Boots settles into his seat, clearly not invited to the party inside, but I'm definitely going to crash it. I scramble out of the car, almost tripping over the bundle of seatbelts hanging loose, slam the door behind me and run up to the adults. I can't imagine what it is we're here to do or what role Sophie's grandfather has to play, but I'm about to find out.

Sold

Jones knocks authoritatively on the door, three strong knocks. I wonder if my mother will think it's the police. Nothing happens for a moment. He clutches his bag to his chest and looks up at the top of the door, like he's wondering what the hell he's doing here and hoping he can find the answer there. Miss Keene stands just behind and to the left of him, Sophie behind her, and I'm behind Sophie, my eyes trained on the back of Jones's head. I want to ask Sophie what he's doing here, but I'm too afraid he'll hear me. I'm sure his ears are as sharp as his eyes. He huffs in irritation and knocks three times again, louder than before.

'Open up, Miss . . . What is the woman's name again?'

'MacNally,' Miss Keene supplies.

'Miss MacNally! Open up, please!' he shouts, as he knocks on the door again, one two three, bang bang bang!

There's another moment of tense silence. Then I hear my mother's voice sounding smaller than I've ever heard it: 'Who is that?'

'Audley Jones, Esquire, ma'am! Please open up. We have things to discuss and I do not intend to be here longer than is necessary.'

Miss Keene turns to Sophie, one eyebrow cocked high up, almost to her hairline. *The audacity*, the eyebrow says.

I know, right? Sophie's wide eyes respond.

Miss Keene clears her throat and turns back. She holds her

hand behind her. Sophie reaches out and gives it a squeeze. *She'll never open the door,* I think, so I'm surprised when I see my mother's face appear in a slim crack of light. Her eyes are wide as she looks at Jones in confusion, scans over Miss Keene. They scrunch up when they rest on Sophie. Her forehead furrows deeply and, all of a sudden, I feel hot. She opens her mouth to spit something out, but just then, Akil wrenches the door open, causing me and Miss Keene to jump.

'Is who –' he begins, but Jones cuts him off.

'Miss MacNally, we are here in the interest of this child. May we come in?' he asks, but doesn't wait for an answer before he pushes his way through the door. Akil stumbles back, his face stuck somewhere between surprise, confusion and anger.

'Hold on, hold on,' Akil says, recovering himself as we all trudge into the house. It seems even smaller now with so many people bundled into it. I've only been at Miss Keene's a few weeks but it feels like I've been gone a whole lifetime, like my house has shrunk in the meantime, the paint peeled off a little more, the dirt accumulated. I look around the space that my grandmother had kept so clean, that I'd kept clean, now in disarray, and I feel a pang of embarrassment. I wonder if Akil lives here now. I wonder if they thought I was never coming back. I wonder if my mother cared.

'Is wah really ah gwaan here?' Akil continues, his head swivelling from Jones to Miss Keene to Sophie and back again. He doesn't look at me at all.

'Who are you, sir?' Jones asks.

Akil huffs out a laugh. 'I am Akil,' he says, and I notice he's trying to curl his accent. 'Who are *you?*'

334

'Do you have any connection to this child?' Jones asks, ignoring the question.

'Him is the father,' my mother says. She's still staring at Sophie, murder in her eyes.

'So she seh . . .' Akil adds. He laughs a little as he says it, but then a thought seems to cross his mind. 'Ay, I not *payin* for *nutten*, you hear? I neva ask fi nuh pickney!'

'We're not here about child support, Mr . . .?'

'Patterson,' Akil says warily.

'Patterson,' Jones mutters softly to himself as he walks the few steps to the dining table. His eyes flick across the surface, looking for somewhere to put down his documents, but it's covered with dirty plates and cups, balled-up napkins, sticky rings from old mugs of cocoa. He clears his throat, turns towards the sofa and rests the papers on the back.

'Well, this may also concern you, Mr Patterson. Miss Mac-Nally, as I'm sure you're aware, Miss Sophie . . . Jones would like to take over legal guardianship of the child.'

It seems like he almost choked on Sophie's last name. His last name.

'Is what you really seh you doing here?' my mother spits at Sophie. Her hands curl into fists and her face screws up in anger. 'I tell you areddi, you *not* getting her.'

'Yes, yes,' Jones says. 'I've been told you're resistant to the idea. May I ask why?'

'Wha?' my mother says.

'Why are you unwilling to hand over legal guardianship?' he says very slowly, enunciating each syllable, as if my mother is slow.

We all look at her. Her mouth is opening and closing like a fish's. I can see she's intimidated by this pass-for-white,

335

uptown man with his crystal accent and his big words. I'm curious if she'll tell him outright that it's not that she cares about me, it's just that she doesn't want Sophie to get what she wants. But it's Akil who answers.

'But see yah,' he says, laughing. 'Den she need a reason to keep her owna pickney?'

'It is certainly her prerogative to maintain guardianship of her own child, yes,' Jones says. Akil's chest puffs up, like he got a question correct in class. 'However, by all accounts, Miss MacNally, you are either unwilling or incapable of taking care of the child yourself. I have reports of severe neglect, Miss MacNally, reports that you are not fulfilling your *responsibilities* as a parent. I'm told, by several witnesses –'

'*Witness?*' my mother interjects.

'– that this child is practically raising herself. I'm told that she is subject to verbal and sometimes physical abuse. I'm told you kept her locked up here in the home, that you've taken no interest in her education, that you take, in fact, no interest in the child herself. Are those accounts incorrect, Miss MacNally?'

'What *witness?*' my mother says, glancing at Akil. He shrugs and leans back on the edge of the dining table.

'That is inconsequential at this time, Miss MacNally. My question to you is, are those accounts false? Are you, in fact, financially and morally prepared to care for this child until she comes of age?'

'I –'

'Are you prepared to be here at home with the child, to make sure there's enough food for her to eat, ensure that she's maintaining her grades at school? Can you afford to pay for her education? Can you afford to pay for her clothes and books and all the things you need to raise a child?'

'But see y—'

'Because it seems, Miss MacNally, you haven't done a good job of that so far. In fact, it doesn't seem that you've been doing this job at all. It was first your mother and then Miss Jones who took responsibility for this child until now. Is that correct?'

'That is —'

'Miss MacNally, if you wish to maintain guardianship of this child, that is well within your rights, but now that I've been made aware of the state of *care* this child is receiving, I can promise you that I will take a particular interest. I do not take these reports of neglect and abuse lightly. I can have you arrested, Miss MacNally, and the child remanded as a ward of the court. As an officer of the court, I have the authority to have this child monitored for the next four years. That means your actions will be under scrutiny, Miss MacNally. We will be watching you closely to make sure you are present and accountable for this child's development. And should we see further instances of neglect, or abuse, we will be prepared to prosecute you to the full extent of the law.'

My mother had been trying to get a word in during Jones's little speech but now she falls silent. Her face has gone grey, her fists shaking by her side. Akil is looking from her to Jones, like he's watching a tennis match. My heart is melting into my stomach. I can feel the panic rising up to my throat. *This is why we're here?* To force my mother to be nicer to me? To force her to raise me right? What about France? What about Sophie? I look at my aunt but she's staring steadfastly at my mother. Miss Keene catches my eye and makes a 'calm, calm' gesture with her hand. *Just relax*, that hand says, so I try to

337

breathe deep, although my breath starts catching in my chest. Suddenly Akil laughs.

'You mussi come from *well* uptown,' he says to Jones. 'Is not suh we do tings here. Pickney haffi *work*.'

'Not according to the law, Mr Patterson. However, there is an alternative, and that is to transfer guardianship to Miss Jones, who is prepared to continue taking care of the child in all the ways a parent *should*. She will take over all financial responsibility, ensure she continues her education, and you, well, you will be free to live as you wish, Miss MacNally. As you've been doing up until now, except this time not at the expense of a minor child. You will have no further responsibilities to fulfil. The choice is yours, Miss MacNally, but it must be made now.'

At this Jones taps the neat pile of documents at his side, perches on the back of the sofa and folds his hands one over the other. For someone who was in such a rush before, he seems now like he has all the time in the world. My mother's chest is heaving. I want to scoot closer to Sophie but I'm afraid to move and break whatever spell Jones just threw out over the living room. We all stand around awkwardly for a very long moment.

'Paulette,' my aunt says softly, breaking the silence. 'Paulette, please. I know that you have no love for me, but I can give Pumkin such a great life, I can –'

'Her name is *Akisha*!' my mother shouts. 'And I don't business what you cyan give her. You too wanty wanty. Is not everyting you want you gwen get, dat you haffi learn.'

'But this isn't about me, Paulette. This is about Pum– Akisha, and what's best for her,' Sophie pleads. 'She's just a child, she can't be . . . she can't be here living alone and taking care of herself. She needs a parent, Paulette.'

'Tcha!' my mother says, flicking her hand at Sophie.

Sophie exhales slowly and looks helplessly at Jones, but his gaze is locked on my mother. Another tense silence descends over the room until the sound of Akil kissing his teeth tears into it. He crosses his arms and looks at my mother.

'Why you don't just sign the paper dem?' he says. 'The whole of this business just . . . chu. Piece a palaver.'

My mother looks at him, surprise etched on her face.

'Because . . . because why she muss always get what she want?' she says, in a whiny voice, like a little kid about to throw a tantrum. 'Everyting she want, she get. Why she muss have her too?'

'Well, what is it that *you* want, Miss MacNally?' Jones asks. 'I think you've made it clear that you don't actually want to be a parent, so, what is it that you actually want?'

My mother looks startled at the question, so startled that she has no answer at all. I don't think anyone's ever asked her what she wants. I feel a little sorry for her that no one has ever cared about her. *But I cared*, I think, and the pity hardens in my chest, like a marble. She's looking at Jones with her mouth open.

'What I want?' she says.

'Yes, Miss MacNally,' Jones says, with a sigh, like he's heavy with fatigue, or negotiating with a four-year-old. 'What do you want?'

She turns and looks at me for a very long moment, and hope begins to crawl its way out of its hiding place in my stomach. Will she choose me? Does she want me? And if she does, what does that mean? But then she tears away her gaze

339

and locks it onto Akil, and the hope storms its way back into its hiding place and slams the door. I can see it very clearly: she wants him. She's only ever wanted him. But keeping hold of him is like trying to keep a grip on a handful of sand. I'm only fourteen and even I can see that. He looks back at her and opens his eyes wide, and wider, like he's trying to tell her something. Then he says, in an almost whisper, 'Ask him for money, nuh!'

As if we're not all in this tiny room together. As if we all can't hear him.

'Gwaan nuh? If she want her suh bad, then you can get summ'n out of it!' he says, a little louder.

My mother looks at Akil. She has a weird expression on her face. I don't know what it means.

'You don't hear what the man seh?' Akil continues. 'You want the whole a the government people faas up in yuh business? Cuz you deh pon yuh own with dat, me nuh eena dat deh business! Yuh on yuh *own*. Me? I woulda tek some funds, set up myself. No responsibility? Chu, easy decision dat.'

He throws up his hands. *I said what I said*, his hands say. I want to ask him what responsibility he's ever taken for anything. I want to ask him who he thinks he is to weigh in on this decision. But all the words are knotted up with emotion and stuck in my throat and, anyway, I'm too afraid to speak. My mother looks at him for a very long moment, but he doesn't look back at her. He's studying his nails. The tension in the room presses against my arms, squeezing me tight, like I've been stuffed into a too-small coffin. My mother sidles up closer to Akil.

'Dat is what yuh want?' she asks him, her voice close to a whisper.

340

He shrugs carelessly, still picking at his nails. She licks her lips and steps even closer.

'And then . . .' she whispers '. . . and then yuh gwen stay, Akil?'

He shrugs again, makes a noise in his throat. 'Look here nuh, I neva ask fi nuh pickney, yuh see mi?' he says. 'Me nuh eena dat pickney-raising business. Man a man. It woulda be different if it was a yoot, still.' He sighs and shifts to his other leg, moves on to the nails on his other hand, pick pick pick. 'But, yuh nuh, if we get likkle funds, cyan start a business, set up weself . . . then, yuh nuh?' He nods slowly, nod nod nod, pick pick pick.

My mother stares a moment longer then straightens her back and looks at Jones. I can see the hope in her eyes, the image of her and Akil together, no unwanted daughter standing in their way, as clear in her eyes as if I was watching a show on TV. She thinks I'm the reason he won't stay around, hasn't been around since I was born. She looks at Sophie, and her mouth curls in a snarl. She's spent all of my life dangling me over Sophie's head, the only bit of leverage she's had over her sister, but now she has to choose: her happiness, or her bitterness.

The sisters look at each other, like two cowboys in a standoff, until my mother turns back to Jones and nods once, twice, three times.

'Yes. Yes, that's what I want.'

'You want money,' Jones says, not as a question, but as though he always knew it would come to this. He looks at me for the first time since we've come inside, as if he'd forgotten entirely that I'm here. He shakes his head a little, then looks to Sophie. 'Does the child need to be here for this?'

'Come, Pumkin, let's go outside,' says Miss Keene.

'I don't want to go outside,' I say, the panic rising up in my throat, pushing through my fear of speaking in front of Jones. I want to know what's going to happen. Sophie has no money: that's what she's told me since she moved away: *Money's tight, Pumkin. I'm working as hard as I can.*

'It's best you come outside,' Miss Keene says, using her hand to usher me out.

'If she's going to sell me, I want to know for how much!' I shout. 'I want to know how much I'm worth!'

Everyone falls silent. I look at my mother and she meets my eye. For a moment it seems she's in pain, her forehead scrunched up, her mouth slightly open, her hand stretched just a little towards me, like she wants to say something, but then her eyes slide away from mine and find a place on the floor, just like that day in the VP's office.

'It's best you go outside.' He says it gently. Even as I stare at my mother, even as I stare at *Paulette*, I have time to wonder at all the different sides of this man. He's like a bunch of different characters rolled up into one person.

'I don't *want* to –'

'Do you want to go and live with your aunt?'

I hesitate, still looking at Paulette. What I *want* is for her to fight for me. I *want* her to want me. I want to be enough for her. I want her to love me. Or, at least, I want not to care that she doesn't.

But I know now, for the first time I *really* know, that she never will. And it feels like someone scooped out the last bit of ice cream from the tub, the last bit of hope being scraped out of my gut. Then Sophie takes my hand, soft and gentle, and rubs her thumb over the back. I look at her and she's gone all wavy and blurry, but still I can see her face. I *love you*, her face says. I'*m fighting for you*.

So I take a deep, hot breath and say, as firmly as I can, 'Yes.'

'Then, please, go outside. Let me do my job.'

And even though he's gentle, there's no more room for argument. Miss Keene reaches for my free hand again and says, 'Come, Pumkin. Come.'

Sophie squeezes my hand and lets me go. I blink away the blur in my eyes and glance at my mother one last time, but she is staring at Akil. He's looking at me now, though, a smile playing around his lips, and I want to slap it so hard off his face that I huff and flash Miss Keene's hand away and storm out of the front door, Miss Keene following close behind me.

She love you bad bad

Outside the sun has set but it's not dark yet, the sky still a dying blue, streaks of red and yellow shooting across it. Everything looks soft and blurry through the tears in my eyes. It makes me angry, because I don't want to cry.

'Bwoy, Pumkin,' Boots says, leaning on the hood of his car. 'It rough, man, I know seh it rough.'

I look at the streaks in the sky and don't say anything. I hear Miss Keene pacing behind me, her little feet crunching up the gravel. Boots takes his car keys out of his pocket, throws them up and catches them three times. Jiggles them a little and throws them up again, one two three. He clears his throat. I can tell he wants to find something to say. But what do you say to someone whose own mother would rather sell her than love her?

'You know, yuh auntie . . .' He starts, stops, clears his throat, starts again: 'Yuh auntie . . . she love you bad bad. Bad *bad*. She will do anything for you. From she go to France, all she do is work to find a way to get you to her. She neva waan call Missa Jones yuh nuh, she did want tek care of it on her own. But you know how it go roun here, Pumkin. Yuh try yuh try but is not till the big big uptown white man come bang pon the door dat people pay any attention. And at first him wouldn't even tek her calls but she call she call she call till him didn't have no choice but to listen to her, and to help her, because she wasn't giving him

345

no peace till him help her get you to her. Yeah, man, she love you bad bad.'

My face crumples into itself and everything balled up in my chest pushes out of me as I start to cry. I cry and cry and cry, my chest heaving. I manage to think that something must be wrong with me, I cry so much, but I cannot stop, and it only gets worse when I feel Boots's arms around me, as I hear him say, 'Hush, hush, yaah, Pumkin, is awrite, hush, yaah,' rocking me back and forth like a baby. We stand like that for a long while, as the red streaks in the sky flush more vibrantly, as the blue gets deeper and deeper, until the cicadas start singing around us, until the sound in my throat dies and the tears dry up and I'm just sniffling and sniffling, until I notice I have wet Boots's shirt with my tears.

I'm startled when the door to the house flies open and Jones and Sophie walk out. Jones strides with purpose, walking again like a very important man in a very important rush, so Sophie has to do a little run-skippy thing every now and then to keep up with him.

'Should we talk about the repayment and transferring the house title to Paulette?' she's saying to Jones, slightly out of breath from trying to keep up. Jones glances angrily at the gate as he walks through it, as if he's still holding a grudge for how it got the best of him on the way in.

'I have most of the money saved up, just need a few more months for the rest, and the transfer of the house title, I have all of that ready to go. I can just stop by your office with all the paperwork or I'll call your secretary and set up a ti–'

'This is it now, you understand!'

Sophie pulls up short as Jones whips around to face her, his finger pointed at her face.

'I am done with this family now, you hear? This is it!'

Sophie blinks twice. 'Yes. This is it,' she says.

As he turns back around, he catches sight of me. He looks at me for a moment, then starts heading for his SUV. But he stops again. He can't seem to make up his mind. Then his shoulders sag a little and he turns again and walks towards me. I move away from Boots and stand up straight, waiting until Jones is right in front of me. We stare at each other and it reminds me of the first time I met Miss Keene. I felt like a mouse in front of a hawk then. Now I feel like I'm facing down an old lion. He turns and looks back at his granddaughter, then down at the ground, then up at the sky. We are all watching him silently as his glance trips around the neighbourhood, stopping to rest on the small, inconsequential houses, the road full of potholes, the streetlights that flicker tiredly or don't work at all, until it lands back on Sophie's face.

'Just . . .' He stops, clears his throat. 'Yes, just . . . call my secretary and . . . we'll make the arrangements about the title. Don't . . . don't worry about the money.'

Sophie just stares at him as he nods once, decisively, spins on his feet, walks to his car, points the keys at it and gets in after it beeps twice with the headlights. He puts his leather case and the papers on the passenger seat, starts the engine and drives away without sparing any of us a second glance. The three of us watch as he carefully navigates the potholes, until the red of the brakelights looks like far-off dots in the distance and the car turns off the road and he is gone.

'Come, let's go,' says Miss Keene.

I walk up to the gate and lift it to pull it closed. I glance up and see Paulette at the window. She's staring out at me but it's

347

too dark to see her expression. I stop and look at her and we stand there like that for moments, minutes, hours, years, until Sophie puts her hand on my arm and gently pulls me away. 'Come, Pumkin. Let's go home.'

*

When Miss Keene goes through the pile of mail her house-keeper put neatly on the table, she finds the letter from the exam centre, my name typed on the front. Time stops as I rip open the thin envelope.

Sophie and Miss Keene hover in front of me. Miss Keene is calm as ever but Sophie's hands are fluttering like the wings of a bird that can't find its way out of a house it's flown into. I unfold the letter and I read it, and I read it again, and then once more. My heart slides slowly down into my stomach and everything blurs and I have a moment to wonder when I will ever stop crying. Sophie grabs the letter out of my hand in a fit of impatience and hunches over it, Miss Keene squooshed up beside her. There's a moment of silence. Then I hear Sophie as if from far away as she starts to scream, holding the letter high in her hands, like a medal. Even Miss Keene, ever poised and straight-backed, does a little yip and starts to shimmy her shoulders, their faces spread wide in grins.

'You PASSED, PUMKIN! YOU PASSED!'

They descend on me, grab me by the shoulders, dance me around and around the room, hug me close, squeeze me tight, and I spread my own mouth wide in a grin and I laugh and I hold their hands and I jump up and down and squeeze them back. I'd made it, I'd done it, I'd passed. I was on my way. On my way to a new life with Sophie. But I can see myself as if from the outside, grinning and laughing and jumping up and down, Sophie and Miss Keene delirious with joy for me. The outlines of their bodies are blurry and fuzzy like ghosts, but sharp and clear in front of me is my mother's face: she's staring blankly at me, blank like a mask, not even the memory of an emotion written on her face. I should be happy now – I got what I wanted, what I worked so hard for, what we all worked so hard for – but all I can see is that face, and I can't feel anything. I can't feel anything at all.

'Walk good'

'Wishing you good fortune on your journey'

Two years later . . .

The smell of breakfast forces my eyes open: eggs and bacon frying in the pan, toast, coffee. Made in a French press, of course. I think about which of my organs I would sell for some ackee and saltfish right now. My appendix, maybe? I heard only rabbits use those. I extricate myself from my duvet, wrapped tightly around me, like a roti, and peek out of the window. The sun is fat and yellow, even though it's early in the morning, and the lawns are green green green. Did I notice how lush they were before? How fresh the air smells, how tall the trees that push their way out of the sidewalk, fighting to take up space? I shake my head and stretch my arms. It's almost time for school — there's no time to waste.

When Sophie and I landed in Paris two years ago, I was overwhelmed by the sheer number of people. Everyone seemed to know where they were going, while I stood stock still and wide-eyed in the centre of a quiet little storm. Those first few days, living like tourists, visiting all the museums and monuments and everything you're supposed to see in Paris, were a complete blur. In the train to Marseille, my head was plastered to the window, my eyes straining so hard to take everything in, I had a headache. I was finally here! After everything I'd gone through, everything that Boots and Miss Keene, Mandy and Tamara did for me, and Sophie too, of course, after every setback, I'd overcome the odds and achieved my goal. I was with Sophie, in France! And I waited for that feeling: of finally being home, of being where I belonged, but restlessness had dug its way into my belly and churned relentlessly there.

You're here, I told myself. *You're free!* But free to do what?

As we settled into our lives together, I thought we would shed the pressures we had felt back home to be different, to be *better*, but nothing really changed except our environment.

There were a lot of black people in Marseille, most of them French-speaking Africans, but we were still a small minority. Imagine my surprise when I learned that I'd moved halfway across the world, crossed the ocean, stepped into a different time zone, and still I did not fit neatly into a box. Not quite black enough for the African kids, certainly not light enough for the white kids. Still a square peg in a sea of round holes. They made fun of my accent, the funny way I spoke French, my Caribbean mannerisms. They didn't really like bread pudding, but maybe it's because I could never find the right bread. Or coconut shavings, or the exact type of brown cane sugar I needed, so I had to give up all my little Jamaican pastries and make regular cake instead, but who could compete with the little pâtisseries that lined every block? My dream of opening my own little shop seemed even further away than before. Still, I made a few friends. Fabiette – Fabi – whose parents were from Cameroon, and Ondine, born and raised in Marseille, were my closest.

But Sophie . . . Sophie was as she ever was.

In Jamaica, she'd refined her uptown accent so much you could cut yourself on it; in Marseille, she did the same.

'I don't want people to think we're African,' she'd said, as she made me practise and practise my pronunciation, just like she did back home.

'Why not?' I'd asked.

'Well, we're not African so why should people think we are?'

'But we're not French either and you definitely want peo—'

'Pumkin, don't *argue* with me about this!'

I thought about what Boots had said about being stuck in the roles we had held as slaves on our island, of never escaping our colonialist roots. Auntie Sophie had met a man soon after I arrived, a Frenchman, and she was a completely different person with him. Not like she was with Boots, relaxed and at ease, but tense, as if she was always looking over her shoulder, afraid to let her mask drop. As I watched her working hard to fit in with her new French friends, watched her try to act as if she'd been born and raised in the city of Paris, how she was careful to say we were 'expats' and not 'immigrants', how she raised her eyebrows when Fabi came over but gushed and smiled over Ondine, I realized it was Sophie's own skin she was trying to shed. I realized, with sadness, that she would never feel she was good enough, no matter where she went. And I knew it wasn't really her fault, but I also knew I didn't want to be that way. Not any more.

I was tired of always trying to fit in. Why couldn't I just be myself? Why couldn't I enjoy people's company not because of what they could do for me but just because I enjoyed it, no matter where they were from? Why should I deny where *I* came from?

I don't need to be 'better' than someone else. It's enough just to be myself — my worth isn't relative. I know that now. I left Jamaica, went to France, but I was still the same person with all the same fears and worries as before — they didn't all magically disappear. I learned that, no matter where I went, there I was. I love Sophie, but I no longer want to be like her, always desperate to escape herself, unable to see that she's perfect just as she is, flaws and all . . .

Now I clump down the stairs in my school uniform, the smell of breakfast pulling me forwards, like a magnet. I sit in my usual chair and wait for her to bustle out of the kitchen.

'Ah, we're up! Eggs for breakfast, *et voilà*!'

I smile and wiggle in my seat as she plops the plate of scrambled eggs and toast in front of me, the plate of bacon in the middle.

'No ackee and saltfish, then?' I say.

'Child, who has time to make ackee and saltfish in the middle of the week?'

'Not even a johnny cake?'

She tuts and plonks down in the chair across from me, but I see the smile on her face. She knows I'm only joking.

'I'm just playing, Miss Keene. You know how much I missed ackee and saltfish – I feel like I want it every day now.'

Her head bobs up and down.

'I must have gained twenty pounds when I got back from Paris all those years ago,' she says. 'I stuffed everything I missed right down my gullet – patties, jerk chicken, festival, bammy –'

'Bammy! Oh, Miss Keene, you have bammy?'

She chuckles. 'We'll do a big Jamaican breakfast on Sunday – ackee and saltfish, johnny cakes, bammy, fried plantain, the works. You'll have Mandy and Tamara here and you can ask Boots and Grace and the kids if they want to come.'

My mouth starts watering. I look down at my eggs. They are a poor substitute.

'And, Pumkin, remember, you can call me Bev. You can't be living here and still calling me Miss Keene.'

'Okay,' I say, resolving not to call her anything at all if I can help it. I feel like my mouth will catch fire if I call her by her first name.

Sophie did not understand when I told her I wanted to come back to JA. She yelled, she cried, she gave me the silent treatment, she talked me half to death. She called me ungrateful and I really felt that I was. Everyone had gone to such lengths to get me to Marseille, and here I was bawling to go home.

'You know how many people would *kill* for this opportunity?' Sophie had raged. 'Nobody wants to go back to Jamaica!'

But Miss Keene understood. She knew exactly how I felt when I told her how much I missed the way the earth smelt after it rained, the way the streets would flood in a downpour and you didn't have to go to school because the buses couldn't run. I missed the way the air smelt at Christmas, which is not a thing I can describe – you just have to smell it for yourself. I missed the explosion of colours on all the trees, the way there was always music playing somewhere, always someone dancing on the street. I missed the way people yelled at each other from across the road, smiles wide as they made plans or caught up, the way people gave big juicy hugs, the tiny little nice things they would do for you, like give you a free mango, or help you fend off a man when you're alone on the road. I missed the way people looked out for each other.

I'd thought I was alone there, but I'd had Boots with his booming laugh, Tamara and her sarcastic comments and Mandy's complete ignorance of normal Jamaican things. Miss

Keene's stern face that masked the softness right underneath. Maybe I was a fish out of water in my hometown but it was water I knew, water warm and deep and blue, containing multitudes within it, flowing every which way. I would rather swim there than anywhere else.

I'd tried it Sophie's way, but only when I got to Marseille did I realize I had been fighting for Sophie's dream, instead of figuring out what would make me happy. Transplanted myself but not escaped any of the things I had been trying to escape. So Miss Keene helped. We spoke to Sophie, we worked out a plan. I'd come back and stay with Miss Keene for the two years of sixth form, and then we'd take things from there.

I've barely had a few bites when I hear the familiar toot-toot of Boots's horn outside. I stuff the last of the toast into my mouth and grab my backpack, running out of the door as Miss Keene bawls after to me, 'Mind you don't choke!'

Tamara is leaning out of the side window. 'Hurry up nuh, man!' she shouts, as if I'm not already rushing down the little driveway. I can see Boots's mouth wide open in that great, booming laugh, and I shake my head at her impatience. I jump into the back seat.

'You have my stuff?'

'And good morning to *you*, Tamara,' I say pointedly.

'Yes yes, mawnin mawnin, you have my stuff or what?'

I laugh and open my backpack, pull out two brown-paper packages tied with red string. Tamara snatches them from me, opens one right away, pops the rock cake into her mouth. I watch her sit back in the seat, eyes closed, a smile on her face as she chews.

'You're welcome,' I say, laughing.

'Mm-hmm.' She nods.

I take out two more packages and lay them in the space beside the driver's seat. 'For you and Grace and Ricky and Keisha,' I say.

'Awrite!' Boots booms, letting out his great big laugh.

'Wait, you have more in there?' Tamara says, springing forward in her seat, pawing at my bag.

'Those are Mandy's coconut drops!' I say, batting her hand away.

She sighs and takes another bite of rock cake, then puts her hand on my shoulder and smiles. 'I really missed these rock cakes.'

'I really missed you too, T.'

Maybe one day I'll return to France, join Sophie for good, go to university, build a French life, open the bakery that serves the King. Or maybe I'll stay here in JA, open a baking school for kids like me who want to lose themselves in the sifting and pouring and grating and folding. Who knows what life will bring? What I know is, it won't matter where I am, or who I'm with, because I have already found the sweetness in my own skin.

Acknowledgements

When I started writing *Sweetness in the Skin*, my only goal was to finish it. Writing a book is hard and frustrating, and downright painful at times – there were lots of tears, and countless times I wanted to give up. Except I didn't, and in the end, I finished it. Here are the people who helped me get there:

Nicolai Christ, who gave me a personal coaching session that changed everything for me: thank you for showing me how to set myself free. Ben Fergusson, who ran the novel-writing workshop where the idea for *Sweetness* was born: thank you for encouraging me to run with it. Victoria Gosling, who created this amazing space for English writers in Berlin: thank you for reading my manuscript, giving me notes and connecting me with the best literary agent ever (more on her later)! Jane Flett, my writing midwife: this book would not exist without you. Thank you for unlocking me, teaching me, encouraging me, being such a cheerleader and all-round superstar. Sarah Van Bonn and Sharon Mertins, my first readers: thank you for your careful and considered feedback, for being so supportive and excited for me, and for letting me know 'it's good and it's ready' (I'm still not sure I believe you).

My agent, Jenny Hewson: I don't even have the words to say how much I appreciate you. You literally changed my life.

Thank you for being the absolute best at what you do. My US agent, David Forrer: working with you has been a blast, truly so much fun. Thank you for holding my hand while I navigated North America. Gin & tonics on me when I'm stateside! My UK editor, Jessica Leeke: you had me at hello! Thank you for taking such good care of Pumkin, for your guidance and your direction. You might be British but your heart's Jamaican! It is such a joy to work with you and the entire team at PMJ. Speaking of, special thanks to Clio Cornish for swooping in to get Pumkin in readers' hands and for being such a support to me as I navigate this new journey, and to Madeleine Woodfield, Gaby Young, Ciara Berry, Lily Cooper, Hattie Evans, Nick Lowndes and everyone who wrote me one of the beautiful, handwritten letters that I will keep forever. Emily Griffin, HarperCollins US, and Janice Zawerbny, HarperCollins Canada: thank you for loving Pumkin as hard as you do and for getting her ready for her North American debut. Alai Ganuza and Lauren Wakefield: thank you so much for my absolutely stunning cover!

Amina Blackwood-Meeks and Joan 'Bumpy Head' Hutchinson: thank you both for digging up the right Jamaican proverbs to fit *Sweetness* out of the gazillion that exist. Hazel Orme, thank you for your eagle-eye and also how much care you took with our Jamaican dialect.

My friends, and family, all around the world, who yelled with excitement at every step of the way, who always asked me for updates, who told me they couldn't wait to read it. You are too many to name*, but you know who you are. (*But I have to mention Kimmy Barrett, who will 'strap the book to her back' so everyone she knows will see it: did you catch the line?) Your support and enthusiasm kept me going. Thank you.

To Daddy, who snuck away the first short story I wrote at age eleven and submitted it to *The Gleaner*. Seeing my name in print for the first time gave me such a thrill, I've been chasing it ever after. Thank you for always encouraging me, believing in me and supporting me, no matter what I choose to do. To Mum, my biggest cheerleader, president, founder and sole member of my fan club! The sheer power of your love for me propels me through all the things I'm scared to do, but do anyway. I would never have achieved this without your positivity and your support. We screamed and jumped together for every step forward, even when we were far apart. 'Celebrate every little success,' you said, but I would have no success without you. Thank you for being the best.

To Schatzl, my place of peace and calm and tranquility, no matter what storm is raging outside. Thank you for giving me hugs when I was so frustrated I wanted to quit, for listening to me rant and rave about characters, for brainstorming ideas when I felt stuck and for repeatedly and ever more loudly offering to translate *Sweetness* into Czech. Miluji tě!

And if you bought this book and got this far: thank you! I hope you love Pumkin as much as I do.